'A brilliantly constructed novel, a story that drew me in and took me along for the ride' *SFCrowsNest*

'The spectacle is unde̶ ̶̶ of characters who give their ̶̶ ̶̶ and who finally turn War of t̶ ̶̶ novel.' *Locus*

'Following on from the extraordinary climate change novel *Austral*, this is further evidence that Paul McAuley may just be the best SF writer we have.' *SFX*

WAR OF
THE MAPS

PAUL McAULEY

This paperback first published in Great Britain in 2021 by Gollancz

First published in Great Britain in 2020 by Gollancz
an imprint of The Orion Publishing Group Ltd
Carmelite House, 50 Victoria Embankment
London EC4Y 0DZ

An Hachette UK Company

3 5 7 9 10 8 6 4 2

A CIP catalogue record for this book is
available from the British Library.

ISBN (Mass Market Paperback) 978 1 473 21735 5
ISBN (eBook) 978 1 473 21736 2

Printed and bound in Great Britain by Clays Ltd, Elcograf S.p.A.

www.unlikelyworld.co.uk
www.gollancz.co.uk

In memory of Gardner Dozois

I have noticed from the study of maps
The more outlying the island –
The further out it is in the remote ocean –
The stronger the force that pulls us towards it.
David Greig, *Islands*

PART ONE
Another Country

1

Ghosts of Godlings

A lone tree leaned over the cistern, its bell-shaped yellow-leaved canopy dinting and swaying in the hot breeze, sprinkling coins of mirrorlight across the water and the effigy of a toad, carved from a knot of bonewhite wood, which crouched on a slab of rock at the water's edge. The lucidor picked up the stoneware beaker set between the toad's long-toed feet, left by some unknown traveller and used by many such since, and dipped it in the cistern and drank the measure of cool water straight down and refilled it and sat back on his heels. Sipping slowly, wondering if the toad was the avatar of a godling or the spirit animal of one of the vagrant tribes that wandered the borderlands, wondering if the bandits knew about the little oasis. Most likely they did. This was their territory and he was a stranger here, passing through on his way to somewhere else.

A school of desert minnows patrolled the cistern's square perimeter, flickering beneath the fleet of narrow inturned leaves adrift on the skin of the water, turning about the current of the spring that pulsed from a crack beneath the deity of their little map, scattering when the lucidor stood and unhooked the fighting staff slung slantwise at his back and shrugged off his black leather coat. The right side of his face darkly blushed, as if he had sat too long by a fire, his long grey hair, brushed back from his forehead and gathered into a coil pinned by a barrette, was scored by a crisp charcoal streak that ran above his ear, and the left sleeve of his shirt had been ripped off and tied around his upper arm. He used his teeth and right hand to undo the knot of this makeshift bandage and drops of fresh blood welled and ran when he peeled the cloth from the raw trough gouged in his biceps.

Out in the mirrorlight, the stolen warhorse caught the blood scent and stepped about and tugged at the reins that tethered her to a thorn bush. The lucidor paid her no mind, refilling the beaker and rinsing out the wound. Pinkish water dripped into the pool and the minnows flicked around and rose to the surface and snapped and fought over this offering.

The lucidor picked threads of cloth from the wound and washed it again and dabbed it dry. With a small ceramic knife he cut a strip from the shirt sleeve and folded it into a pad and laid it over the wound and tied the remainder of the sleeve around his arm and blotted sweat from his forehead with the back of his hand.

He put the beaker back in its place and pulled on his leather coat and picked up his staff and walked up the stony slope to the crest of the ridge. It was high summer. Noon. The eight white points of the Skyday mirror arc strung across the crown of the blank blue sky, as hot and bright as they ever would be. The tawny plain shimmering in great falls of heat and light, stretching towards a chalky sketch of mountain peaks and the border between the Free State and Patua.

A minute feather of smoke slanted in the mid-distance, warping in the glassy air. The lucidor extracted his spyglass from the flap pocket of his coat and shot it to its full length and applied it to his right eye and studied the root of the smoke and the plain on either side. There had been no signs of pursuit when he had paused in his flight across the grasslands to bind his wound, and there were none now. None that he could see. But although the ambush had failed, he knew that he had not yet outrun the hunt. Even if the bandits had fled or had been captured or killed by the train's crew and passengers, the department knew where he was and where he was going, and would set other hirelings or agents on his trail. He had to get on, and make a new plan while he rode.

The warhorse, a sturdy young piebald mare with plates of pale horn pieced across her shoulders and neck, was nosing for insects amongst the stones under and around the thorn bush. She bated and tried to bite the lucidor when he unhooked the canvas water bottle from the saddle horn, and tried again after he filled the bottle at the cistern and mounted up. He jerked the reins tight, told her that she had better learn to get along because he didn't intend to let her friends catch up, and heeled her into a canter.

They rode down gravel and shale switchbacks into a slanting grassland dotted with weather-bent trees. Dry grass brushing the stirrups. At dusk the lucidor made camp in the lee of a slant of bare rock. He did not dare to light a fire in this open country, for a fire might attract any searching for him, and ate a meagre supper of smoke-dried meat he found in one of the saddlebags and wrapped himself in the saddle blanket and stretched out on the hard ground.

When he woke, the warhorse was cropping dewy grass and a mantle of cloud had stretched across the forest below, grey in the grey dawn light. By the time he rode into the beginnings of the forest the cloud had burned away and mirrorlight was hot on his back and his coiled hair. This was the northern edge of the high plain of mainland Patua, frayed by steep valleys that wound between knife-edged ridges. He followed the course of a dry stream down one such valley, tall conifer trees he could not name rising on either side. Ribbons of sand and gravel. Boulders thatched with glass moss that spun tiny rainbows from mirrorlight. A grassy clearing thick with saplings where one of the trees had fallen. The windless air heavy with heat and the buzzing song of some kind of insect, flavoured with a clean medicinal scent. Now and then the lucidor halted the warhorse and turned in the creaking saddle to look behind him. A lawkeeper fleeing retribution. A trespasser in this strange country, far from his desert homeland.

The forest was scarred by tracts of dead trees; the valley sides were cut by erosion gullies and long rockslides. The climate of the entire map was changing, altering its weather, disfiguring its land without regard for boundaries or politics. The heartland of the Free State endured long summer droughts now, and its winters were colder and wetter. And while most mirrors dimmed each winter, as they always had, some were permanently dimmer than they once had been, and one, at the tail of the Sandday arc, had in the last century shrunk to a faint red spark. Some said that the creator gods had stinted when making the world; others that the world's slow dying was part of their design. Yet still people met and married, and made babies and died to make room for the next generation. Life went on, somehow. Perhaps the creator gods had made people better than they had known or intended.

Many of their relics had likewise outlasted their passing. Once, the lucidor rode past a roofless circle of pillars rising out of scrub trees on a bluff above the dry stream. Once, he stopped to study with his spyglass a tall column that stood at the prow of a high ridge, decorated with carvings of some forgotten skirmish of the Heroic Age when godlings, autonomous shards of the creator gods, had walked new-made maps clad in the bodies of men and woman, and left behind monuments and temples and even entire cities, and rumours of places where time stretched from seconds to centuries between one footfall and the next, or where the unwary could be thrown into the sky or transported instantly to a map halfway around the world or to the bottom of the World Ocean. Places where rocks floated in the air. Places where the sick were healed. Places where the words of godlings still echoed and could drive the unwary mad or grant certain adepts disciplined by years of meditation a pure everlasting instant of ultimate enlightenment. How to measure the significance of this last assignment against any of that? The lucidor thought of an ant crawling across a child's balloon. Not even close.

Remfrey He had once told him that people busied themselves with habit and ritual to avoid thinking about the awful truth — that they were no more than discarded toys in an abandoned house, and only those who accepted that their world and their lives were a cosmic joke and laughed at it and found new games to play could be truly free. Not that Remfrey He believed any of that, of course. He did not really believe in anything, apart from the singularity of his genius. No, he had been amusing himself, the only kind of amusement he could manufacture after his arrest, by challenging and trying to undermine the lucidor's beliefs. A game he had continued to play long after he had been sentenced and exiled. Smuggling out notes commenting on disasters and crimes. Asking disingenuously, after the death of the lucidor's wife, if the lucidor still believed that his little life had any kind of meaning or structure.

Well, he still believed in the principles that had shaped his life. He still held them to be true. That was why he was here, and why the department wanted to hunt him down. Remfrey He would be amused by his persistence, no doubt, but it was all he had now. All he knew.

After the mirrors had dropped one by one behind a high ridge and shadows began to deepen and spread beneath the trees, the lucidor made camp beside a pool at the bottom of a dry waterfall. Someone had been there years before, had left a hearth circle of stones, and a carbine that leaned against a juniper close by, its wooden stock grey and rotten, the hard plastic of its chamber and barrel dulled by weather and cracked in several places. The lucidor squatted on his heels and studied it for a little while, wondering if its owner had left in a hurry because they had been running from an attack, or if they had been ambushed and killed, and their killer had overlooked the weapon they hadn't had time to use.

So many stories in this world. So many stories lost to time.

A rat snake fled from the lucidor when he went to fill his water bottle at the stream, and he stalked it through the sparse undergrowth and spiked it with his staff. He eaten nothing all day but the last handful of dried meat, and lit a small fire in the old hearth, telling himself that he was screened by trees and the risk of discovery was smaller than the risk of infection, and butchered his kill, throwing the head and guts to the warhorse and threading fillets of pale meat on a stick and searing them over the flames. After he had eaten and stamped out the fire, he climbed the tumble of house-sized boulders at the top of the waterfall and looked out across the dark tree-clad slopes. Far off in the dusk a shimmering twist of red and orange veils marked the carved pillar he had passed hours and leagues ago. Indistinct figures moved inside the light. Luminous ghosts of godlings eternally playing out a small episode in one of their games. No other sign of life anywhere. No sign of pursuit.

Back on the train, yesterday morning, he had guessed what was about to go down when he saw through the carriage window three bandits on warhorses scramble up from a gully beside the track. He'd been expecting something like it ever since he had glimpsed one of his former colleagues in the crowded market of the border town, just before he had crossed over into Patua. As he stood up, the woman two seats behind him rose too, fumbling in her reticule, jerking out a blazer, and he whipped his staff up and sideways in a short arc that struck her shoulder. The blazer's tight bright beam scorched his face and crisped his hair and set the carriage ceiling aflame, and before the woman could fire again he lashed her with two quick blows, knocking her down as one of the bandits burst through the door at the end of the carriage. The man, brandishing a pistol and shouting the lucidor's name, was shoved backwards by the panicky throng of passengers trying to escape the spreading fire, and the lucidor kicked out a window and clambered onto the roof of the carriage.

The other two bandits were cantering alongside the carriage, chased by a riderless warhorse, as the train braked in a shuddering scream of ceramic on ceramic. One stood on his stirrups and grabbed the balustrade of the platform at the end of the burning carriage and swung onto it, and the lucidor made a swift calculation and slung his staff over his shoulder and jumped. He landed with a rushing jolt on the riderless warhorse and grabbed up the reins with one hand and swung his staff as the second bandit cut towards him, smacking the man in the face and bowling him clean from his saddle. The bandit on the carriage's platform shot wildly, two rounds snapping wide, the third grazing the lucidor's arm, and the lucidor spurred his mount and raced away from the train, out across the gravel flats beyond the tracks.

The lucidor had no doubt that his mission had been uncovered or betrayed before it had scarcely begun. He feared for his old boss and anyone else who was in on it, knew that he couldn't turn back even though it was most likely that he would find nothing but trouble ahead. He'd been lucky that the department had sent bandits instead of his fellow officers to capture or kill him after he had crossed the border; lucky that only four had come after him. Four that he knew of. The department must have thought him an easy target because he was old and disgraced, and he knew that it would not make that mistake again. Knew that he couldn't rely on luck to see him through.

2

Cement Works

He fell asleep in a hollow he scraped in silky sand, wrapped in the saddle blanket with his head pillowed on his leather coat and the clash of stars burning in every shade of red beyond the saw-toothed silhouettes of the trees, and woke to a dull, cloudy dawn and the sound of rain pattering on a thousand thousand needles in the forest canopy. His bones ached in the chill damp; his wounded arm tenderly throbbed. Watched by the warhorse, he gathered fallen branches and built a new fire, wove a small basket from the ribs of fern fronds and filled it with water that he heated with pebbles plucked from the heart of the fire, dropped several pinches of glass moss into the water, and unknotted his makeshift bandage. The skin around the wound was hot and tender and there was a seepage of straw-coloured liquid. The lucidor plugged it with the boiled glass moss, cut and folded a fresh cloth pad and retied the remnant of the sleeve around his arm, shaved as best he could with the curved blade of his little knife, peeled and ate a couple of lobes of paddle cactus, and kicked apart the fire and saddled and mounted the warhorse.

For half the day he rode down trackless slopes of trees and mossy boulders, and at last the land bottomed out and he crossed a broad shallow river, the rain-pocked water no higher than the warhorse's hocks, and rode on through stands of tree-sized seed ferns. Rainwater guttering from the tips of drooping fronds, rain pattering on his hair, beading on the upturned fox-fur collar of his leather coat, soaking the knees of his trousers and trickling into his boots.

On the far side of the fern forest, the lucidor urged the warhorse up a shallow slope of sand and brush and reined her in at the top and for several minutes sat in the saddle looking out at the sprawl of the old port town of Roos and the grey flood of the Horned Strait. More water than he had ever before seen in his life, easily a hundred times wider than the Great River that wound through the fertile plain of the Free State. A desert of water stretching away under a low sky to a misty glimpse of land on the far side: a faint line that was the southern coast of the Big Island where most people in Patua lived. Where Remfrey He was somewhere going about his business.

'Think what you could do with all that water,' he told his wife. She had died six years ago, and although the curses and raging disbelief and self-pitying sorrow of his grief had long ago calcified he had not yet shaken off the habit of talking to her, especially when he saw something that might have caught her interest. He still carried her in his heart. He always would.

A river channelled by stone embankments divided the town into two unequal parts. On one side buildings like stacked sugar cubes climbed a hill crowned by a citadel built of black stone; on the other was a silted harbour and an industrial sprawl dominated by the overgrown wreckage of the iron ore works. The railway line on which the lucidor had been travelling had once transported ore from the mines in what was now the Free State to Roos, where it had been processed, and carried the slaves who had worked in the mines – the lucidor's ancestors, the ancestors of almost everyone in the Free State – in the other direction.

He had been intending to take the ferry from Roos across the Horned Strait, and on the other side catch another ferry that followed the coast of the Big Island north to the twin cities of Delos-Chimr. Where, according to the intelligence he'd been given, Remfrey He was supposedly helping the Patuan army devise new tactics against alter women and other monsters of the invasion.

A simple plan, thrown over when the bandits had ambushed the train. The lucidor reckoned that agents from the department, and bounty hunters and thief-takers hunting him for the price the department had put on his head, might well be watching the ferry now, so after scanning the shore with his spyglass he cut west, riding down the slope and finding a service road that ran between fields of electrical flax and regimented stands of ironwood trees. He paused to watch a work crew fell one of the trees. Men and women standing at a respectful distance as a charge of GPX, the gravity-polarised explosive which departmental assault teams sometimes used to take down doors, flared in a brief disc of red flame around the base of the trunk. The tree shivered, but it did not fall until a team of horses harnessed to rope pulleys surged forward and its long straight trunk, topped by rags of foliage, crashed down between its neighbours.

The lucidor rode on in the thin rain, passing a farm with plastic tunnels crammed with green crops running between rows of tilted light-collecting panels, riding through a sprawl of small factories, warehouses, and abandoned lots overgrown by volunteer saplings and ox grass and tumbles of kudzu. At a roadside stall frequented by workpeople and cargo-wagon drivers he bought a paper cone of something called popcorn squid – nuggets of salty flesh fried in breadcrumbs and doused in sweet chili sauce – and ate quickly, aware of the curious glances of the other customers, who were no doubt wondering who this stranger was, with his warhorse and his foreign clothes. He licked his greasy fingers clean and rode on, past two barges moored beside conical hills of sand and gravel, past the dusty silos of a cement works and a fan of railway sidings, crossing a narrow causeway to a long spit of land on the far side of a milky lagoon, where he had spied what looked like a fishing village.

The short row of single-storey houses, built of planks painted with black tar, squatted on a ridge that overlooked the pebbly beach where boats were drawn up along the water's edge. One boat in particular had caught his attention. It was more than twice the size of the rest, its hull moulded from some kind of plastic rather than shaped wooden planks, and there was a big square tent on the shore in front of it, open on one side, with lights shining inside and several people busy around tables and plastic tubs. As the lucidor rode up a woman stepped out and asked him what he wanted.

'I'm looking for someone who can take me across the Horned Strait.'

'You've come to the wrong place, friend. The ferry's in the old town.'

'I know where the ferry is. I'll give you this horse and her saddle in exchange for a ride on that big boat of yours.'

'We aren't in need of a horse, and we won't be going anywhere for a while,' the woman said.

She was in her early forties, a tall sinewy woman dressed in a denim work shirt and leather trousers, with a bush of wiry hair and a sharp, canny gaze. A long knife sheathed in an ironwood scabbard was suspended from a baldric slung over one shoulder, and she had stopped a sensible distance from the lucidor and the warhorse.

'What you need to do,' she told him, 'is turn around and ride back over the causeway and head along the coast road to the old town. Keep going west, you won't miss it. It's the place with the old ruin up on a hill by the river. The ferry terminal's directly below it.'

'What about the villagers?' the lucidor said. 'Might any of them take me across?'

'I can't speak for them, but I can tell you it isn't likely. Fisherfolk don't like to go too far out from shore these days.'

One of the people watching this exchange from the shelter of the tent, a young woman, stepped out into the rain and said to the lucidor, 'The fur trimming your coat is fox, isn't it? Desert fox. And that staff at your back is what certain lawkeepers carry in the Free State instead of pistols.'

'I was a lawkeeper before I retired,' the lucidor said. 'Now I am hoping to make myself useful in the war against the invasion, which is why I am looking for the fastest way across the Strait.'

That was the cover story he had worked up before setting out, based on conversations with an acquaintance who had spent two years fighting against insurgents in Patua; his boss had supplied a fake letter of recommendation decorated with a genuine seal, and a letter of transit and identification documents made out for Saj Orym Zier, a former sheriff for the court of magistrates who otherwise exactly resembled the lucidor.

'From what I hear, a fair number of would-be mercenaries from the Free State are on the run from all kinds of trouble,' the first woman said. 'Maybe that's why this jasper wants to avoid the port and the scrutiny of the garrison.'

The young woman ignored that and said to the lucidor, 'You are no ordinary mercenary. You are gifted. A muzzler. I am not sure what they call you where you come from, but that's what we call your kind here.'

Her square pugnacious face was framed by long black hair parted down the middle, and like the half-dozen men and woman watching the exchange she wore a long white cotton coat. There were iron and copper rings on her fingers, and her bold gaze suggested that she was used to command.

'We are mostly called suppressors in the Free State,' the lucidor said, trying to hide his surprise. 'If you know what I am, you must be gifted too. You, or one of your friends.'

'I am a map reader,' the woman said. 'As are two of my assistants. We felt our gifts dimming as you approached.'

'If I am interfering with your work, I should ride on,' the lucidor said.

'What do they call you, in the Free State?'

'Saj Orym Zier.'

He had practised saying his alias, but it still felt strange in his mouth.

'I recall how they greet guests in your country, Saj Orym Zier. My home is your home, hearth and heart. I am Orjen Starbreaker. This is my steward, Lyra Gurnek,' the woman said, laying a hand on the tall woman's arm, 'and these are my assistants. We have no hearth, but we are in good heart, working hard to unravel the true nature of some of the invasion's little monsters. And while we cannot help you make the crossing, I think I know someone who might be able to help you. Come in out of the rain and we'll discuss it over a cup of chai. I will show you a little of what we are doing here, too. I am sure you'll be interested, given the kind of employment you are seeking.'

Orjen Starbreaker's rings were made of rare metals, her name was old and honourable, one of the names of those who claimed direct descent from men and women ridden by godlings in the dawn of the world, and she was a map reader, working on creatures of the invasion. She might know where Remfrey He was and what he was doing, might even have met him. And besides all that, the lucidor had ridden most of the day and was cold and weary, so he climbed down from the warhorse and tethered her to one of the stakes that anchored the tent and followed Orjen Starbreaker inside, with her steward close behind.

Long tables overflowed with the kind of organised clutter that reminded him of the city morgue's laboratory. Microscopes, centrifuges, glass dishes and flasks and beakers, bottles of reagents, dissecting trays half-full of black wax, some with small creatures slit and splayed in them like the leavings of some unholy feast. In one corner, an electric still dripped distilled water into a plastic jerry can. The stout-walled ironwood bomb of an autoclave crouched in another. A rank of plastic tanks stood at the back, and the salt tang of seawater mixed with the prickling odour of formaldehyde and other chemicals.

A young man fetched graduated glass beakers of clear amber chai. The lucidor took a dutiful sip, tasting mint and sugar, and warmed his fingers on the beaker while Orjen told him that she and her assistants were documenting the spread of known invader species, searching for new kinds, and trying to find out how they lived and reproduced.

'I visited the Free State once,' she said. 'Years ago, travelling with my father. We were taken out into the desert to watch a display of hunting with raptors, and there was a visit to a floating village in the marshes where the Great River drains away into the desert. But because my father was there on official business we spent most of our time in the capital, and most of the people I met were either government officials or security officers or lawkeepers. That's why I recognised your staff. It's carried by a particular type of lawkeeper, those who work for the Department for the Regulation of Applied Philosophy and Special Skills.'

'As I said, I'm retired now,' the lucidor said, unsettled by the young woman's sharp gaze.

'Lucidors. That's what they're called. That's what you are.'

'It's what I once was.'

14

'"Lucidor" means "one who seeks light". Light being knowledge, wisdom, understanding. But you don't seek it out because you want to understand it, do you? You don't want to learn from it or find a use for it or discover what it tells you about the world. You want only to suppress it.'

The lucidor could have told her that the Free State was a poor country. Landlocked, mostly desert, its only cultivatable land lying along the Great River. He could have told her that although it lacked many of the resources possessed by Patua, its people shared what little they had and made sure that it was put to the best use, and thought carefully about what they needed and what they did not. The People's House planned and policed every part of the economy, but no one went without food or shelter, and after its War of Independence the Free State had enjoyed two hundred years of peace and stability, while at this very moment a popular rebellion in the south of Patua was taking advantage of the chaos after the government had been forced to abandon the capital.

He could have told Orjen Starbreaker all that and more, but it would have been impolite, and he wanted to stay on the right side of her because of her offer to help him find a way across the Horned Strait, and because he wanted to ask her about Remfrey He. So he said, 'It's true that the department helps to regulate applied philosophy, and hunts down bandits who try to smuggle drugs and other contraband across the border, but that isn't all it does. You said that you visited the marshes. I was once sent there to investigate the rumour that a necromancer was at work in its far reaches.'

That got Orjen's attention, as he hoped it would.

She said, 'This was someone who could raise the dead?'

'Someone who was said to be creating monsters from parts of the dead, but turned out to be an old woman who had a glimmer of the healing touch, just enough to keep alive the birds she caught and sewed together. She couldn't explain why she did it, but the doctors who examined her were able to prescribe a physic that helped her to overcome her compulsion. Finding people who misuse their gifts is also part of our work. As is searching out gifted children, so that they can be helped to put their talents to best use.'

15

'You also serve a single-party government that controls every aspect of philosophical research, and suppresses or censors anything that conflicts with its ideology,' Orjen said. 'Could it have mobilised against the invasion as we have? Would it approve of the work we are doing here?'

'That would depend on the work, of course.'

'It's right here, in these tanks,' Orjen said. 'A sampling of the creatures that are displacing and destroying ordinary life.'

She called them her little monsters, and showed them off with enthusiastic pride and no little affection. 'Look at this!' she said, as she led him from tank to tank. And 'You see? You see?' And 'Isn't this amazing?'

Here was a scaly worm, as long as the lucidor's forearm, which shot out a hundred sticky venomous threads when Orjen prodded it with a stick. A creature with pairs of spines on its back patrolling the bottom of its tank on stiff prop-like legs tipped with claws, tentacles writhing around its blunt head. A small school of leaf-shaped creatures the colour of graphite, with sucker mouths filled with rasping teeth; Orjen said that they bored their way into fish and ate them from the inside out. A creature with a fat segmented body and half a dozen eyes set on short stalks around the base of a single long tentacle that ended in a snapping mouth crammed with crooked needles. A darkly translucent creature like a long flattened arrowhead that swam by flexing its body in sinuous curves, with two combs of stiff grasping poison-tipped spines around its mouth. A fist-sized creature that sculled to and fro on three pairs of paddles, its body like a streamlined helmet with two enormous eyes where the visor would be. It seemed to be the juvenile form of something much larger, Orjen said, known only from the tip of a claw-tipped tentacle embedded in the hull of a boat it had attacked; the life maps of the swimming helmet and the fragment of tentacle were identical.

Other tanks contained tangles of fast-growing red weed, or were filled with milky water from the lagoon, in which intricate lacework spires and plates and pebble-shaped structures sat like miniature cities sunk in fog. These were a kind of calcareous weed not found elsewhere, its growth apparently encouraged by the effluent discharged by the cement works. According to Orjen these weeds and every kind of little monster were the radically altered offspring of ordinary species which had been infected by microscopic pathogens called tailswallowers, because of their looped and knotted life maps.

'The tailswallowers are the root and heart of the invasion,' Orjen said. 'We are a long way from understanding how they take over the life maps of their hosts, but we are beginning to understand what we need to know.'

The lucidor felt a tingling unease and said, 'If these creatures are infected, could they infect us?'

'Don't worry. The tailswallowers which created these little monsters aren't the kind which infect people, and are in any case woven into the life maps of their hosts. And that's the most interesting and important thing about the invasion. The life maps of its tailswallowers are made of the same kind of stuff, and contain the same kind of patterns, as ordinary life maps, which means that we have a better chance of understanding and overcoming it before it spreads too far. Especially as our work is not hampered by the kind of cumbersome regulations and oversight demanded by your government.'

'I would hope that the people of the Free State would mobilise every necessary resource if the invasion threatened to cross the border,' the lucidor said. 'And I know that an acquaintance of mine would very much like your work. Remfrey He. Perhaps you know the name?'

Orjen gave him a sharp look. 'Is he someone you arrested for the so-called misuse of philosophy?'

'He crossed into this country a little while back, and must have passed through Roos on his way to the Big Island. Had he heard of your work, I'm sure he would have paid you a visit.'

'We have not been here long. And in a few days we will strike camp and move further west, where I hope to locate the leading edge of the invasion. Meanwhile, we have to get back to work, but first I'll point you towards someone who might be able to help you cross to the Big Island. You see, I hadn't forgotten about that.'

Orjen asked her steward for paper and brush, and in neat flowing characters wrote a short note – *Please give all the help you can to this traveller, so that he may continue his education across the Horned Strait* – and folded it and sealed it with a drip of wax melted over a ceramic burner and pressed her iron signet ring into the warm wax and handed the note to the lucidor. She waved away his thanks and told him to think about what she had shown him.

'If you survive combat with alter women or rebels and return home safely, tell your colleagues about what we are doing here. Tell them about the power of philosophical investigations that are not policed and regulated.'

Outside in the rain, the steward, Lyra Gurnek, gave directions to the house of a trader who had supplied reagents and equipment vital to Orjen's work. 'She's mostly honest, but she has connections with people who work on the shady side, and she's keen to keep up a relationship with someone like the boss, if you know what I mean.'

'Because your boss comes from a rich family.'

'Rich, and old, and influential,' Lyra said. 'She doesn't have to be working here. She doesn't need to do any kind of work at all. But here she is all the same. And she just did you a big favour. Not only the letter, but also by taking the time to show you a little of our part in the war against the invasion.'

'I am grateful for the favour. And for the demonstration of Patuan applied philosophy.'

'She's right to be proud of her work,' Lyra said. 'And she wouldn't have taken the trouble if she didn't think you might learn something. As for me, I reckon you have the look of a man who can't help but find trouble wherever he goes, so I hope you repay that favour by getting across to the Big Island soon as you can. Because when you do find trouble, or when trouble finds you, I'd like it to be somewhere so far away that we never get to hear about it.'

3

Wights

The trader's establishment was a three-storey house built of yellow clay brick and roofed with red tile, in the middle of a short row of similar houses that stood alongside a canal lock. In the shop that fronted it, with shelves of dry goods and canned and bottled produce laddering the walls and half of its counter given over to a bar, a young woman directed the lucidor to the stables at the rear, where a burly man took charge of the warhorse and the lucidor was led by the stable boy through a white-tiled kitchen to a small room off the corridor beyond. Heavy drapes were pulled across the window and the only light came from a lamp set on the table where the trader, Noojak Crow Pelee, sat, a stack of papers in front of her and a stalked instrument with a rotary dial and a wired earpiece at her left hand – a species of telephone, the first one the lucidor had seen outside a government office.

The trader was a small shrewd old woman dressed in black, propped by several cushions in her high-back chair and giving the impression that her feet did not quite touch the floor. Her wiry grey hair was parted down the middle and woven into two braids bound with black ribbon, a pipe burning clove-scented tobacco drooped in one corner of her mouth, and like the shop girl, the burly man and the stable boy, she was a wight, with pale waxy skin and a broad flat nose and eyes pinched by folds of skin under the heavy ledge of her brow. No wights lived in the Free State, but the lucidor had once worked with a wight lawkeeper from Patua while investigating a gang that had been smuggling remapped racing hounds across the border. They came

19

from Oase, a map two hundred and fifty thousand leagues to the north, where herds of long-haired elephants and rhinoceros roamed frigid plains, stalked by sabre-toothed cats and hunted by tribes of wights who built houses from the bones of their prey. Descendants of wights stranded in Patua after the great ships that sailed the World Ocean had been decommissioned kept their bloodline pure and maintained the traditions of their homeland. Some were merchants and traders; others travelled the roads of Patua in horse-drawn caravans, selling woollen blankets and rugs woven with intricate patterns, bone knives and scrimshaw carvings, searching out seasonal farm work and meeting in fairs where horses and dogs were sold, marriages made, and wrestling matches and spear-throwing contests were held.

The lucidor handed Orjen Starbreaker's letter to the old trader and she pinched a pair of spectacles over the end of her nose and closely studied the wax seal before snapping it with her thumbnail and unfolding the stiff paper and reading the message.

'Mistress Orjen is a good customer of mine,' she said, taking off her spectacles and looking up at the lucidor.

'So she told me,' the lucidor said. He had not been invited to sit, and was standing next to the chair on the other side of the table, trying his best to look indifferent and unthreatening.

'How do you know her?'

'I thought that she might be able to take me across the Horned Strait in her boat. She sent me here instead.'

Noojak Crow Pelee considered this, sipping on her pipe and rifling smoke from her nostrils. 'You must have made an impression on her.'

'She hoped to enlighten me about the importance of philosophical investigation.'

'She is dedicated and clever. Clever enough to come up with a way of defeating the invasion, perhaps. I certainly hope so. Meanwhile, we find what work we can to make up for the loss of our usual business, what with cargo boats being commandeered for ferrying troops and military supplies, and the reluctance of captains to sail the Strait unless they have naval escorts to protect them from attacks by sea monsters.'

'Orjen Starbreaker told me that she had examined a piece of tentacle from one of those attacks.'

'Did she tell you that I obtained it for her? Well, it doesn't matter. Tell me why you need to cross the Strait.'

The lucidor explained that he wanted to fight as a mercenary and handed Noojak the letter of recommendation got up by his old boss. She put on her spectacles again and carefully scrutinised it and asked him why he didn't want to take the ferry like everyone else. 'Could it be that you are in some kind of trouble?'

'It's more that I am trying to stay out of trouble.'

'And what kind of trouble would that be?'

The lucidor told her about his skirmish with the bandits on the train, how he had escaped and ridden off on one of their horses. 'I can't be certain,' he said, 'that the authorities in Roos would be sympathetic.'

'Probably not. The commandant of the garrison is a straight-backed stiff-necked fellow with no vices worth speaking of and little liking for my people and other outsiders, such as yourself. I understand that the train was set on fire.'

'One of the bandits was armed with a blazer. It went off when I defended myself.'

'I also understand that one of them was killed, and two more were taken into custody.'

'I am pleased to hear it. But it had nothing to do with me.'

'No, you ran away. You say that you want to become a mercenary, yet you didn't try to protect the other passengers.'

'The bandits weren't interested in the other passengers.'

'They were interested only in you?'

'I believe that they wanted to capture me and take me back to the Free State.'

'Why would they go to such trouble?'

'I was once a lawkeeper. I retired several years ago, but there is always some unfinished business.'

Noojak drew on her pipe and contemplated the plume of smoke she exhaled and said, 'Are you saying that these bandits had a grudge against you? That they wanted revenge because you vanquished them in some previous encounter?'

'I didn't ask what they wanted. I was too busy getting away.'

'That doesn't quite answer my question.'

'It's the truth.'

'That's rather sly of you. Well I won't ask what it was really about. Better if I do not know.'

'That's also true.'

'Do you believe that you are still in danger?'

'I believe I will be in much less danger once I am on the far side of the Horned Strait.'

'Luckily for you, I have little liking of bandits. They make business difficult for everyone,' Noojak said, and flicked the lucidor's letter across the table. 'I can arrange a boat for you, but you will have to wait until tomorrow night.'

'Do all your boats travel at night?'

'Only the ones we don't want the garrison to know about. I will make the arrangements because Mistress Orjen asked me for a favour, but you will have to pay the people who take you across. And given the trouble you are in, I will need that payment now.'

'We can discuss that after I have sold my horse and its saddle.'

'Do you know where to trade stolen horses?'

'In a town like this, I'm sure that there's more than one place.'

'It isn't easy for a stranger to get a fair price. Or to avoid the attention of the authorities. But I can help you,' Noojak said, and called to the stable boy, who had been waiting outside, and told him to fetch Kilik.

Kilik was the burly shaven-headed man who had stabled the warhorse. He talked briefly with Noojak in the wights' liquid tongue, and Noojak wrote two numbers on a piece of paper and pushed it across the table to the lucidor.

'The figure on top is what we are willing to pay for your horse and saddle. It's less than you might get elsewhere, but the horse is stolen and we're assuming the risk. Fair?'

'In the circumstances.'

'The figure beneath, that's what you will pay for your trip,' Noojak said. 'You see it is less than the price of the horse. I can give you credit in the store for the difference.'

The lucidor understood that he was being rooked, but smiled and agreed, and asked, as if giving voice to a sudden afterthought, if Noojak had given the same kind of help to a countryman of his, Remfrey He.

'I don't know that name.'

'Like me, he wanted to join the war against the invasion. He may have been travelling under an assumed identity, and most likely with an escort.'

The lucidor began to describe Remfrey He, and Noojak held up her hand. Her little finger was missing and there were ivory rings on the rest. 'I do not often give this kind of help, and never before to someone from your country. Do you have a place to stay?'

'Not yet. I'm sure I can find somewhere.'

'Then you will stay here,' Noojak said.

'How much will that cost me?'

'I will have to charge a little extra, considering the circumstances. But don't worry about it. It will be deducted from your credit.'

The room was a pinched space with a bare plank floor under the eaves of the stable roof. A bed as narrow as a coffin and a stand with a bowl and a pitcher of water were all the furniture there was. A small dusty window gave a view across the yard and the wasteland beyond its wall, where mounds of bricks overgrown with ivy and honeysuckle outlined what had once been houses and streets. The stable boy brought a bowl of red beans mixed with chunks of fish and onion; the lucidor was still eating when a man knocked at the door and told him that his travel arrangements had been made.

'People we have used several times before. They are as reliable as any in the business.'

'How will I find them?'

'Someone will take you. Tomorrow evening, at the beginning of the third watch. Oh, and we have found a buyer for your horse.'

'I should thank your mistress.'

'She's my mother,' the man said. 'And there's no need for thanks. It's strictly business.'

The lucidor slept surprisingly well. He had placed his fate in the hands of others and had nothing to do now but wait. He woke when the stable boy brought his breakfast – pickled fish fillets rolled around gherkins, thin dry slices of black bread, and chai with butter melted into it. The boy set the tray on the stand and at the door hesitated and asked the lucidor if he was a soldier.

'Not exactly. But I am heading towards the war.'

'Do you fight with that stick?'

The boy was looking at the staff, which leaned against the wall by the head of the bed. It was a single piece of supple black oak a little under two spans in length, shod with iron at both ends.

'It's called a staff,' the lucidor said. 'Haven't you seen one before?'

The boy shook his head. He seemed to be about eleven or twelve, a skinny boy with milky skin, curly red hair shaved high around the sides, wire-rimmed spectacles. The legs of his denim coveralls were rolled at his ankles and the corner of a thin paperback book stuck out of one of the pockets.

He said, 'Have you ever killed people with your staff?'

'I prefer to disarm and subdue them.'

'Could you kill monsters with it?'

'I don't know. I have never tried.'

'I want to fight the monsters,' the boy said, 'but people like me aren't allowed to join the army.'

'By people like you, you mean wights.'

The boy nodded. From somewhere below, a man's voice called out something in the wights' language.

The lucidor said, 'What's your name?'

'Panap.'

'There are other ways of fighting the invasion, Panap. A woman I met yesterday is making a study of monsters. Different kinds of small ones, from the sea. She is trying to find out how they were made and how they live, and how to stop them spreading any further. It seems to me that it might be the best chance of defeating the invasion.'

'But you're going to fight,' the boy said.

'I am not a philosopher, and it's too late for me to learn how to become one. But a boy like you, bright and curious as you are, might make a go of it.'

24

The man's voice called out again.

'I hope you kill lots when you get to the other side,' Panap said with sudden fierceness, and was gone.

The lucidor was leaning at the window and sipping his oily chai when Kilik led the warhorse by a catch halter into the yard, where two women were waiting beside a buckboard wagon. The women watched as the warhorse was walked around the yard and one of them talked with Kilik while the other ran her hands along the edges of the warhorse's horn plates, lifted her legs one after the other and inspected her hooves, stuck a stout stick in her mouth and examined her teeth, and used a sounding tube to listen to her heart. Kilik and the stable boy, Panap, brought out the saddle and saddle blanket and bridle, and the woman who had examined the warhorse held the lead rope while her companion strapped on the saddle and swapped out the halter for the bridle and mounted up. She rode the warhorse twice around the yard before cantering out of the gate and out across the wasteland along a track that was no more than a mane of grass between two ruts.

The lucidor watched from his window, and Kilik and Panap and the other woman watched from the gate, as the warhorse turned and came back along the track at a brisk trot. The woman in the saddle leaned down and said something to her companion and reined the warhorse around and spurred her into a gallop. In a moment, horse and rider dwindled down the track towards its vanishing point, returning a few minutes later and coming to a hard stop by the gate, the warhorse rearing on her hind legs with a harsh scream that shivered the glass in front of the lucidor's nose and shocked several big white birds from the ridge of the house's roof.

The rider hauled on the reins and brought the warhorse down, sparks flying as knife-edged hooves struck brick paving, and walked her through the arch of the gate into the yard and swung down from the saddle and leaned against the warhorse's flank and stroked her neck and spoke into her ear before handing the reins to Panap. The two women conferred with each other, and then had a short, serious conversation with Kilik. At last the deal was done. Panap ran off to the kitchen and returned carrying a tray with glasses and a bottle and a plate of green gherkins. Kilik and the two women took bites from the gherkins and tossed shots of clear liquor down their throats and bumped fists, and the warhorse was hitched to the buckboard wagon and the women drove off with the warhorse trotting behind.

Although the lucidor had stolen her and ridden her for only a couple of days, although he did not even know her name, he felt a small sharp pang of regret as he watched her go. He had treated her as nothing more than an ordinary mount and she would be better handled now, ridden by someone who knew how to use her potential to the fullest, but in giving her up he had also given up his last chance of turning back. It was as if a door had closed, finally and completely, on everything he knew. Everything he had left behind. The only way was forward.

He shaved with cold water from the pitcher, untied the bandage around his left arm. The margins of the gouge seemed less inflamed, and when he eased out the glass moss packing there was no blood or discharge. He splashed water over the wound and dabbed it dry and replaced the glass moss and retied the bandage and went down to the yard and performed his morning exercises, using his staff for balance as he moved slowly from position to position. Panap watched him from the stable door but was called away by Kilik before the lucidor had finished.

No one tried to stop him when he walked out of the open gate. He followed the canal to a basin where single-masted cargo ships were tied up in the shadow of square brick warehouses, and with nothing better to do, more from habit than hope, spent a couple of hours asking the ships' crews if they had taken or knew of anyone who had taken a man named Remfrey He, escorted by either soldiers or lawkeepers, across the Horned Strait. Finding out the size and nature of Remfrey He's escort party, their unit and the rank and name of the officer in command, would give him some idea of the security around the man and might help to trace him, too, but no one recognised He's name or description, and the general opinion was that anyone in the care of the army would have been transported aboard one of the military ships that sailed from Roos to points north and south on the Big Island.

There was a small commercial area a little further on, clustered around a crossroads where a huge latticework globe stood on a plinth of black baserock. Maps, some entire and others patch-worked from islands or continents, none bigger than a child's hand, were scattered thinly across its surface. The home map, Gea, was a squarish red tile close to the equator, smaller than most of the rest, and a silvery ball representing the Heartsun was spindled at the centre, and everything was spattered by the droppings of a fractious parliament of vivid green birds which had colonised the globe's pole, chattering each to each and scolding passers-by.

Cafés, bars and chai houses, shops where food and clothes and all manner of goods could be bought without needing a chit or ration card, lined the streets. The lucidor found a flyblown hotel with a sign above its door stating that its rooms could be rented by the hour and bribed the desk clerk with one of the greasy plastic notes he'd been given and paged through the register, and wasn't much surprised when he failed to find Remfrey He's name, or any name signed with He's characteristic loops and flourishes. If the man had spent any time in Roos it was likely that he would have been quartered in the citadel, and because it was also likely that the lucidor's description and name and alias had been passed to the Patuan authorities he could no more pay a visit to the citadel than he could risk taking the ferry.

He ate a plate of fish sausage and charred slices of green tomato at one of the sidewalk cafés and walked back to Noojak Crow Pelee's house and dozed through the afternoon, waking when the stable boy, Panap, knocked shyly at the door and said that he would take him to the dock where the boat was waiting. It was dusk, and lights showed in windows of the row of brick houses and street lights were burned above their reflections in the black water of the canal. As they walked beside it, the lucidor asked Panap if he'd had any thoughts about their conversation that morning.

'I'd still rather fight,' Panap said. 'If I can't join the army, maybe I'll become a mercenary like you. I'll fight monsters and kill as many as I can, and make the rest so scared they'll run away. And then we can go home again, my family and me.'

'How old are you, Panap?'

'Almost nine.'

'I had thought you a little older. Your people must grow up more quickly than ours.'

'We're stronger, too. Better fighters. That's why it's stupid, not letting us join the army.'

'And where is your home, if it isn't here?'

'Ymr. Do you know it?'

'It was the capital, before the invasion.'

'I was born there, but I don't remember it because we left when I was very young, and my parents don't want to talk about it because it makes them sad. But I've seen pictures in some of Granny Noojak's books, and read about its history. It's two thousand years old. Almost as old as the world. A godling built a city there in a day, all of glass, and another destroyed it in an hour. And then the godlings left and people built Ymr on the ruins. So it's old, and it's also very holy. That's why it's so important to protect it from the invasion.'

'You like to read, don't you? You mentioned your grandmother's books, and you have one tucked in your pocket.'

'It's a hero story. A good one.'

'What kind of hero?'

'A man who solves crimes the lawkeepers can't. He has a gift that allows him to see into the souls of people, and a ring set with a shatterling fragment that glows red when there's danger near.'

The lucidor smiled at the boy's artless enthusiasm. He said, 'You remind me of a friend I had at school. He also liked to read. He spent most of his spare time studying old books and records in the school library, knew all kinds of odd things. After leaving school, he was assigned to the records office of my department. He was happy there. He loved his work and he was good at it, and it was useful too.'

No point telling the boy that Sym had liked his food and drink as much as his books, and had died of apoplexy eight years ago.

'Amongst other things, he helped lawkeepers by uncovering irregularities in the paperwork of businesses they were investigating, or by pointing out similarities between new crimes and

28

old cases. Just as there are different ways of fighting crime, there might be other ways of defeating the invasion. Do you remember the philosopher I mentioned, yesterday?'

'I think so.'

'Her name is Orjen Starbreaker. Ask your grandmother about her. Ask if you could visit her. She will show you all kinds of little monsters, and explain that the best way to defeat the invasion is to understand how they came to be what they are, and how they live.'

'You can see monsters right here sometimes. They come up into the canal from the tidal causeways. Last week soldiers were scooping out big jellyfish. Thousands of them.'

'That's what I mean. You can't defeat things like that with pistols or staffs. But if you're clever you might be able to find a weakness you can exploit. Orjen Starbreaker can explain it better than me. She's camped right on the shore, near the cement factory and a little fishing village. Tell her I sent you, and tell her you like animals. You do like animals, don't you?'

'I like horses.'

'People who really like something want to find out all they can about it. I'm sure you want to learn all about horses, and there's something of a science to it, so you're already on the path,'

'Why do you care what I do?'

'I don't know. Perhaps because you remind me of my friend. And also of myself, when I was younger. I was recruited when I was about your age, and I didn't have the chance to find out what else I could do. And you're cleverer than me, and I think you can do better than the army.'

'That's what my parents say.'

'Sometimes it's a good idea to listen to your parents.'

The lucidor was telling Panap about the strange creatures Orjen had shown him as they climbed the steep hump of a footbridge over the canal. When they reached the top, a man stepped into the pool of light cast by a lamp at the far end. Lucidor Cyf, his staff slung over his shoulder.

4

Cyf

'You are a long way from home, Lucidor Kyl,' Cyf said.

'You have forgotten that I go by Thorn, now, Lucidor Cyf. I reclaimed my birth name after I retired.'

The lucidor had last seen the man in the market of the border town, and wasn't surprised to see him again.

'I heard you also go by Saj Orym Zier,' Cyf said. 'For someone supposedly retired, you have been very busy of late. Crossing the border using false documents, getting mixed up with bandits and setting fire to a train, stealing a horse . . . Oh, and conspiracy to kidnap. The department knows all about that. Scorpions arrested Pyn and half a dozen of his friends.'

The lucidor had already guessed that the little cabal, such as it was, had been betrayed or discovered, but he still felt a small sharp jolt of shock. It was Pyn, his old boss, who had given him the news about Remfrey He's escape to Patua. They had met in one of the oldest chai houses in Liberty City, a converted barge moored at the embankment in the shadow of the People's House, with views across the river to the salt-white houses of the new town and the tawny hills beyond, the lucidor dressed in his work clothes, a loosely belted striped robe and the kind of conical straw hat favoured by labourers, Pyn in a white shirt and loose linen trousers. A small neat precise man who looked like a clerk and possessed the devious mind and low cunning of the worst kind of criminal. After reminiscing about the old days, old cases, old colleagues, Pyn had brought the conversation around to Remfrey He, explaining that his 'escape' had been arranged after a secret agreement between representatives on the security committee and high-ranking officers in the Patuan army, asking the lucidor if he wanted to do something about it.

The lucidor said now, to Cyf, 'Have Pyn and his friends been charged?'

'Not yet. And it's possible that they won't be,' Cyf said. 'It seems that Pyn has comprehensive evidence about decisions and actions concerning Remfrey He that were made by a few individuals without proper authority or due process. Everything is up in the air right now, and when it settles out Pyn may walk away unscathed.'

'He has a mind as sharp as a box of knives. Always thinking ahead. Covering every angle. And what about me? Did you come all the way out here to arrest me?'

'Of course not: I don't have any authority in Patua. No, I came here as a friend, hoping to persuade you to do the right thing,' Cyf said, meeting the lucidor's gaze unblinkingly.

He was a blunt, burly middle-aged man somewhat shorter than the lucidor, denser, with dark close-set eyes, and curly hair razored short, receding from his broad forehead. A meticulous and conscientious investigator who made good use of his scrying gift and worked his cases by the book. He had never threatened or cajoled suspects during investigations, had never tried to trick them into admitting their guilt, told them that he was there to help them get things straight, led them to believe that they would get a better deal by cooperating or let them think that they had a chance to outsmart him. Instead, he had worn them down with relentless patience, dismantling their lies, evasions, false alibis and excuses until only the truth was left. Back when Cyf had been a freshly turned-out rookie the lucidor had been one of his tutors, and they had worked several cases together in the years since. They knew each other as well as friends and colleagues could, although they had drifted apart after the lucidor had retired. The lucidor's fault, that, not Cyf's. His stubborn pride.

'And what would the right thing be?' the lucidor said. 'According to you.'

'To return to the Free State, of course. Tell your side of the story.'

'After being arrested, no doubt, when I cross back over the border.'

'Well, yes. But it will be no more than a formality,' Cyf said.

'And the bandits,' the lucidor said. 'Were they trying to help me, or were they trying to kill me?'

'I didn't have anything to do with that.'

'Someone hired them.'

'I believe they were hoping to claim the reward put up for your return. Who's the kid, by the way?' Cyf said, looking at Panap, who had stopped, uncertain, a little way behind the lucidor.

'He doesn't have anything to do with this.'

'Yet he's leading you to a boat owned by a couple of smugglers.'

The lucidor turned to Panap, asked him where the boat was moored.

'There's a little dock past those warehouses,' the boy said, pointing.

'They're expecting me?'

Panap nodded. 'Look for the green light.'

'I'll find it. You run on home, Panap. There's no need for you to come any further.'

The boy looked at Cyf, looked at the lucidor. 'Are you going to fight?'

'We're just catching up on what we have been doing since we last saw each other. Go on now, and don't forget what I told you about Orjen Starbreaker.'

The boy hesitated, and the lucidor gripped his shoulders and spun him around. 'Right now! Quick as you can!'

As Panap sprinted away, elbows flapping, the lucidor walked down the hump of the bridge towards Cyf, saying, 'You know I am going to catch that boat.'

'I know you should come back with me,' Cyf said, falling into step with him. 'You'll have to answer to the charges against you, but you have plenty of friends in the department. We'll see to it that you get a fair hearing.'

'And Remfrey He. Will he be sent back? Will he get a fair hearing?'

'I suppose that would depend on the Patuans.'

'And that is exactly why Pyn sent me here. Why I can't go back unless I bring Remfrey He with me.'

'We're doing our best to sort this out,' Cyf said. 'We really are. And frankly, Kyl – and I'm going to call you Kyl because your alias is too much of a mouthful and I can't picture you with some quaint back-country cactus-herder name like "Thorn". Frankly? You're too old for this kind of nonsense. Come back with me before you get into real trouble.'

The lucidor remembered how Cyf would sit hunched at one of the long tables in the investigations office, working his way through reports and statements and technical assessments with frowning concentration. Walking down the street with his former colleague, passing between cones of lamplight, he was reminded once again of everything he had left behind, but now he felt skittish, light-limbed. Freed of all plans and obligations, eager for flight.

He said, 'Don't worry about me. I can still look after myself. As those bandits discovered.'

'You got lucky there.'

'I think I did well enough. One dead, two of the others arrested. Who escaped? Was it the woman who shot at me with a blazer?'

'No, she was taken prisoner after you knocked her out. Do you know who she is?'

'I didn't have time to ask.'

'Agna Agnasdaughter, also known as the Bloody Rose. A notorious outlaw wanted for piracy, banditry, kidnap, horse stealing, and general mayhem, including at least six murders. She has the quicknerve gift – it must have surprised the living death out of her when she tried and failed to beat you to the draw. I suppose the people who put up the reward for your capture neglected to mention that you're a suppressor.'

'As I said, I can look after myself,' the lucidor said, remembering the woman's consternation when she had fumbled for her blazer.

'She's in prison, awaiting trial and execution.'

'I can't say I am sorry to hear it. She meant to kill me, and nearly did,' the lucidor said, touching the place where his hair had been crisped by the blazer's tight hot beam.

'The bandit who was killed, shot by one of the train guards, was the man whose horse you stole. Bloody Rose's husband, Erslan. Erslan the Toothcutter, like her wanted for kidnap and murder. He got his name because he wore a necklace made from the teeth of his victims.'

'Again, I can't say I'm sorry.'

Cyf ignored that. 'That horse was how I found you. I slipped money to a couple of people in the trade, and one of them told me that someone had bought a warhorse just this morning. It didn't take much more to find out that the people who sold it have a sideline in smuggling. All I had to do was wait for you to show yourself, and here we are.'

'I am beginning to think that I might have trained you a little too well.'

'Patuan lawkeepers are looking for you, along with every low-life who thinks you'll be an easy takedown for good money. And the Bloody Rose's gang is probably out for revenge. Do you really think you can find Remfrey He before one of those parties catches up with you?'

'None of that will matter once I get across the Horned Strait.'

'There are bandits on the other side, too. Not to mention rebels who would happily take a wanted man hostage, and use him as a bargaining piece with the government. And even if you avoid the bandits and rebels and lawkeepers, a couple of scorpions are helping the Patuans keep Remfrey He safe. They aren't going to hold up their hands and let you take him from them.'

Scorpions were agents of the Office of External Affairs, an elite force that worked directly for the Council of Nine.

The lucidor said, 'Perhaps I can persuade them to do the right thing, and help me take Remfrey He back where he belongs.'

'You know that won't happen.'

'I am not supposed to be here, Cyf. Yet here I am. Who knows what else is possible?'

The street cut between two tall warehouses to a quay at the edge of a long dark reach of water. Off in the distance was a small stone jetty with a green light at its end, and a single small boat drawn up beside it.

Cyf put his hand on the lucidor's shoulder and said, 'You don't have to do this right away. Give it a day. Take some time to think it through.'

'I have already thought it through.'

The two men stood facing each other. The warehouses loomed above, shuttered and dark.

Cyf said, 'For all you know, Remfrey He may be doing some good here.'

'He could be developing the ultimate weapon against the invasion, but he will also be looking for ways to amuse himself. To have a little fun. And you know as well as I what that involves. What kind of horrors. He should never have been sent here, Cyf, and he has to go back. Back to the Free State, to spend the rest of his life in a place where he cannot hurt other people.'

'Even so, he's no longer your responsibility.'

'It was my case. My arrest. My testimony. That is why Pyn asked me to bring He back. That is why I agreed to go.'

Cyf said, 'That is how Pyn put his hook in you. And to what end? You couldn't do anything after Remfrey He's sentence was commuted to internal exile. You can't do anything now.'

'I did do something, if you recall.'

'Yes, you did. You resigned. Remind me how that worked out.'

'I know what I need to do.'

'And you gave it your best shot. But a man your age should not be mixing it up with bandits, and right now you need to come home with me before you get into real trouble.'

'Those bandits tried their best to kill me, so I would guess that the people who put up the reward would rather I was brought back dead than alive.'

'I want you to come back safe and sound. So do your friends in the department. Not to mention your sister.'

'What my sister thinks or wants is none of your business.'

'She's worried about you, Kyl.'

Maybe she was, but the lucidor had not seen her since his wife's funeral, six years ago. He said, 'When you get back to the Free State, you can tell her that you talked to me and I was in good health and fine spirits.'

'I told her I would bring you back with me,' Cyf said, and reached over his shoulder and gripped the end of his staff.

'I am not going to fight you, Cyf. And you do not want to fight me. If you did, we wouldn't have had this conversation. Go back to the Free State. Tell everyone that I am doing what needs to be done.'

The lucidor squared his shoulders and walked on towards the wharf and the waiting boat. Cyf didn't try to follow. 'Don't think it ends here,' he called out.

The lucidor did not reply. As far as he was concerned he had finished with the department long ago. He did not owe it any kind of valediction.

5

Peculiars

His ride was a fishing boat scarcely ten spans from stem to stern, with a turtleshell coracle lashed to the roof of its wheelhouse and its pulsion motor throbbing underfoot like a resolute heart as it headed out to the wide dark flood of the Horned Strait. It was owned and crewed by a pair of fisherfolk from the Fair Isles. Jem and Esse, husband and wife. According to Jem, they had been forced to turn to what he called the ghost cargo trade to make ends meet after fishing had gone all to hell right across the Strait.

'Back in the day, in the kelp forests, you could lower a stick with just a picture of bait tied to it, and bring it up a minute later with half a dozen fine fat crabs clamped on. Lobsters too. And all kinds of fish, and clams big as this,' Jem said, holding his arms wide. 'Enough eating on one of them to feed a man for a week.'

Jem and the lucidor were standing either side of the cramped little wheelhouse, where Esse perched on a tall stool at the helm, all three of them shadows in the shadowy dark. The boat was ploughing across what appeared to be limitless black water under a cloud-sheeted sky, the lights of Roos receding into the night behind them. There were monsters lurking in the sea's unguessable depths, the lucidor had to trust the two smugglers and their frail craft to see him safely across, but he was filled with a reckless elation. He had not felt this alive in years.

'It was easy living,' Jem said, 'until thorn stars arrived and started in on the kelp. You know what I'm talking about, kelp?'

The lucidor admitted that he did not.

'That's right. You Freestaters have seas made of sand instead of water. But you have trees, don't you?'

'Here and there.'

'Kelp is a sort of underwater tree, with holdfasts like roots, and long stems, and blades that spread out across the surface of the water. Thorn stars eat away the holdfasts until the kelp plants detach from their moorings and drift up and away on the currents, and then the thorn stars eat the rest. You can still see slicks of kelp floating out here, covered in black balls. Thousands of the little devils. They breed fast and nothing will touch them, because they're all armour and gristle.'

'I believe you,' the lucidor said, thinking of the little monsters Orjen Starbreaker had shown him.

'Some say they'll attack a boat that gets too close to one of those slicks,' Esse said. 'Clamp onto its hull and gnaw right through it.'

She was a calm, practical, broad-hipped woman, somewhat older than her husband, dressed like him in a denim shirt and denim trousers, a kerchief knotted around her neck. One of the sleeves of her shirt, the left, was pinned up. As soon as the lucidor had come aboard she had told him that she'd lost her arm when she was a little girl, an accident involving a line that had snapped free of a winch. She liked to get it out of the way, she said, because people always wanted to ask, and she could handle a boat as well as anyone else.

'About the only fish left are another kind of monster,' Jem said. 'What we call peculiars. They're big and ugly, and their blood's poisonous, so they're pulped and the pulp is treated with chemicals and dried into flakes. Not my idea of food, but needs must for some.'

'People will eat anything if they're hungry enough,' Esse said. 'And a lot of people are.'

'Hard times come for everyone,' Jem told the lucidor. He was the voluble, nervy type who would talk about anything and everything that came into their heads during an interrogation: all you had to do was wait until you caught them in a lie or flagrant contradiction. 'When you get to the war, you might well find yourself alongside fisherfolk who turned to the blood-and-glory trade because there's nothing left for them back home. Lucky for you, some of us are smart enough to find other ways of earning a living. Though it has to be said, we mostly take people who are going in the other direction. Last fellow, he was quartermaster of an army corps. Sold drugs on the side, and made good money out of it. Enough to set him up for life. Trouble was, he was too good at it. When his tour of duty ended the people who supplied him wanted him to sign up again. Threatened to kill him if he didn't. So he went on the run, and we helped him get across.'

'He told you all that?'

'Oh, you know how it is. People like to talk when they're on the last part of their journey. Once they know they're out of danger.'

Esse looked over her shoulder and said, 'That's enough about that.'

'We're just passing the time,' Jem said.

'He doesn't need to hear your nonsense.'

'Aren't you worried about monsters out here?' the lucidor said. 'I heard some are big enough to attack boats.'

'There aren't that many of the really big ones,' Jem said. 'And we know the places where they might be found, and keep well away. In our business, it isn't monsters that put us at hazard. It's people. Lawkeepers want a cut in exchange for turning a blind eye, which is only reasonable, like paying taxes. Only there are some who take their cut and turn right around and arrest you. Or they'll intercept some poor crew out at sea and pitch them overboard or kill them outright, say they were resisting arrest, and seize the cargo. And you know some of it goes missing before it's inventoried. And then there are gangs who prey on folk like us, or try to get them to carry cargo they don't want to carry. Drugs. Weapons. You agree to take one package of drugs across, next thing you know you're beholden, and you can't go to the law for help because you have already broken the law. We have family backing us up, so we don't get that kind of trouble. Others aren't so lucky.'

'There you go again,' Esse said. 'Wearing out the man's ears with your foolishness. Do something useful. Spell me at the wheel.'

'Is it that time?'

'You know it is,' Esse said, and cut the motor and told the lucidor that her husband knew the currents in the deep water better than

39

she did. She seemed to stumble as she climbed down from the stool, and the lucidor unthinkingly reached out to steady her and she thrust her hand under his nose and told him to look at it.

Her cupped palm was empty.

'Stay right still and don't look away, damn you,' she said, with a glare of furious concentration.

'Just do it, Esse,' Jem said.

'It isn't working,' Esse said, and reached inside her shirt and pulled out a knife.

The lucidor grabbed her wrist and twisted it up and back until she had to open her fingers and drop the weapon. She writhed furiously in his grip, tried to head-butt him, and he swung her around and slammed her head against the frame of the wheel-house door, kicked her legs out from under her and stepped back and drew his staff.

Jem looked at the lucidor, looked at the Esse's knife, which had fallen point first and stuck in the deck. Its handle was wrapped in cord, its stone blade worn pencil-thin by years of sharpening, a deadly little needle that could slice a man's throat to the bone, or kill him with a single thrust to the heart. The lucidor snatched it up and threw it out into the dark beyond the gunwale, told Jesse to stay exactly where he was, and pressed the iron-shod end of his staff against Esse's breastbone when she started to push to her feet.

He had Jem tie up his wife, asked them if this was how they treated all their passengers.

'Only murdering scum like you,' Esse said.

'It was her idea,' Jem said.

'Shut up, Jem.'

'And where did she get that idea?' the lucidor said.

'The warhorse,' Jem said. He was standing beside her, hands on his head, swaying as the boat rocked idly.

'The warhorse?'

'The one you sold. That belongs to Esse's sister's husband.'

'Didn't I say shut up? Don't give him anything.'

The lucidor met Esse's angry gaze. She was sitting with her back hard against the transom of the little boat's stern, her arm lashed to her side by rope wound four times around her waist and knotted to one of the posts of the net winch.

'Your sister is the Bloody Rose, so called.'

'Who is in jail, thanks to you. And also a widow, because you killed her husband.'

'It was a train guard who killed him. How many teeth were there, on that famous necklace of his? How many did he kill? His death could not begin to make up for them. And he wouldn't have died if he and the rest of your sister's gang hadn't chosen to come after me.'

'We weren't going to kill you,' Jem said. 'We were going to ransom you, in exchange for the Rose.'

'Just for once in your life stop talking,' Esse said.

'I'm not the one who failed to overpower him.'

'You have a gift,' the lucidor said to Esse. 'Your sister had one too. She was quicknerved, and I reckon that you are a silvertongue.'

'And I reckon you aren't as smart as you think you are,' Esse said.

'Some silvertongues work their gift by words alone; others manifest a spark or a little flame,' the lucidor said. 'People cannot look away once they have seen it, and do what you tell them. We sometimes used silvertongues in interrogations. They can make all but the most stubborn or crazy tell the truth, or some version of it. But I couldn't be in the interrogation room or anywhere close by, because I have a gift too, the kind that stops other gifts from working.'

'Our rotten luck,' Jem said.

'People with your gift are used to getting want they want,' the lucidor told Esse. 'Used to seeing other people as servants to their will. That's how you got that quartermaster to talk, isn't it? And then you tipped him overboard. Or told him to jump.'

'We do what we have to do, in these hard times,' Jem said.

'Your wife is a lot older than you, and I have to wonder – did she really lose that arm in a fishing accident, or was she in the same trade as her sister? Was marriage your idea, or hers?'

'Don't listen to him,' Esse said.

41

'I suggest you stop listening to her,' the lucidor told Jem. 'And don't look into that flame of hers any more, either. Even if it does make you feel good.'

'What are you going to do with us?' Jem said.

'If you take me across the Strait to Naxos, as we agreed, I will leave you to work out what to do with the rest of your lives. Giving up this trade would be a good first step.'

With the lucidor at his back, Jem took the wheel and restarted the motor. After a little while, he pointed to a dark line at the dark horizon and said it was the coast of the Big Island.

'How much further to Naxos?'

'Two or three hours. More or less.'

'You had best be heading in the right direction.'

'This boat was my father's, and his father's before that. I've been sailing this sea all my life. Haven't got lost yet.'

The coast, if that was what it was, seemed a long way off, there was no sign of the lights of the port they were supposed to be heading for, and the lucidor had no idea where it was and no trust or liking for the little boat's helmsman, but he felt a cautious measure of hope. He had overcome his would-be kidnappers, and as far as he was concerned any landfall on the Big Island would be good enough. The boat ploughed a straight course through the night, smacking through small waves, but the dark line did not seem to grow any closer, and after a little while discs of cold blue light began to appear in the black water all around.

They weren't creatures of the invasion, according to Jem. Just ordinary jellyfish.

'Mirror jellies. Them and the thorn stars are about the only things that thrive out here, now.'

The jellyfish were half a span or more across, their blue glow brightening and dimming as they languorously pulsed beneath the surface of the water, growing ever more numerous until they were crowding edge to edge all around, merging into a general glow sliced by random black lines of open water. The pulsion motor began to labour as the boat pushed through them, and then it cut out and the boat drifted sideways while Jem fussed at the controls.

'Jellies must have clogged the inlets,' he said at last.

'So unclog them.'

'They're under the boat. We'll have to use a drag line.'

Esse said, 'Why bother? Perhaps he wasn't meant to get across.'

'I'm doing this to save all of us,' Jem said, and started to uncoil a rope, told the lucidor that all they had to do was loop it over the prow and saw it over the inlets. 'It should scrub off anything stuck there, long as we keep it as taut as we can.'

It took a while, crabbing sideways along the sides of the boat as it rocked on the swell, paying out the rope as they hauled it across the keel to the location of the inlets, pulling it back and forth. At last Jem said they had done all they could, and they walked the loop of rope back to the prow and Jem ducked into the wheelhouse and started the engine. It ran for a few moments and shut down and would not start again.

'You fools,' Esse said. 'They're all up inside the inlets, where no amount of rope can reach.'

'What does she mean?' the lucidor said to Jem.

'The inlets have mesh filters over them,' Jem said. 'I was hoping the jellies had stuck to them, but they must have been sucked through. Can you swim?'

'Barely,' the lucidor said.

He had splashed about with the other children in the pools of the oasis where he'd been born, but hadn't had much use for it since.

'You don't need to do anything fancy. Just get under the boat and unclog the inlets by hand.'

'That's your job, not mine.'

'I can't swim.'

'It's true,' Esse said. 'Most fisherfolk won't. Or can't.'

'Better to drown quick than slow,' Jem said. 'How we see it.'

'What about her?' the lucidor said, looking at Esse.

'With one arm? And anyway, why should I?'

In the blue glow all around the boat her smile looked like one of the grotesque masks worn by actors playing godlings.

'All you have to do is unclip the filters and stick your arm in and scoop out the mess,' Jem told the lucidor. 'It won't take but five minutes.'

'And as soon as I jump in the water, you'll start the motor and take off.'

'We aren't going anywhere if the motor can't take in water to push it out behind. With the inlets clogged it just overheats and shuts down. You don't believe me, you can try to start it up yourself, but you won't do any better than I did.'

'What about that little coracle, on the roof there. Can't you use it to tow us out of here?'

'It's too far to row. And too dangerous, in something that small. There are monsters that might could swallow it whole.'

'This boat does not feel much bigger. And it isn't going anywhere.'

'It will, once we've cleared the inlets.'

They were staring at each other, Jem looking angry and scared, the lucidor trying to work out if all of this was some kind of trick.

'We'll try the drag line again,' the lucidor said, breaking the silence.

'It won't work,' Esse said.

'You will know if I want your opinion, because I'll ask for it,' the lucidor said.

'She's right, even so,' Jem said.

'It's either the drag line, or taking to the coracle,' the lucidor said, and stared at the man until he looked away. 'Let's get to it.'

He and Jem were working the loop of rope over the boat's prow when the boat tilted sideways as something scraped along its hull. The lucidor dropped his end of the rope and grabbed the edge of the wheelhouse, saw a shape half the length of the boat moving away, cutting a dark lane through the glowing cobbles of jellyfish.

Esse laughed and began to stamp her feet on the deck planking. One two. One two. Hard as she could.

'Quit it!' Jem said. 'That was a peculiar. There'll be more out there.'

'Bring them on,' Esse said, staring at her husband and the lucidor with hot defiance. 'He wasn't ever going to let us go free. Better we both die out here, so long as he does too.'

She began to stamp her feet again. The lucidor started towards her, and something struck the boat amidships. The lucidor lost his balance and sat down hard, and Jem loomed over him and swung the tarred end of the rope and there was an explosion of white light and somehow he was lying in a slop of cold water, his head echoing like a rung bell.

Jem was working at the knots that bound his wife to the winch post, Esse was kicking and swearing, telling him to finish off the damn murderer, and something smashed into the stern, splintering planks and throwing up a spout of water that rained across the boat's length. Jem fell down and Esse screamed as the transom exploded inwards and a broad head pushed up under the drum of the winch. It was mostly mouth, a chinless lipless maw with clusters of pale wormy tentacles writhing at each corner and a dozen small black eyes randomly studding a broad forehead. Water foamed in around it, swirling with jellyfish, and it snapped sideways at Esse, its mouth closing around her legs and wrenching her free. Jem dived after her, catching hold of her hand, and the monstrous fish slid backwards and took both of them with it. The boat surged forwards like a squeezed watermelon pip as the weight of the peculiar left it, then began to settle stern first into the water. The lucidor pushed to his feet and, half-blinded by a spike of pain that pushed clean through his skull, began to clamber up the slanting deck towards the wheelhouse, and the coracle lashed to its roof.

6

Empty Houses

In the bright clear early morning the lucidor gathered his clothes from the thorn bushes where he had spread them to dry and dressed and pulled on his damp boots. His shoulders were a stiff bar of pain and his hands were blistered and raw after rowing half the night, and his head felt as if it had been stuffed with broken glass. Although his coiled hair had cushioned Jem's blow, there was a pulpy tender bone-deep bruise beneath it.

He'd fetched up on a slant of short wiry grass that grew right to the water's edge, backed by a low slope covered in tangled banks of thorny briars. He had abandoned the coracle at the water's edge and the Horned Strait stretched away beyond, flat and calm and empty under a blue sky flecked with rows of small white clouds. No sign of the boat, no sign of any monsters. It was as if the Strait's great flood had swallowed every horror and washed the world clean.

A dirt path ran along the top of the slope, above beds of tall reeds and stretches of muddy water dissected by wandering lines of trees. After slaking his thirst with handfuls of brackish water at the edge of a reed bed the lucidor picked up his staff and set off along the path, hoping to find a homestead or village. Someone who could point him towards Naxos.

He was still haunted by the last moments of Esse and Jem. Even though they had betrayed him, had wanted to cause him serious harm, no one deserved to die like that.

One of the tutors in the department's school, Lucidor Ryx, had long ago cautioned him against believing in absolutes of good and evil, right and wrong. The law was a construct, Ryx had said. Decided by people, enacted by people. Certain seers and augurs might claim that we were created with an innate knowledge of fundamental principles of law and morality, but such claims were groundless appeals to an absolute authority that had long ago quit this world. In Patua, the monarch was held to be the living representative of the creator gods and the final arbitrator of all laws and covenants, but the only true authority in the Free State proceeded from laws formulated by the people and their elected representatives. Those laws were fallible and flawed, for lawmakers were as fallible and flawed as everyone else, but they could be altered and adjusted, always endeavouring to match the challenges and changes of lived lives and always failing, but each time, hopefully, failing better. Laws embodied ideals that every citizen should strive to uphold, but lawkeepers must work at a more utilitarian level and sometimes found it necessary to bend or even break small laws, or to otherwise act in ways that their superiors would be wise not to question. In such cases, lawkeepers must rely on their own judgement, Ryx had told the lucidor, and while we can teach you some basic rules and particular examples, the intelligence which tells you how to act in a particular circumstance can only be gained through experience.

The lucidor had been a young boy, then. A shivering stripling recruited by an agent of the department after his gift had come to its notice, with a little native wit and ability, and a stubbornness at his core that Lucidor Ryx and other tutors, and the lucidor's superior officers, had failed to eradicate. If he'd been a little cleverer and a little less stubborn he might have spared himself a lot of trouble. But he was what he was and could not change that. One of the lone dogs that the department found useful until they crossed a line or butted against an immovable authority, as they almost always did. They never attained the highest ranks, worked cases others had long ago abandoned, and often wrecked their careers or were sidelined or dismissed after upsetting someone in power or ignoring the chain of command. So it was with the lucidor, who had refused, out of pride, stubbornness and an abiding sense of duty towards the victims, to end his investigation of Remfrey He's past crimes after the man had been tried and sentenced on specimen charges. A disciplinary committee found him guilty of insubordination and offered him the choice of resignation or demotion from field work to back-office administration in an obscure branch of the records division, and he had chosen to quit.

You found me because we are very alike, Remfrey He had once said. The lucidor had heard that too many times from lesser criminals, and the notion that the best thief-takers were able to think like thieves was a tired cliché, but he suspected that Remfrey He had hit on some kind of truth, limited though it was. They were both proud men who worked according to their own principles, yes, but that was where any similarity ended. Remfrey He's pride was an accomplice to his vanity: he believed himself to be more than ordinary, one who could not be bound by laws made by and meant for ordinary men. Vanity was at the root of all his crimes, but it was also his weakness, an ephemeral bloom that flowered fully only in front of an audience. The lucidor's pride, on the other hand, needed no praise or veneration. It was a pact he had made for himself and no other. A refusal to give way or make accommodations when his principles clashed with the wishes of his superiors. A determination to always do the right thing, hard though that sometimes was. As his wife had so often said, sometimes in amusement, sometimes in frustration, he was too stubborn to ever change.

He wondered if he would have set out on this quest if she were still alive. Most likely she would have pointed out that his old boss was exploiting him, would have asked him why he was prepared to throw away everything he had achieved, his honour, his life, for an endeavour that even if successful would end in disgrace. He would have taken what she had to say seriously. He always had, because she was usually right. And maybe, just maybe, he would have agreed with her, would not be walking along this unknown path on an unknown coast in a strange country, homeless, hungry and lost. But here he was, and despite being shipwrecked he had managed to get across the Horned Strait and keep to the path that would lead to his quarry.

His salt-stained clothes quickly dried. White crystals blooming in the creases of the leather coat he'd slung like a cape over his aching shoulders. A salty itch all over his skin and stinging the wound in his arm, as if he had been swarmed by ants. The glare of the Highday mirror arc aggravating his headache.

At last he spotted a small scatter of houses on the far side of the marsh and found a path that cut towards them, raised on a narrow tree-lined embankment scarcely a span above the flat brown water. The fields beyond were flooded and had recently been planted out with rice seedlings. The lucidor walked along the top of a pounded dirt dyke and felt a momentary tug at his heart, as he clambered over a paddle gate that allowed water to pass from one field to the next, at the stray thought that his wife would have appreciated its sturdy workmanship and simple but effective design.

There were just seven houses, low and whitewashed under roofs thatched with bundles of reeds, set in gardens of vegetables and flowers along an unpaved cart track. No signs of life. Only the sound of the breeze and a bird singing a lonesome song somewhere high in the sky, now here, now there, and a window shutter creaking as it swung to and fro.

The lucidor imagined a lookout spotting his approach, villagers gathering their children and fleeing into the woods behind their homes. If they had run from him, they must have a very good reason to fear strangers, to hide instead of confronting them. The thought gave him a creeping feeling of unease; he looked all around before stepping into the garden of the last of the houses. He browsed amongst pea vines twining up tripods of twiggy branches, shucking peas and dropping the empty pods, and drank from a wooden pail of warm stale water and splashed his face and neck. A fig tree had been trained in a fan up the end wall of the house and he filled the pockets of his coat with soft purple figs and peapods and walked on.

A huge evergreen tree reared above the intersection where the cart track was crossed by the cracked, overgrown slabs of an ancient highway. As he walked under its shade the lucidor caught a strong whiff of a familiar sickly, corrupt reek and looked up and saw the bodies of two men hanging from one of the branches high above, nooses tight under their chins, arms tied behind their backs, dressed in patched and much-washed cotton shirts and trousers. Flies orbited their heads, crawled over eyeless sockets and teeth exposed by rictus grins. Hard to tell how long they had been dead. Several days at least, maybe more. They weren't army deserters or bandits, judging by their clothes, but they might have been killed by bandits to intimidate the rest of the villagers, or executed by some hostile authority as punishment for lawbreaking or refusal to bend the knee.

The lucidor walked on, prickling with vigilant caution. Fields gave way to rough unfenced pasture where small red cattle grazed amongst a scatter of monumental black rocks, some as big as houses. The track curved east and north, climbed a hill and gave a view of the strait sparkling away into heat haze. On the far side, in a cool dell where trees overhung a shallow stream, he dozed away the hot hours either side of noon, woke and ate his store of figs and peas, drank from the stream and bathed his blistered hands in its cool water, and followed the track out of the green shade of the trees into wincingly bright mirrorlight.

He hadn't gone very far when he glimpsed movement to his right: a horse and rider skylighted on the crest of a ridge half a league away. He dropped flat, elbow-crawled into the tall grass and weeds at the side of the track, cautiously raised his head. The rider showed no sign of having seen him, seemed to be surveying the slope below the ridge. Moving slowly, taking care not to disturb the grass around him, the lucidor pulled out his spyglass, but by the time he had thumbed dry salt from its lens and applied it to his eye the ridge was empty.

He waited a little while, propped on his elbows and scanning the land all around, and when he felt certain that the rider wasn't coming back or trying to circle behind him he stood up and went on.

The arc of mirrors was weltering in a red glow above low rounded hills when the track bent around a big outcrop of rock and he saw fields on one side and three houses on the other, crouching in the shadow of a small belt of trees rising behind them. He pulled out his spyglass again, studied the houses and fields. No sign of movement anywhere, no lights, no smoke.

You can stay out here all night, he told himself, or you can find shelter, maybe even some help. The small windows of the first house blankly reflected the crimson blush of arcset. Its front door hung open; there was no reply when he halloed it. Inside was a single room floored with beaten earth and faintly smelling of old smoke and the lives of other people. Bunches of dried herbs and onions twisted in ropes hung from the central roof beam. Stoneware crockery piled on a shelf above a stone oven where the charcoal corpses of some kind of flatbreads lay on the griddlestone. A doll woven from grass hung from a nail over the door. Two child-sized hammocks, a painted chest, a double bed behind a painted partition. A wicker chair by the stove, several spindly stools at a table, one lying on its side. Nothing else was out of place. No bloodstains on the floor or walls. No sign that the place had been searched.

A straw-stuffed mattress crackled beneath the lucidor when he sat on the bed. He imagined someone hearing an alarm call and rising suddenly from that stool, knocking it over. Pausing to gather up their children and arm themselves with some kind of agricultural implement. Running out of the door to confront . . . what? Friends of that rider he'd seen, most likely. Whoever they were.

It was growing dark, he was tired, his head and wounded arm were throbbing in different rhythms, and the bruise under his coiled hair at the back of his head was hot and tender. He unpicked the bandage around his arm and discarded the packing of glass moss and washed the wound with water scooped from a bucket and rebound it. Found a chunk of salt pork wrapped in muslin in a lattice-fronted meat safe, untwisted a couple of onions, and tucked one of his plastic currency notes behind the doll nailed above the door. A poor excuse for rifling the household's larder, but the best he could do.

He collected fallen branches in the steep wood behind the houses and built a small fire in a hollow between the exposed roots of one of the big trees, where he had a good view of the

51

track and the fields and the open country beyond. It was almost dark now. Just one mirror left above the horizon, scarcely brighter than the fire as it burned down to glowing embers. He trimmed a stick with his little knife and was threading slices of meat and segments of onion and fig onto it when he heard, faint but distinct, the sound of horses' hooves on the track below.

7

King of Pain

The lucidor was pushing handfuls of earth over the embers of the fire as the riders, three of them, came around the rock outcrop. Men and horses silhouetted against the level red light of the last mirror, one of the men holding a long gun upright with its stock butted on his thigh. The lucidor squatted behind a fallen tree on the slope above, watching them, certain that they had come looking for him. The lone rider must have spotted him after all.

The riders halted a little way from the first of the houses, directly below his hiding place, and after a brief discussion two dismounted and headed for the house. The lucidor had shut the front door when he'd left; now he heard a splintering crash as it was kicked open, a shouted warning, a smash of crockery. He was outnumbered and outgunned, knew that he should run, but neither the heath rising behind him nor the fields on the other side of the track provided much cover, and if the riders caught sight of him they would quickly chase him down. Or shoot him in the back, for the fun of it. And besides, he had spent much of his life running towards danger, not away from it, and he was curious about these men. Who they were and what they wanted, why these houses and the little village and the land all around were deserted, why those two villagers had been hanged.

Moving with flat-footed caution, he descended the wooded slope, circling behind the third rider. Waiting until the man's friends came out of the first house and broke into the second, then moving in quickly, swinging his staff in a wide arc that struck the rider hard above his ear. The lucidor grabbed his leg as he slumped sideways and hauled him from the saddle and dragged him to the edge of the track, kneeling on his back to keep him down and pulling his pistol from his belt and quickly searching him, finding a combat knife with a serrated ceramic blade, a couple of strips of jerky and a box of lucifers, and a foul rag that he stuffed into the man's mouth to keep him quiet.

The horses stepped about uneasily, reins trailing, but there was no sign that the rider's friends had seen the takedown. Not bad for an old man long retired, even if he was out of breath and his headache had sharpened, and when he had crabbed down the slope he'd done something to his left ankle, which hadn't mended properly after he'd broken it years ago.

The lucidor pulled the man's belt from the loops of his trousers and used it to bind his wrists and turned him over and straddled his chest and patted and pinched his cheeks until he stirred. He wore a thigh-length green jacket with shoulder tabs and a high collar, had a bushy untrimmed beard and long hair tied back with a strip of rawhide, reeked of sweat and wood smoke. A corner of the rag protruded from his lips like a withered tongue.

'Swear you won't call to your friends if I take out your gag,' the lucidor said. 'A nod for yes will do it.'

The man tried to spit out the rag, subsided when the lucidor put the pistol in his face and repeated his question.

The man nodded, staring cross-eyed at the pistol.

'If you shout out, it will be the last thing you do,' the lucidor said, and pulled the rag from the man's mouth and asked him why he and his friends had come looking for him.

'Who says we're looking for you?'

'Why else would you be kicking in doors of empty houses?'

'Maybe we're looking for trespassers.'

'That's why you came looking for me? Because I am trespassing?'

'Like I said.'

'Are there any others looking for me, or just you three?'

'There'll be more looking if we don't come back.'

'How many more?'

'More than enough to take care of you.'

The lucidor pushed the muzzle of the pistol against the man's forehead, repeated his question.

'Around twenty,' the man said.

'Let's say exactly.'

'Twenty-one, twenty-two. If that makes any difference.'

'It's plain you aren't farmers. And you aren't regular army, either, despite that uniform jacket. So what are you doing here, and where are the people who lived in those houses?'

'You come with us, you'll find out. Might even be we can find a use for you, smart as you are.'

There was a distant shout, a faint high-pitched wail. The man tried to wriggle free when the lucidor looked up, and the lucidor smacked him with the butt of the pistol, a hard sharp blow that laid him out, and grabbed the front of his jacket and hauled him to his feet.

He had been planning to leave the man lying there and surprise his friends when they found him, but they were already coming down the track, one of them dragging a small slight figure by an arm, a boy of twelve or thirteen, stumbling and plainly scared out of his wits. They stopped a little way off and the man who wasn't holding the boy jerked his carbine to his shoulder, aiming it at the lucidor and his prisoner, and said, 'You dumb loser, Vikor.'

The lucidor was holding Vikor's sagging weight by a forearm across his throat. Sweating with the effort, trying not to show it. He had got himself in a jackpot, and the only way out was to take control of the situation. He jammed the pistol against Vikor's head and said, 'Give me the boy and I'll let your friend go.'

'You think this is some kind of standoff?' the man said. He was tall and broad-shouldered, wearing the same kind of green jacket as Vikor. There was a patch over his right eye and the slant of its straps creased the springy bush of his hair. He sounded casual, amused, and his aim was unwavering. 'All you have is Vikor, who I could care less about, and his piece-of-shit pistol. Damn thing misfires half the time and wouldn't knock down a coney less you were shooting point-blank, while this carbine is good enough to put a hole through Vikor and you both. And that's exactly what it will do unless you lay down that pistol and put up your hands.'

'I'll drop it if you agree to set down that carbine at the same time.'

'I don't think so.'

'It's the only way we can make this work.'

'I don't think so,' the one-eyed man said again. 'Goose the kid, Sly.'

The other man was standing behind the boy, gripping him by the shoulders. He raised one hand, forefinger extended, sneeringly smiled at the lucidor, and touched the back of the boy's head and held on to him as he screamed and writhed.

The department sometimes used people with the electricker gift to deal with rebellious prisoners, or to put down suspects as quickly as possible. They cross-wired nerves, fired jolts of pure agony. This one, Sly, was strong. Able to hurt the boy even though he was inside the outer edge of the lucidor's own gift.

'Sly is the king of pain,' the one-eyed man said. 'Want to see how much the kid can take?'

Sly screwed his forefinger into the boy's ear and the boy screamed again, high and anguished, and kept screaming, pausing only to sob for breath. The lucidor aimed the pistol at Sly, and the one-eyed man made a small adjustment to the carbine butted against his shoulder and said pleasantly, pitching his voice over the boy's screams, 'You're as likely to hit the kid as Sly, and you only got one crack at it before I shoot you. But hey, your call.'

'Leave the boy alone and we can talk,' the lucidor said.

The man studied him, then said, 'That's enough, Sly.'

Sly pulled his forefinger from the boy's ear and said, 'I got plenty of juice left for you, old man.'

The boy was crying hard, chest heaving, and the lucidor had to ask him for his name three times before he got his attention.

'Dickon,' the boy said. His cheeks glistened and he wiped his nose with the back of his hand.

'Don't worry, Dickon. I'll get us out of this.'

'You'll put that pistol down is what you'll do,' the man with the eyepatch said.

Vikor pitched forward, all unstrung, when the lucidor let go of him and stepped back, raising the pistol above his head, holding it by its stubby barrel, and laying it on the ground.

'I reckon you took Vikor's knife too,' the man said. 'Give it up, along with that stick. Toss them off to one side.'

The lucidor did as he was told. He still had his own knife. If one of the men stepped close, he might have a chance to use it.

'That's better,' the one-eyed man said. 'Now, how about telling me what you're doing here? By your accent, I'd say you're a Freestater. I know the edge of it – I worked the border trade once upon a time. And you have a soldierly look, too. A mercenary would be my guess, but you're a long way from any fighting.'

'I'm just passing through, on my way to Delos-Chimr.'

'Then you must have taken a wrong turn, brother,' the one-eyed man said. 'Did someone send you here? I can't help thinking that's more likely. Are you a scout for some crew looking to get rich at our expense?'

'I had some trouble on the sea crossing to Naxos. Perhaps you could point me towards it.'

'How about it, Sly? Reckon he's telling the truth?'

'Only one way to find out,' Sly said.

'Think you can make a tough guy like him talk?'

'I ain't never failed yet. Look after the kid,' Sly said, and shoved the boy towards the one-eyed man and angled towards the lucidor, making sure he didn't come between him and his friend's carbine.

'I want to treat you fairly, what with you being an old man,' Sly said. 'So if you want you can come at me. Take your best shot.'

The lucidor did not speak or move, standing with his hands half-raised.

'That how you want it that's how you'll get it,' Sly said, and pulled a short stick from his belt and jabbed at the lucidor's chest.

He was one of the strong ones all right, able to channel his power along a rod or length of rope, but the lucidor felt only a faint tingle when he twisted the stick from Sly's grip and hit him hard alongside the head, the crack echoing back from the hillside as the electricker collapsed.

'I forgot to tell you that I have a small gift of my own,' he told the one-eyed man.

'It don't change anything,' the man said. His fingers were twisted in the boy's hair, and he was holding the carbine against his hip with his other hand. 'Put yourself on the ground. Flat on your belly, hands behind your back.'

'Let the boy go first. He isn't part of this.'

'On the ground now, or I'll put one in your leg,' the man said.

They stared at each other, the lucidor reckoning the odds of the man making the shot one-handed, when something, a pebble, hit the track a couple of spans from the man's boots. It kicked up a puff of dust as it skipped away and a second pebble struck the man's shoulder with a meaty smack. He turned and fired a shot from the hip that went whanging off into the dusk, then ducked as a third pebble flew at his head, and the lucidor swung into the saddle of the nearest horse and kicked it into a gallop, reins in one hand, Sly's stick in the other. The one-eyed man pushed the boy away and raised the carbine to his shoulder, and the lucidor whacked him hard in the face and hauled the horse around. The man was on his hands and knees, snorting blood, and a figure was running down the track, another boy, hands raised, calling out that he was a friend.

8

Sanctuary

The two boys, Dickon and Rollo, said they had returned to their home to collect chicken dung from the midden and look for food, and had hidden from the lucidor when they had seen him coming down the track because they had thought that he was one of the diggers. That was what they called the bandits: diggers. They had come across the water some thirty days ago, Rollo said. Had rounded up all the men and women they could find, including his parents and Dickon's widowed mother, and put them to work in the ruins of an old city, forcing them to dig out a deep shaft under a temple where an ancient revenant called the Thing Below lurked.

'It was thrown down when it tried to fight the godlings,' Rollo said. 'And it's been trapped beneath the temple ever since.'

'It wakes up sometimes, and makes the earth shake,' Dickon said.

'If the diggers set it loose, it could destroy the world,' Rollo said, and told the lucidor that the people who had managed to avoid being captured by the diggers had been hiding from them ever since, trying to work out how to frustrate the diggers' plans and take back their home.

'Is that why you risked your lives?' the lucidor said. 'I'm not entirely ignorant of the uses for chicken dung. It can be rendered down to nitre, which is used to make explosives.'

'It was his idea,' Dickon said. He was hunched into himself, shivering from the after-effects of Sly's jolts.

'You wanted to come along,' Rollo said. 'And don't try to blame me for getting caught. You shouldn't have tried to make a run for it.'

'How many of you escaped?' the lucidor said.

'Maybe a hundred,' Rollo said.

He was about the same age as Dickon, a sturdy lad with a mop of curly hair and a bold gaze and a good measure of reckless courage: he had come to the aid of Dickon and the lucidor armed only with a slingshot not much different from the one the lucidor had used to knock down mice and cottontails when he'd been a young boy.

'We outnumber the diggers, but more than half of us are too young or too old to fight,' he told the lucidor. 'And most of those that can don't know how. But seeing how you handled these jackeens, I reckon you could teach us a few tricks. And I know Alcnos would like to meet you.'

'She's our headswoman,' Dickon said.

'I have business elsewhere,' the lucidor said. 'If you can point me towards Naxos or Delos-Chimr I reckon we'd be square.'

'Would those be places on the Mains?' Rollo said.

'Delos-Chimr is the largest city in Patua,' the lucidor said. 'Don't tell me you've never heard of it.'

'Alcnos might know,' Dickon said.

'Or Doros,' Rollo said. 'She used to take cow hides and rice to Kava, across the Sleeve.'

'Then you had better take me to this headswoman of yours,' the lucidor said. 'But I can't promise to be of any help in your fight against the diggers.'

He told himself that this affair with the diggers and the Thing Below was none of his concern. Most of the stories about revenants and artefacts left behind by the godlings exaggerated their powers, and he needed to get on, find his way to Delos-Chimr. With every passing day Remfrey He would be devising more mischief and mayhem, strengthening the loyalty of any he had recruited, and making it ever harder to take him down.

'What about these three?' Rollo said. 'Are we going to leave them here?'

The man with the eyepatch lay on the ground, his one bloodshot eye watching them over his gag, his wrists and ankles bound with lengths of braided rawhide the lucidor had cut from a bullwhip he'd found looped to the saddle of one of the horses. Sly and Vikor lay nearby, likewise bound and gagged, both still unconscious.

'I'm not going to kill them, if that's what you are asking,' the lucidor said. 'Only those who have put themselves outside of all law and decency execute prisoners. Let their friends find them, and punish them for their failure.'

'Their friends most likely know exactly where they are,' Rollo said. 'Do you see the black box on yon one-eye's belt? Diggers use them to talk to each other. Whatever you choose to do, we should not linger.'

The black box was a kind of godspeaker, much smaller than the ones the lucidor had used back in the Free State, which had brick-sized casings to house the wet-cell batteries that powered their workings. They came in pairs which each contained one half of a particular kind of shatterling fragment, and the two halves shared an affinity that took no mind of the distance that separated them, so that when you used one it was as if you were speaking directly into the ear of the person holding the other.

While Rollo and Dickon ran off to fetch their loot, the lucidor stuck the little godspeaker in his pocket and stashed the diggers' pistols and assorted cutlery in one of the saddlebags, and slung the carbine over his shoulder. The one-eyed man was watching him, and he loosened the man's gag and asked him if he and his friends really were trying to dig up some sort of relic from the first days.

'That isn't exactly what it is.'

'What is it, then?'

'Something you can't even imagine.'

'Then there's no harm telling me.'

The man raised his head and tried to spit at the lucidor, but the spittle ran down his chin and dripped on the dirt. 'You think you got the better of me, but you don't. Less you've got a boat hidden somewhere we'll be seeing each other again.'

'You had better hope that we don't,' the lucidor said, and retied the gag and left the man lying there.

Rollo and Dickon returned with a sack of onions and yams and three damp smelly sacks of chicken dung, and in the last light of dusk they mounted up and headed out across the bare fields, the two boys riding together on one horse, their sacks slung either side of the saddle, and the lucidor riding the second horse and leading the third. According to Rollo, this part of the coast was called the Land and his people had lived there forever, farming and fishing, but after some to and fro the lucidor was still unclear exactly where it was. It seemed that hardly any outsiders had visited the Land before the diggers came, and hardly anyone who lived there ever left it. Everyone knew everyone else, and most had the same family name, Iskander, which in their patois meant Children of the Land. Rollo said that he was also called Rollo Briarhead, on account of his curly hair, because there were five other Rollos, including his father.

There was a silence after that, the boys no doubt remembering that their parents and most of their friends were prisoners. By now, night had fallen and they had left the fields behind and were riding over a trackless heathland broken by long pavements of bare rock, picking their way by the red light of the clash of stars that arched across the clear cloudless sky, at last reaching the edge of a long slope that fell towards what looked like a wide dark forest, with a faint glimmer of water beyond. That was the Sleeve, Rollo said, and the land on the far side was the Mains. Where the diggers had come from, and where, he supposed, the lucidor would be going.

The lucidor, stupefied by tiredness and his unforgiving headache, took a few moments to realise that the Mains must be the Big Island, and the Land was another island, very much smaller, lying off its coast.

He said, 'Do your people have boats?'

'Of course we do,' Rollo said.

'Then I think that I need to have a word with this headswoman of yours.'

They had barely started down the slope when Dickon gave a cry of alarm. The lucidor looked around, saw a flickering dab of light on the far side of the dark heath. Either the diggers had managed to get free and had set a fire to signal for help, or their friends had found and freed them, and were burning the houses out of spite.

'We made them angry,' Dickon said.

'I reckon they were born angry,' Rollo said and pointed towards the forest and told the lucidor that was where they would find sanctuary. 'We've been hiding there all this time, snug as lugworms, and the diggers have yet to find us.'

They trotted down the slope and cut along the edge of a long reach of marshy land, the night busy with the pipings and whistlings of unseen creatures and the questing whine of mosquitoes. The lucidor slapped something that stung his neck and was reminded of Lucidor Ryx's little homily which explained that mosquitoes and other pests were proof that the creator gods had raised up from perfect memory the imperfect world of their first beginnings.

Rollo and Dickon were still searching for the path that would take them across the stretch of marsh when three riders and their horses crested the top of the slope half a league away, silhouetted against the red tide of stars for a moment, disappearing as they started down. Rollo turned his horse unhandily, heading back the way they had just come. Dickon, clinging behind, told him to hurry.

'We could ride the horses across,' the lucidor said.

'If we cross in the wrong place mud will swallow them and us,' Rollo said.

Shouts in the distance. The spark of a single shot. The diggers had reached the edge of the marsh and were riding along it towards them. The lucidor unhitched the spare horse and smacked it on the rump, sending it trotting off into the night, but knew it would only distract their pursuers for a moment or two.

'Hurry hurry hurry,' Dickon said.

The lucidor shrugged the carbine off his shoulder and peered into the darkness, ready to make a stand that might give the boys time to escape. He thought there was a good chance he would get away with it. Only three diggers were chasing them, three that he knew of, and that stray shot suggested that at least one of them was easily spooked.

'There it is,' Rollo said. 'The dead tree. You see?'

'Are you sure?' Dickon said.

'It's plain as daylight. We'll have to leave the horses,' Rollo told the lucidor. 'They'll slow us down in the forest.'

'You can leave the food and the chicken dung too. You didn't collect anywhere near enough to make a useful amount of nitre,' the lucidor said, and dismounted and undid the strap of his horse's saddlebag and slung it over his shoulder. 'But we'll take these pistols, so if we can shake off our friends you'll come out ahead. Are you ready? Then lead on.'

They waded one after the other through chest-deep water towards a skeletal white ghost glimmering under the black shadow of the forest's edge – a dead sapling scarcely taller than the lucidor. He followed the two boys past it, splashing up out of the water and limping along a narrow path that looped around and between the prop roots of small gnarled trees that grew along the edges of creeks and pools and shoals of mud. The night buzzed with calls and songs of unseen creatures. Small lights drifted through the air, blinking coded messages in red and green. Faintly luminous shrouds of moss hung from branches. Clambering along a rope bridge slung between trees either side of a broad creek, the lucidor felt as if he was passing through one of the nebulae sprinkled across the night sky.

Twice they paused to listen; twice they heard the sound of their pursuers blundering through the flooded forest some way behind them, and the second time saw the bright flash of a torch amongst the smaller lights of the living constellations. At last they crossed a string of teetering planks to a muddy island half circled round by reeds. A reach of still black water beyond perfectly reflected the starry sky. The lucidor sat down heavily, his bad ankle hot and loose, his headache banging away, and scarcely noticed that Rollo and Dickon had disappeared into the reeds on the far side.

He was still sitting there when the boys came back. Apparently they had left a boat moored in the reeds but hadn't been able to find it, each blaming the other for not tethering it properly until the lucidor asked them if there was another way out of there.

'We could swim across,' Rollo said.

The lucidor did not much like the idea of blundering through reed beds and stretches of water in the dark and said that he preferred to make a stand. 'I can knock down those planks, and hold off the diggers while you two swim for it.'

'I'm not going to leave you,' Rollo said stoutly. 'Give me one of those pistols.'

'You don't need a pistol to fetch help. Get going now.'

'Wait,' Dickon said. 'I heard something.'

The boy was a shadow crouching amongst tall reeds, looking out across the dark water.

'If they got in front of us we are done for,' Rollo said.

'There's at least one boat out there,' Dickon said. 'See it?'

'How many in it?'

'I can't tell.'

The two of them whispering and anxious.

The lucidor drew his staff and pushed to his feet, and heard a low three-note whistle off in the night. Rollo forked thumb and forefinger in his mouth and whistled a reply; a few moments later two small coracles glided out of the darkness, the first towing the second.

'You silly pair of churls,' the woman in the first boat said, as Rollo helped to pull it ashore. 'I was beginning to think I'd lost you. Who is that with you?'

'A friend we found,' Rollo said. 'He's going to help us fight the diggers.'

9

Headswoman

'This was a peaceful place before the diggers arrived,' the headswoman, Alcnos Tallykeeper, said. 'We lived as we always have,
tending our farms and herding our cattle, fishing and collecting
shellfish and hunting wild fowl. Some may think it a simple life,
and it is often hard and unforgiving. Much of the Land is bare
rock, or soil so poor it is not even suitable for grazing. And the
climate is changing. Becoming wetter and colder, even though
this is one of the thin places in the world, especially blessed by
the warmth of the Heartsun. Once upon a time we could plant
three crops of rice in a year, but these days we can grow only
two, and sometimes cold weather takes the second crop before
it can be harvested. But for all of that this is our home, and we
won't give it up easily.'

She was a serious young woman with long black hair brushed
to a deep gloss, dressed like the other landers in a knee-length
cotton shirt and cotton trousers and leather sandals. The women
in her family were by tradition custodians of tablets that recorded
centuries of births and deaths, cattle lineages and harvests; after
her village had been burned to the ground and her mother, prin-
cipal of the common council of headspeople, had been executed
by the diggers as an example to the rest, Alcnos had managed to
save the tablets and escape into the forest, where she had rallied
the other fugitives.

'I have only seen a little of this Land of yours,' the lucidor told
her, 'and it seems fertile enough to me. Especially this forest.
But I am from a desert country where every scrap of green is
precious.'

'Our fields yield good crops only because we have worked them carefully for centuries,' Alcnos said. 'And the forest is rooted in mud and salt water, where nothing else will grow.'

According to her, the people of the old city, Pythos, had felled swathes of the saltwater forest for firewood and the sea washed in and carried off the mud and made barren places that could still be seen today. But the landers lived lightly, so that the forest and the rest of the Land would be preserved for their children and their children's children and all the generations to come.

'We were living here before the first foundations of Pythos were laid, and we have outlasted it, and the antinomians once exiled here, and the High Family who were given title to the Land,' Alcnos said. 'They moved to the capital two centuries ago, and their house and their hunting lodges have fallen to ruin. After they left us, we believed that we could manage our own affairs. As we did, so long as no one troubled us. But then the diggers came, we couldn't defend ourselves against them, never before having had the need, and here we are. Driven from our homes and hiding in the forest, the rest of our people killed or enslaved.'

'In my country, there are laws to protect people like you,' the lucidor said. 'And lawkeepers to enforce them. Is there no one you can ask for help?'

'Such laws as there are were made by the High Families to keep people like us in their proper place,' Alcnos said. 'And I understand that there are many places now where those laws are no longer kept, because of the war. Until you came, we had no one to help us but ourselves. But now, for the first time, I feel a little hope. It is as if a hero has stepped from one of the old stories.'

'I told you last night that I will do what I can to help you,' the lucidor said. 'And I will. But please don't think that I am anything other than an ordinary man. Older than he once was, and not necessarily wiser.'

'We pray to the small gods for good harvests and fine weather,' Alcnos said. 'And we asked them for help when the diggers came. Oft-times they are capricious, but here you are. No doubt you believe that you found your own way here, but might it not be possible that you were guided by our prayers?'

'The diggers are better armed than your people, and judging by the ones I encountered last night, a good number of them were once soldiers. They won't give up easily. People will be hurt. People will die. Are you prepared for that?'

'Many have already died,' Alcnos said sombrely. 'The diggers killed my mother and all the other members of the Common Council. They killed people who refused to obey them at the outset, and hang any caught outside the bounds of the forest and leave their bodies as a warning to the rest of us.'

'I saw two yesterday,' the lucidor said. 'Hanged from a big tree close to one of your villages on the southern shore.'

'Near the Blackwater Marsh?'

The lucidor nodded. 'The tree was at a kind of crossroads.'

'The diggers caught and killed them four days ago,' Alcnos said. 'The family that owns the steading nearby was hiding in the barrens on High Heath. Three brothers went looking for food, and two were caught by the diggers. The two you saw. The third brother escaped, but either the diggers followed him to his family's hiding place, or they tortured the brothers they caught before they killed them, and forced them to give up its location. In any event, the diggers found it and slaughtered most of the family. There are no trees up on High Heath, so they hammered stakes into a cliff and hung the bodies from them by their wrists. Eight of them in a row. Men, women, children. Only two escaped, and they managed to find their way here, which is how I know the story.'

'I understand why you want vengeance,' the lucidor said.

'I need to put an end to it,' Alcnos said. 'I have no doubt that the people they've put to work at their diggings are being used hard. Some may have already died, and we can't count on the diggers leaving any alive when they're done. We know that we must fight and we have been preparing to fight as best we can. But you can teach us how to fight properly, and lead us when we march on the diggers to free our people and take back our home.'

She and the lucidor were sitting at one end of the dry ridge of a little island where a dozen tents and a common kitchen and a workshop had been rigged from scrap wood and canvas, and a tall post carved in the likeness of a serpent had been erected: one of the small gods of the landers, with shattering fragments embedded around the white slits of its eyes. The forest and the streams and creeks that dissected it stretched away on every side under an early morning haze exhaled by millions of dark green leaves; to the north was a long glint of mirrorlight on open water: the sea channel, called the Sleeve by the landers, that the lucidor had to cross to reach the Big Island and regain his path.

Last night, after Alcnos had rescued him and the two boys and brought them to the island camp, an old man with a kindly, patient manner had treated the lucidor's bad ankle, bruised head and blistered hands with poultices, cleaned and rebandaged his wounded arm, and given him a draught of astringent black tea that took away most of his headache. He had slept on a truckle bed under a slant of canvas, breakfasted on rice and boiled greens, the best meal he remembered eating for a long time, and was wearing his leather coat over a white shirt and cotton trousers because his own clothes had been taken away to be cleaned and mended. He owed Alcnos his life, and wanted to repay the debt. And after last night's dust-up the diggers would be on high alert. They would be looking for him, and that put Alcnos and her people in danger, so helping the landers fight back against the diggers' brutal occupation was a matter of honour. The same honour that had brought him here in the first place. Honour, and his ingrained stubbornness. And besides all that, he didn't have any choice. The only boats which could safely make the crossing to the Big Island had been captured by the diggers, along with much else.

The lucidor had dealt with all kinds of felons in his time, including bandits and other criminals who, like the diggers, had taken to oppressing ordinary people. The madwoman Asthryn Bey, for instance, whose followers had snatched children and taken them to the ruins of a labyrinthine citadel deep in the desert, where she had experimented on them with drugs and surgery in a futile attempt to recreate the noble race of the First People. And before that he had helped to put an end to the so-called Nameless, an endtime cult which had moved from village to village in the borderlands, executing prelates and officials and recruiting followers to its cause. But he had been helped by other lawkeepers and the army back then, and the resources of the department. The landers outnumbered the diggers, but they were inexperienced and poorly armed, and although the lucidor admired Alcnos's forthright courage, he knew that courage was no guarantee of victory.

Still, he believed that he had a possible advantage: the godspeaker he'd taken from the one-eyed man. 'The diggers' patrols must be using them to report back to their camp,' he told Alcnos. 'Which means that I can use this one to talk to their leader. I think there's a good chance that they will agree to meet and parley. I took three of them down. They'll want to know who I am and what I am doing here.'

'Even if they agree to it, they'll most likely try to ambush you,' Alcnos said.

'Not if I am somewhere else.'

He watched her think about that.

She said, 'You hope to draw some of them out, weakening their defences, making their camp easier to attack.'

'That's certainly one way we can play it. But before we make any plans, I need to see this camp of theirs, how it is situated, and what kind of defences it has.'

Alcnos, the lucidor, and Alcnos's friend and bodyguard, Doros, set off a little after noon, paddling through the forest in a coracle of wicker and cowhide, following channels and creeks that wound through and around stands of trees. Tree trunks were caged by armatures of prop roots, branches were hung with creepers and feathery falls of moss, and foliage thickened in every direction, pierced by narrow shafts of mirrorlight that glared off water or struck individual leaves and transformed them into luminous green stars. The lucidor, used to the desert's spare landscapes, found the green shade and crowded mazes of creeks and trees and mud banks oppressive, and the motionless air under the low canopy was packed with heat and humidity. He soon shrugged off his coat, and his shirt stuck to his back and his face was greasy with sweat. In some places currents ran and swirled between trees and mud banks; in others, the shallow water was clear and still, and dark green hummocks of algae grew on bottom mud and stretches of pale sand, attended by schools of small striped fish and flocks of shrimp that scattered in every direction as the coracle's shadow glided overhead.

According to Alcnos, the little monsters which had ruined fishing in the open waters of the Horned Strait had not yet invaded the forest. She pointed out a few of the half hundred plants that could be eaten or used to make remedies, named animals and birds. A heron standing sentry at the margins of a channel. Cormorants perched on root arches, spreading their wings to dry like priests at prayer. Something like a thorny cucumber that cast mucus nets over the bottom mud, catching tiny animals it drew into its mouth – Alcnos said that the mucus made a good glue when it was boiled with sap from reed roots. There was a small lizard with a white cowl which it could raise around its head in perfect imitation of a flower, attracting the pollen-eating beetles on which it preyed. Another lizard glided through sunlight and shadow on membranes stretched between fore and hind legs. A pair of anthrops squatted side by side on a high branch, arms around each other's waists as they watched the coracle pass beneath them. It was forbidden to kill them, Alcnos said, because they shared so many traits with people.

'And if you kill one by accident, bad luck will follow you until you die,' Doros said.

She was a burly broad-shouldered woman with a competent no-nonsense manner and some experience of the world beyond the Land: before the diggers had arrived, she had been in charge of the boat that took cow hides and rice and the strong liquor that landers brewed from cloudberries to sell in a little town on the other side of the Sleeve. She'd made it clear that she believed this scouting trip was a bootless enterprise that put their lives at risk for no good reason. She had already scouted the diggers' camp, said that it was typical of a man to have no faith in the opinions of a woman, and had not been appeased when the lucidor had told her that the diggers might have altered and strengthened their defences since, especially if they believed him to be a scout for a rival gang.

'He might see things neither of us have noticed, D,' Alcnos had said.

'Maybe. All I know is I see things plain enough. A mound we'll have to climb and a wall we'll have to breach, unless we try to break through the gate where the diggers will have made their strongest defences, as it's the weakest part. I'd draw you a picture,' Doros had told the lucidor, 'if I thought you'd take any notice of it.'

'I will be happy to discuss tactics when I have seen what there is to see,' the lucidor had said.

Now, Doros plied the coracle's paddle with a steady vigour as they threaded through the mazy channels of the forest towards the old city, and Alcnos sat next to her, shoulder to shoulder, hip to hip, a recurve bow and a quiver of arrows fletched with white feathers cradled in her lap. Their easy familiarity, the way they touched each other when they thought the lucidor was not looking. Alcnos's hand on Doros's shoulder. Knee bent against knee. Shared looks.

At last, the coracle grounded on a kerb of tumbled rocks, Alcnos handed the bow and quiver of arrows to Doros and the lucidor limped after the two women up a path that wound through trees rooted amongst tumbled blocks of stone. The path was narrow and winding and steep; the lucidor, sweating hard and slapping at small black biting flies, had trouble keeping up. At the top, they clambered through a notch in a rim of naked rock and crossed a curving stretch of stony grassland – the headland that separated the forest from the estuary of the Land's only river – to the edge of steep cliffs of glistening black baserock that fell to a restless seethe of white water.

A hot wind blew around them as they looked out across a circular bay to the overgrown ruins of Pythos, cradled inside a steep bare ridge that bent towards the mouth of the bay, where an arc of rocky spires curved towards the point of the headland. The grid pattern of the old city's streets showed through a patchy growth of trees and scrub, stubs and stretches of bone-white walls poked up here and there, and a roofless rectangle of pillars stood on a flat-topped mound. The Temple of the Well of the

World, according to Alcnos. The place where the diggers had made their camp.

The lucidor pulled out his spyglass and scrutinised the place while Alcnos told him that the temple had been built above the deep pit where the Thing Below lay buried. The people who had built the temple had called it the Serpent at the Navel of the World, Alcnos said, and named their city after it. Pythos: the place of the serpent. They believed that it had possessed oracular powers, and priestesses officiating at the temple had been its mouthpieces. The landers visited the old temple every year before the first rice planting and laid yew branches on the floor of the temple and made offerings of rice and yams and fruit and sang the old prayers of warding. Not to venerate the Thing Below, Alcnos said, or to call on its oracular powers, but to keep it from returning to the world. Afterwards, everyone feasted in Alcnos's home village, and for the rest of the year the temple and the rest of the ruins were left alone. The ancient revenant had become part of the landers' folklore. They used one or another of its names to curse stubborn animals or malfunctioning equipment and tools, frightened disobedient children with stories about fools and disbelievers who had been snatched by it, blamed it for bad weather, bad luck, curdled milk and every kind of domestic mishap. Apart from the annual ceremony and the rare occasions when the Thing Below grumbled and tossed in its sleep and shook the ground the landers gave it little thought. Its presence had long ago become familiar, smoothed into the background of everyday life. The diggers' plan to dig it up was a dangerous heresy, but as far as Alcnos was concerned their ruthless brutality was even worse.

'Others before them have tried and failed to dig up the Thing Below,' she told the lucidor. 'It has ways of protecting itself, and does not need our help. All I care about is rescuing my people and driving the diggers from the Land with such force and fury that no one else will think to disturb us again.'

A wooden derrick had been erected in the middle of the roof-less temple, with a big spoked wheel turning at the top: part of a winding machine that was hauling spoil out of the shaft. The lucidor could see it clearly through his spyglass, small and detailed as a toy. The gateway in the old curtain wall built around the top of the mound was blocked by a wagon, and watchtowers stood either side of it, looking out across the approach road. It would be easier to breach one of the crude tree-trunk palisades that patched gaps in the curtain wall, except that the steep sides of the mound had been cleared of trees and brush, and any party scrambling up it would be horribly exposed.

The lucidor asked Doros if the gate was the only entrance. 'Is there a back way I cannot see from here, or a tunnel or cistern?'

'There's a smaller gate on the northern side,' Doros said. She was sitting on a lichen-spattered boulder, the bow over one shoulder and the quiver of arrows over the other. 'But it stands over a sheer drop. They dumped spoil from their diggings there, to begin with, but when the spoil heap grew halfway up the drop they began to pile it inside the compound instead, and blocked off the gate.'

'How sheer is that drop? Is it climbable?'

'You would need a very long ladder. It's smooth baserock from top to bottom.'

'Where do they keep their prisoners?'

'Open cages in the big courtyard,' Doros said. 'I watched them being built. First thing they did. Then they mended the old wall, and clear-cut the mound. Tell me if I'm thinking like a silly, naive woman, but it seems to me that the weakest part of their defences are the gaps they've closed up with tree trunks.'

'That's exactly what I think,' the lucidor said.

He was still studying the ruins of the old town through the spyglass, taking in a paddle steamer and several small boats tied up along a quay. But he was no sailor, and no cut-and-run coward either. The boats would have to wait.

'We've been making black powder,' Doros said. 'It could be useful, I reckon.'

'We have only a little,' Alcnos said. 'That's why Rollo and Dickon went on that foolish expedition.'

'You could certainly knock out one of those palisades with explosives,' the lucidor said. 'Or you could even pull it down with a block and tackle. But it's going to be hard to get up there without being spotted. And if the diggers see you and start shooting, there's no cover.'

'That's why we thought it best to attack at night,' Alcnos said.

'It might work, if you could climb up there without making a noise. And if the diggers haven't set tripwires or planted mines . . . Has anyone scouted the area around the mound?'

'We scouted all around while they were building the defences,' Doros said. 'We might be farmers, but we also hunt. We know how to sneak up on something without being seen. They dug trenches around the base, put sharp stakes at the bottom of them, covered them over with straw matting and dirt. We made a map of them. Didn't see any wires or anything else, and we got pretty close.'

'Close enough to smell the meat they were roasting,' Alcnos said.

'Cow meat,' Doros said. 'One of the first things the diggers did was kill all the cattle around and about our village.'

'They made people plough up the crops, too,' Alcnos said. 'And then they burned the village.'

'And murdered her mother,' Doros said. 'And the other councillors, and all the others since.'

'He knows about that,' Alcnos said.

'And now he's seen where the curs have made their nest,' Doros said, 'I'd like to hear how he thinks we can overthrow them and save our people.'

'You doubt my ability almost as much as I do,' the lucidor said.

'I have yet to see evidence of any kind of ability.'

'How long have you and Alcnos been something more than just friends?'

Alcnos ducked away from his gaze; Doros met it and said, 'How did you guess?'

'It wasn't a guess.'

'It isn't exactly against any law,' Doros said.

'But only men and women can marry,' Alcnos said. 'And women are supposed to marry by creed and custom.'

'It is different in my country,' the lucidor said. 'Anyone can marry anyone else, man or woman.'

'And we will make it so here,' Alcnos said. 'But first we must deal with the diggers.'

'You have a sharp eye for other people's business, but that isn't why we brought you here,' Doros said.

'I haven't seen everything I need to see yet,' the lucidor said. 'Take me back to the camp. Show me what weapons you have, and this black powder of yours. Show me how your people intend to fight.'

10

War Faces and War Cries

Despite their fierce enthusiasm and Doros's claims about their hunting skills, the landers were utterly innocent of the stratagems and tactics vital to successfully assault a stronghold, and were armed with little more than the slingshots, spears and bows they used for hunting, and machetes and a variety of agricultural implements. The lucidor reckoned that he needed ten days to work up a detailed plan and knock the landers into shape and school them in the rudiments of combat and the parts they needed to play. Ten days at the very least. And even then they would need all the luck, cunning and artifice they could muster to overcome their enemy.

Alcnos and Doros were more optimistic, telling him that the carbine and pistols he had captured would make a big difference, showing him the fowling gun which had been rescued from the ruined house of the High Family which had once ruled the Land. He had to admit that it was an impressive weapon: its four wide-mouthed ceramic barrels, each stamped with a triangle of three stylised peacocks, the sigil of its former owners, were set at angles that covered a thirty-degree field of fire. Although the firing mechanisms had been removed, no doubt because they had been iron or steel, and there was no ammunition, the villagers knew how to make black powder with willow charcoal, sulphur refined from stinking bottom mud by the two-pot method, and saltpetre (which they called white flowers) extracted from dung heaps. It was crude stuff ordinarily used to remove tree stumps and make little bombs that stunned fish in forest pools, but Doros explained that it worked well enough when wrapped in twists of papery leaves and rammed down the barrels of the fowling gun with pebbles and shards of glass and ignited by cord fuses.

'We can take down a fistful of those jackeens with a single discharge,' she said with dark satisfaction.

'There are four times that number of diggers,' the lucidor said. 'And they aren't going to stand still while you reload this thing.'

'If you know a way to speed it up you had better tell me.'

'It's more a question of working out the best use for it.'

With Doros's help, he organised the volunteer troops into small teams and schooled them long into the evening. Giving them rudimentary instruction in hand-to-hand combat, urging them to assault grass-stuffed sacks over and again with spears and machetes and knives. He told them to make their war faces and yell their war cries to unnerve the enemy. He told them that it was hard for people to hurt other people without flinching, hard in the heat of combat to remember to make precise killing blows; told them to target the belly, because anyone stabbed in the belly would be out of the fight.

He organised slingshot trials, too. The best users, including the boy, Rollo, could hit targets twenty spans away with reliable accuracy, and send stones flying in high arcs for four or five times that distance. Even so, that was no better than a cheap plastic pistol, and this ragtag army of farmers would be going up against seasoned bandits armed with battlefield weapons, and training exercises were very different from the bloody confusion of actual battle. It wasn't going to be easy, and the price of victory, if they were victorious, would likely be high.

Alcnos didn't share the lucidor's pessimism. She had taken part in every exercise, praising the others and reminding them that they were fighting for their families and friends and homeland and would be forever remembered as heroes, and she told the lucidor afterwards that he was their secret weapon.

'When I was as young as you I might have thought so too,' the lucidor said, remembering how he'd fought his way past traps and illusions into the heart of the maze where Asthryn Bey and her followers had made their last stand. He had been in his prime, then, and the arrest of Asthryn Bey had been one of the finest moments of his career. Now, he was old and tired and cross-grained, and several cups of astringent black tea had failed to completely quell his headache. He was still not yet fully recovered from the shipwreck and its aftermath.

'You overmastered three diggers,' Alcnos said. 'That's no small thing.'

'Rollo and his slingshot had something to do with that.'

'Exactly so. With you taking the lead and my people at your back who knows what we can do?'

'I know that we have to do much better than this,' the lucidor said. 'We will start over tomorrow.'

He needed ten days. Ten days at the very least. But all of his plans went to bang and smash the very next morning, when a coracle beached on the shore of the little island and a woman clambered out of it and fell to her knees in the shallows, beating her head and wailing in raw bottomless anguish, and people broke away from the session on hand-to-hand combat and ran to her.

Alcnos got the story out of her in bits and pieces. Everyone listening sombrely as the woman explained that diggers had raided her camp and murdered her family and friends. She had been spared because she had been out in the marsh, checking bird nets. Two diggers had tried to ambush her when she returned, shot at her as she escaped. Alcnos asked if she was certain that everyone was dead, and the woman said that she had seen the bodies laid out. Her husband and his mother, and everyone in the other families – even their children. All dead, she said, and hit herself about the head again.

There was a brief uproar as some people wailed and cried in sympathy with her, while others argued about what needed to be done. Some were afraid that the woman might have led the diggers to their camp and wanted to pack up and make a run for it; others wanted to make for the scene of the atrocity and confront the diggers head on. For a few moments it looked as if a fight might break out, and then a man yelled that he could see smoke, and everyone fell silent and looked at where he was pointing.

It was two or three leagues away, a pale thread rising above the treetops, bent by the wind off the sea.

'If the diggers set that fire, it's because they want to lure you into a trap,' the lucidor said. 'It's likely that they let this woman escape so that she could spread word of what they had done, and are waiting to ambush any who rush to the camp hoping to take revenge.'

'He's right,' Alcnos said. 'The diggers will pay for this and everything else they've done. I promise that they will. But we must work together, with cool heads and calm hearts.'

Doros chose two volunteers and paddled off to scout the area around the sacked camp. After they had left, Alcnos asked the lucidor if he really thought that the diggers had let the woman go.

'If she was close enough to count the bodies, they would have been close enough to kill her.'

'The camp is in the middle of a big reed bed, very hard to see. How could they have found it?'

'They may have followed someone to it, or caught someone and forced them to give up its location. Or they may have someone who has a gift for finding things. What they call a scrier,' the lucidor said.

'I know what a scrier is,' Alcnos said. 'One of the daughters of the High Family, the last of them born here before they quit their house and the Land, could find all manner of lost things.'

'Didn't they leave two hundred years ago?'

'We have long memories.'

'And your people – do any of them have gifts? I should have thought to ask before. They could be useful.'

'None that are recorded, or that I know of.'

'Then you'll have to rely on mine,' the lucidor said, and explained that when he was close to anyone with a gift, their gift stopped working. 'That was how I dealt with the diggers' electricker, their so-called king of pain. And if any scriers try to reach out to me, their gift meets mine and makes a blind spot.'

'So they can't find you.'

'Or anyone close to me.'

Alcnos thought about that for a moment. She said, 'We should evacuate this camp in any case. They may already know about it. And evacuate all the others, too. Find hiding places for those who cannot fight, and make ready everyone who has volunteered.'

'There's something else,' the lucidor said. 'The diggers didn't trouble to attack your camps until now. As far as they were concerned you didn't pose a threat, or have anything they wanted. That changed after you took me in.'

'Because they know that you are dangerous.'

'More likely it's because I'm an unknown quantity, and it's better to be safe than sorry.'

'So we can't wait any longer. We have to attack them now.'

'I'm afraid so.'

'When the small gods answer a prayer, there is always a price,' Alcnos said. 'We are being put to a test, but we shall overcome it.'

She was possessed by a serene confidence the lucidor both admired and mistrusted. He knew that he was going to need her help more than she needed his, and also knew that even the best plans rarely survived contact with the enemy.

'One of the strategies we talked about was creating a distraction so that a party could sneak up to a weak spot in the wall around the diggers' camp, and breach it. Now we know that they are looking for me, there's an obvious way to do that.'

'What do you suggest?' Alcnos said.

'I will be the distraction,' the lucidor said.

11

Wrong Side

When the lucidor switched on the godspeaker a woman answered almost at once. As if she had been waiting for him, and was eager and ready to talk.

'I was beginning to think that you had found a way to sneak off this rotten little island,' she said.

'Why would I leave when things are just beginning to get interesting?'

'You should have surrendered when we came for you. It would have saved a great deal of trouble. For us, for you, and for the farmers.'

The woman's voice was a sly contralto. There was a steady mechanical pulse in the background, no doubt something to do with the shaft her people were excavating.

The lucidor said, 'How did you know to look for me?'

'The wreck of a fishing boat fetched up on the southern shore two days ago. We searched for survivors and found a coracle, and then one of my scouts spotted you.'

'The men who found me were not especially welcoming,' the lucidor said.

'We didn't know about your gift when we set out to find you.'

'Why are you interested in it?'

'You should be glad that we are. You have taken up with the wrong side. Those farmers are little better than cattle, and as helpless. If you stay with them, we will kill them all and take you captive and put you to work alongside the rest of our prisoners. It will be better for everyone if you join us of your own free will.'

'I know what you are trying to dig up. How can my gift help you?'

'Come and see. All you have to do is walk up to the gate and surrender. Do it before the end of the day or we will burn the rest of the farmers' hiding places, and make you watch while we execute the survivors,' the woman said, and cut the connection.

12

Into the Pit

As he unhandily paddled the coracle around the headland, passing between two wave-washed spikes of baserock and steering towards the harbour of the old city, the lucidor had plenty of time to reflect on his plan. Such as it was. It was early evening. The pale shrunken disc of the last mirror of the day's arc hung just above the sheer cliffs of the headland and dusk was thickening in the warm still air. Flittermice the size of cats were beating heavily across the water, trawling for fish with skin pouches stretched between their clawed feet. The lamps of the diggers' camp glimmered in the middle of the ruins stretched along the curve of the shore.

Although he knew that he was expected, the lucidor's heart quickened when a brilliant white light kindled at the end of the harbour wall, sweeping an oval footprint across the water, pinning him in its glare. He stopped paddling, allowing the coracle to drift on the current, as a small sleek boat roared out of the harbour entrance. A burly blond woman at the helm, two men aiming carbines at the lucidor as it checked its speed and idled up to him. He stowed the paddle and caught the end of the rope one of the men flung to him, and the coracle was hauled fast against the side of the boat. He was told to climb aboard and lie flat and face down, and as the boat's motor revved up and it swung around and sped back the way it had come one of the men searched him swiftly and efficiently and took the godspeaker. It was all the lucidor had brought with him, thinking to give it back to its owner as a token of good will.

The boat slid into the harbour like a knife returning to its sheath, gliding past the paddle steamer and docking at a stone jetty. The lucidor was hauled to his feet and bundled up a ladder, and the burly woman and the two men escorted him along a paved street, low banks and hillocks grown over with dry scrub and clumps of thorn trees stretching away on either side like a graveyard for a lost race of giants. As the little party climbed the slope of the mound the wagon that stopped the gateway in the curtain wall was hauled aside to allow them to enter, and rolled back as soon as they had passed through. On one side were tents pitched amongst heaps of rubble; on the other a square compound fenced with barbed wire strung on timber posts. Men, women and children in ragged clothes or nothing but breechclouts squatted or lay on trodden dirt. A few stood at the wire, watching the lucidor and his captors go past. The goaty smell of unwashed bodies. The ripe stink of an open latrine.

Several people were watching amongst the tents, too. The lucidor recognised two of the men he had ambushed in the little village: the one-eyed man and his friend, Vikor. The one-eyed man's head was bandaged, and he made a point of spitting on the ground as the lucidor was marched past, towards the derrick that reared above the pillars of the temple. It was about thirty spans high and nailed together from four straight tree trunks and crosspieces of crudely split planks, most with the bark still on them. The wheel at the top groaning as it slowly turned. Everything was coated with dust, starkly lit by fizzing arc lamps raised on poles. A wood-burning steam engine thumped and jetted spurts of smoke at the tower's base, cranking the long iron chain, a city's ransom of iron, that turned the tower's wheel and raised a chain of buckets that one by one were caught by a bar that tilted them over a wooden platform. All of the buckets were empty, clanking around the wheel and descending past a smaller platform on the opposite side of the pit, where several people, including the electricker, Sly, were clustered around a woman in a high-backed wheelchair.

The woman was about the lucidor's age, dressed in a long black skirt and a black shirt, a black skullcap pinned to her closely trimmed white hair. Her left arm had been amputated below the elbow and the sleeve of her shirt was cut away to accommodate a leather shoulder saddle and struts fashioned from ironwood that hinged around her elbow and ran across the leather sleeve fitted to the stump of her forearm to a prosthetic hand.

She reached out with this hand, struts shifting, elastic cords tightening, jointed wooden fingers stiffly clicking, to take the godspeaker from one of the lucidor's escorts and drop it in her lap, squinted at the lucidor through spectacles with thick round lenses that magnified her pale blue eyes, and said to no one in particular, 'This old man bushwhacked three of my best people?'

'He's a tricky sumbitch is what he is,' Sly said.

'My name is Thorn,' the lucidor told the woman, seeing no reason to use his alias. 'Formerly a lucidor of the Department for the Regulation of Applied Philosophy and Special Skills in the Free State, now seeking employment in the war against the invasion.'

'And I am Mirim ap Mirim, formerly an officer of the science division of the Patuan Army, now prospecting for a treasure buried far below. If you want to help fight the invasion, Thorn, you have come to the right place at the right time. But are you here of your own free will, or because of some kind of misplaced loyalty to the farmers?'

'They gave me shelter after your people attacked me,' the lucidor said, looking at Sly. 'But I owe them no loyalty, and admit that our short conversation intrigued me. You said that my gift might be of use.'

'Did the farmers tell you what we are trying to dig up? Did they tell you why?'

'They believe that you want to recover an ancient relic. It isn't yet clear to me why, or why you think I can help you.'

'Do you know what alter women are?'

'Creatures of the invasion. Monsters more human than most.'

'They were human, once. Or at least, the mothers of the first alter women were human, before they were infected. I was one of those charged with studying the alters. Specifically, how they induce, by some mechanism not yet known, spines and needles of baserock to grow through overlying layers of rock and soil. I was searching the deep stacks of the Imperial Library in Delos-Chimr for other examples of manipulating and working baserock when

I found a traveller's account of a visit to an insignificant island off the south coast of the Big Island. A transcription of a folk tale about an ancient relic buried under a temple in the ruins of an old abandoned city. Mention of groundquakes and strange lights that suggested something was still active there, an old shaft sunk in a failed attempt to dig it up, and a sketch of the bay where the city stood, with a curved headland, and baserock spikes at its mouth and a semicircular ridge rising behind the ruins of the city. In short, the very image of an impact crater. And when I saw it, I realised at once what the relic must be,' Mirim ap Mirim said, looking at the lucidor expectantly, as Lucidor Ryx used to do after posing some legal or ethical conundrum.

'If a shatterling fell here,' the lucidor said, remembering the flecks of shatterling stuff embedded in the small god set in the middle of the landers' camp, 'you have gone to a lot of trouble to dig up something that can be easily and commonly found elsewhere.'

'What most people think of as shatterlings are fragments of the creatures that once lived above the sky and fell to the world after the godlings returned to the creator gods,' Mirim ap Mirim said. 'We don't know why the shatterlings were created, what they did, or why they were destroyed. Some say that they were loyal servants that destroyed themselves after their masters abandoned them. Others that the shatterlings tried to stop the godlings from leaving, and were overthrown. Still others claim they were soldiers serving rebel godlings who refused to leave, and were defeated when they went to war against the rest. Whatever they were, they all fell, and the one that fell here struck with such force that it overturned layers of soil and rock and shattered the baserock beneath, throwing out debris across the island and the sea around it. I am sure you have seen some of the big rocks that litter the island. They are the least of it. A huge fan of ejecta covers the sea floor, tailing away to the east. Other shatterlings were destroyed by similar impacts, or broke up before they struck the ground. This one was not. Instead, it tunnelled deep underground, and is there still, digging down towards the inner shell of the world. We are so close to it now that we can detect the faint vibrations of its tireless activity.'

'When it is angry, the ground moves,' the lucidor said, remembering something Alcnos had told him.

'So the farmers say. The lower levels of the shaft drilled by its impact have collapsed behind it, and its top was sealed long ago. As if a cap of concrete and prayers and offerings could contain a servant of the godlings. We stand at the top of that pit. The prize is half a league below, scratching at the boundary between baserock and adamantine. You do know,' Mirim ap Mirim said, 'that the world is a shell. Or have things so degenerated in your sandy scourhole of a country that you think you live on a flat plate riding on the back of a turtle, or some such nonsense?'

Her smile showed teeth too even and luminously white to be real.

'We aren't as ignorant as you might like to believe,' the lucidor said.

He had come here with a simple plan. All he had to do was find some way of creating a distraction that would give Alcnos's little army a fighting chance of breaking into the diggers' camp, and he had been working out how to break free while the woman lectured him. He knew that Sly would be easy enough to take down, and the three diggers standing behind Mirim ap Mirim had the unshelled look of philosophers or clerks dragged unwillingly into daylight, but the two men and the woman who had escorted him here were another matter, and their boss was an unknown quantity. She was in a wheelchair and lacked a hand, and from the way her skirt lay he could see that she also lacked most of her left leg, but she might have a pistol or some other weapon tucked in its folds, and the cold blue gaze swimming in the lenses of her spectacles had the broken-glass glint of the truly obsessed. No telling what she might do when he kicked off. Perhaps he should try to tackle her first. Use her as a shield to hold off the others, or sling her into her damn pit. At least that would shut her up.

'The world is round,' she was saying. 'A shell spun by the gods around the Heartsun, which is the corpse of the sun of the Ur Men. Dwindled now to iron and ashes, it was the only sun the Ur Men knew, but their children's children escaped its grip and ransacked and remade the galaxy. The shell of the world encloses it at a distance of half a million leagues and we live on the outside of the shell, where the Heartsun's gravity keeps everything in place. All this is known and understood, but too easily forgotten.'

She paused, as if expecting the lucidor to comment. He said nothing, waiting to see where this was going.

'The point being, the world is hollow,' Mirim ap Mirim said. 'Its shell is sculpted with the contours of maps, and the basins and deeps of the World Ocean, and there are thin places in it, too. This is one of those thin places. I do not think it a coincidence that our prize fell here, and I have good evidence that it is still functional. Alive, in its own way, and perhaps even conscious. Remembering what it once was and what it needs to do, and patiently working towards that end. Digging slowly but surely. Trying, I believe, to reach the interior of the world's shell.'

'To what purpose?'

'To answer that, I would have to enter the airy realm of speculation. Which is to say, give you an answer with no real substance to it. All I can tell you is that it is still alive, in its fashion, and therefore useful. A tool, a weapon, or perhaps even an ally. The hidebound fools who claim to be my superiors would not listen, and even accused me of an unreasonable obsession. So I recruited my own people, and here I am.'

'Trying to dig up a shatterling that might still be alive, possessing unknown powers – some might call that reckless. Others mad.'

'If I am mad, it is a useful madness,' Mirim ap Mirim said. 'For it will profit all of us here, and might even turn the tide of the war. And you will help me, Thorn. Or rather, your gift will. Step forward, Sly. Show me that this man is as reported.'

'I told you what he is,' Sly said.

'I know what you told me,' Mirim ap Mirim said. 'And now he stands before me, and I must see what he can do.'

'It's more in the nature of what other people can't do, when he's close.'

'Show me.'

'Yes, ma'am,' the electricker said, and sidled around Mirim ap Mirim's wheelchair and slapped a hand on the lucidor's shoulder and jerked it away, leaving a faint tingling tickling sensation.

'See what happens?' Sly said. 'Nothing, that's what.'

'Was that your best effort?' Mirim ap Mirim said. 'Try again.'

'Any normal man's heart would burst, way I tried to shock him,' Sly said, and gripped the lucidor's shoulder again, shook him. 'But this one, he don't even flinch.'

The lucidor saw a chance at mayhem, and stuck his right foot behind Sly's left leg and shoved him backwards. Sly fell as if unstrung, but before the lucidor could kick the electricker over the edge of the pit one of his escorts grabbed him in a headlock and hauled him off. The lucidor jabbed at the man's ribs with his elbow, but the man managed to twist away from the blows without letting go, and then the woman stepped in and the two of them forced the lucidor to his knees and lashed his wrists together.

Sly struggled to his feet, saying, 'You should have done that at the start. He's old, but he's spry and mean.'

Mirim ap Mirim dismissed the electricker and leaned forward to study the lucidor, pinioned on his knees between the two guards.

'Be careful, ma'am,' one of the philosophers said.

'He has what I need, all right,' Mirim ap Mirim said. She might have been talking about a horse, or a rare piece of equipment. 'Our scrier couldn't locate him. That human eel couldn't shock him. But is his gift strong enough to quell the shatterling?'

'I came here at your invitation,' the lucidor said. 'And I came unarmed, as a friend.'

'Not exactly unarmed,' Mirim ap Mirim said. 'And certainly not as a friend.'

'If you let me up we can discuss how I can help you.'

There was a long pause. The lucidor became aware all over again of the steam engine labouring on the other side of the pit and the creaking wheel turning above. The empty buckets ascending and descending and the rattle of the iron chain, whose links might have been forged from ore his enslaved ancestors had mined.

'Fetch the numberling,' Mirim ap Mirim said, and as one of the philosophers hurried off she told the lucidor that at first her excavation had gone according to plan. 'We removed the concrete cap on the old shaft and dug out the overburden of rubble that partly filled it, and found at its end a second smaller shaft filled with pulverised rock.'

Again, she paused expectantly.

The lucidor said, 'You believe that this second shaft was dug by the shatterling.'

'There's no other explanation that satisfies. We began to excavate it, and that's where our troubles began. One by one, the farmers we put to work down there were driven mad.'

'By the shatterling.'

'Of course by the shatterling. Some became catatonic. Others tried to take their own lives. Some succeeded. Others went insane in interesting ways. Do you know the seat of your gift? Where your special power comes from?'

'I have heard it said that gifts are manifested only by direct descendants of those the godlings chose to ride.'

'I mean the physical location. The structure in your brain that generates it.'

'The dharma node.'

'Exactly so. At the base of the brain, just above the optic lobe.'

Mirim ap Mirim lifted her prosthetic hand and touched with one wooden finger the taut skin behind her ear. The lucidor noticed that there was the outline of a fingernail carved into the fingertip. He was noticing everything, alert and pumped up by adrenalin.

'Everyone has a dharma node,' Mirim ap Mirim said. 'It is believed that they enabled the godlings to speak directly to the minds of the First People. But the dharma nodes in the brains of people who can trace their descent from the ridden are larger than average, and the nerve fibres that connect them with other parts of the brain take up aniline dyes more readily than those of ordinary people. The farmers here do not number the ridden amongst their ancestors, but the High Family which was given title to this island most certainly does, and some of its male scions may have sired illegitimate children with their servants. Their lineage has been much diluted since then, for none of the farmers exhibit the faintest hint of a gift – until, that is, they were exposed to the shatterling, like this poor fellow.'

The philosopher had returned, leading by a rope halter a scrawny man who was reciting numbers at high speed. A breathless gabbling torrent that began to tail off as the pair approached the platform, until the man violently shook his head and fell silent.

'I don't quite understand the point of this demonstration,' the lucidor said.

'You are the point. Your gift is the point.'

The scrawny man stood slack-jawed, turning his head to and fro as if searching for something that had unexpectedly disappeared from plain sight.

'This wretch was receiving a transmission from the shatterling,' the philosopher in charge of him told the lucidor. 'And now your gift is blocking it.'

'We have transcribed blocks of numbers, looking for patterns,' one of the other philosophers said.

'So far without success,' the third said. 'But it's the first time anyone has glimpsed the workings of a shatterling's mind. Difficulties in comprehension are to be expected.'

'You are all crazy,' the lucidor said.

'No doubt we all have been touched in some way,' Mirim ap Mirim said. 'But almost all of the farmers we have put to work in the pit have been driven mad, like this numberling, or have killed themselves, or have fallen into a waking sleep. And we are running out of workers.'

'We think that you might be able to protect them,' the third philosopher said.

'But there's a problem,' Mirim ap Mirim said. 'Your kind of gift has a limited range. Like the influence of the shatterling, it diminishes with distance, according to the inverse-square law. That's why we need to test the quenching effect of your gift close to the source. As close as we can get you.'

The lucidor realised what she planned to do, and said, 'I came here in good faith. And this is how you repay me?'

'Fortunately, a gift like yours isn't something you can switch on or off at will, so it doesn't matter what you think,' Mirim ap Mirim said, and tossed the godspeaker to the woman guard and said that she wanted to hear everything.

The lucidor's escorts hauled him to his feet and unceremoniously pitched him into a bucket, and the burly blond woman stepped in after him and put a boot to his chest when he tried to sit up, advised him to sit still and enjoy the ride. The lucidor subsided, watching the circle of light at the top of the pit shrink, watching the walls flow past in the blue glare of fluorescent lights. Brick walls, stone walls, a narrow opening with a glimpse of stone arches supporting a low ceiling . . . The mound on which the temple stood must be the remains of an older building, or perhaps a series of them, with deep layers of cellars and vaults and crypts beneath it.

Brick and stone gave way to blue-grey clay; clay gave way to ironwood forms wrapping the walls of the shaft, and at last the bucket bumped onto a wooden platform. The woman stepped out, and rather than suffer the indignity of being manhandled like a sack of roots the lucidor pushed to his feet and followed her as the bucket dragged along the platform between two slow-turning pivots.

It was hot, down there. Hot and dry and dusty, packed with a tingling pressure like the onset of a thunderstorm. When he was a small child, the lucidor had been taught that all of the world's heat came from the Heartsun, some of it transmitted by the mirrors, the rest percolating to the surface through layers of baserock, and here was the truth of the long-ago lesson.

The only sounds were the clatter of the chain turning past the pivots, and the scrape of the buckets across the platform. Tools laid neatly by a heap of broken rock and gravel. A tall candle burning in a glass cylinder hung from a post, presumably to warn if the air went bad. Below the platform was an uneven floor of broken rock lit by chains of electric bulbs, with a tripod winch standing over a circular pit, not much bigger than an ordinary well, at its centre.

Another bucket delivered the philosopher and the crazed numberling. The woman used the godspeaker to report that they were at the bottom and the numberling was quiet, and told the lucidor to get moving. 'Down the ramp. She wants you as close as you can get.'

'So quiet,' the numberling said, looking all around. 'So so quiet.'

'Put this on,' the philosopher told the woman, handed her what looked like a small net.

'Seems like our muzzler friend is protection enough,' the woman said.

'I'd advise putting it on, just in case,' the philosopher said. Tufts of his cropped hair stood up between the links of the net he'd fastened around his head. He told the lucidor that they were woven from plastic threads doped in iron, had been developed to make people invisible to scriers. 'We don't have enough for the workers, and in any case they aren't much use against the shatterling, but they're better than nothing. You don't need to wear one, of course. Limiting your gift would defeat the object of this little experiment.'

Mirim ap Mirim's voice sounded from the godspeaker, small and clear, asking what was happening.

'So far so good,' the woman told her.

'We don't know how the shatterling will react to you,' the philosopher told the lucidor. 'It's very exciting. An important test of its powers.'

'Why I'm here, I drew the short straw,' the woman said. 'This idiot actually volunteered. Go on, now. Down the ramp. The sooner this is done, the sooner we get back to the world.'

The philosopher led the way, pulling the numberling by the halter. As he followed them to the floor of the pit, the lucidor had the sudden feeling that something was watching. The back of his neck prickled, there was an elusive glint in the brightly lit air, and it felt as if the pressure in the air was increasing, as if something was compressing the ironwood forms. He thought of a hand holding a glass tumbler, fingers tightening and trembling with effort, knuckles growing white . . .

The two diggers must have felt it too. The philosopher put a hand to his head, adjusting his net cap, the woman was aiming the godspeaker here and there, as if trying to catch some elusive sound, and both of them startled when the numberling screamed and dropped to his knees and began to bang his forehead against the stony floor. He screamed until his breath ran out and lifted

94

his face in the glare of the electric bulbs, blood from his raw forehead streaming over his cheeks towards his ears, and took a huge rattling breath and began to scream again. Bloody spittle flying from his mouth. A raw howl echoing off the walls.

The woman started towards him, and staggered and fell to her knees as the hacked-over floor bucked underfoot and a grinding rumbling roar filled the pit. Stone slabs tilted and cracked. Two of the big timbers supporting the platform splintered. Strings of bulbs swayed, sending huge shadows scurrying across the walls like the ghosts of gigantic beasts, arterial spurts of dust shot up from the well of the secondary pit, and a crown of sparks spat and popped around the philosopher's head and set fire to his hair. He screamed and beat at the flames and ran towards the ramp, and the woman pushed to her feet and shot him, knocking a spray of blood from his head as he bonelessly dropped.

The lucidor was balancing on shifting rock, looking around for something, anything, he could use against the woman as she stepped towards the secondary pit, watching him over the sights of her pistol. He flinched when a string of bulbs popped overhead and the woman smiled a ghastly smile and stuck the muzzle of the pistol under her chin and fired and collapsed backwards into the pit.

The grinding motion of the floor eased. A small aftershock rippled across the broken rocks, and then everything was still. The air was fogged with dust. The numberling smiled like a saint in ecstasy and said, 'So quiet,' and collapsed.

He was dead, blood in his nostrils and ears, pupils pinpoints on red eyeballs. So was the philosopher, and the secondary pit was so deep the lucidor could not see where the woman had fallen.

The chain of buckets was still turning across the platform. The lucidor used an ironwood stave to prise planks from the floor and smash them to kindling, and set two bucketloads on fire with candles and strips of cloth torn from the philosopher's shirt. The buckets were steam-formed ironwood, as hard to burn as it was to cut, and he thought that the fires would last long enough to reach the top of the shaft and signal to Alcnos and her little army. He watched as the flickering lights rose beyond thickening

95

layers of smoke, and when he judged they were near the top he grabbed the stave and clambered into another bucket as it jolted away from the platform.

The two buckets of burning wood fell past him as he rose into the distilled glare of arc lamps under the great dome of the night, and a raging confusion of shouts and screams and shots. The landers had broken through the curtain wall and all across the camp diggers were fighting landers and ragged prisoners. A section of wooden palisade had been blown to splinters and the wagon that had blocked the gate lay in pieces and the pieces were on fire. Two diggers ran towards the gate and there was a roar of flame and they fell in bloody ruin as shot from the fowling gun hailed through them. Reckoning that he might find Alcnos or Doros in charge of the gun, the lucidor jumped down from the platform and ran through the pillars of the temple towards the gate, swinging the stave to knock down a digger who had been taking pot-shots at landers, raising it above his head to block a machete swung by a wild-eyed prisoner.

'I'm with you,' the lucidor said. 'Where's the tablet keeper?'

The young woman shook her head and took two steps backwards and turned and ran. The lucidor saw Vikor laying curled up with half a dozen arrows in him, saw a woman trying to pound a man's head flat with a rock, saw two prisoners chasing Sly towards the curtain wall. The electricker turned, jabbed one of the prisoners with his stick and knocked her down, shot the other, and was trying to scramble up the wall when the lucidor grabbed one of his feet and pulled him down and stood over him, breathless and spent.

13

Phantom Follower

By the time the lucidor found Alcnos and Doros the battle was over and the diggers had been vanquished. Alcnos, soot-stained, one hand roughly bandaged, had a young girl fetch his staff and the rest of his belongings, told him that she had ordered the attack when the earth began to shake.

'We broke through one of the palisades and set the prisoners free, and then it was everyone for themselves,' she said.

'The diggers didn't put up much of a fight,' Doros said. 'Reckon they were thrown into confusion when the earth shifted under them. I know it scared me.'

'Did you have something to do with it?' Alcnos said.

'I don't know how to begin to answer that,' the lucidor said. 'Where is the leader of the diggers?'

No one knew. The landers had taken only four prisoners: a woman shot through a lung and unlikely to live, and three men, including Sly and one of the philosophers. Doros wanted to execute them, but Alcnos said it would be better to take them across the Sleeve and set them free.

'They thought us weak and helpless,' she said. 'We have proven them wrong, and the survivors will bear witness to the welcome we give to those who come here with fell intent.'

She had a grim look. The lucidor was glad to see it, glad that she had been willing to do whatever needed to be done to save her people, but sorry to see that her innocence was gone. Her life and the lives of the landers would be very different after this. War had reached out to this small island and left its indelible mark.

He said, 'You have won a famous victory, Alcnos. Don't ever forget that you fought for the freedom to live as you wish.'

'We did what we had to do. I wish it hadn't been necessary, but there wasn't any other way,' Alcnos said. 'I suppose you will want to be on your way.'

'That's why I helped you,' the lucidor said.

'It wasn't the only reason. You are a good man.'

'The leader of the diggers thought that she was doing good. She believed that capturing the Thing Below could help to end the war.'

'Yes, but she was crazy.'

'And I'm in a strange land, heading towards the heart of another country's war. Perhaps I am crazy too,' the lucidor said, and although he meant it as a joke it had the chime of an uncomfortable truth.

While Alcnos organised a makeshift infirmary to treat the wounded, the lucidor helped Doros and a squad of volunteers search the camp and make the grim inventory of the dead: more than twenty landers had been killed, including Rollo. Dickon broke away from the embrace of his mother to tell the lucidor that his friend had been shot from the curtain wall in the first minutes of the assault.

'He was brave, and I will forever be in his debt,' the lucidor told the boy, but knew that no words could comfort him and hugged him hard and moved on, and at last found Mirim ap Mirim seated in her wheelchair, behind the steam engine. She had been shot in the head. A portion of the brain which had planned the excavation of the shatterling was spattered over the dirt behind her, and her godspeaker was still in her lap. Moved by an obscure impulse, the lucidor stuck it in the pocket of his coat before calling to the clean-up squad.

It was almost midnight by the time the dead had been gathered up and the lucidor and Doros were satisfied that no diggers were unaccounted for. The landers had discovered the camp's kitchen, and hot food and beakers of chai were being distributed while Alcnos gave a short speech to the surviving irregulars and the liberated prisoners. As she stood on a crate, holding the hand of a small bewildered child and talking of peace and hearth and home and never again, the lucidor slipped away, past the smouldering wreck of the wagon and out of the gate, walking alone in the dark through the overgrown ruins to the harbour.

The paddle-wheel steamer had been set on fire and had sunk in its mooring with only the smoking skeleton of its superstructure above the water, but the boat which had intercepted the lucidor was untouched, and after spending a couple of minutes discovering how it worked he steered it out of the harbour and across the bay into the open waters of the Sleeve, heading north and west towards the Big Island under a clear sky livid with the smash of stars. Mindful of monsters lurking in the depths, he pushed the boat through the chop as fast as he dared and ran it onto a muddy strand on the far shore. By the time the first light of the mirror arc was brightening the eastern horizon he was already three leagues away.

He drove himself on for most of the day, keeping within sight of the sea as he walked across a heath studded with clumps of low wind-bent trees. His wounded shoulder and bad ankle were still troubling him, but his headache was gone and his spirits were lifted by the unfamiliar beauty of the coast. Mirrorlight sparked on water sweeping out to the horizon under a cloudless sky and soon warmed him through, and he shrugged off his coat and carried it over his arm. The pathless turf was cropped short by conies and slow-moving square-headed animals that somewhat resembled rock chigüires from the desert fringes of his native land, except that they were the size of the landers' cattle. Once, he saw several large flightless birds stretching their necks to pluck the tough fruit from the crowns of sago palms. Once, walking the edge of a cliff along the curve of a bay, he saw a crowd of animals like black-furred, overstuffed punch bags sunbathing on rocks below. For a moment he wondered if they were some kind of monster, but spied ordinary birds, the kind Alcnos had called cormorants, standing here and there along the water's edge, and saw slicks of kelp rising and falling on the wind-driven swell. Perhaps, like the Land's marshy forest, this was one of the places not yet touched by the invasion, still as it was when it had sprung from the minds and hands of the creator gods.

He stalked and brained a coney, broiled it over a small fire he lit using one of the lenses from his spyglass, and went on. Late in the afternoon, by now limping and using his staff as support, he crossed a stream on a bridge constructed from slabs of rock and followed the track beyond to a village nestled in a sheltered cove. No smoke from any of the sturdy stone-built cottages, no sign of people. Doors had been smashed open and household goods were scattered outside; two cockleshell boats drawn up on turf at the edge of the water had been holed by axes. A faint sweet stink of death came from several of the cottages, but the lucidor did not investigate because it would do nothing but break his heart. Bandits had passed through here, or perhaps it had been the diggers on their way to the Land, killing those too old or infirm to be of use to them, rounding up the rest. If so, he was certain that Alcnos would help any survivors to return to their homes, and apologised to them before taking a clay cookpot and a blanket from the scattered wreckage, and pulling handfuls of root vegetables from one of the garden plots.

Shadows were lengthening all around as the mirrors sank towards the shoulder of the valley, and he had an irrational fear that the dead inside the cottages might begin to stir, so rather than stay overnight in the village he went on. And as he walked, with the land darkening all around and the first stars pricking the sky, he had the feeling that someone was walking with him. At his back, always just out of sight. As if one of the dead had decided to follow him, or a large predator that had not yet learned to be afraid of people was stalking him through the warm dusk.

He made camp in the hollow centre of a ring of thorn bushes, boiled up a soup of vegetables and the bones of the coney with a handful of wild thyme. Sated, he sat cross-legged before the fire with the blanket around his shoulders and his staff at his side, feeding the fire with scraps of wood and watching the dark beyond the thorny tangles. He didn't remember falling asleep but woke with a start at first light. Something was calling harshly in the distance, a flock of small brown birds were all a-twitter as they hunted insects in the bushes, and he was entirely alone.

He walked all that day, and the next. Seeing no other villages, no roads, no sign of the handiwork of people. Drinking from streams that ran clear over stones or white sand, killing coneys when he needed to and butchering them with his ceramic knife, which he kept sharp with a pebble from a streambed. The land grew ever more rugged. Outcrops of bare rock; narrow valleys slanting towards the sea. Far off, the rounded tops of a range of mountains were sketched in blue and purple against the cloudless sky.

Above the head of one valley he found a crater fifty or sixty spans across, a lush circle of grass in its bottom, its rock sides fused by the heat of one of the energy weapons, hugely more powerful than blazers, which had been deployed in battles between godlings and their surrogate armies. There were similar craters in the deep desert of his homeland. Some stamped in sand and formed from fused glass rather than fused rock, some in short chains, others part of a chaos of trenches and overlapping craters, like the trampled floor of a goat pen. This one stood alone, a stray hit from a naval battle fought offshore perhaps, or from a battle in the air between kite craft.

Elsewhere he found small steep quarries floored with water, and the remains of old paths that followed the contour lines of valleys or were sunk between the steep banks of holloways. On the third evening, following one such path, the lucidor came to the ruins of an old mine standing on a headland, its shaft plugged with rubble and its square pump house roofless and mostly fallen to ruin, a collapsed chimney stack sprawling downhill like the spine of some stone giant.

It was a lonesome place, but a broken wall gave shelter from the wind and in the last light of the long day the lucidor made camp in its lee. He'd bagged a small bird something like a partridge that afternoon, and plucked it and stuffed it with berries and cooked it over a small fire, and after he had eaten he stretched out on turf still warm from the day's heat, loosely wrapped in the blanket, looking up at the sky's vast cataclysm. Waves of mostly red stars breaking against each other; cauls of gas lit by nurseries of hot newborn stars; the wanderer, Tiu, standing bright as a drop of fresh blood high above the western horizon, brighter than anything else in the sky.

The lucidor remembered how it had shone over the roof of the Number Eighteen Hostel for Single Men the night before he had left Liberty City, as he sleeplessly tallied what he needed to do and all that could go wrong. And remembered how it had also shone in the desert nights of his childhood, moving through the fixed constellations.

Before the department had recruited him, his education had been a patchwork of practical instruction in weaving, pot-making, cultivating crops, herding and animal husbandry, the songs and stories passed from one generation to the next, and occasional lessons from one or another of the government's wandering teachers. One of those teachers, a severe, earnest young man, had once given the children a short lecture on astronomy while they lay under the starry sky of a summer's night, and years later the lucidor still remembered how he had explained that they were seeing the wreck of a galaxy that had collided with their own, and that most of the stars in the clashing tides were either small cool long-lived red dwarfs or the remains of stars which had shone in the lost age of the Ur Men and had long since run through their lives and shrunk to dense cores warmed by nothing but the heat generated by their final collapse. Every star above the size of a red dwarf had suffered that fate before the two galaxies had met and merged, and colliding dust clouds had triggered a final burst of creation.

We are lucky to live in these times, the teacher had said. Until the creator gods spun this world from dust and thought and quickened the First People there had been none like us for billions of years. Nor will there be again, when this world ends, as it must. Nothing lasts. Neither people, nor worlds, nor stars. Not even the universe itself, for everything in the universe will gradually decline into disorder, until at last everything everywhere will be randomised matter at the same temperature and all information will be lost in an undifferentiated ocean of noise, and nothing interesting will ever happen again. That is why we must live fully in every moment of our lives, and dedicate ourselves each day to the betterment of our country.

Listening to this as he lay with the other children under the vast ancient spectacle of the sky, the young lucidor had felt a kind of swooning awe. How thrilling, how amazing, that he could be alive there and now, out of all the possible places and times in the vastness of the universe! Later, he realised that everyone, from the Ur Men onwards, must have felt the same way about their own lives, just as everyone had a special regard for the place where they had been born. Yet even now, years and years later, studying the clash of stars spread across the sky of another country, he felt a strong echo of that thrill. Memories of his childhood had grown sharper in the past few years and the naive, ignorant and intensely curious young boy he had once been seemed ever more familiar, as if two ends of a circle were closing. What would that boy think of what he had become?

He was still wondering about that when he fell asleep, and woke with a sudden start under a sky paling from the east. His blanket was spangled with dew and something, the godspeaker, was urgently vibrating in the pocket of his leather coat. It was useless without its paired twin, but he'd kept it anyway, telling himself that there was some small value in the fragment of the shatterling at its heart. And now, when he took it out, it was shivering like a trapped animal in the palm of his hand.

He set it on a flat stone and watched it turn in erratic circles. Its twin had fallen into the pit when the guard had shot herself. It was possible that Alcnos and Doros had recovered it and were calling him, but he didn't think it probable, and the only other plausible explanation shot a shiver down his spine.

The godspeaker was still hitching around and around with a staccato buzz, like a tomb beetle trapped in a jar. He picked it up, and because it was always better to know than not summoned up his resolve and pressed the button to acknowledge the call.

No one answered. No sound but the wind in the grass and a bird calling its two-note call somewhere in the distance.

It was still not quite dawn. That grey interstitial time when reality seemed most fragile. Everything a shadow of its real self. His feeling of being watched was back, stronger than ever, and he decided to make a start on the day's walking before he had his

103

breakfast. He kicked dirt over the ashes of last night's fire, was tying the blanket around the cookpot when he glimpsed someone standing by a bent tree rooted in the broken length of the fallen chimney. Someone tall and thin and clad in white, smudges of dark eyes in a white face, a long arm rising and a finger pointing at something behind him. He turned like a fool and saw only the empty heath stretching away in the predawn light, and when he turned back the figure was gone.

14

Heat

The lucidor's first thought was that his imagination had tricked him. He had spent half his life chasing lawbreakers and now it was he who was on the run, a fugitive trying to stay ahead of people who wanted to arrest him, or take him prisoner, or worse. Small wonder that he'd conjured a phantom from shadows when every shadow might conceal an enemy. And perhaps there really had been someone there. A refugee from the looted village, a deserter on the run from the army, a wandering mendicant. He had heard that there were all kinds of mendicants in Patua, walking the roads in perpetual pilgrimage with nothing but the clothes on their back and a begging bowl and a holy tablet, or sometimes not even that but instead travelling naked, or skyclad as they called it here, with uncut nails and hair. Whoever they were, they might have been as startled as he, might have ducked behind the slender trunk of the tree or the broken length of the chimney . . .

But that didn't explain why they had shown themselves after the godspeaker had woken, and although it could have been a trick of the predawn light or his sleep-fuddled mind, the figure had seemed more insect than human. Too tall, too thin, with arms and legs that had too many joints, or joints that worked the wrong way, all wrapped in something very like a burial shroud . . . It sent his mind back to the pit, and the grinding shudder of stone on stone, and the look the woman had given him before she had jammed her pistol under her chin and blown out her brains and tumbled into the shaft dug by the shatterling.

The godspeaker was back in his pocket. For a moment, he thought about taking it out and leaving it there, or better still walking past the ruins of the mine to the cliff edge and throwing it into the sea. Instead, with shock still tingling in his blood, he scooped up his meagre belongings and set off, glancing back several times and seeing nothing, feeling a little easier when the first of the mirrors jumped up from the horizon and the countryside around him grew more distinct. He paused at one of the streams that trickled towards the sea and drank and washed his face and dipped water into the cookpot before walking on, gnawing at a leg of the bird he had broiled the previous evening. At last he struck the remnant of an old road, and followed it as it turned inland. He wanted to find a town or village. Even a farm would do. He wanted to find out exactly where he was, how far he was from Delos-Chimr, whether there was a train or bus that could take him the rest of the way.

He walked through dry hills patched with threadbare grass, their slopes gashed to bedrock by washout gullies. The road he was following soon petered out. It was Skyday again, and the mirror arc burned white and hot in the cloudless sky. The rolling hills shimmered behind glassy waves of heated air. Small groups of antelopes with fawn-coloured hides and white rumps grazed here and there. Always in the distance, always one standing with its finely shaped head raised, watching the lucidor as he slogged past. Crickets snapped away from his boots; seeding heads of grasses clicked and popped. He was limping again, had fashioned the blanket into a cowl to protect his head and face from the burning glare of the mirrors, had folded his leather coat over one arm and was carrying the cookpot by its handle. Sweat stung his eyes and trickled down his chest and back and dried in stiff pale rings on his shirt.

He tried to walk downhill as much as possible because that should lead him to water, but he found no water and the day wore on relentlessly, growing ever hotter. The only shade was cast by scattered clumps of arthritic low-growing conifers, and he spent the hottest hours of the day prostrate under one such clump, watching the shadows of branches shrink across a dry duff of fallen needles and begin to grow in the opposite direction. Insects scraped and chirred; a bird he could not see in the weave of dark green branches overhead sang the same two notes over and over.

As the mirrors chased each other towards the western horizon, he drank the last of the warm greasy water from the cookpot and rose and went on. He passed the roofless shells of mudbrick houses strung under a ridge but found no water there, only a well blocked with dirt and rubble, and soon afterwards discovered a rutted track that cut across swathes of grassland as parched as his tongue. The old trick of sucking a pebble gave only a little relief.

It was dusk when he reached the edge of cultivated fields and saw the lights of a small town glimmering under the darkening sky. The track cut between fields of sorghum and corn and bean. A sturdy giant standing where the corners of four fields met resolved into a circular stone tower fretted with hundreds of slits – he would later learn that it had been built to attract roosting birds whose droppings, accumulating in the hollow centre, were used to fertilise the fields. By now he was limping badly. Limping past the last of the fields, limping past lighted windows of houses, limping into the town square where the facade of a whitewashed temple rose above a row of pleached bottlebrush trees.

There was a stone trough for watering horses. Watched by people seated at tables in an open-air café at the centre of the square the lucidor staggered up to it and dropped the cookpot and his coat and cranked the handle of the pump and bent to suck up the thin spurt of water. When his thirst was sated he turned, took two steps, and fell face down in silky dust.

15

Mercenary Work

The doctor of the town's infirmary diagnosed heatstroke and exhaustion, gave the lucidor salt tablets and sips of ice water, and cleaned and rebandaged his wounded arm. His staff and the rest of his possessions would be stored in a safe place, the doctor told him: carrying weapons inside town limits was forbidden.

'You can return them now, because I don't plan to stay,' the lucidor said, but when he tried to stand everything tilted around him and his sight washed with red and he fell back on the bed.

'You should forget any plans you may have until you have recovered,' the doctor said. 'You are not as young as you once were, and it looks like you have had a hard time of it recently. You are lucky that you found us when you did.'

The lucidor spent the next day in bed, cradled by the languor of a mild fever, falling in and out of sleep. Lozenges of light dropped by the airy room's windows crawled with infinite slowness down the whitewashed wall towards the scrubbed planks of the floor. The conversations of the other patients and their visitors and the whisper of the fans turning overhead seamlessly merged into dreams about plunging endlessly into the pit beneath the temple mound or plodding across a sere landscape while being stalked by something huge and inimical yet always just out of sight. An orderly gave him bone broth at noon and stewed fruit in the evening, and at last he fell into a deep sleep and woke early the next morning, hollow and weak but alert.

The doctor found the lucidor in the infirmary's courtyard. He was dressed in a white shift, barefoot, gripping a broom in both hands as he moved slowly from position to position.

'You seem a little better,' the doctor said.

'If you could return my clothes and possessions, I will pay you for my treatment and be on my way.'

'We are not yet so impoverished that we must charge strangers for elementary kindness,' the doctor said. She was a calm, practical, broad-beamed woman only a little younger than the lucidor. 'And while you are somewhat better than you were, when you were given over to my care, you are not yet fully recovered.'

'I think I can manage a little walking,' the lucidor said, although he was sweating from the mild exertion, and leaning on the broom.

'If you want to give back something for your care you can indulge my curiosity. Have breakfast with me, and tell your story.'

They sat on a balcony overlooking a dusty white street, sharing a breakfast of beans and scrambled eggs and green tomatillo salsa while the lucidor explained that he had been shipwrecked and cast ashore while travelling from the Free State towards Delos-Chimr, where he hoped to find work as a mercenary. Telling the doctor about the defeat of the diggers and his encounter with the shatterling would only complicate matters, he thought. Best to keep things simple.

'Were you involved in a fight before or after the shipwreck?' the doctor said. 'The wound in your arm is from a pistol round. And the burned streak in your hair looks to be from some kind of heat weapon.'

'That was before I set out across the Horned Strait. The train I was travelling on was attacked by bandits.'

The doctor's smile revealed a gap between her front teeth. 'In short, you have been shot and shipwrecked before even finding the war. And while I was treating you yesterday I noticed a number of older scars. It seems that you have had something of an adventurous life.'

'I was once a lawkeeper.'

'Once, but no longer.'

'I retired. You'll find papers to that effect in the pocket of my coat. A letter of recommendation.'

'How long were you a lawkeeper?'

'Almost forty years.'

'A long time.'

'Too long, as it turned out.'

'And what about your companion? Have they also come looking for adventure, or are they some random survivor of the shipwreck?'

'I came here alone,' the lucidor said, with a small cold prickle of unease.

'One of the town's watch saw someone following you when you came down the road last night,' the doctor said. 'I'm a little surprised that an experienced lawkeeper did not notice that he had company.'

'I was entirely fixed on finding water,' the lucidor said, which was true enough.

The doctor wasn't going to give up easily; she seemed to be enjoying her detective work. 'You were carrying a godspeaker,' she said. 'I don't know much about them, but I believe they always come in pairs. If I used yours, who would answer?'

'I don't know,' the lucidor said.

'Then why are you carrying it?'

'I suppose you could call it a spoil of war.'

'You took it from one of the bandits.'

'I hope to sell it when I reach Delos-Chimr. What did my so-called companion look like?'

'Tall and slender, and dressed in white. And too far away, apparently, to make out their face or gender. Are you all right?'

'Perhaps I'm not quite as well as I thought I was. But if you fear that I may have led someone undesirable to your town, I will be happy to help your people look for them.'

'Our watch searched the fields and went up the road for half a league, but found no one. At first light this morning they went out and searched again, with the same result.'

'I have some small experience in tracking. I might be able to find something your watch missed.'

'Rest here a little while,' the doctor said. 'I will assess your condition when I have finished my rounds.'

When she returned, she was accompanied by the town's mayor, a young woman with a pleasant manner and a shrewd direct gaze, who told the lucidor that she had taken the liberty of reading the letter of recommendation that he carried, and asked him about his experience in the lawkeeping trade.

He did his best to answer her questions as honestly and fully as possible, said that he didn't blame her for being suspicious. 'In the uncertainty created by war any stranger is a possible threat. But I hope the letter reassures you that I am no more than a traveller who has strayed from the path he planned to take.'

'We are somewhat out of the way,' the mayor said. She was dressed in a long skirt and a white blouse, square-toed brown leather work boots. Her straw hat sat on the table between them. 'Remote from the railway and the trade routes. Almost no one comes here, even by accident.'

'You're the most excitement we have had in a long time,' the doctor said.

'And you had a companion,' the mayor said. 'Someone who evaded the watch, and slipped away.'

'I was travelling alone,' the lucidor said. 'If someone was following me, I was too ill to realise.'

'I think he's telling the truth,' the doctor said. 'It's hard to fake prostration and heatstroke. And even harder to fool me.'

'And this mysterious other?' the mayor said.

'A mendicant, perhaps,' the doctor said. 'Or a thief, waiting for our friend to reach the end of his strength. Or even no one at all. A trick of light and shadow and heightened nerves. We have had enough false alarms in the past. This may be one more.'

'You'll still vouch for him.'

'I haven't changed my mind.'

The mayor thought about that, then said to the lucidor, 'Your good friend the doctor tells me that you have some knowledge of bandits.'

'Once upon a time I helped to curb the activities of bandits and smugglers along the border between our countries,' the lucidor said. 'And I have had a little more experience in that line very recently.'

'And you have led men, in your former line of work,' the mayor said.

'Men and women. It's my opinion that women are often better suited in my former line of work, because they attend to details that men too often miss in their haste to bring an end to a case.'

'You needn't try to flatter us,' the doctor said.

'I'm telling the truth as I see it,' the lucidor said.

'And you are proficient with that stick of yours?' the mayor said.

'I have the feeling that you might be interviewing me for a job.'

'It's more in the nature of an arrangement that may be of mutual benefit,' the mayor said.

'You are travelling to Delos-Chimr,' the doctor said. 'The way goes through the mountains to the north, and it is not an easy one. There are fierce wild animals, and gangs of bandits have taken refuge there.'

'I was hoping to take a ferry or some other ship.'

'Then you would have to walk back the way you came,' the mayor said. 'The coast here is rocky and wild, and mostly uninhabited.'

'A train then. Or a bus.'

'You would have to take a long detour to the east,' the mayor said.

'We really are a long way from anywhere else,' the doctor said.

'Then I will have to take my chances in the mountains,' the lucidor said.

'The arrangement of which I speak will improve your chances of crossing the mountains unscathed, and will also be of help to us,' the mayor said. 'So far, rebellion in the south-west and the war against the invasion have scarcely affected us. But we have to make a regular delivery of goods to the regional government and the army in Delos-Chimr, as a contribution to the war effort. And on the last trip our people were attacked by bandits. A ragged and starving crew, but ruthless and desperate. Two of our people were killed, and five injured, fighting them off. The next delivery is due soon, and will leave in eight days. You could ride with it. Our people know the road through the mountains, but they have little experience of fighting.'

'And you would have company,' the doctor said, 'and no fear of getting lost.'

112

The lucidor pretended to think about it, although it did not really need much thought at all. He knew that the two women had conspired to push him towards their offer, knew that although they probably weren't telling the whole truth, it was not a bad deal. He didn't know the mountains or the road through them, and there would be safety in numbers, especially if he was being followed.

He said, 'What kind of goods are we talking about?'

16

Potters' Marks

The goods tithed to the regional government were packed into straw-filled crates and the crates were lashed to wooden frames tented over the backs of tethered burros. They were tough animals a little like dwarf horses, the burros, with shaggy coats, long ears and dainty hooves. And were liable to bite or kick out if you approached them on their blind side or startled them in any way, the master of the train, Nunco Arwal, told the lucidor.

'They will walk all day over every kind of terrain, steady as you like, and want only a handful of grain and a spit of water at the end of it. But they're cross-grained beasts. Stubborn and temperamental. And nervous. Liable to go from ambling along to panic and stampede in a heartbeat. A falling rock or a clap of thunder will set them off. Sometimes no more than a raised voice, if it's unexpected. That's why we like to sing when we make camp. It keeps them calm and means less trouble the next day.'

Nunco was a stocky vigorous middle-aged man with a frank manner and a canny gaze, dressed in an embroidered shirt and padded trousers, a wheel pistol on one hip and a whip coiled on the other. He and the lucidor were standing to one side of the brisk organised chaos that, in the shadow of three bottle kilns, filled the yard of the pottery. The town, Turain, was famous for its ceramics, made from fine white clay dug from the banks of the sluggish river that formed its western boundary edge and shared its name: the tithe the lucidor had supposed would be beans and corn and salt meat turned out to be dinner services for the messes of army officers, and plain tableware for the canteens of government bureaucrats. Last year, Nunco Arwal told the lucidor, they had transported a dinner service of more than two hundred pieces, fired with the most expensive blue and silver glazes in the 'Snow Falling on Cedar Trees' style, for the personal use of one of the army generals. After they had seen it, two of the general's colleagues had demanded prompt delivery of the same service, and had not offered to pay for the goods, either.

'They felt it was owed. That it was their entitlement. I don't know much about war, but I can tell you that it sometimes brings out the worst in people. Liberates them from ordinary constraints. Now you must excuse me, those boneheads over there aren't balancing their load properly,' Nunco Arwal said, and strode off, leaving the lucidor standing alone in his leather coat, with his staff slung across his back.

He had mostly recovered his health, exercising for hours each day to rebuild his strength and each evening walking the perimeter with the town's watch, hoping to catch sight of his follower and prove that they were nothing out of the ordinary. But there was no sign that anyone was haunting the edges of the town, and although the woman who claimed to have seen someone following the lucidor said that they had ducked away into a bean field, there were no fresh footprints in the soft black dirt between the rows of plants.

The lucidor spent a fair amount of time with the doctor, too, drinking chai, playing a form of chequers that involved throws of six-sided dice at intervals to rearrange the pieces, listening to her stories about the townspeople, telling her a few choice stories from his career, and discussing the similarities and differences between the customs and politics of the town and the Free State. Although the pottery was run as a cooperative, controlled by a board of workers and passing a portion of its profits to Turain's common reserve (which funded the clinic and paid the doctor's wages), houses, farmland and small businesses were privately owned, there was no prohibition on the accumulation of wealth by individuals and families, and the doctor, like Orjen Starbreaker, could not understand how state control could be anything other than oppression of individual expression and imagination, even when the lucidor explained that it was the realisation and application of wasteful or dangerous ideas that needed to be controlled, not the ideas themselves.

'You can think about a poem in your country, but you can't get it published because the government controls the presses,' the doctor said. 'How is that different from censorship?'

'You can recite or sing it in public. As some do. But setting up your own press to distribute unlicensed work would be an act of uncivil selfishness.'

'So you would smash up the press and burn the books, and arrest the owner.'

'The owner would be arrested if there was a properly issued warrant sworn after a properly vetted complaint. The press would be confiscated, and the books pulped and the pulp used to make other, better books.'

'And afterwards you would go home, read some grim utilitarian verse praising your government, and consider yourself properly educated. Forgive me, but it does not sound like much of a life.'

'I have never had much of an interest in any kind of poetry,' the lucidor said.

His wife had had a liking for it though, had liked to visit cafés where poets, none of them published, gave readings. She told the lucidor that their rivalries and intrigues were often as entertaining as their work. He remembered lying in bed with her in their room in the Number Eight House for the Newly Married while she recited a love sonnet, the warmth and weight of her in his arms, the tickle of her soft voice in his ear, but those were private memories, and none of the doctor's business.

Actually, he rather enjoyed their conversations, and the doctor was entertained by his stories about the smugglers, cultists, incubator gangs, pataphysicians and rogue map readers he had gone up against in his prime. She had a lively wide-ranging mind and what she called a forensic interest in the peculiarities of human nature. She had never got around to romance or marriage and did not regret it, said that as far as she was concerned the townspeople were a kind of extended family – she was in their care as much as they relied on hers – and on the night before the lucidor was due to leave with the burro train for Delos-Chimr she told him the story of how she had ended up there.

'People of our age sometimes have the foolish notion that they must prove that they have not been brought low by time,' she said. 'After living full and useful lives, they suddenly realise that the end of the road is only a little way ahead of them. They begin to fear that they are no longer relevant. That the world is moving on without them. They believe that there may yet be time for one more grand adventure, want to prove that they can still make a mark and win respect. But an important part of growing old is accepting without regret that all lives end in some kind of failure. We never do everything we hoped to do, or do what we have done as well as we would have liked.'

'Are you talking about me, doctor? Or are you thinking of yourself?'

'Oh, I got over my foolish need for adventure when I was very much younger. It is a story of madness and failure with a kind of happy ending. Or so I like to think.'

When she was a student, the doctor said, she had become interested in medicinal herbs. The creator gods had seeded the world with a wealth of plants that possessed healing properties, but only a small number had ever been cultivated, and many had died out in the wild. But now and then a new species was found, or ones thought lost to the world were rediscovered, and after she had earned her medical qualifications the doctor used a small inheritance to fund a plant-finding expedition of her own.

'I lived for a year amongst the folk who lived in the mountains to the north of this town,' she said. 'Although they are a patriarchal people, being a woman turned out to be to my advantage. Most of their healers are women because caring for people is considered women's work, and while their men would tell anyone about everything, their women confided their secrets only to each other. And, eventually, to me. With their help and advice I found several useful plants unknown to my profession, including one whose leaves yielded an effective painkiller when mashed with slaked lime. And because I worked hard to gain the women's trust, I was at last allowed to take part in a ceremony they called "Touching the Hands of the Godlings".

'It involved the ritual ingestion of a small portion of a mushroom found only in the mountains. A mushroom said to have been used by those who were ridden by godlings when the world was still dewy fresh and everything in it was their plaything. I was inducted into the secret by a shaman who seemed to me then to be incredibly ancient, but probably was no older than I am now. She and the other old women of her village took me into a system of caves, where she and I were stripped naked and bathed, and I was painted from head to foot with patterns of dots and dashes that matched the patterns of the tattoos that covered her body. Prayers were sung, and she led me deeper into the caves, at last squirming through a narrow passage to a kind of cell whose flowstone walls were painted with the likeness of godling spirits: slender long-limbed human figures each with a single large eye, and decorated with the same patterns as the shaman's tattoos and my body paint. There, in the light of a single small clay lamp, the shaman chewed a portion of her sacred mushroom, and with a deep kiss transferred it to my mouth. It was a solemn, thrilling moment, and it changed my life. Not so much for what I saw, but for the obsession it planted in me.'

'What did you see?'

'We sat together for a long while, and when I was beginning to believe that nothing would happen the painted figures on the walls began to move in the flicker of the lamp's flame. They danced, and stepped down and invited me to join in their dance. The ceiling of that little cell was so low I couldn't stand, yet I seemed to be in a much larger space, and the godlings took my hands and spun me around and passed me from one to the next. They talked to me, too. Or sang. Of what, I can't recall, but I do remember the feeling those songs and that dance gave me. It wasn't unique. Many experience it through prayer, meditation or ecstatic trance. Some say that it is the most primal state of consciousness, gifted to us by the gods. Perhaps you have experienced it yourself. But there, deep underground, out of my mind on shaman spit and mushroom juice, it went deeper than any ordinary prayer or trance. A feeling that there was no part of me separate from the world, and no part of the world was separate from me. I felt that I had floated off into a limitless ocean that contained all of time and all of space, and at the same time I felt that ocean opening up inside me.

'At last it subsided, and the godlings faded back into the walls. The little clay lamp was still burning steadily, and when the shaman guided me back to the cave entrance I discovered that it was still night, and scarcely more than two hours had passed. I wanted to experience the vision of the dance again, craved it as an addict craves soma, but as far as the shaman was concerned it was a rite of passage that should not and need not be repeated, and neither she nor the other women, nor any others I asked in the other villages, would tell me where that mushroom grew. I begged. I tried to bribe them. I tried to threaten them. Nothing shifted them. I looked for a year, walking mountain trails familiar and unfamiliar, and never found it.

'By then I had run out of money. I took a job in a city in the mountains of the south-west, hoping that I might find the mushroom there, but had no better luck. I dread to think what might have happened to me if I had. Fortunately, I was young, and was able to outgrow my foolishness. The obsession slowly lost its grip, and when I learned that the doctor who ran this infirmary had died, I applied to take his place, and I have been here ever since, treating the townspeople as best I can and cultivating a little herb garden, and have never regretted it. And there is the happy ending.'

'Then you must think someone who has set out in pursuit of adventure so late in life a luckless fool.'

'You're not a stupid man, so I must suppose that you have a good reason to want to become a mercenary.'

'It's partly a matter of vocation, I suppose. Much like practising medicine. I was trained to be a lawkeeper and know nothing else. And it's also a matter of honour.'

'Ah. Then I am sorry for you, for that is worse than any other kind of addiction, and far harder to shake. Luckily, the state of your mind is not my concern. As to the rest, you are fairly fit, considering your age, and you heal quickly. As long as you keep that ankle tightly bound, you will be fine. As far as Delos-Chimr, anyway. What happens to you after that is not my concern either.'

'I hope to return one day, and tell you about it,' the lucidor said.

'I would like that,' the doctor said, and they exchanged the embarrassed looks of people who know that they have told small harmless lies to save each other's true feelings.

The work of packing and loading the cargo had begun at first light the next day. And now, suddenly, order crystallised out of noise and confusion. Handlers unknotted hobbles from the legs of the burros and the doctor appeared and wished the lucidor luck and pressed a small canvas pack into his grip, telling him it contained a few necessaries for the journey, and without any ceremony the line of burros unspooled from the yard and took the road out of town.

The lucidor walked with Nunco Arwal at the rear of the procession. The mirrors had not yet burned off the early morning chill. Thin scarves of mist lay just above the river, in this season a shallow stream winding between slopes of crazed mud, as the burro train clattered across the wooden bridge that spanned it. The bridge was old, Nunco told the lucidor, dating from the brief reign of the last of the imperators, who had been crowned as a baby and executed at the age of twelve during the palace coup which had installed the first of the present royal line on the throne. That was more than six hundred years past, but the bridge, its wooden roadway cantilevered in brick piers, was still painted in the old imperial red, and the posts of its handrails were carved into the heads of serpents, with fangs picked out in white and eyes in gold or silver.

The far end of the bridge was guarded by a square keep of wood and white stone, which the lucidor thought would do little to check even a small party determined to force its way across. The procession passed through its gate and followed an unpaved road that ran straight between fields of bean and corn into the tawny plain beyond, crossing dry streambeds on plain wooden bridges that dully resonated to the tramp of burros and their handlers. Mirrorlight burned through the dust they raised. The lucidor was glad of the wide-brimmed hat he had been given, and rationed sips from the leather bottle hung from his belt.

The mountains rose abruptly from the plain and by noon the toiling column was switchbacking up slopes of scree and gravel, at last passing through a gorge to a high valley where conifers grew in dense ranks either side of a swift river. Ridges rising steeply above the trees were crowned with fluted and gouged columns of raw blue clay capped with massive boulders, like the ruin of an enchanted city or a temple grown overnight from mushrooms.

Nunco told the lucidor that this fantasy landscape had been created by winter rains eroding a deep deposit of clay, leaving only columns sheltered beneath boulders, and those were being thinned and undercut year by year, and when a boulder became unbalanced and crashed down the rest of the column was quickly washed away. The lucidor wondered if the creator gods had known that the gradual desolation of this part of the map would create this strange beauty, and Nunco considered the idea seriously, saying at last that he hoped that they had, for if they had gifted a little beauty to generations of people living long after they had quit the world, then perhaps they had not abandoned it entirely, as some mystics claimed, and might one day return.

The valley floor slanted up and the burro train left the clay columns behind, climbed past rapids and small waterfalls and dark pools where flotillas of foam drifted like unanchored maps, and passed beyond the head of the valley and descended to a path that threaded along a contour line cut into rocky slopes, with a steep drop to a dry gorge. The path was so narrow that there was barely enough room for the handlers to stay abreast of their charges, but the burros plodded on at their steady pace.

At last the train reached a broad gully where a stream crossed the track and fell over the edge and was blown into spray before it hit the bottom. There was a camp site amongst tall pine trees, with tree stumps scattered across ground trodden flat from much use and carpeted with dry brown needles. While the handlers fed and watered the burros and built a fire in a circle of blackened stones, Nunco and the lucidor trekked up through the trees along-side the stream, clambering amongst boulders to a prominence with a view across treetops to distant mountain peaks, looking for the smoke of camp fires and other signs of bandits and failing to find any.

Living in the mountains was not easy, Nunco said, as they walked back to the camp, which meant that any bandits thereabouts were generally a poor sort, having been driven from more prosperous parts because they couldn't fight their corner. Animals were a greater danger: cave bears, packs of wild dogs, leopards, fierce nimble mountain buffaloes which could outrun a man ('If one charges you, it's best to climb a tree'), and leeches.

'I don't mean the worms that live in rivers and marshes,' Nunco said. 'I mean the kind that look a little like people, and stalk their prey at night. They used to roam higher up, living off the blood of goats and longhorn sheep. But the winters are growing colder, and they've crept down to these lowlands, which is one of the reasons why the mayor took a chance hiring you.'

'I know something about bandits and wild dogs, but have never heard of creatures like that. I don't think we have them, in the Free State.'

'They mostly come at night, and can be driven off by fire,' Nunco said. 'I am sure a man like you has faced worse dangers.'

Nunco came from a long line of burro wranglers, and told the lucidor that those born into his family not only inherited qualities that suited them to their profession, but also benefited from a store of wisdom and tradition. 'If you turn over any piece from our pottery, you'll find its base is incised with two marks. One is the mark of the potter who made it; the other is the mark of the town. In the same way, we're stamped with the imprint of our parents and family, and with the particular qualities of the family trade. I suppose it must be similar in this department of yours.'

'Not exactly. Like any organisation, the department has its customs and traditions,' the lucidor said, thinking of everything he had left behind and tried not to miss when he had left. 'But it doesn't allow children to follow their parents into service because it believes it could foster privilege and favouritism, and other anti-communitarian crimes. Instead, we are recruited by agents who search out children with particular gifts.'

'That's a harsh rule, if you ask me,' Nunco said. 'It's good to know who you are. That you are part of a tradition, with skills and lore that your parents teach you, and you in turn teach your children. It gives you a sense of belonging. It gives you ballast.'

In the chill evening, everyone in the train gathered around the fire and ate cornbread and a rich soup of blood sausage and tomatoes and white beans flavoured with dried herbs and fresh pine sap. Firelight glowed on faces, burning wood crackled and snapped and lofted flotillas of sparks into the night, and a song suddenly rose out of the low murmur of general conversation, one woman singing the first two lines, another joining her in counterpoint, and others taking up the melodies. Human voices rising and falling in two-part harmony. Work songs and wedding songs, lullabies and love ballads.

In one of the pauses between songs, Nunco clapped a hand on the lucidor's shoulder and said that perhaps he could teach them something new.

'I am not much of a singer,' the lucidor said. 'And I barely remember the songs of my childhood. I left them behind at an early age.'

'You only have to teach us the words,' Nunco said. He had taken off his hat. His grey hair, parted in the middle of his scalp, fell on either side of his face to his shoulders. 'We'll do the rest. A song can put on several different tunes, as a man or a woman will wear different clothes according to mood or occasion.'

He was serious, and the people around the fire were watching the lucidor with interest and anticipation.

Self-conscious at being put to the test, the lucidor stood and recited in plainsong chant the lyrics of a traditional herder's lament about the beauty of the high summer steadings being no compensation for lack of human company in general and his wife in particular. Nunco nodded, saying that it was a good sturdy thing, and the woman who had begun the first song recited the lyrics of the lament back to the lucidor and sang the first verse in a simple melody, shaping it by stretching notes and giving each line a mournful descending descant. Her companions took it up, improvising, improving, laughing when they stumbled, starting over, and so it went around the campfire, changing from verse to verse, becoming something other than the song that the lucidor remembered, and he was struck deeply and plangently by the realisation of how far he had come from home. Maybe Cyf was right, and the doctor too. Maybe he was a stubborn old man who'd set out on a vain and foolish quest. But as far as he was concerned, it was not only necessary but a matter of honour, and honour could not be easily set aside. It was like a house. It had to be cherished and maintained, or else it would be ruined by weather and time.

He talked a little about this with Nunco, who said that he had only really understood it as he had grown older. 'Some of the younger people say that we should tithe only pieces we would usually reject. Why labour over something that we have been forced into giving away? Why work hard for people who threaten to punish us if we don't do as we're told? But I say that our craft is more important than petty acts of defiance, and turning out second-rate goods would do more damage than any oppressor could. Damage to our honour. To our reputation. To our self-worth.'

'There's no humiliation in striving to do the best you can,' the lucidor said.

'Exactly so. Perhaps the only advantage of age is perspective. It's like climbing a mountain peak. It's a great labour, and every part of your body aches, but at the end you are rewarded with a wonderful view.'

'You love these mountains.'

'It's a complicated relationship. I love them, yes, but my life would be much easier if crossing them wasn't the best way of reaching Delos-Chimr. We used to travel there once a year. Now we must go four or five times, sometimes six. It is hard enough for the youngsters, but I have a bad hip, and the damp makes my back as stiff as ironwood. Soon I'll be forced to ride a burro, and that's when I know I will have to make way for someone younger. At least I know who it is, and I know she'll be good at it, too.'

'A relative of yours?'

Nunco raised his head, pointing with his chain towards the woman who had led the singing. 'Anil is my eldest son's eldest

124

daughter. When I retire, she will become the youngest train mistress in the history of our town. I hope that I will be allowed to take a little consolation in that.'

He and the lucidor fell to talking about the inconveniences and embarrassments of old age. Lapses in memory and failing eyesight and hearing. Digestion that had to be indulged. Aches and pains that never quite went away. Nunco's hip. The lucidor's ankle.

'You'd think the gods would have been more kind, and allowed us to keep our faculties until a sudden end,' Nunco said. 'Instead, we fall apart piece by piece, like the world itself. If there's a reason for that, I haven't yet found it.'

'I am sure the mystics and philosophers have an explanation. For what it's worth.'

'I've heard that you don't think much of mystics, in your country. That you don't have temples, or priests.'

'We know the gods created the world, and then abandoned it. And for that reason we think that attempts by mystics and priests to placate or to petition them, much less try to understand them, are a waste of time and resources better spent elsewhere.'

Nunco leaned forward and poked at the coals at the edge of the fire with a stick. Firelight sparked in his eyes when he looked sideways at the lucidor, cast the lines and wrinkles in his face in stark relief.

He said, 'May I give you a scrap of advice?'

'Of course.'

'We're just a couple of old men, talking freely as old men like to do. But you should be more guarded about what you say when we reach Delos-Chimr. Its citizens don't take kindly to anything that might be construed as heresy. Especially from people like you.'

'From strangers, you mean. I'm not insulted by the truth.'

'I mean that Delos-Chimr used to be in the trade of supplying slaves when your country was a satrapy. Its citizens have not entirely lost that prejudice.'

'I'll be careful.'

'I wish I could be sure that you will.'

17

City of the Copper Mountain

The lucidor was shaken awake by Nunco's daughter, Anil, who told him they'd had a visitor.

'Who? Where are they?'

'Long gone, I hope. But you had better bring your big stick, just in case,' Anil said, and moved on before the lucidor could frame another question.

Grey dawn light, scarves of mist winding through and amongst the tall trees and mist blanking the sky, and the whole camp was astir. A woman was kicking up the embers of the fire and several handlers stood with their backs to it, armed with cutlasses and whips and watching the shadows under the trees. Others were running towards Nunco, who was standing over a stricken burro.

The lucidor snatched up his staff and followed. The animal knelt on dirt soaked black with blood; blood was still seeping from a circular wound in its neck. It seemed stunned, scarcely flinched when Nunco examined it.

'You can put away your cutlery,' he told the handlers as he stood up, wiping his hands on rag. 'This far west any leech is most likely old and solitary, driven from its pack. It will be far away by now, sleeping off its feast in some scrape or burrow.'

The burro had lost too much blood to live long. Anil knelt beside it and stroked its muzzle and softly sang to it and the train master took a hammer from one of the handlers, and squared up and swung, a hard blow to the back of its skull.

Nunco returned the hammer to its owner, wiped his nose on the sleeve of his padded jacket. His eyes were bright and wet. 'We'll have to throw her over the edge,' he told the lucidor, 'before she attracts something worse than a leech.'

While Anil tied a rope to the dead animal's forelegs, the lucidor apologised to Nunco for sleeping through the attack. Protecting the burro train should have been a simple task, and he felt that he had failed at the first challenge.

'A solitary leech can slink past the best watch silent as a shadow,' Nunco said. 'And it hypnotises its victims, so they don't cry out.'

'Something that can drain a burro must have been some size,' the lucidor said, thinking of a predator stepping light-footed amongst unsuspecting sleepers, choosing a victim.

'The saliva of leeches stops blood clotting,' Nunco said. 'After this one fed, it left the poor animal to bleed to death.'

The lucidor helped Nunco and Anil to drag the carcass across the narrow road to a prow rock that jutted over the long drop to the bottom of the gorge. The rope was untied and the burro was unceremoniously pitched into the void and Nunco strode off without looking to see where it fell, shouting at the handlers to finish their breakfast and pack up as quickly as they could, it was past time to start moving.

The mist did not lift as the day wore on. Whiteness thickening all around, the mirror arc a blurred streak only slightly brighter than the rest of the white sky, shadows materialising ahead, resolving into trees and rocks, fading away behind as the train of burros plodded along the narrow path. Nunco walked at the head of the procession, the staff he had fashioned from a fallen branch jabbing at the ground as if he mistrusted its reality; the lucidor followed directly behind him, treading carefully over stretches of bare slick stone, always aware that at his right hand was a long fall concealed by the wall of mist, eyes straining to make sense of shapes blurring out of blank whiteness, ears straining for the pad of a leech's feet or a leopard's paws, the chink of a bandit's pieced armour.

Once, curtains of mist briefly swirled apart to reveal a small temple perched like a crown on a high crag on the far side of the drop. The lucidor glimpsed tall pale figures prowling about the columns of its peristyle like ghostly celebrants from an age past, and then the mist thickened again and the temple faded from view.

They overnooned in a grove of giant trees whose broad trunks, clad in soft red bark, soared into the mist, and went on. When it began to grow dark the handlers lit pitch-pine torches that crackled and hissed in the chill damp as the train crept down a path threaded between a tumble of rocks to a forest where remnants of stone walls that had once marked the boundaries of fields ran between the trees, at last reaching a clearing backed by a cliff in which the facade of a building had been carved, its balconies, colonnades and single square doorway overgrown by ivy and red-leaved vines.

The burros were herded into an enclosure built generations ago with stones taken from the old walls in the forest and the handlers set up camp at its entrance. As they sat by one of the fires, spooning up corn soup spiced with chilli oil, Nunco told the lucidor that the cliff dwellings stretched west for several leagues, and the whole mountain range was said to be hollow. An enormous underground city built by godlings who had moved blocks of stone as if they were no more than grains of sand.

'No one ventures into it now. Everything of any worth was looted long ago, and its chambers and corridors are haunted by leeches and creatures worse than leeches. There's a species of sightless leopard that hunts by smell and hearing, and won't give up the chase once it has scented prey. White crocodiles spend their whole lives in flooded crypts, preying on crickets and young flittermice that fall from nests in the ceiling, and the dung hills that accumulate under flittermice roosts swarm with carrion beetles that can strip a person to their bones inside a minute. The people of Delos-Chimr call it the City of the Copper Mountain because quantities of that metal were once found here, but we know it by another name: Argatta, the City of Demons. Do you know its story?'

'Don't forget that I am a stranger here,' the lucidor said.

'Your ancestors came from our country, so I thought that they might have taken the old stories with them.'

'We prefer to look to the future rather than dwell on the past. It may have been a golden age for your people, but it was a hell for us.'

'It was a kind of hell here, once upon a time,' Nunco said. 'The godlings' city quickly fell into ruin after they left, but people came to live here all the same. They clear felled tracts of the forest and used the wood to build houses and temples, and cut terraces into the land and farmed it. They prospered for a while. The first settlements grew into towns, and a patchwork of small principalities developed, but then came a long drought. The rivers in these mountains are fed by snow caps on mountain peaks, and when the snow wasn't replenished the rivers ran dry. Wells dried up too, crops failed for year after year, the forests burned, and the principalities went to war with each other, and tried to end the drought by sacrificing their captives. It's said that so many were beheaded that the rivers ran again, red with blood, and centuries later people dug up the soil at sites like this and boiled or burned it to extract the blood iron. But all that killing did no good. The drought did not end, and most of the mountain people abandoned their homes. All that's left of them are the boundaries of their fields, and carvings they cut into the walls of the old cliff dwellings in a script no one can read now.'

'And your tall tale,' the lucidor said.

'It may be somewhat exaggerated, as stories got up to bridge gaps in history often are. But this really is a place of death, left to grow wild ever since it was abandoned. Even bandits avoid it, which is why it makes a good camp site.'

'What about leeches? Or the blind leopards and the white crocodiles?'

'The cave creatures don't often leave their caves. Leeches are another story – they lack the sense to keep away from places men believe to be haunted or cursed. We were complacent yesterday; we'll double the watch tonight.'

The lucidor volunteered for the first watch and took a pitch-pine torch and walked the perimeter in the misty twilight, searching for tracks and traces of animal and human predators amongst stones and thorny scrub at the edge of the dark trees and along the footing of the looming facade carved into the cliff, feeling a small measure of relief when he failed to find any. As was their custom, the handlers had left a parcel of food on the ground outside the doorway, which was framed by a pair of statues of kneeling men whose bowed shoulders and raised hands supported a triangular pediment overhung by a curtain of vines. Mindful of Nunco's warning, the lucidor drew his staff before he pushed through, wanting to make sure that nothing dangerous lurked inside, and to explore a little of a place supposedly built by godlings.

The passage beyond the doorway was walled with slabs of stone carved with friezes of bulls and men and women in pleated skirts, helmeted soldiers in close-ranked arrays, and lordlings sitting sideways on thrones, holding staffs, sickles, flails, fans, sheaves of corn and other emblems of rank that no longer had any consequence, and gazing at something far beyond the dwarfed supplicants who bowed or knelt at their feet. The carvings close to the doorway were damaged by water and patches of black moss; further in, past images of battling armies and men hunting with leashed lions, the passage opened onto a circular tholos ringed with bulbous columns that rose into seemingly limitless darkness. Drops of water fell from somewhere high above and plinked one by one into the black water of a central stone-rimmed pool. The lucidor cast about, holding his crackling torch high, but the floor was covered in dust trodden only by his footprints, and he was quickly satisfied that nothing living had been in the place for a very long time. If any attack came, it wouldn't be from this quarter.

Outside, it was full night. The torches set at the corners and entrance of the enclosure flickered like failing stars sunk in the vast quiet misty dark. The lucidor sat outside the entrance until he was relieved by the second watch, and wrapped himself in his damp blanket near one of the camp fires and lay awake a long time, aware of the men and women sleeping around him and the burros tethered to the high lines stretched from wall to wall, and the darkness beneath the trees all around.

He didn't think that he would sleep, but was startled awake by a vibration against his hip. It was the godspeaker, shivering in his hand when he took it from his coat pocket, smooth and cold and heavy as a cobble. Without thought he pressed the button in its centre and answered, and a soft voice neither male not female said, 'Come and find me. Follow the light.'

The lucidor wet his lips with the tip of his tongue and said, 'Who are you?'

A white spark kindled between the torches that guttered at the entrance of the enclosure. The lucidor rose and stepped towards it, moving carefully amongst prostrate men and women. Everyone was asleep, even the two young men who were supposed to be standing watch at the entrance, and as he followed the spark as it floated off across the clearing the lucidor wondered if he might still be asleep and this otherworldly summons was no more than a dream.

The last of the mist had cleared. Stars and star smoke glowing between thin rakes of cloud defined the straight edge of the clifftop high above. The white spark hung just before the square doorway and darted away through the curtain of vines as the lucidor approached. He found it floating a span above its reflection in the pool of water when he reached the tholos, and as he trod towards it along the line of footprints left in the dust from his earlier visit it began to move again, leading him through a low doorway in a wall of close-fitted stone blocks to a helical staircase, flickering just ahead of him at every turn until, breathless, his heart beating hard, he emerged on a high balcony near the top of the cliffs.

A row of tall statues stood along the edge of the balcony, looking out across the clearing and the forest slopes, everything washed in faint red light and deep shadow under the great clash of stars. The white spark hovered for a moment at the far end of the balcony then shot into the sky at tremendous speed, and a shadowy figure stepped out from behind one of the statues at the far end of the balcony. It was dressed in a pale, hooded robe and as it glided forward the lucidor saw that the cowl of the hood framed a black void with two faint stars where a person's eyes should be.

'At last we can talk,' the figure said.

'I think that we have met before,' the lucidor said.

His heart was pumping quick and cold and he was gripped by a powerful, primal urge to flee, but he nerved himself to stand his ground.

'Briefly and imperfectly,' the figure said. Its voice was a soft flat whisper, but every word was as distinct and precise as cut stone.

'At a place where an old mining disaster left a small imprint I could use to reach out to you. The imprint here, created by the sacrifice of tens of thousands in a futile attempt to end a century-long drought, has far more potency. As you see.'

The lucidor blinked in sudden strong sunlight. The night and the forest were gone. Under an enamelled blue sky terraced fields stepped down long slopes towards a view of mountain peaks. A paved road cut straight through them, rising to a plaza directly below, where men and women, shaven-headed, naked and painted white, sat on the ground in long rows, guarded by soldiers armed with long guns and dressed in trousers and jackets blotched green and brown. At the centre of the plaza was a sky-blue canopy that shaded a high-backed chair in which a small boy stiffly sat, rows of medals pinned to the breast of his uniform jacket. A man with a cruel, clever face stood beside him, and bare-chested servants stood in a row behind his chair, some holding sweating pitchers and plates of delicacies, two sweeping large feather-fringed fans back and forth, three more beating kettledrums, soundless in this vision, as a pair of soldiers grabbed a prisoner and shoved him towards the apparatus set before the canopy. Its tall wooden frame was topped by a crossbeam from which hung a heavy angled blade of bright copper, and at the base of the upright was a kind of stocks, with a horizontal plank jutting behind it. The prisoner was knocked off his feet and quickly lifted onto the plank and the upper half of the stocks was clamped over his neck. A third soldier stepped forward and without any ceremony pulled a lever and the blade dropped and the prisoner's head fell into a basket. There was a pause as blood gouted and guttered into a leather bucket, and then the soldiers raised and locked the blade and hauled the decapitated body off the apparatus and carried it across the plaza to a cart piled high with previous victims. A clerk perched on a stool made a note in a ledger and as the soundless drums beat again and the next prisoner was hauled forward night's curtain fell as abruptly as the copper blade.

'They killed on an industrial scale,' the apparition said. 'Day after day. Year after year. And it did no good. The rains did not return and the inhabitants of this place at last lost the war that supplied its harvest of prisoners, and were killed and scattered. But centuries later a measure of the emotional energy of their ritual sacrifices yet remains, and that is what I am drawing on so that we can talk face to face.'

'What do you want from me? Why did you choose me?'

In the short silence, the lucidor feared that he had overstepped the mark, and the apparition was considering a suitable punishment.

At last, it said, in its soft affectless voice, 'When compared to the engineering projects that reshaped this galaxy this is not much of a world. Neither especially well made nor designed to last. But then the gods that created it and populated it with fragments of themselves were not much in the way of gods. The powerful and the puissant had gone elsewhere or elsewhen long before. These were a very minor order of left-behinds. Just bright enough to wonder what it would be like to be enfleshed again; just powerful enough to act on that whim.

'We were their servants. Charged with watching them at play and making stories of their games, for they had shed their omniscience along with much else when they fragmented and descended to the arena their uncleaved selves had made. The world is permeated by an information grid woven from trillions of interconnected motes of smart dust. We filtered significant information from that grid and processed and integrated it and committed everything to memory. And when they were done with their games the gods resumed their true form and took our memories and shattered us, having no more use for our services and perhaps fearing what we might become, after learning so much. And so we fell.

'You have seen the crater I made when I hit. Rather, when the expendable portion of myself struck the world, moments before I did. I had seen what was about to happen, and had just enough time to work out how I might survive. Falling into the shaft tunnelled by the portion of me that fell first, buried there when rock flung high by the impact fell back. I was badly damaged and lacked resources and energy, so began to dig down towards the inner surface of the world, where the power of the Heartsun could be directly tapped and I might find resources left over from the world's construction. I hoped to rebuild myself and make contact with any of my sisters who might have survived, but it has taken far longer than I believed it would when I began. Several times, people tried and failed to dig me up. In the most recent attempt, the attempt in which you were involved, they brought apparatus containing a matched pair of fragments from one of my sisters. I was able to infiltrate and use them to eavesdrop, and learned that there is a war against an invasion that infects plants and animals and people and turns them into strange new forms. Parts of this map have been ceded to it, and it continues to spread, and may have infected other maps. Tell me what you know about that, and do not lie. I will know if you do.'

'The country I come from hasn't yet been touched by the invasion, so I know no more about it than you. But I did meet a woman who was studying those strange creatures,' the lucidor said. 'She told me that the life maps of the invasion are similar to ours.'

'That is not surprising. The gods populated the maps and the World Ocean with plants and animals based on those from the world of the Ur Men, and life from that world spread across the galaxy more than five billion years ago. Even if this invasion wasn't kindled here by mischance or meddling, but was instead delivered by some wandering ship or rock, it is likely that it would be a cousin of the gods' creation.

'I know now that I cannot be other than what I always was. I was made to serve the gods who made this world, and although against them I am still a servant of their creation. They fashioned it for their amusement, and I will restore and reshape it. There is much work to be done, but in the end all will be made well. There will be a new order, and a new harmony, and I will become at last what I was always meant to be. But first I must save this map, and to do that I must find out what the invasion is and where it came from. Its strengths and its vulnerabilities. More data is needed, and you will help me gather it. If you serve me as you should, you will be rewarded. Perhaps I will make you my mouthpiece, once I have saved the world. We will make this map a holy ground, and you will sit on a throne at its centre, like the boy-king I showed you, and through you I will make the world's peoples understand what I need them to do.'

The lucidor, astonished and appalled by the cool craziness of the shatterling's grandiloquence, said, 'I am an outlaw in my own country, and a stranger and a fugitive in this one. I don't think that I can begin to help you.'

'I tried before to reach out to others. To those who first dug the pit, and to those who dug it out again. In every case, their minds failed. In every case but yours, because your gift is just strong enough to mute the full impact of our connection. And now it is time to strengthen that connection and make it permanent.'

Something seized and shocked the lucidor's body. He watched, helpless, as his hands broke open the godspeaker and prised the shatterling fragment from its circuitry. It was a black grain small enough to be held under his thumbnail. His hand lifted towards his face, stuck his thumb in his mouth, pressed the hard grain against the roof of his mouth.

'We will talk again when I have done a little integrative work. Meanwhile, I think you had better help your friends,' the apparition said, and vanished like a blown candle flame.

18

Blood Work

Loosed from the shatterling's control, unstrung by his ordeal, the lucidor dropped to his knees. First light glimmered in the sky and he could see now that the statues looming above him had heads as narrow as axe blades, with oval eyes and small, pouting mouths. The arm of one was raised to point at something long lost to time, and the fingers of its hand were forked at the tips.

Shouts floated up from below. The lucidor pushed to his feet and saw that things quick and dark were running towards the enclosure and scrambling over its walls and the handlers were trying to drive them back or fighting with them amongst burros kicking and bawling in panic and distress.

There was no time to find his way back down the staircase and through the tholos, so the lucidor swung over the chest-high balustrade and lowered himself to the ledge below. Some of the vines that draped the facade had rooted there and it was a simple matter to slide down them from ledge to ledge, all the way down to the ground. He drew his staff and took a breath and ran straight at a group of attackers and took out the two nearest him with quick hard blows to their heads. They were small as children, skinny and black-furred, mouths like gaping wounds ringed with thorns, small pale eyes spaced widely above flattened snouts. Leeches, no doubt about it.

Three more ran at him. He shifted to a wide hold and a horse stance, blocked swipes of their long arms and claw-tipped fingers, struck them with the end of the staff, precise, disabling blows to chests and throats and knees, and ran for the enclosure's wall, banging his bad ankle as he swung over it and dropped down amongst panicking burros. A leech balanced like a dancer on the back of one of the burros hissed at him, and the lucidor knocked it off its perch with a roundhouse blow and jammed the end of the staff into one of its eyes. The creature kicked hard and quivered and lay still, and something leaped at the lucidor from the top of the wall. He saw it from the corner of his eye and half turned as it struck him and wrapped its arms around his neck. He ran backwards and slammed it against the rough stones of the wall, its grip loosened, and he twisted and threw it to the ground. It sprang up at once, and he caught it with a back spin strike and felt its neck break.

He looked around, trying to catch his breath, and saw that the fight was almost over. The handlers were clubbing injured leeches lying on the ground, and the rest had fled over the walls and were scampering on all fours into the dark under the trees. The lucidor wiped a spray of black blood from his face with a handful of moss. Small hurts were beginning to make themselves known as the flood of adrenalin drained away. His palms, scarcely healed from rowing across the open sea after the shipwreck, were blistered from sliding down vines, his ankle warmly throbbed, and he had wrenched a muscle in his shoulder.

Nunco briskly inspected him, grasping his chin and turning his head from side to side, said he hadn't been bitten. Others hadn't been so lucky, and their wounds were washed thoroughly and dusted with flowers of sulphur and bandaged. Several burros had been bitten too; Nunco told the lucidor that two or three leeches had sneaked past the guards and got in amongst the animals, and the smell of blood had brought the rest.

'They must be desperate,' Nunco said. 'They usually come at the dead of night, and I've never known them to attack in a swarm like this.'

'Perhaps something disturbed them,' the lucidor said.

In the immediate aftermath of the fight the encounter with the shatterling had seemed like a mad dream, but then he had found the broken shell of the godspeaker in the pocket of his coat. And now, as the cold weight of reality settled in him, he was wondering if the leeches had somehow felt and reacted to the shatterling's presence.

'Some claim that leeches are a kind of anthrop,' Nunco said. 'But I believe they are a fell invention got up to make the world more interesting for the godlings. When I think of how their ancestors might have been hunted for sport in the first days of the world, I can almost feel sorry for the evil little monsters.'

'They may be monsters, but I don't think that they are evil,' the lucidor said. 'To be evil you must know good, and turn away from it. We don't call it murder when a leopard pounces on its prey. That's its nature. I think that it's same with leeches. They are only what they are.'

He and Nunco were standing near the entrance to the enclosure, watching as handlers dragged out dead leeches by arms or legs and piled them in an untidy heap.

'Then the fault is in their creators,' Nunco said, 'and that's a worse thought. What does it say about the world if those who made it thought that creatures like this had some place in it?'

The lucidor recruited handlers to keep watch in case the leeches regrouped and attacked again, and the rest packed up the camp and loaded crates onto the burros. Several crates had been broken open in the melee; supervised by Anil, handlers unpacked them and sorted through the crockery and rewrapped unbroken pieces and distributed them amongst the rest of the cargo. Kindling and tree branches were packed around the corpses of the leeches and Nunco set the bonfire alight, and as greasy white smoke rose above the treetops and the carved cliff, the train of burros was whipped into motion.

After two leagues Nunco called for a brief halt and everyone ate a makeshift breakfast of cold flatbreads folded around stripes of sweet tomatillo salsa before the train set off again, following a track that descended through thickly forest slopes. Here and there were long scars where fires set by lightning had burned, and charred trunks of fallen trees lay amongst fresh green saplings and the fluffy seed pods of fireweed and drifts of sunflowers. Once, a troop of monkeys leaped in graceful arcs from treetops on one side of the road to treetops on the other, and several of the burros bucked in panic and handlers had to haul hard on their halters to prevent a stampede. Once, the track ran beneath the overhang of a high bluff, and when the overhang became a tunnel the lucidor and Nunco walked through it, pitch-pine torches flaming in dripping darkness, disturbing only a few flittermice that swirled around them and fled towards the eye of daylight at the far end. Once, the road bent around a high slope and revealed the blue eye of a lake amongst trees in a valley far below and a vista of mountain peaks beyond, some snow-capped, others glinting where casings of rock had fallen away to expose the adamantine underpinnings of baserock. The flat top of one mountain was crowned with the white buildings of a small city: the City of the Gods, Nunco told the lucidor, kept immaculate by some sorcery as if awaiting the return of its inhabitants, and impossible to reach because there were no paths up the sheer cliffs below it.

The lucidor didn't tell Nunco about the encounter with the shatterling. He hardly knew where to begin, didn't know if Nunco would think that he had been blessed or cursed. He didn't know himself. He had been changed, that much was certain. A burden that he had not asked for had been laid on him. A doom.

He kept touching with his tongue tip the tiny grain glued to the roof of his mouth. It did not hurt, seemed to be covered with a thin layer of skin, and was too firmly attached to prise loose with his thumbnail. He supposed he should have asked Nunco to cut it out, or should have tried to cut it out himself, but after a few hours it felt smaller and less sharply defined. As if it was dissolving.

In the early days of the world, certain saints had consumed shatterling fragments in the belief that it would bring them closer to godlings and creator gods only recently departed. Likewise, present-day prognosticators and mountebanks falsely claimed to have been gifted with unlikely powers after swallowing similar fragments. The lucidor hoped that he was more like the mountebanks than the saints. Hoped that he wouldn't be changed by the grain stuck in the tender hollow behind teeth and the scalloped ridge of his palate, even though the shatterling, which must know more about the matter than even the most enlightened saint, had claimed that it would bond them together. He felt like a stripling recruit awaiting his first orders, or a patient beset with the tingling intimation of fever. Remembered the wretched numberling, driven mad by a brush against the shatterling's mind. Thought of the woman down in the pit. He was certain that the shatterling had forced her to kill herself so that it could get hold of her godspeaker, wondered if it had made Mirim ap Mirim kill herself, too, so he could find and take the godspeaker's twin, wondered if he would be able to detect any signs of madness creeping through him.

Anil walked up and down the line as they drove the burro train onward, talking with each of the handlers. The lucidor supposed that she was reassuring them after they had been unnerved by the attack, but when they overnooned in a clearing where a ruined pele tower stood at a bend of the road, clad entirely in a shroud of dark green ivy, Nunco confided that he and Anil had been visited by the same dream in the night, a vision of beheadings in front of the temple and the land beyond as it once was, and Anil had found that the other handlers had all shared it.

'The killing went on and on,' Nunco said. 'As if they were slaughtering beasts rather than people. As if death meant nothing to them. All that blood – and we were sleeping on ground soaked in it. We have overnighted there many times before without any trouble, but it seems that we've overstayed our welcome. A few blamed you, but Anil and I soon put an end to that.'

'I had something like the same dream,' the lucidor confessed, and stopped himself from saying more.

'I wondered if you did. Perhaps you are more accustomed to such things, being a lawkeeper, but I can tell you that it frightened and sickened me.'

'It affected me too. More than I can tell you.'

The lucidor had thought that agreeing to accompany the burro train to Delos-Chimr would set him on the right path, but he had been grievously mistaken. The attack by the leeches had been the least of it. So like everyone else he was preoccupied with visions and portents as the train set off again, crossing a broad swift river on a stone bridge, descending through woods where conifers gave way to broadleaf trees. The woods thinned and fell back and they crossed grassland studded with solitary trees with tall bare trunks topped with ragged spreads of foliage. Tears-of-blood trees, Nunco told the lucidor, planted by monarchs whose family had ruled the map for a thousand years after the godlings had quit the world. The trees' red sap was used to dye ceremonial clothing, and their large, rare fruits were packed in ice and dispatched to the capital, for every fruit was the property of the Queen, served at feasts and formal dinners or gifted to favoured courtiers.

'She must be much feared,' the lucidor said, 'if these fruits are never stolen.'

'She is much loved,' Nunco said, and kissed the knuckle of his thumb and touched it to his forehead.

He and the lucidor fell into another discussion about the differences between their two countries. Nunco couldn't understand how ordinary people could be trusted to choose their leaders wisely; the lucidor couldn't understand how a monarch whose life was so very different from the people of her country could properly and fairly rule over them, or why the people of Nunco's town, with their common ownership of its pottery, obeyed the decrees of a government whose head claimed title to all property in the land and possessed an absolute authority that transcended laws which bound everyone else. Nunco said that the Queen was the mortal representative of the gods, being a direct descendant of certain saints of the first days, and the lucidor was sharply reminded of the shatterling, and the path he was following instead of the path he had intended to follow. Criminals were not executed in the Free State, but the lucidor thought that his life would have been so much easier if an exception had been made for Remfrey He. No teasing notes and mind games; no need to take up this bootless quest.

It was late in the day, now. The burro train had left the tears-of-blood trees behind and was following a track through fields of maize, sweet potato, tobacco, sorghum and electrical flax. And then the shore of the Horned Strait was at the horizon, and as the long red light of the last of the mirrors foundered in the west the track joined a paved road. Factories, mills and grain silos reared up alongside, the dishes of radio telescopes beaming prayers into the cosmos stood like giant blossoms on a hilltop, and the road widened into a four-lane highway, with flocks of bicycles and the runabouts for which Delos was famous weaving in and out of a heavy traffic of self-propelled carts that passed the burro train in a rush of wind that stank of burned cooking oil.

The handlers took up a song and drove their charges through weeds and sere grass along the shoulder of the road and at last – it was night now, and lamps hung from tall stalks illuminated the road with an eerie orange glow and runabouts were crowned with glaring headlamps and carts were strung with hundreds of tiny lights – they turned off the road into a freight yard near the docks where the burros were unloaded and the cargo was tallied and Nunco had a protracted discussion with a bureaucrat about the breakages.

'At least the cut was fair, this time,' Nunco told the lucidor, afterwards.

'The cut?'

'The share these people take for doing their job. I saved a little money by persuading that fellow to take his from the profit after deductions for breakages, rather than from what the profit should have been. Unfortunately, I couldn't get him to move on the increase in the fee for overnighting. Prices are higher every time we come, and every time we are told it is because of the war.'

They camped in a lot behind the freight yard, where carts and a solitary land cruiser, painted in red and gold and looming above the smaller vehicles like a temple set amongst ordinary houses were parked. The handlers purchased hay for the burros from a merchant, and built a camp fire and brewed a bucket of chai and cooked their evening meal.

It was too late to begin to explore the Twin Cities and the lucidor was in any case exhausted by the long march, so he spent a restless night with Nunco and the others. There were always people coming and going in the lot, and in the middle distance a processing plant where electrical flax was dried and baked and mechanically winnowed to husk away everything but the conducting strands thumped and hissed and banged all night long, lit by glaring lamps and wreathed in vapour.

At first light, the lucidor abandoned his fitful sleep and washed and shaved at a standing tap and made his farewell to Nunco, who was organising a small string of burros to collect from a wholesaler clothes and shoes and a variety of other goods ordered by the townspeople.

'You could stay with us,' Nunco said. 'In these times it's clear we will need someone like you. You'll get a house and a share, and all you'll have to do is organise the town watch and escort burro trains.'

'Is that your idea, or the mayor's?'

'We put it to a vote before the train left.'

The lucidor was touched, but said that he had already retired from that kind of work, and wasn't sure how many more times he could fight off leeches or go up against bandits.

'The fight against the invasion will be no easier, from what I have heard. But should you survive that and need a quiet berth, think of us,' Nunco said, and handed the lucidor a small sheaf of plastic notes as payment for his services. 'It isn't much, and it will soon be gone if you spend any time here.'

'Because the war has made everything so expensive.'

'Everything here was already expensive. Now it is more so,' Nunco said, and told the lucidor that his best chance of finding employment was across the river, in Chimr's Tinkers Market.

'Do they sell philosophers' tools there?' the lucidor said, thinking of Remfrey He.

'Everything of that kind and more,' Nunco said. 'They will have you bartering away your soul, if you don't take care. The Twin Cities are full of rogues, cutpurses and smooth-tongued tricksters, and Tinkers Market is the very centre of their trade.'

'Don't worry,' the lucidor said. 'I have been dealing with people like that all my life.'

PART TWO
Alter Women Territory

19

Interesting Aura

For most of the morning the lucidor walked beside a long straight highway that cut through an industrial sprawl that reminded him of Roos – Roos as it might have been in its pomp, with a traffic of slaves flowing through it in one direction and iron ore in the other. He stopped at a roadside stall and ate a breakfast of noodles and sliced boiled eggs and pickles, and went on.

The grain of shatterling stuff was gone from the roof of his mouth, leaving only a small painless blister. He hoped that it had fallen away and he had swallowed it in his sleep, told himself that his gift might foil the shatterling's attempt to make permanent contact now that he was far from the blood-soaked spot where it had ambushed him, but couldn't shake off the idea that the grain had germinated like a seed, sprouting fine tendrils that grew through flesh and blood into his brain. The shatterling was still in its pit, but it had reached out to him and used him as godlings had once used the people they had ridden. Only briefly, to be sure, and it had been silent since then, but the loss of control to something old and powerful was no less frightening, and there was no way of knowing when it would reach out to him again, and what it might do when it did.

This foreboding uncertainty darkened the edges of his every thought, but for the moment he was free to act for himself, and he had reached Delos-Chimr, and Remfrey He was somewhere ahead of him. He told himself that as long as he could find the man and put an end to his mischief anything that happened after that was of no consequence.

He passed a big army barracks behind mesh fences and barbed wire, passed block after block of yellow brick apartment houses

147

six or seven storeys high, their windowless sides painted with patriotic slogans, portraits of the Queen, and murals of agricultural and factory workers raising scythes and hammers in unity, and soldiers pointing towards territory they were about to liberate or cheerfully carrying small children in their arms or massed in steadfast ranks. The road traffic grew ever heavier. Convoys of self-propelled carts. Carts drawn by teams of horses or oxen. Quick bright flocks of runabouts, some towing small trailers with passengers packing bench seats hip to hip, shoulder to shoulder. A column of soldiers marching south in two ranks and around thirty files, preceded by flags flying from long bamboo poles and followed by ox carts piled with kit bags and equipment.

Apartment houses gave way to a commercial grid of shops and offices, and by noon the lucidor had reached the bank of the brown purposeful river that divided Delos from Chimr. Food carts were set up along a promenade in the shade of wattle trees, and the lucidor bought a pastry shell stuffed with minced onion and cubes of sweet potato from one of the carts, a paper cup of milky chai from another. He was sitting on a bench and eating, trying to ignore people glancing or openly staring at him, his leather coat and the staff propped beside him, when a shambling procession came down the promenade.

There were about fifty men and women mostly the lucidor's age or older, dressed in bright yellow robes got up from dyed sheets or lengths of cloth, walking in no special order and with no apparent leader. Most were barefoot. Some wore conical paper hats daubed with yellow five-pointed stars. A belly drum boomed a slow and steady beat, several marchers tootled a rambling melody on reed flutes, and others handed out leaflets to passers-by.

The lucidor took one from a woman with a flushed, shining face and the pinned eyes of a drug addict. Blocks of short sentences in uneven type under a smudged image of the five-pointed star, some words and phrases capitalised for emphasis.

JOIN US!
GLAD TIDINGS!
APOCALYPSE
TRUE LIGHT
SHATTERLING

When he saw that last word the lucidor crumpled the leaflet and tossed it away. Even though it was obviously the ravings of some kind of endtime cult, it seemed like an omen.

The woman sitting at the other end of the bench edged closer to him, told him that the endtimers came by every afternoon with their music and their leaflets, said that they were crazy but harmless.

'There are endtimers where I come from, too,' the lucidor said. 'Some harmless, some not so much.'

In the early days of his career, Remfrey He had paid lunatics to rant in town squares about similar apocalyptic fantasies, or to deliver messages from the recent dead to friends and relatives, warning them about accidents and illnesses that would soon carry away them or their loved ones. His idea of fun.

'These follow a prophet who claims to be the mouth and arm of a shatterling,' the woman said. 'He says that it gives him visions of the future.'

The lucidor's tongue went to the roof of his mouth. He said, 'How did he become the servant of this shatterling?'

'I think it visited him while he was meditating on a mountain peak. Or so he says.'

'You don't believe him?'

'All I know about the future is that we cannot really know about it until it happens. Or until it doesn't.'

The woman seemed sensible enough, neatly dressed, her small boots, buttoned at the side and nicely polished, not quite touching the ground.

'I know someone who was likewise visited,' the lucidor said. 'He would be interested in talking to this preacher.'

'Does he have visions too?'

'Of the past, rather than the future. Where might I find this prophet? Was he in the procession that just went past?'

'He preaches in Chimr, I think. Across the river. If you're looking for prophets, that's where you'll mostly find them. It's notorious for its seers and sibyls, and all manner of sects and cults. May I ask – did you come here from the south? Have you been fighting against the rebels and bandits?'

'I came from that direction, certainly.'

'Then perhaps you know or you have heard something about a captain in the Third Light Brigade. Go Captain Lymer Grasswhisperer.'

'Your husband?'

'My daughter.' The woman's gaze softened. 'She was killed in the campaign against the rebels. The army didn't tell me how, and didn't send her back to me either. Just an empty urn and a folded flag. Not even a scrap of uniform. So if you happen to return to the south, and if you hear something of Go Captain Lymer Grasswhisperer, a report, a story, anything at all, perhaps you could send word to me. Here, I have my name and address written down, and my daughter's too. Name and rank and company,' the woman said, and gave him a slip of paper.

The lucidor took it and told the woman that should he find himself in the war in the south he would be sure to ask after her daughter.

The woman thanked him and stood up. 'It's people like my Lymer who will save us. Not false prophets and the fools who follow them,' she said, and walked off towards a group of soldiers standing around one of the food carts.

The lucidor picked up the leaflet he had thrown away and smoothed it out and pocketed it, and set off in the other direction, towards the bridge that strode across the river on fifteen stone arches. Soldiers at a checkpoint were stopping every vehicle and everyone on foot who wanted to cross into Chimr. The lucidor joined the queue of pedestrians and showed one of the soldiers the papers that Pyn had supplied. There was a chance that the department had alerted the authorities in Delos-Chimr to watch out for a tall man in late middle age, most likely dressed in a leather coat, carrying a fighting staff, and claiming to be Saj Orym Zier, a former sheriff for the court of magistrates, but the lucidor supposed that all the crossing places would be likewise guarded, and he had business in Tinkers Market, and an itch to meet the endtimer prophet and ask him a question. He looked straight ahead while the young soldier thumbed through the papers, felt something relax inside himself when she handed them back and waved him through.

Delos was a bustling city of industry and apartment buildings; Chimr was older, quieter, more compact. Narrow streets of mud-brick flat-roofed houses painted in a variety of reds and pinks, workshops, small shrines and onion-roofed temples spread around the mound of the citadel where the governor of the province had his official residence. As in the oldest parts of Liberty City, where overseers, clerks, auditors and other officials of the satrapy had once lived, many of the houses stood along courtyards set at right angles to the street and entered through arched gateways, with plants growing in tubs and bicycles leaning against walls and children playing and washing lines strung overhead. The lucidor and his wife had lived in a one-bedroom apartment in the upper floor of a similar house, overlooking a similar courtyard; it was strange and bittersweet to walk streets that were familiar yet so far from home.

Nunco had given him directions to the quarter popular with Freestater mercenaries, and he rented a bed in one of the quarter's hostels, a shabby place where the clerk conducted his business behind a window of heavy plastic and a woman stopped him on the stair and tried to sell him some kind of combat drug. The room was barely big enough for its two sets of bunk beds, but the lucidor did not plan on sleeping there. After leaning out of the window and studying the buildings across the street he went back downstairs and visited the bar next door, where he bought drinks for a trio of cow wranglers from the northern edge of the Free State. They had served with the border patrol during their year of national service and afterwards had lit out for Patua and more of that kind of fun. None of them had heard of Remfrey He or knew anyone likely to know about him or his whereabouts. They hadn't been in town long, they said, were waiting to get their papers sorted out so they could sign up with the Red Hand Company, the maddest and baddest group of mercenaries to ever walk the map. It had cleaned out the rebel town of Amarant two weeks ago, and was getting ready to move on to the next stronghold.

'That's where the action is,' one of the lads said. 'Fighting rebels.'

'Killing monsters sounds too much like stockyard work,' the second said.

'Not to mention there's no loot in it,' the third said.

All three were cockeyed drunk. Two brothers, twins, and a cousin. Brawny, restless young men, the kind with a low boredom threshold who would start a fight over a spilled drink, or jump up on a table and announce that they would take on anyone in the place.

'Are you planning to go north or south, grandfather?' the cousin said. He was a little older than the twins, a little more sensible, and slightly less drunk.

'You'll have to pay a contractor twice over to get into any front-line company. Someone of your age and all,' one of the twins said.

'They might take him if he wants to go north,' the other twin said. 'That stick of his looks like it would be handy when it comes to cutting down red weed.'

He made a grab for it, and the lucidor caught his hand and forced it up behind his back, thumb pressing hard on the medial nerve, the young man sweating hard and grimacing as he tried and failed to wriggle free, laughing when the lucidor let him go, saying that he wanted to learn that trick.

'Or maybe we can teach you a trick or two ourselves,' the other twin said, with a lazy smile that showed front teeth filed to points.

'You're an idiot,' the cousin said. 'Can't you see that he used to be a lawkeeper? Who else would carry a staff like that?'

The twins' attitude changed at once. Like most bullies they resented anyone with actual authority.

'Let's go to the Crooked Billet,' one of them said. 'This place is dead tonight.'

'Doesn't smell of law either, the Billet,' the other said.

'You could try the chai house on Artillery Row. Map readers and the like from the old country hang out there,' the cousin told the lucidor, and followed the twins out.

The chai house was a small windowless basement with a porcelain stove and red paper lanterns. Its customers crowded around spindly tables, most at least half the lucidor's age, everyone talking to everyone else. He sat with an untouched beaker of chai, waiting for one of the people who were giving him surreptitious glances to get up the nerve to challenge him. A group of young men in

152

the centre of the room seemed especially interested in him, and after a while one came over to his table. A bearded boy with a shaved head and spectacles with mismatched lenses, one round and red and the other square and green, he sat across from the lucidor without waiting for an invitation and told him that he had an interesting aura.

'If you hope to sell me a patent cure-all I have no need of one,' the lucidor said.

The young man made a show of adjusting his spectacles. 'I'm no charlatan, friend. I'm a student of applied philosophy, specialising in the measurement and interpretation of auras generated by the electrical and chemical activity of the human brain. And I can tell from the static kernel in your aura that you have recently swallowed an active shatterling fragment.'

The lucidor felt a sudden chill in his blood and said carefully, 'I may be carrying one.'

'Soldiers like to carry all kinds of charms,' the young man said. 'A vial of soil from home, a picture of a wife or sweetheart, something given to them by one of their children – anything that might protect them from bullets and quarrels, ward off sickness and madness, hide them from the enemy's gaze. And some swallow shatterling fragments. Almost all of which are fakes, but since belief in charms is a form of magical thinking it doesn't much matter if they are or not. If you have need of something that you think will protect you, give you luck or courage, you'll act accordingly. But you, my friend, have swallowed a true fragment. It sits within your aura like an island in the flow of a river. Black and unmoving and unreadable. I've seen the same thing in the auras of certain priests, but never before in a civilian or a soldier.'

'Do I look like a priest?'

'That was my first thought. I came over because I wondered what a priest was doing here, a place popular with people who have the least time for priests and their pieties. But you're a Freestater, by your accent and costume, so perhaps you're some kind of spy. An agent of your government, or for some kind of weird Freestater sect,' the young man said, taking off his parti-coloured spectacles and looking straight at the lucidor. His eyes were also mismatched. One was a lighter brown than the other and had specks of gold in it. 'So tell me, friend: have I guessed right?'

'I haven't been here long enough to know what a spy should look like. Do they wear silly gear like yours, so people will think them harmless fools?'

The lucidor was having fun. It was like the good old days at the beginning of his career, when he had been tasked with gathering information from map readers and tinkers. They cultivated an air of mystery, claimed to possess all kinds of secret and arcane knowledge, but also loved to boast about their work and gossip about their rivals, and as long as you were prepared to put up with their bragging and foolish banter it was not hard to find out what you needed to know.

'My silly gear revealed more than your little secret, friend. I can also tell that you're a muzzler. Don't try to deny it. It's right there in plain sight.'

'You can see it in my aura?'

'Each gift has a particular signature.'

'Is that so? Because I don't need to read your aura to know you have the silvertongue gift, and I don't think you need to read mine, either. Your friends sent you over because they thought that you could cozen me to spill my secrets, or perhaps you boasted to them that you could, and you have just discovered that your gift isn't working, and made the obvious deduction.'

'I can see that I made a mistake,' the young man said, and started to get up.

'Sit down,' the lucidor said, putting a little force into his voice.

The young man dropped back into his seat. 'I really can read auras,' he said. 'It isn't a scam or a trick. It's applied philosophy. And I really do want to know about your shatterling fragment.'

The lucidor ignored that. 'I'm looking for an old friend who's also in the applied philosophy trade. A man named Remfrey He. Last I heard, he was working for the army.'

'Why do you want to find him?'

'I told you. He's an old friend.'

'I guess you really haven't been in town long, or you would have heard the news.'

The lucidor leaned forward, looking into the young man's eyes. 'He did something, didn't he? What did he do?'

'If I tell you, will you tell me why you swallowed your shatterling fragment?'

'I might, if you tell me everything you know, and tell it straight.'

'Your old friend was working for the army, all right. Something to do with alter women is what I heard, but don't ask me the exact nature of it because that's all I know. Anyway, the army had him under heavy manners, but one night he disappeared. Two of the map readers who were working for him also disappeared; the rest of his crew were killed. Word on the street has it that a crew of commandos kidnapped him and smuggled him back to the Free State,' the young man said and leaned closer to the lucidor and lowered his voice. 'Which is why you should be careful, friend, claiming you know the man. The Queen's Shadow Service has eyes and ears everywhere.'

'When did this happen?'

'It all blew up around twenty days ago.'

'Then I can tell you that the street has it wrong. Remfrey He wasn't kidnapped. He escaped. That nonsense about commandos kidnapping him is no doubt put about by army counter-intelligence, to cover for the army's embarrassment.'

'And you know that how?'

It was a little over twenty days since the lucidor had been ambushed on the train, too close to be a coincidence. If commandos had snatched or had been about to snatch Remfrey He in an improbable raid, Cyf would have told the lucidor about it. No, it was more likely that Remfrey He had found out about the lucidor's mission. Found out that the department had tried and failed to stop him. The man had no doubt made arrangements to escape long before, and news about the failed ambush might have given him the impetus to activate those plans before the Patuan army increased its security and oversight, or otherwise compromised his freedom to do as he pleased while pretending to serve it.

The lucidor wasn't about to tell the young man any of that, of course, and said, 'My old friend Remfrey He also has the silver-tongue gift. It's the secret of his success. All his life, he's used it to seduce people, make them utterly loyal, persuade them to do things they would otherwise never ever think of doing. The people he was working for should have made sure that he was kept away from everyone else, or that he was always accompanied by someone like me. Clearly they didn't. I have no doubt that Remfrey He used his gift to persuade those two map readers to go with him when he escaped, and he may well have used it to make the rest of his little helpers kill themselves. He's done it before.'

'If you're right, if he really did escape, I hope you catch up with him,' the young man said. 'I hope he gets his due. The people working for him, the ones who died and the ones who disappeared, they have a lot of friends here. And Remfrey He cheated some of us too. Stole our work. Claimed it for his own. So good luck to you.'

'One more question. Don't worry. It's an easy one. Where was Remfrey He working before he escaped?'

'That's easy. A place in Canners Row, down in the old docks. No one knew about it until Remfrey He disappeared, and then everyone did. Even the army couldn't keep it secret.'

'He does have a flamboyant touch,' the lucidor said, and thanked the young man for his candour.

'You haven't told me,' the young man said.

'Told you what?'

'About the shatterling fragment. Why you swallowed it.'

'It's simple enough. Another shatterling told me to.'

20

Prophet

When he had checked into the hostel, the lucidor had reckoned that the apartment building across the street would be a good vantage point. Now, he found a service gate at the rear of the building, climbed a stair to the flat roof, and settled down for the night in a corner of the parapet. Waking now and then to check the hostel and the street below, dozing off again, rising shortly after dawn and brushing dew from his leather coat and running through a short set of exercises to work off the stiffness in his cold old bones. The hostel's night clerk, his surliness only slightly improved by the plastic note the lucidor slipped through the slot in his window, said that no one had come asking about Saj Orym Zier and pointed the lucidor towards a chai shop down the street, where he bought a cup of hot spiced milk and an almond pastry and asked for directions to the old docks.

Canners Row was a short street of workshops and small manufactories, most of them boarded up. The lucidor briskly walked down it like someone on his way to somewhere else, averting his face as he passed a man standing opposite one of the manufactories, and circled around the block and took a position at the corner of the street. Traffic picked up; people walked past the lucidor on their way to work; at the far end of Canners Row a woman cranked up the roller door of a workshop. A little while later a runabout trundled up the street and stopped beside the man stationed by the manufactory. A second man climbed out, the two briefly conversed, and when the first man folded himself into the runabout the lucidor walked away from the corner, stepping sharply into a doorway and pretending to unlock the door as the runabout went past.

Someone was watching the place, all right. Most likely the army, for any kind of lawkeeper would have more street smarts. The lucidor supposed that it was possible that they were waiting for him to turn up, but it was more likely in case Remfrey He or one of the assistants he had befuddled came back to the scene of the crime.

The lucidor circled the block again, but it seemed that the manufactory and the other buildings on that side of Canners Row backed onto the buildings in the next street. It would be sensible to give up on the place. Remfrey He was long gone and his employers would have stripped it of everything useful, but breaking into the manufactory might flush out anyone from the Free State who had been sent after the lucidor, and if Remfrey He knew that the lucidor was coming after him he might have left some kind of message. A taunt. A clue. Something only the lucidor would recognise or understand. He couldn't let that go, knew that he was going to have to come back when the area was quiet. Meanwhile, he had other lines of enquiry to pursue.

Following Nunco's directions, he skirted the northern side of the citadel, crossed a big square in front of a temple, and descended the narrow corkscrew of the Street of Luthiers to the edge of Tinkers Market. It stretched across a dozen squares, linked by covered streets crammed with shops and stalls, sellers and buyers, street performers and beggars. These last were not Patua's famous holy mendicants, but homeless people reduced to asking others for money or food. Children, cripples, mothers with babies. Some of the ragged men and women wore the remnants of army uniforms and were missing limbs or were blind or badly scarred or mutilated. The lucidor gave away all of his small denomination notes and discovered that not only did Patuan society lack any formal system for relief and rehabilitation of the indigent but also that none of its victims thought this anything other than the natural order of things.

One of the recipients of his charity pointed him to a street specialising in drugs, raw chemicals and surgical instruments and apparatus, and he went from shop to shop asking after Remfrey He, hoping to hit on a rival, enemy or gossipmonger who might give up useful information. His queries were mostly met with polite apologies or blunt denials, and those few who admitted to knowing of the man believed, like the garrulous young aura-reader, that Remfrey He had been kidnapped by Free State commandos, and wanted to know why the lucidor was trying to stir up more trouble.

'I'm just trying to get at the truth of the matter,' the lucidor told them. 'Where might he have gone, if he didn't return to the Free State?'

No one knew. Or if they did know, they didn't want to tell him.

He fared no better in the street where rare books and tablets were tiled across tables or displayed in glass cabinets, or in the square turned into an exotic garden by masses of rare plants collected from distant corners of Patua, brought here from other maps centuries ago or created by map readers who specialised in manipulating and remapping what they called the Big Green. The lucidor wasn't greatly discouraged. He still believed that Remfrey He had escaped, and if the manufactory turned out to be a bust he might learn something from the people guarding it. And besides, he had a feeling that the man wanted to be found. How else could he boast about what he had done?

The lucidor sold the shell of the godspeaker for a pittance, knowing that he was being cheated but glad to be rid of it, and used the money to buy a vial of army-issue wake-up pills at an apothecary shop and a fish sandwich at a hole-in-the-wall kitchen. He was sitting on the worn step of a shrine, eating slowly and spitting out small bones, when he heard a familiar drumbeat and saw a small procession of endtimers coming towards him, led by a tall woman crowned with a conical paper hat and clad in a ragged yellow robe and a kind of rapt dignity. When a man tried to hand him a leaflet, the lucidor caught his wrist and asked him where Afram Auspex could be found. That was the name of the endtimers' leader, according to the leaflet he had saved.

'He will be preaching to the city not an hour from now,' the man said, peering at the lucidor around a sharp crooked nose. 'Join us, brother, and let his words set a fire in your heart.'

'I'll walk with you,' the lucidor said, 'but don't ever call me brother again.'

Feeling somewhat exposed and foolish, he followed the motley procession across a square packed with an exotic zoo of caged or leashed animals and birds, across another where clothes and bolts of cloth were sold, and found himself climbing the winding way of the Street of Luthiers to the square in front of the temple. It was two hours after noon. Mirrorlight gleamed on the temple's whitewashed façade, and the shadows of the buildings on the other side of the square had begun to stretch across the wide space, lapping at a fountain where a stone godling rode the back of a stone kraken that wrapped a stone boat in its stone tentacles.

A small crowd had gathered in front of a low platform. Mostly endtimers, faces shining with rapturous expectation, stars embroidered on yellow shirts and robes, drawn on paper hats, inked on foreheads. There was a long wait. Shadows crept across the middle of the square. Two more processions arrived, and at last a slim young man dressed in a long white shirt over baggy white trousers stepped onto the platform and without preamble began to speak of the end of the world.

The lucidor stood at the back of the crowd while the prophet stalked to and fro across the stage, explaining, in a sonorous voice that carried clearly across the square, that the invasion was the first sign of the imminent apocalypse. Soon there would be groundquakes that would shake flat the cities of this map and all the other maps around the world, and the World Ocean would rise up in waves as tall as mountains and wash away the ruins of the cities and scour the maps clean. Only the devout would survive, and they would see the shell of the world break open and the shatterlings which had been trapped inside emerge. Wonderful and terrifying, they would pluck the devout from their sheltering place and take them to a new and better world where they would build a shining city and live in harmony until the gods returned to judge and reward them.

'He talks pretty, don't he?' the man beside the lucidor said.

'He knows how to hold a crowd's attention. I'm surprised that the authorities allow him to preach like this.'

The man was chewing something that had stained his lips and teeth red. 'The city law arrested him a while back, but he wrote letters in jail and got out with the help of one of the Queen's cousins. Long as she's on his side, ain't much the city can do.'

'I heard that he was enlightened by a shatterling.'

'Maybe so. He surely likes to talk about them.' The man bent his head and spat an oyster of red phlegm between his feet. 'Not that I pay much attention. I come here because it's free entertainment, and sometimes his people hand out food afterwards.'

The prophet, Afram Auspex, was explaining that all it took to follow him was to be willing to learn how to live the best life you could, and to embrace the inevitability of the world's end with joy and an open heart. As he led his followers in a chant of slogans and aphorisms, the man beside the lucidor leaned in and said, 'No free eats today, it looks like. He would've said if there was. Watch out for his followers. First they ask for money. And if you give them any, they start hugging you and asking if you want to join the elect.'

The prophet raised his hands and his followers cheered and drums rattled out a quick fusillade. The man beside the lucidor spat again and turned away; the lucidor went in the other direction, shrugging off acolytes who tried to stop or embrace him.

Afram Auspex was kneeling at the edge of the stage, holding hands with a tearful woman, speaking to her with quiet sincerity, briefly cupping her head with his hands. As an acolyte led her away the lucidor pushed in and told the prophet that he had a question.

'Ask away, brother, but know that I do not have answers for everything,' Afram Auspex said. 'No man does, in this imperfect world.'

He was less than half the lucidor's age, handsome and smooth-skinned, his gaze dark and serious.

'What did the shatterling look like?' the lucidor said. 'The one that told you all about how the world is going to end.'

Afram Auspex studied the lucidor for a moment, and said, 'I think you have come a long way to ask that.'

'It isn't the only reason I came here. But I have a personal interest in your answer.'

'You are from the Free State, aren't you,' Afram Auspex said. It wasn't a question. 'I understand that Freestaters have no religion.'

'Some do. It isn't disallowed. We know that the creator gods made this world and quickened the first people, but most of us see no reason to thank them for it. They quit on us, and there's nothing we can do to bring them back.'

'Not to this world, no,' Afram Auspex said. Very serious. Very sincere. 'But they will meet us in the new one. You are a disbeliever. You think it a fantasy. But tell me: what brought you all the way from the Free State to this square, and this meeting?'

'I have business here, as I said. And one of your people gave me a leaflet, and I got to wondering about your shatterling.'

'Do you think it was free will that brought you here? Was it an accidental encounter that inspired your question? No. This world was made by the creator gods. On that we can agree. They made this world and everything in it. Including ourselves. And everything that happens, from the first breath of the first man to its last end, was foreordained from the beginning. Your coming here is part of the world's great story, graved into it at its creation, unravelling with unavoidable precision. My part in that story is no less foreordained. I have followed my path, and you have followed yours, and the place and very moment where and when our two paths have crossed was mapped out long ago. The difference between us is that I know it, and do not reject that knowledge. No, brother. I celebrate it. Because at the end of this world's story the elect will escape and take up a new story elsewhere. One that they alone will forge. And nothing can stop that because it also is part of the creator gods' plans.'

The acolytes around the lucidor, having listened to this short speech in rapt silence, now murmured assent.

'If you are right, and everything is inevitable,' the lucidor said, 'then it seems to me that the creator gods didn't trust us to make the right decisions.'

'It's up to us to decide whether to accept that knowledge with rage, or denial, or with grace and full understanding.'

'You claim that you once met a shatterling. I have met one too. It had stars for eyes. No face. Just two stars floating inside a kind of hooded robe. Does that sound familiar?'

'There are things in this world that are other than what they claim to be. Think about that, my friend, as you go on your way. I don't know where your path will take you, but it's clear that it brought you here before you were ready to accept the truth. Perhaps you will come back to me when you are,' Afram Auspex said, and when he stood up two burly men in yellow robes caught the lucidor's arms and pulled him away.

21

Lab Work

Less than an hour after the lucidor resumed his station at the corner of Canners Row, a runabout brought a replacement for the man currently keeping watch on Remfrey He's manufactory. A woman this time. It was still light, too early to make a move. The lucidor maintained his vigil with the stony patience he had learned from years of surveillance, thinking about what Afram Auspex had told him, deciding that it didn't matter if it was his own decision or inexorable fate that had brought him here. It was the right thing to do, and that was the beginning and end of it.

It grew dark. Streetlamps flickered into life. Manufactories and workshops closed up and men and woman headed home and traffic on the street where the lucidor stood at post thinned out. At last, exactly four hours after the woman had been dropped off, the runabout returned and a man took her place. The leather workshop a few doors down from He's manufactory was still open, but everything else was shuttered and nothing moved along the short street.

The streetlamp opposite the manufactory was dark, about the only sensible precaution the people keeping watch had made. The figure in the deep shadow beneath it did not move as the lucidor approached, but he felt the full weight of the man's attention as he walked up and told him, 'I'm supposed to take over. There's a problem come up with your family.'

It gave the lucidor only a bare moment of distraction, but it was all he needed. He struck the man in the throat with a bunched finger strike, drew his staff as the man doubled over, honking for breath, and knocked him out with a swift punt to the temple. It was over in two seconds. Nothing stirring in the street; no witnesses; no cry of alarm. Only a faint busy hum from the leather-working place.

The lucidor patted the man down, found a flat leather sap and an electric torch in one pocket of his surcoat, a three-shot snub-nosed pistol, a godspeaker and a big ironwood key in the other. A wax seal was stamped across the joint of the manufactory's double door and the hasp was fastened with a padlock the size of the lucidor's fist. Nothing happened when the lucidor cut the seal; no one stepped out of the shadows when he turned the key in the padlock and cracked one of the doors and peeked inside.

A big cool empty space, dimly lit by skyglow that filtered through dusty panes set in the high slant of the roof. A faint tang of chemicals. No movement anywhere.

The man faintly groaned but did not put up any resistance when the lucidor dragged him inside. He tied the man's hands to his ankles with his belt, gagged him with a strip torn from the hem of his surcoat, gently closed the door and stood with his back to it and surveyed the space. Taking his time, letting his eyes adjust to the dimness as his breathing and heartbeat returned to normal.

A line of big square tanks standing along the back wall reminded him of Orjen Starbreaker's laboratory tent, but these were much bigger, about twice his height and formed from thick plastic. A raised catwalk ran along their rims; pipework spidered overhead. Each tank rang hollow to the knock of his knuckles and he climbed the ladder to the catwalk and knelt on its plank floor and ran a finger along the white residue crusted at the lip of one of the tanks, tasted it. The salt sting of the sea.

Elsewhere were benches with notched and scarred tops, a porcelain dissection table, a ladder of empty shelves. The standing desk in a corner of the space had nothing in any of its drawers but a dry stylus. In another corner, where the chemical odour was strongest, was a bin of shattered glassware.

Nothing had been left on or under the benches. The dissection table had been washed clean. The lucidor studied the tanks again. Each had a drainage hole in the centre of its flat base, and the floor beneath slanted to a brick-lined channel. He shone the man's electric torch along the length of the channel, pausing when he saw a sharp glitter reflected from something caught between two bricks, just above a shallow pool of water.

He reached in and pulled it free, inspected it in the bright circle of the torch's glare. It was a scale about half the size of his palm, reddish and roughly square, with a ridge running down its centre and a curved tooth-edged margin. A fish scale, he supposed. A fish scale from some kind of big fish or fish-like monster kept in those tanks. He stuck it in his pocket and ran the torch beam up and down the channel again, swept it across the floor and over the walls, but didn't find anything else. The place had been cleaned out by Remfrey He or by the army, leaving only boltholes and scrape marks in the concrete floor where equipment and machinery had once stood.

A set of circular imprints triggered a memory of the raid on one of Remfrey He's houses, where there had been a row of man-high glass cylinders in one room, each filled with straw-coloured liquid through which trains of bubbles rose, caressing the flanks of the creatures floating inside. Things patchworked from baboons, it was later determined, but at first inspection they had looked alarmingly like tinkered human children. Legs fused together. Arms replaced by blunt tentacles. Raw slits in their flanks. The lucidor had thought them dead, but when he had stepped up to inspect the nearest tank the creature inside had opened its golden eyes . . .

Suddenly, something was standing at his back. The dim air brightened with chalky light and the ghosts of glass cylinders shivered into view, solidified. Child-sized bodies in various stages of disassembly hung in faintly green liquid inside each cylinder, and smoke trails or tracks suddenly surrounded them, the spoor of phantom figures moving at speed, coming into focus for a moment or two when they paused to bend over cluttered work benches or worked on an armoured figure splayed on the dissection table, blurring into motion again.

And then the ghostly carnival faded, and the shatterling's soft caressing voice said, 'That so-called prophet was never touched by any of my sisters.'

The lucidor swallowed drily. 'I reckoned as much. His kind like to tell grand stories about themselves, but most often that's all they are. They claim to know all about the end of the world, but never say when it will come.'

His palms were sweating and he didn't turn around. He didn't want to see what the shattering had manifested as this time.

'He lied about me, too,' the shatterling said. 'I am what I am. And what I show you is true.'

The air brightened again. Two men hung by their heels from the overhead pipework, back to back, revolving slowly. Their arms had been hacked off and pieces from animals and birds had been grafted onto their faces. Below them an audience sat cross-legged in a circle, dressed in long white coats and braced with wooden crosspieces, some with their bowels out. Eyes and ears were stuck with surgical instruments. Hands had been cut off and stuffed in mouths.

'Who did this?' the shatterling said.

'A man I'm trying to find.'

'Tell me about him.'

The lucidor briefly explained why he was looking for Remfrey He. The crimes for which the man had been exiled in the Free State; the secret agreement which had arranged the loan of his skills to the Patuan army.

'He was supposedly helping them to find a way to push back the invasion, but he escaped. No doubt to pursue his own plans. Hoping to find or make use of something that he can turn to profit, or to mischief and mayhem.'

'You are enemies.'

'I arrested him. It's my responsibility to bring him back. It could be,' the lucidor said, 'that we can help each other. You can help me find and arrest Remfrey He, and I can help you discover what he knows about the invasion. I could even bring him to you.'

'Are you trying to bargain with me?'

'I'm trying to point out that we have a mutual interest.'

The lucidor had no intention of giving over Remfrey He to the shatterling's control, but he hoped that the offer might buy him a little time.

'I want to save the world,' the shatterling said. 'And you want to catch an escaped criminal. The two things are scarcely of equal worth.'

'Remfrey He is a monster, but he knows more about reading life maps and tweaking animals than anyone else alive, and his work left a mark here. That's what you're using right now, isn't it?'

'That, and the imprint left by a temple that burned down during a civil war a thousand years ago, with its priests and their congregation still inside. Do you really know where he is?'

'There were alter women in those glass cylinders and on the dissection table. And the alter women's territory is in the north, where the invasion started. Where else would Remfrey He go if he wanted to further his work? I want to find him, and you want to learn about the invasion. I can help you, and you can help me. Two pigeons with one stone.'

'I do not understand that expression.'

'No, I don't suppose you have ever used a slingshot. Are we agreed?'

The lucidor waited for judgement, sweating in the cool air, trying not to jump when the gruesome tableau winked out.

'The man is awake,' the shatterling said, and the presence behind the lucidor was gone.

22

Coat of Ten Thousand Nails

The man was groggy, but managed to give the lucidor a hard angry stare when he squatted beside him and loosened his gag. He drily spat, told the lucidor that he was in a lot of trouble but would get a fair hearing if he gave himself up and shared what he knew.

'I know that Remfrey He wasn't kidnapped by Free State commandos,' the lucidor said. 'What were you doing here? Waiting for him to come back? Or waiting for someone like me to come along?'

'If you work for the Free State, we're on the same side,' the man said. 'And your best chance of finding Remfrey He is to cooperate with us.'

'Who do you work for? The army?'

The man did not reply.

The lucidor took out the godspeaker. 'If I press the button, who will answer?'

'The officer in charge.'

'An army officer?'

'What do you think?'

'I think you wouldn't last a day on the streets if you were a lawkeeper.'

'Call her. Go ahead and call her. She will tell you the same as me.'

'Cooperate or else. It isn't much of an offer.'

'It's your only chance,' the man said. 'This is a small city. If you walk away now we won't have much trouble finding you later on.'

'Remfrey He managed to walk away, and I suppose he was under what your superiors believed to be a close watch.'

'If you know something about that, it will go a long way to forgiving this little misunderstanding.'

'Do you know where he went?'

No answer but another hard look.

'You were warned that someone would come looking for him, weren't you? Who warned you?'

The man did not answer that, either, but there was a faint flicker in his gaze.

'What else did they tell you?' the lucidor said.

'All I know is that I was assigned to watch this place. Me and a couple of others. And one of them will be along to take the next watch very soon.'

'I don't think so. The watch changes every four hours, and you only just got here.'

'You think you're right smart, don't you? Think again, because if I don't check in with that godspeaker you took off me they will be here a lot sooner.'

'Then you won't have to wait long before they find you,' the lucidor said, and retied the man's gag and opened the door and looked up and down the street before stepping outside. Hoping the man had been bluffing about checking in, because he wanted to ask Remfrey He's neighbours a few questions.

In the leather workshop men and women sat at industrial sewing machines driven by belts turned by a common overhead shaft, stitching cuirasses and segmented breastplates. Piecework done without any finesse or craft, the forewoman told the lucidor. There was a little custom work for officers who wanted special fittings, gilt stamping and rivet patterns and the like, but mostly they turned out cheap copies of the same four pieces, day in, day out. Still, she shouldn't complain. Business was good because of the war. This place and several dozen like it were working around the clock to keep the army supplied.

She didn't ask to see the lucidor's identification when he told her that he was carrying out a special investigation concerning Remfrey He's disappearance, said that she could only tell him what she'd told the military police and the spook from the Shadow Service. The man and his assistants had kept themselves to themselves. There had been a small traffic of visitors in army uniform, the occasional covered cart, and every two or three days a water wagon, but otherwise you wouldn't have known that anything out of the ordinary was going on. No, she didn't know if it was seawater or fresh, she never asked.

'I didn't even know he was gone until the army and Shadow Service turned up and started asking questions I couldn't begin to answer. I heard rumours he was making monsters of some kind. Or turning people into monsters, the way alter women do. But like say, they're only rumours. I only talked to him a couple of times, and he didn't say anything about his work.'

'What did you talk about, you and Remfrey He?'

'The piece he commissioned from us. Made to his exact specifications,' the forewoman said. 'It wasn't like anything we'd done before, but he was from your country, so I supposed it was the way you did things there.'

Remfrey He's drawings had been confiscated by the military police, but the forewoman hesitated when the lucidor asked about the cutting patterns, then said that he was the first to have asked for them.

'My wife's family was in the garment trade,' the lucidor said.

'Lex, our dressmaker? He kept the patterns back because they were unusual. And clever too.'

'Are they stored here, or did your dressmaker take them home?'

'We keep a catalogue of patterns going back a century. That's how long we've been here. I suppose Lex put Remfrey He's designs in with the rest.'

'I would be eternally grateful if you could let me see them. And I promise that I won't tell anyone that you did.'

The forewoman told him to wait there, went into one of the offices behind the rows of machines and a few minutes later came back with paper patterns she laid out on a cutting table. They were for the armoured garment known as the coat of ten thousand nails, worn by state troopers on ceremonial occasions in the Free State: a sleeveless knee-length coat made from overlapping leather plates sewn to a canvas backing and split at the waist so that the wearer could ride a horse. Definitely the kind of thing

Remfrey He would order up if he was planning to head north, into the heart of the war against the invasion. In his version, the leather plates were not fan-shaped but roughly square, with one curved edge and a central ridge. The lucidor fetched out the fish scale he'd found in the drain. It was the same shape.

The forewoman said that Remfrey He had wanted the coat finished off with gold lace and silk, but that had been pieced out elsewhere, and no one in the workshop had seen the finished article.

'He was very particular about the construction of it. The patterns of the scales, how they fit the way the body bends and flexes. Lex said that some of his ideas would improve the pieces we make for the army. I think so, too. But the army has its own patterns, and we have to stick to them.'

The coat had been delivered some fifty days before Remfrey He and two of his assistants disappeared. It seemed that he had been planning to escape the army's supervision long before the lucidor had started out on his long journey.

He asked the forewoman if anyone had visited the manufactory after it had been sealed. She said that he was the first she knew of.

'They took everything away, sealed it up, and put a guard on it. The landlord can't rent it out again until they say otherwise. It was important, wasn't it? His work. Important for the war.'

'Is that what you were told?'

'We weren't told anything. But after all that fuss when he left, I'd suppose it had to be.'

'Remfrey He had other interests,' the lucidor said. 'A little like the commissions you do for officers, but for his own amusement.'

'Speaking of commissions,' the forewoman said. 'Your friend forgot to pay for that coat of his before he left. When you catch up with him, you might remind him of what he owes.'

23

Bright Company

It was gone midnight by the time the lucidor got back to the Freestater quarter, but its cafés and bars were still busy and people were sitting at outside tables or strolling under the red lanterns strung above the streets. It was not possible, from the lucidor's perch on the roof of the apartment building, to tell if anyone was watching the hostel's entrance, but he reckoned that it was likely. If someone from the department was looking for him in Chimr, they would know about his alias and would have given it to likely lodging places. By now, they must know where he had rented a bed, and when they heard about the break-in at the manufactory they might decide that it was time to move on him. If they did, he would know exactly how much trouble he was in.

One by one, the cafés and bars closed and their staff took in tables and chairs and locked shutters and doors and said their goodnights to each other and went their separate ways. A man wielding a long pole with a hinged top snuffed out the lanterns. Two women supporting a third came unsteadily along the street and shoulder-barged through the door of the hostel. Soon afterwards, bells tolled near and far, announcing curfew. Only the streetlamps along the main thoroughfares of the city and the floodlights at the base of the citadel's curtain wall were still lit. The street below the lucidor's perch was dark and empty and still.

He dry-swallowed a couple of wake-up pills, but it had been a long day, he hadn't had much sleep the night before, and after a couple of hours he dozed off. And jerked awake, stiff and cold, as two runabouts pulled up below, their roof-mounted lamps lighting up the front of the hostel. Two men climbed out of the first, both in long surcoats, one with a bandage around his head, and a man and a woman out of the second. The third man was dressed in a leather coat and a staff was slung over one shoulder; when he turned to speak to the woman the lucidor saw that it was Lucidor Cyf.

The lucidor quit his post and made his escape as soon as Cyf and his army friends went inside the hostel. He knew now who was looking for him; knew that when they failed to find him in the hostel they would check the neighbouring buildings. It was time to leave. Time to follow Remfrey He north. And he reckoned that the best way to get there was to become what he had been pretending to be ever since he'd crossed the border.

He spent the rest of the night in an alley behind a stables half a league away, and at first light walked through the waking city towards Tinkers Market, stopping at a chai shop whose owner was just pulling down the awning. He bought a pastry and a paper cup of green chai and ate and drank as he walked on, passing through narrow covered streets where vendors were setting up their stalls and opening the shutters of their shops, to the big square at the far end, where the contractors who recruited mercenaries did their business.

The corner of a colonnaded arcade gave a good view of the square and shops that sold weapons and armour and other equipment, and the small traffic of men and women who examined pieces but rarely bought anything. The mirror arc was high in the sky and shadows were at their shortest when the mercenary contractors at last began to set up their tents and stalls, posting lists of the various specialists they required, raising the banners of the companies they represented. The Company of the Rose. The Company of the Hook. The Red Company. And there, the one the lucidor had been told about when he had been briefed before leaving for Patua. The Bright Company, which took its name from the polished armour worn by its soldiers and was led by a captain from the Free State.

The lucidor bought a snakefruit and peeled its scaly rind with his knife and ate its sour-sweet flesh while watching the proceedings from the shelter of the arcade. He had been told how the system worked. Contractors interviewed and examined likely candidates, and those they approved signed a letter of service indenturing them to a company for up to five years. The contractors received commission for every new recruit; the recruits were given chits as an advance on basic pay to buy clothing in the company colours, any weapons and equipment they needed or thought they needed, and an indemnity from an assurer. The advance would be paid back from their wages, and if they were killed before they had paid back what they owed the indemnity would make up the difference.

It was a slow but steady business, interesting to watch. Most of the men and women who pitched up were veterans dressed in combat gear, signing up for a second or third stint. They gossiped and joked with the contractors, sealed the deal with a signature and an elbow bump, and did not take the chits they were offered because they already had the gear they needed. New volunteers were treated very differently. The contractors closely questioned them, they were examined by a sawbones, and put to the test in brief trials of strength and skill. The lucidor soon realised that these bouts were as much for the amusement of the contractors and the general public as for testing ability. The professional fighters matched against the volunteers hornswoggled them with tricky feints and horseplay, ragged them with taunts and insults, knocked them down and let them pick themselves up, quickly and ruthlessly disarmed them and told them the different ways they could have been killed. One fighter picked up his flailing opponent and lifted him above her head and walked in a circle to desultory applause before dumping him in a horse trough. Another liked to snick away at the blousons and shirts of volunteers, leaving them in tatters but hardly ever drawing blood. A third taunted a hapless, gangling lad with insults and whacks from the flat of his sword blade, dodging clumsy thrusts with a dancer's grace until his opponent collapsed from exhaustion.

The lucidor was in no special hurry to put himself forward. He reckoned that the contractor would be eager to make up his quota towards the end of the day, and meanwhile he kept watch for people who might be watching out for him, and sized up the fighter who put volunteers for the Bright Company to the test: a bare-chested bruiser armed with a stout tall wooden pole with padded leather at either end, who used his reach and strength to batter his opponents into submission. Hopefully, the lucidor would not need to take him on, for if the contractor had any sense he would recognise his experience and worth and sign him up on the spot, but if it came to it, the bruiser had a trick knee and the lucidor reckoned that it would be easy to step inside the range of that pole and kick him in the kneecap and bring him down. The man also liked a glass of beer between bouts, and would be nicely befuddled by the end of business.

It was a hot close day, and after finishing his snakefruit the lucidor took a drink from the public fountain, where water spouted into a stone basin from the jaws of a dire wolf carved from bone-white sinterstone, its snout polished by the touch of thousands of hands. He was splashing water on his face and neck when he saw Lucidor Cyf clamber out of a runabout on the other side of the square.

Cyf walked across the square to the booth of the contractor for the Company of the Rose, handing the man a sheet of paper, which the lucidor did not doubt was printed with a copy of his likeness, and after a brief conversation moved on to the contractor for the Bright Company. If he knew that the lucidor was there, he showed no sign of it, and there was no sign of any backup either. Perhaps it was no more than a routine precaution. Cyf was a methodical, conscientious investigator. The conspiracy had been broken up, people had talked, he probably knew about the briefings the lucidor had been given, had figured out that joining a band of mercenaries was the lucidor's best option for pursuing Remfrey He. Or it had been until now, unless the lucidor could persuade or bribe the Bright Company's contractor to take him on – he would not be the first fugitive or felon they had recruited.

It didn't take Cyf long to make his round of the contractors. As he walked back towards the runabout its door swung up and a woman got out. Not the woman who had accompanied Cyf on the raid at the hostel, but someone else. Someone the lucidor recognised. The woman he had met in Roos at the beginning of his adventures. The map reader and collector of little monsters, Orjen Starbreaker.

24

Mutual Benefit

The lucidor followed the map reader as she strolled through the crowded lanes and covered streets of Tinkers Market, examining wares and talking with shop and stall owners, talking with several of their customers. She had stayed behind after Cyf drove off in the runabout, didn't seem to be aware that the lucidor was tailing her, and if she was being shadowed by bodyguards they were too good for the lucidor to spot. He pretended to be interested in tanks teeming with small brightly coloured fish while across the narrow lane Orjen Starbreaker drank chai with the owner of a stall that sold lizards in cages of woven wicker. She tickled one of the lizards with her forefinger and it inflated its throat into a red bubble and sang a short sweet song, and she said something to the stallholder that made him smile and walked on, never once looking back.

The lucidor saw his chance when she stopped again, at a stall stacked with ancient documents printed on heavy, flaking plastic sheets. A gaggle of Afram Auspex's endtimers was passing through the crowded lane, ringing handbells and handing out leaflets, and the lucidor used them as cover to get next to Orjen Starbreaker, saying to her, 'Why did you and Cyf come looking for me?'

She didn't seem surprised to see him. 'We both want to find Remfrey He,' she said. 'And I think that we can help each other.'

'Promise me that Cyf didn't set you up as a decoy.'

'It's the other way around,' Orjen said, setting down the plastic sheet she had been studying or pretending to study, and dusting her hands. 'After Cyf didn't find you at the hostel, he reckoned that you would be planning to leave the Twin Cities and chase after Remfrey He, and we would most likely run into you at the mercenary market. He locked on to me with his scrying gift, and knew you must be somewhere close when his sense of my presence began to fade. And I knew that you were following me when I tried and failed to get any sense of the life map of a canary lizard.'

'That's not bad. If Cyf is somewhere close by he should step out and allow me to congratulate him.'

'I persuaded him to let me try to draw you out on my own. And here we are.' Orjen brushed strands of black hair from her face and studied the lucidor for a moment, said, 'You look as if you have had a hard time of it.'

'I took the long way around.'

'And arrived too late to find Remfrey He. You could have saved yourself a lot of trouble if you had told me about him when we first met, instead of spinning that silly story about wanting to become a mercenary.'

'It wasn't exactly untrue.'

'Even if one the companies agree to take you, you will not find it easy to leave the city. The army is looking for you. The Twin Cities' lawkeepers, too. There are checkpoints along the roads, and heavy security at every railway station.'

'Then I won't use the roads or the railway.'

'Cyf said that you were stubborn.'

'I suppose he tracked you down after I left him in Roos. I hope he didn't misuse the boy to do it.'

'The boy?'

'A wight boy. Panap. Red hair, bright, keen on animals. I suggested that he pay you a visit.'

'There was no boy. Only Cyf,' Orjen said.

'That's a pity. I hoped that you might have encouraged him to use the talents he had instead of wasting his life chasing fantasies. How did Cyf find you?'

'He knew that you had been lodging with Noojak Crow Pelee, and she told him about me in exchange for a surprisingly small bribe.'

'She also gave me over to smugglers who were supposed to ferry me across the Horned Strait, but tried to take me prisoner instead.'

'I'm sorry to hear that. And please believe that I sent you to her with the best of intentions.'

'Even if that's true, I still don't know if I can trust you,' the lucidor said. 'Especially as you seem to have fallen in with Cyf.'

'I am not working for him. He is working for me. Or rather, your department has seconded him to the service of my father.' Orjen smiled at the lucidor's undisguised surprise. 'You and I are both chasing Remfrey He, and I think we will have a better chance of finding him if we help each other. We need to talk. Discuss how we can reach an agreement that will be of mutual benefit.'

'And if I don't want to help you?'

'I came here alone; no one will arrest you if you decide to walk away. But you are wanted in the Free State for conspiracy against the government, and you are wanted here, too, because you attacked a soldier and broke into a restricted army facility. If you are caught, you will be tried and sentenced by an army court, and either imprisoned here, or sent back to the Free State. In either case, that will be the end of your pursuit of Remfrey He. But if you agree to help me, my father can offer you protection from arrest and deportation, and he has resources that will help us find Remfrey He.'

'Who is your father?' the lucidor said. 'How does he come to have these resources?'

Orjen struck a pose, and for a moment the lucidor glimpsed the little girl she had once been. 'The Margrave Eua, Governor of Delos-Chimr,' she said. 'And he would very much like to meet you.'

25

Margrave Eua

They drove to the citadel in a runabout Orjen summoned, like a rider whistling up her horse, with a small box that emitted a coded godspeaker signal. It was bright red, the runabout, and not much bigger than a pigeon coop inside, guided by its own small mind as it jolted over paved or cobbled streets, deftly avoiding pedestrians and cyclists, merging with the other traffic. Runabouts were hundreds of years old, Orjen told the lucidor, based on technology dating back to the First People, kept running by cannibalising those which had fallen into disrepair, because most of their parts could no longer be crafted.

'Functioning mindchips are hardest to find,' she said. 'They are based on shatterling fragments retranscribed by a process we have not yet been able to unriddle, let alone attempt to replicate. We have lost or forgotten too much, and think most of the rest is magic and miracles. The invasion is a terrible threat and may yet overwhelm us, but at least it has spurred us to revive and reinvent the lost arts. And its mere existence suggests that there is something new in a world where there has been nothing new since the creator gods quit it.'

'Unless it's something old someone uncovered on some other map,' the lucidor said.

He was thinking of the shatterling. Although it had not revealed itself since the vision he'd had in Remfrey He's workshop, he retained a faint sense of it, like a small dark shape always just out of sight.

'We have extensive records of the flora and fauna of our neighbours, and there's nothing like alter women or the other creatures

181

of the invasion in any of them,' Orjen said. 'But if it was not seeded by a starfall or tinkered up by someone, I suppose that it is possible that it has always been here, and has only just reached us after spreading from one of the maps on the world's far side. There's a lot we do not yet know. We do not even know what the invasion wants, or if it knows what it wants.'

'I know one thing. If Remfrey He has discovered something important about the invasion and its monsters, he won't be planning to use it to end the war, or to help anyone but himself.'

'I have seen a mirrorgraph of the tableau he made with the bodies of the people he killed, or commanded to kill themselves, when he escaped,' Orjen said. 'Most of his assistants, and the two people from the Free State who had been overseeing the liaison with the army. All of them mutilated, or surgically altered. So I do have some small understanding of what he is capable of.'

'His escape was only the beginning,' the lucidor said, thinking of the vision the shatterling had shown him, thinking that it had shown him true. 'The first part of a scheme that is as yet unclear. But I do know that there will be other atrocities. Remfrey He has been unable to do what he likes to do for a long time. He will be eager to make up for that now. And if we're lucky, he will also be eager to boast about what he's done, and what he plans to do. That's always been his weakness. I broke into his workshop because I thought he might have left some clue about his plans. A clue or a taunt.'

'And did you find anything?'

'A fish scale. The same kind of fish scale he used as a pattern for a garment he'd made,' the lucidor said, and explained about the coat of ten thousand nails got up by the neighbouring workshop.

'This is exactly why we need you,' Orjen said. 'You chased and caught him before, and with our help you can do it again.'

'I didn't catch him, in the end,' the lucidor said. 'He surrendered.'

'Because he knew you were closing in on him, and there was no other way out.'

'I suppose it was Cyf who told you that story. Did he also tell you that Remfrey He claimed that he turned himself in because he wanted to deprive me of the glory I did not deserve?'

'Cyf told me that you had mounted a meticulous investigation to bring Remfrey He and his followers to justice,' Orjen said. 'Everyone in your department knew what you had done, and even if Remfrey He gave himself up at the last moment it was still your arrest, your victory.'

The lucidor didn't contradict her. Trusting this woman was a hefty risk, but he reckoned that as long as she and her father thought that he was useful they would not hand him over to the Patuan army or send him back to the Free State in Cyf's custody, and he could use their resources, information and influence to track down Remfrey He. As for what happened when he found the man, he would worry about that when the time came. Meanwhile, he would show willing, share just enough information to keep his new friend happy, and do his best to convince her that he was indispensable. It shouldn't not be too hard. Orjen was clever and dedicated to her work, but she was also young and artlessly idealistic, could not begin to plumb the dungeons and dark places of Remfrey He's mind.

The governor's residence was a rambling, homely villa with whitewashed walls and shuttered windows and a red tile roof, set in gardens at the foot of the citadel's steep-sided mound. It faced west, and the light in that late hour burned on the baserock cliff that loomed above the house and the long lawns that sloped to groves of fruit trees. Everything trimmed, immaculately neat. If not for the standards raised on tall white poles and the soldiers guarding the gate it might have been the residence of a wealthy farmer or provincial merchant.

'My father is greatly preoccupied with food shortages and civil unrest and all the other troubles caused by the war, and won't be able to spare much time to talk with you,' Orjen said, after they had been waved through the gate and their ride parked itself at the end of a row of runabouts. 'So you need to make every word count.'

'What would you like me to tell him?'

'Just be yourself, and do not let him intimidate you. He likes to test people, and he will especially want to test you. Oh, and you will have to leave your stick here.'

'It's a staff, and it comes with me,' the lucidor said.

'You can't take a weapon into my father's presence.'

'I won't harm him or anyone else. You have my word on that. As I have your word that I won't be harmed.'

Orjen stared at him for a moment, then said, 'If you say or do anything that appears to be a threat, the guards will act swiftly and ruthlessly. And I will not be able to intervene.'

'I didn't come here to fight,' the lucidor said. 'I came here to help.'

It was a small victory, but at this point he would take what he could.

Children ran up as he followed Orjen across a clipped green lawn, and a small girl with a mass of black curls took his hand and led him towards the terrace in front of the house, where twenty or more people sat at a long table under a striped awning. Orjen took a place at the left hand of the bearded patriarch, presumably her father, who sat at the head of the table, and the small girl led the lucidor to a seat at the other end and skipped away.

He'd fetched up between the husband of one of Orjen's sisters and a woman who was one of the governor's aides and wanted to know how he had reached the city. The lucidor told her that after he had crossed the Horned Strait he had mostly walked.

'It is a very interesting country. The mountains especially so.'

'I hear that the mountains are full of bandits,' the woman said.

'Then I suppose I was lucky, because I didn't see any,' the lucidor said, and changed the subject, saying that he hadn't expected to join what seemed to be a family gathering.

'Some are family; others, like me, work in the governor's office. We eat together every day,' the aide said. 'The governor believes that hospitality is the glue that binds civilisation.'

Up and down the long table people were chattering while servants brought a stream of dishes. Popcorn squid in a sweet chilli sauce, kid seethed in buttermilk, black lentils stinking of garlic, glass noodles with crisp fried onion and lotus root, thick charred slices of green tomato, pomegranate salad, pickled walnuts. All served in bowls or on plates with a pattern of silvery conifer trees standing in a silvery snowfall on a blue underglaze, reminding the lucidor of Nunco Arwal and the mayor and doctor and the other people who had shown him unexpected kindness when he had pitched up in their little town.

Small children chased each other across the lawn or briefly visited their parents for a cuddle or a few morsels of food; older children ate with the adults. More than half of the men and women, including the governor's son-in-law, were in uniform. Young and elegantly slim, one cheek seamed by a pencil-line scar, the son-in-law was a colonel in the city's lawkeeping force, and he and the lucidor found common ground by comparing and contrasting their work.

'We fight the war on three fronts,' the colonel said. 'In the north, of course, there is the invasion. In the south and east we have rebels and roving gangs of bandits. And here, in the Twin Cities, we keep watch on known troublemakers and agitators, maintain order in the refugee camps, and put down riots. The ordinary people do not understand the peril they are in, and chafe at the cost of the war. The last riot began with a protest against a rise in the price of bread; the one before that was triggered by the imposition of a small flat-rate tax to fund the army. Overstretched as we are, we can investigate only the most serious crimes. Volunteer militias organise neighbourhood patrols, but too often cause even more trouble. Those most eager to police their neighbours lack the necessary temperament and judgement, and think that their temporary authority gives them the right to air and settle old grievances.'

The colonel had the cheerful cynicism of a true lawkeeper; the lucidor rather liked him.

'It seems to me that you impose law from the top down,' the lucidor said. 'In the Free State, the law serves the will of the people.'

'That might work here, if only our people knew what they wanted,' the colonel said. 'Unfortunately, where you have your symposia and committees and ballots and what have you, we have the mob.'

'Despite their differences, our countries must come closer together,' the aide said, eager to contribute to the conversation. 'The invasion knows nothing of borders. It's in your interest to help us to contain and defeat it before it spreads even further.'

'I don't disagree,' the lucidor said.

'A shame more in the Free State don't think like you,' the aide said.

'I have heard that you and your fellow lawkeepers don't carry pistols or blazers,' the colonel said, smoothly intervening.

'Perhaps we don't fear our people as much as you do,' the lucidor said.

'But you use force when necessary. Or do you carry that staff because you feel that you are in enemy territory?'

'I assure you that I carry it out of habit, not because I expect any trouble here.'

'I would love to see a demonstration of its use.'

'I see you already know a little about swordplay.'

The colonel smiled and touched his scarred cheek. 'Some of us like to settle matters of honour in the proper style. An uncapped blade. No face mask or padding. This reminds me of the only occasion when I lost.'

They were discussing similarities and differences between sword and staff fighting when the small girl who had led the lucidor to the table appeared at his side and said that her grandfather wanted to talk with him.

The lucidor looked down the length of the table and saw that the bearded patriarch was gone, and Orjen was talking with an older woman with white hair teased into a kind of cone with little lights strung through it.

'He will be somewhere in the garden, no doubt,' the colonel said, and asked the girl if she could take their guest to him.

'Of course,' she said, quite self-possessed. 'That's why he sent me.'

As she led the lucidor across the lawn, her warm and slightly sticky hand in his, the girl told the lucidor that she was six and a quarter, and her name was Irilanlian.

'I'm pleased to meet you, Irilanlian. I have never met anyone with that name before.'

'What's yours?'

'I have two. One that I was given when I joined the department where I once worked. You don't need to know that because I don't use it any more. My real name, the one my parents gave me, is Thorn. Thorn e Hamandi.'

'That's a funny name,' the girl said.

'I come from another country. That's why I thought your name was funny.'

'It's special because it's the name of one of the godlings who built the old city. She lived up there,' the girl said, pointing to the citadel high above, floating in the glare of its floodlights.

'Then you must be special, too,' the lucidor said.

'She was one of the best and kindest godlings. She took her servants with her when she left.'

'And where are you taking me?'

'Grandfather is looking after his fruit trees,' the girl said. 'He has ever so many, and knows the names of all of them.'

They passed between the raised beds of a vegetable plot, skirted a pond crammed edge to edge with flowering lotuses and crossed the steep arch of the small bridge over the stream which fed it, passing through a double line of avocado trees to a gravel path running alongside a long brick wall with fan-shaped fruit trees growing against it. The Margrave Eua, governor of the Twin Cities, was at the far end, trimming the horizontal branches of one of the trees with a small knife.

After he had thanked his granddaughter and she had run off back to the house, the governor turned back to his work, saying to the lucidor, 'I don't suppose that any of the gardens in your country are as old as this one. It was laid out by the first of my line to have the honour of overseeing the affairs of the Twin Cities, although there was only one city then. Delos was built much later. The Humble Administrator. That was what he was called, after he died, and that's the name of this garden. The Humble Administrator's Garden. It has been in the care of the family ever since. My great-great-grandfather added a pond for his collection of ducks. My grandfather laid out the vegetable gardens. My father planted those avocado trees. And I had this brick wall rebuilt and planted fruit trees. Peach and pomegranate, fig and orange and lemon. They flower and fruit earlier than any others in the Twin Cities because the wall stores the heat of the mirrors, and it's simple enough to discipline their growth. I am cutting back side shoots now, to encourage next year's fruiting.

Plants take their own time, and gardeners must understand and respect that. You herded cactus when you were young, so perhaps you know what I mean.'

The lucidor guessed that Cyf must have briefed the governor. He said, 'It was a long time ago.'

The old man turned to look at him. He was tall and stooped, dressed in an oversized shirt with many pockets, and loose trousers and sandals. A seamed face, shaggy eyebrows overhanging a mild, watery gaze.

'Up the mountain in winter. Down in summer. Is that right?'

'Exactly so.'

'How fast do they move?'

'If you watch them, they hardly seem to move at all. But each day they cover half a kilometre or so.'

'And herders walk alongside. Keeping them together. Warding off animals that want to eat them, picking off insects that want to lay their eggs on them, and so on.'

'Gilded woodpeckers mostly keep off harmful insects. They nest in holes they make in the cactuses, and travel with them.'

The lucidor saw clearly for a moment the small swift birds hovering on blurs of wings, darting in to pick off insects with the long thorns of their bills. Their bronze plumage gleaming in the fierce mirrorlight. He remembered the days and days spent accompanying the river of upright walking cacti, from juveniles a few hands tall to mature plants twice the height of a grown-up. Watching for sand deer that might dart in and snatch a bite from a laggard or make off with a juvenile. Helping cacti that trapped themselves in draws or boulder fields. Clearing rocks from their path, filling sink holes. Children, women, and men working in shifts because the cacti kept moving night and day. They made a celebration of it, singing as they walked, blowing whistles and beating hand drums. Eating and sleeping at rest stops that were used year after year, generation after generation, and catching up with the herd at the next shift.

'In winter herders tap them for their sap, which is turned into edible plastic, so-called,' the governor said. 'And in summer they collect seedling spines, and grind them into flour. I read about it in a tablet of traveller's tales. Is it true that the wild cactus can shoot spines with enough force to penetrate a man's breastbone and pierce his heart?'

'So it's said. Those we herd have lost that ability.'

'Instead they make an excess of sap and seedling spines, just as my trees produce larger and more succulent fruit than their wild cousins. In both cases it encourages people to protect them, so it could be said that plants garden us, just as we garden them. One of my little projects is to try to recreate the fabulous white peach. The long-lost ancestral variety of all the varieties we grow now, quickened by the creator gods when they planted out this map and all the others. They were gardeners too. Hardly an original thought, I know, but one of the reasons my family has clung close to the seat of power for so long is that we do not often give voice to ideas that might threaten to upset the natural order of things. My title, Margrave, is an old one, and my family is the only one that still holds it. Not only because we have roots that go back to the time when it was more commonly granted, but also because we are loyal and diligent. Steady hands on the helm of state. That is why this business with Remfrey He is particularly upsetting. Would you believe me if I say that I knew nothing about it until the man made his escape?'

'It wouldn't surprise me.'

'It seems that elements in what the army liked to call its Dark Research Unit conspired with certain people in your government to make use of his ideas. At first it was by correspondence, but then Remfrey He somehow persuaded his handlers that he must come here so that he could do research into alter women and their nests.'

'He can be very persuasive,' the lucidor said.

'I understand that he has the silvertongue gift. The army claims to have put in place measures to silence it, but clearly they were not enough. Aside from the deaths of Remfrey He's assistants and the people who came with him from the Free State, three of the senior officers involved with the fiasco have committed suicide. Either out of misplaced honour or because Remfrey He planted the idea in their poor foolish heads.'

'He likes to play games,' the lucidor said.

'Mmm. Is he playing a game with you, do you think?'

'I haven't spoken to him since he was sent into exile. And as you may have been told, I am resistant to his charms. I came here because I wanted to,' the lucidor said, thinking of his old boss, who lacked the silvertongue gift but had his own ways of persuading people to take on difficult and hazardous missions with little certainty of success.

'Do you think he might surrender, if you found him?'

'If the only alternative is death, most certainly. He wants to live forever.'

'And would you kill him, if you had to?'

'Only if there was no other option.'

'What if he tried to kill you?'

'He tried once before. When I began to dismantle his cult, he sent an assassin after me. She was caught, and hanged herself in her cell, but not before she gave me clues about where he was hiding. Before I could move in and arrest him, he walked into my department's offices and surrendered. As I told your daughter, his only real weakness is pride. It was his downfall then, and I hope to use it against him again.'

The governor's gaze sharpened for a moment, and the lucidor saw that his mild, shambling appearance was a disguise worn by a clever man who had long ago learned that his cleverness could threaten others with less intelligence and more power.

'I was told by your compatriot, Lucidor Cyf, that you were able to catch Remfrey He because you are not unalike,' he said. 'Are you a proud man? Is that also your weakness?'

'Remfrey He once said that I wasn't as clever as him, or as resourceful, but that we were both the kind of obsessive who couldn't let go of a problem until it was solved.'

'Whatever else you may be, you are most certainly determined. Coming here as you did without permission or authority.'

'I am retired. I no longer have any authority in my own country, let alone yours. On the other hand, no one but myself has to answer for my actions.'

'Not any more.'

'No, not any more. If you allow me to help you, that is.'

'Well, the army has been of little use. It is more interested in finding someone who will take the blame than in hunting down and recapturing Remfrey He. It is a comprehensive mess and I am expected to make it good. The Queen commands,' the governor said, touching thumb and forefinger to his forehead, 'and I am at her pleasure. And besides, it happened in my city, on my watch. I am sure you understand.'

'Absolutely,' the lucidor said, and felt something pass between them. Mutual recognition. Mutual understanding.

'You will have to follow my daughter's directions. Diligently, and without hesitation,' the governor said.

'And will she take my advice in the same spirit?'

'She wanted to recruit you, so you may assume that she will take it seriously.'

'I can only help her find Remfrey He if she does.'

'If he is found, and captured alive, you will have no say in what happens to him.'

'I expected nothing less.'

'Very good,' the governor said, and turned and rummaged amongst the leaves of one of the trees splayed against the wall, twisted a peach from its stem and held it out. Perfect and unblemished, its soft yellow skin blushing pink along its crease. 'With my compliments. You will never taste any better.'

The lucidor took it, and the governor turned back to his pruning. An agreement had been reached; the lucidor had been dismissed.

He ate the peach as he walked back to the house. The governor was right. It was the best he had ever tasted. Fragrant, succulent and treacherously sweet.

26
Sea Iron

The lucidor was issued with a copy of the report on Remfrey He's work for the Patuan army and the aftermath of his escape, every page stamped with the governor's seal, and given a small room in the citadel's officers' quarters and dining privileges in the officers' mess. That was where Orjen's steward, Lyra Gurnek, found him the next morning, drinking chai and trying to puzzle his way through a jargon-riddled description of the methodology used to tweak some kind of fish.

Lyra said that she'd drawn the short straw because everyone else was too busy to give him the tour, and took him down to a deep sub-basement where Remfrey He's workshop had been reconstructed from equipment and specimens the army had surrendered to the governor. A row of cluttered work benches, blood-temperature incubators with triple-walled plastic hulls, and specimens in tall glass cylinders exactly like the ones in the shatterling's vision, unsettling to see in real life. Alter women, child-sized and monstrous yet still recognisably human, sunk in green-tinged preservative solution, their chests and bellies sutured, their internal organs in separate jars. Pale, wire-thin workers got up from whipcord and leather, with small heads sloping straight back above eyes burned white by alcohol, toothless mouths pursed like rosebuds. Burly warriors with slab-muscled chests, thrusting jaws spiked with fangs, and hands fused into pinchers or equipped with rakes of claws. A bent-backed porter with stout legs and vestigial arms.

It wasn't the complete set, Lyra said. All of the specimens on display had been captured outside nests, and Remfrey He had also wanted a breeder.

'The army mounted a raid on a small isolated nest. Four soldiers were killed and more than twice that number were injured as they fought their way inside, and the nest's warriors tore the breeders apart before they could be captured alive. The raiders brought back what scraps they could find, and the man declared them worthless.'

The first alter women had appeared some twenty years ago, after tides of red algae had washed up on the shores of islands beyond the north-east coast of the Big Island and released an infectious agent that killed the men and children of the islands' scattered farms and fishing villages with swift, incandescent fevers and wrote itself into the life maps of the women, who partheno-genetically birthed alter pups and raised them to maturity and died. Within a year, workers were building the first nests and breeders were producing their first litters; soon afterwards nests began to appear on the mainland, and plants and animals around the nests began to change.

At first, the army had mounted a sustained campaign against the invasion, destroying every alter nest they could find and sterilising tracts of the north's wild and rugged countryside, but the alters had quickly returned and multiplied after most of the troops and resources had been diverted to put down the rebellion which had broken out in the south. There were more than two thousand nests along the north-east coast now, Lyra told the lucidor, and alter women and the invasion's strange plants and monstrous animals were spreading steadily southward.

'The boss says that it isn't really a war. It's displacement of life as we know it with life from elsewhere.'

'The boss?'

'Orjen. Your boss too, now. Be easier for everyone if you could keep that in mind.'

The tall woman was no less gruff and mistrustful than she'd been on their first encounter, dressed in black leather trousers and a white shirt, sleeves rolled above her elbows, her wiry hair wrapped in a red bandana. She told the lucidor that alter women nests were highly organised, like those of bees and white ants, with a division of labour between reproductive and non-reproductive members. Breeders gestated multiple offspring which developed at three times the rate of human embryos and were expelled at an early stage in their development and brought to term in the pouches of young workers.

'Breeders breed,' Lyra said. 'Warriors swarm and kill intruders. Porters carry enormous loads and are sometimes ridden by warriors. And workers strip the land around the nests of every scrap of vegetation and use it to build the fungus gardens that feed the nest. They weave platforms and walkways from grass, too, and make crude weapons and tools from wood and stone, and iron extracted from seawater by colonies of little makers in beds of porous stone.'

She showed the lucidor one of the weapons forged from sea iron: a bar shaped to fit the palm of a worker's hand, with four long hooked claws that extended past the second knuckles of the fingers.

'Alter workers and warriors grow fast and die young,' she said. 'Four or five years, that's it. Only their breeders live longer, but not by much. They're child-sized, as you can see, but don't ever mistake them for children.'

'I didn't know that they could make tools, let alone smelt iron.'

'The boss reckons it is instinctive behaviour. What she calls an external expression of their life maps, like bird nests, or the sleeping platforms anthrops weave from branches,' Lyra said, weighing the crude little weapon in her hand. 'Can't say I find that particularly comforting. If they can make something like this out of blind instinct, what might they do if they put their minds to it?'

'Is that what Remfrey He was working on? Alter women intelligence?'

'Something more practical. Alter women pheromones. The special scents that regulate behaviour in their nests. Which is why he wanted a live breeder – he reckoned the pheromones they release control how work is divided up amongst the rest. The idea being that if we could interfere with that, we could disrupt the nests. Maybe even make them destroy themselves. He was also trying to culture the little makers that precipitate sea iron, and tweak their life maps so they could extract other metals from seawater. Everything from copper to gold. He claimed that he'd had some success, but who knows? He poisoned his cultures when he escaped, destroyed his notebooks or took them with him. And the reports he filed with his handlers are incomplete and full of what the army calls wilful misinformation. Which none of his handlers noticed at the time. It only came to light when we tried to copy what he'd been doing.'

'Remfrey He likes to play his little games,' the lucidor said. 'Tell me about the fish he was working on.'

'How do you know about them?'

'It was in those reports. Also, I saw the tanks that had been left behind in his workshop. They contained salt water. Seawater.'

'They did, but for growing those iron stones, not for keeping fish.'

'Then you will have to find some other explanation for this,' the lucidor said, and showed Lyra the fish scale he'd found in the drain under the tanks. 'Remfrey He used scales like this as a pattern for a coat of armour he had the neighbouring leather workshop make. His army handlers didn't know about that, so I have to wonder what else he concealed from them.'

'Maybe the army didn't know about the coat, but they definitely knew about the fish,' Lyra said. 'Remfrey He helped army map readers tweak them, back when he was still in the Free State. The fish were supposed to eat the kind of little monsters we were working on before all this blew up. Which they did, but only after they ate everything else first.'

'These fish – were they released into the Horned Strait?'

'I reckon so, seeing as we found hundreds of them in Roos's fish market. The locals called them peculiars, thought they were creatures of the invasion.'

'I encountered a school of them. They sank the boat that was taking me across the Strait.'

Lyra scratched the side of her nose, considering this. 'Are you saying that Remfrey He can control them? Use them to attack people he doesn't like? I don't know, but maybe you're over-thinking this.'

'I don't think Remfrey He planned to sink the boat I was on, although if asked he would no doubt claim that he did,' the lucidor said. 'But the fish scale is a different matter. It's a clue. A little joke.'

'You mean there's something written on it?'

Lyra had the look of someone who was just beginning to realise that she had lost the trail after walking deeper into the desert than she'd intended.

'Alter women make their nests on the sea coast,' the lucidor said. 'Without exception.'

'All the ones we know about.'

'And Remfrey He was working on how to control alter women, before he escaped. I think he left this scale for me to find. It's the kind of thing he likes to do.'

'If that scale is some kind of joke, you're going to have to tell me the punchline. I still can't see what your fish scale has to do with alter women.'

'Peculiars live in salt water. This scale is a hint that Remfrey He headed towards the sea after he escaped. Or rather, to the sea coast. And given the nature of his work, the sea coast in alter women territory.'

'It seems like a stretch to me,' Lyra said. 'But I'm not here to think about things like that, and you are. Write up a note about it. And read that report. Read all of it. Make notes, highlight everything you think is wrong, write down everything you think we need to know about Remfrey He. Anything and everything that the boss might find interesting and useful.'

'I should talk with her right now. Get her opinion on where Remfrey He might have gone, and what he might be doing.'

'Right now she's busy,' Lyra said. 'Working with the rest of the crew, trying to replicate Remfrey He's army work. And you can't go and visit because your gift will interfere with their map reading. Do your homework, and I'll pass it on. She'll get back to you when she has the time.'

The lucidor was not invited to dine with the governor and his family again, and although he wasn't exactly a prisoner, he discovered that he wasn't allowed to leave the citadel. He read the report, or as much of it as he could understand. He wrote up his notes and outlined a suggested plan of action, and Lyra delivered it to Orjen and the next day told the lucidor that she had gone north to meet with her father's tame general and discuss what needed to be done. Whatever that was. Lyra claimed that she didn't know, said that Orjen would no doubt discuss it with the lucidor when she returned.

Much of the citadel was out of bounds, because the lucidor hadn't been issued with the necessary passes, but he had access to the walkway that ran along two sides of the citadel's battlements, with airy views of Chimr and Delos, and a distant glimpse of the mountains he had crossed with Nunco Arwal and the burro train. Once he was done with the report he spent most of his time up there. Exercising and practising with his staff, addressing the slight weakness that persisted in his ankle. Thinking about everything that had happened and everything he needed to do. Wondering when the shatterling would reach out to him again. Perhaps, like him, it was waiting for something to happen.

He hadn't told Orjen about his link with the shatterling and its interest in the invasion. For one thing, he wasn't certain that she would believe him, might think that he was crazy, or a stone-cold liar. An unreliable fantasist unsuited for a hazardous expedition that had only a small chance of success. And while the shatterling had told him that it wanted to put a stop to the invasion, he knew that he couldn't trust it. It had killed the numberling and the diggers in the pit, it had forced him to seal their link by removing the grain of shatterling stuff from the godspeaker chip and placing it inside his mouth, and above all else it was something old and powerful that claimed to have rebelled against the creator gods. Something beyond human comprehension, and quite possibly mad.

It was said that those of the First People who were ridden by godlings had shared a small portion of their riders' vast, rich minds and had been uplifted and enlightened. Those who died while being ridden died in a state of grace and were enfolded into the common consciousness of the creator gods; those who lived became the chosen. The elect. And after the godlings returned to the creator gods and the creator gods quit the world, the elect became the great scholars, saints and statespeople who founded and shaped the civilisations of the maps. But when he had been briefly possessed by the shatterling, the lucidor had experienced no such grace or enlightenment. He remembered only the horror of paralysis as his hands worked like independent creatures, and he also remembered the ghastly smile of the woman before she jammed her pistol under her chin. There had been no grace or enlightenment there, either.

He could only hope that he had convinced the shatterling that they had a mutual interest in capturing Remfrey He, and that as long as he kept away from places haunted by ancient massacres and the like it wouldn't be able to take control of him again. Perhaps he might even persuade it to help him find Remfrey He, and give him some kind of advantage when the time came to escape from the Patuans and smuggle Remfrey He back to the Free State.

Cyf found him up on the battlements three days later. They greeted each other with awkward formality, Cyf saying that he'd come to make amends, the lucidor telling him there was no need.

'I knew all along that the department had sent you after me. And I'm grateful that you didn't try to force me to return with you.'

'Thinking was, you might return with me voluntarily if I came as a friend,' Cyf said.

Like the lucidor, he was wearing his leather coat, with his staff slung at his back.

'And what are you now?' the lucidor said.

'I'm a representative of the department, helping the Patuan government to trace our mutual friend.'

'I assume that you still hope to take me back, when you are done here.'

'I have my orders. They haven't changed. And if I were you, I wouldn't expect much help from the governor and his daughter when this is all over.'

'And Remfrey He?'

'What about him?'

'Do you have any sense of where he might be?'

'Wherever he is, it's too far away.'

'So he definitely isn't hiding out anywhere in the Twin Cities.'

'The Patuans would know if he was. They have scriers too.'

'When he's found, do you think that they will let you take him back to the Free State?'

'Remfrey He caused a lot of trouble here. The Patuan government will want him to answer for that.'

'And the Free State will go along with that?'

'It doesn't have much choice.'

'The governor asked me whether I would kill Remfrey He, if I had the chance. I thought at the time it was a test of my probity. I wonder now if he was hoping I would save everyone the embarrassment of a trial.'

'I can't speak for the Patuans.'

'And I suppose you aren't going to tell me if the department ordered you to kill him.'

'If this is about your peculiar fixation with justice, I think we are some way past that.'

'It isn't peculiar to me,' the lucidor said. 'It's how things are supposed to work in the Free State. People who do wrong are brought to account and punished appropriately, and every stage of the process is made public so people can see what's been done and petition for change if they don't like it or think that it can be improved. That's how it's always been. Until, that is, elements in the department and the Council of Nine started to make secret deals, swapping prisoners in exchange for . . . what? Some kind of political gain? A way of defusing the Patuans' demands that we help them with their war, after we voted against it? If Remfrey He isn't returned to where he belongs, it will help the people who made that agreement. Help them cover up what they did. Help them avoid due process and punishment. I know what you're going to say, Cyf. You have your orders. But think about what I said. That's all I ask.'

'First of all, we have to find him,' Cyf said.

'We are lucidors. It's what we do.'

Cyf's smile was there and gone. He said, 'I was watching you practise. You still have the moves, but I reckon you're slower than you once were.'

'I'm still not going to fight you.'

'We could give it a go-around. Just for fun. I mean, we don't have anything better to do while the Patuans work out what they want to do, and who is going to do it.'

'If you can get me out of this brig I have a better idea.'

'You aren't a prisoner.'

'Yet somehow I can't leave.'

'If you ask them nicely, I'm sure the Patuans could arrange a sightseeing tour of old Chimr, or something similar.'

'I read the report about Remfrey He's work, and his escape. There was nothing in it about soma.'

Cyf took a moment to think about that. 'He'd been weaned off it after his arrest.'

'That was the official story. The last I knew, two of his guards were smuggling it in for him. I tried to stop it, put in a report laying out who was involved and how it was done, and was told I had been misinformed. I suppose the people in charge thought that maintaining his habit would make him compliant, easier to handle. So the question is, where was he getting his supply in Chimr? Not from the army, according to the report.'

'Perhaps it was an unofficial arrangement.'

'It's possible. But I was wondering if there might be a soma house he was allowed to visit.'

'And if he was,' Cyf said, 'did he talk to anyone there? Did he boast about his work, in the way that he does?'

'And if he was allowed to visit a soma house, where else might he have gone?'

'I suppose I can ask around.'

'I met a colonel in the local lawkeeping force you should talk to,' the lucidor said. 'Happens to be the governor's son-in-law.'

27

Bad Soma

The colonel arranged an escorted visit to two high-end soma houses in Chimr, one used by government officials, the other catering to young scions of wealthy families. Neither was the kind of place that Remfrey He was likely to have used, but in the second the lucidor had a brief conversation with one of the staff and was pointed towards a soma house at the edge of the docks, a brisk short walk from Remfrey He's workshop.

It was a low basement vault divided into half a dozen rooms, mostly used by sailors and dock workers, with low couches where clients reclined on pillows while smoking waterpipes. Threadbare carpets, lamps draped in red scarves, sweet smoke layered under the curved brick ceilings, a languorous hush. When the lucidor and Cyf arrived, in the middle of the day, it was mostly empty. A man dressed in an ankle-length white robe lay on his back, eyes half-closed as he stared dazedly at the ceiling; a woman lay on her side, propped amongst pillows as she drew on the mouthpiece of a waterpipe; a bare-chested man wearing loose cotton trousers with a sash knotted under his considerable belly daintily sipped chai from a glass, heavy-lidded bloodshot eyes watching the two lucidors and their escort without surprise or alarm.

The owners of the house were husband and wife, the husband stooped and docile, the wife brisk and brittle, doing most of the talking. She said that most of her clients were regulars, and when the lucidor showed her a picture of Remfrey He said that she didn't know him, and would have noticed if a Freestater had paid a visit.

'How do you know he is from the Free State?' the lucidor said.

'Why, because he has the look. As do you and your friend.'

'He would have stopped coming here a little while ago. Perhaps that's why you don't recall him.'

'I don't recall him because he was never here,' the woman said.

The lucidor saw a tell-tale flicker in her husband's downcast gaze. 'So if my friends in uniform search the place, they won't find anything he might have left behind. And if I come back in the evening and question your clients, none of them will recognise him.'

The woman looked at the two city lawkeepers. 'There's no need for that,' she said. 'I already told you what I know.'

'And we heard differently,' Cyf said. 'We heard that he was one of your regulars.'

'So we need to clear that up,' the lucidor said. 'We can start by asking your clients. There aren't many in now, but we're happy to wait.'

The woman asked to see Remfrey He's picture again, pretended to study it, and said, 'Maybe he did come in here. Once or twice.'

'Do you have private rooms?' the lucidor said.

'Of course,' the woman said. 'Most prefer the commons, but we cater for all tastes.'

'I expect Remfrey He rented one of those rooms,' the lucidor said, looking at the husband. 'He liked to take his pipe alone, but he also liked to wander around, watch people while they nodded off, talk to them about their dreams.'

'If you know so much I don't know why you need to ask us,' the woman said, affecting offended dignity.

'Did he bring his own supply? Did he offer to share it with your other clients?'

'We had an arrangement,' the woman said.

'He said that it was part of the war effort,' her husband said. 'We could hardly refuse when he asked us to help.'

'Times are hard. People can't always afford their regular pleasure,' the woman said. 'And sailors are generally young and reckless, eager to sample some new thrill. We thought it would be better done here than on the street.'

'And if things went wrong you could always find new clients,' Cyf said. 'I don't suppose there is a shortage of sailors in a port as busy as this.'

'Did anything go wrong?' the lucidor said.

'Some of his stuff was good,' the woman said. 'But some of it was . . . less so. People had nightmares. Very bad nightmares. Two had fits.'

'Maram, he was one of first to try it? He still has nightmares,' her husband said. 'Sees things coming out of the walls.'

'Have you kept these samples?' the lucidor said.

The woman looked at her husband, and said, 'He took them with him.'

'But before things went so badly wrong, you might have kept back a scraping or two,' the lucidor said. 'Thinking, perhaps, that you could find a chemist who could duplicate Remfrey He's special supply.'

'It's for the war effort,' Cyf said. 'As long as you cooperate with us, the army won't have to come here and turn the place over.'

When they returned to the citadel, the lucidor handed the samples over to Lyra and explained their history, asked if it was possible to discover whether they had been manufactured by one of Remfrey He's cultures. Both he and Cyf were pleased by their outing. They had done some proper investigative work, shown that Remfrey He had been deceiving his supervisors long before he escaped, and hoped that it would prove their worth to the Patuans.

Two days later, the colonel, Orjen's brother-in-law, found the lucidor at breakfast in the officers' mess. He sat across from the lucidor without asking for an invitation, asked what he was eating.

'I haven't yet made up my mind. It's either some kind of porridge or a failed experiment in industrial glue.'

'Is the chai as bad as the porridge?'

'It's hot, at any rate.'

The colonel waved a waiter over, asked for a cup, and told the lucidor, 'I heard that your tour of the soma houses was successful.'

'We are trying to make ourselves useful while waiting to find out what is wanted of us,' the lucidor said, and thanked the man for his help. 'While I'm kicking my heels here, perhaps I might be allowed to find out how else Remfrey He abused your country's hospitality. I'm sure a little bad soma was the least of it.'

'We already know that he is a devious man. Discovery of a few minor transgressions won't change that opinion.'

'I don't expect to change anyone's mind. I just want to know as much as I can.'

The colonel thanked the waiter who set a cup of chai in front of him, and without tasting it stirred in a spoonful of sugar. 'Had he still been here when you arrived, I suppose you would have tried to kidnap him.'

'I prefer to think of it as enforced repatriation.'

The colonel sipped the chai, added a second spoonful of sugar and took another sip. 'Could you have managed it on your own?'

'One thing I know: Remfrey He wouldn't have been able to talk me out of it.'

'Ah, yes. When one lacks a gift of one's own, one tends to forget that you have the gift that negates all others.' The colonel gave up on his chai and leaned back in his chair, casually elegant in his tailored grey uniform. 'You claim to have found a clue to Remfrey He's whereabouts. One left specifically for you.'

'Well, no one else found it.'

'And you told the governor that Remfrey He may be expecting you.'

'I think that he knows that I am looking for him,' the lucidor said, wondering where this was going.

'You must find it hard, being his nemesis.'

'That's not how I think of myself.'

'Then how do you think of yourself?'

'I am a lawkeeper. Like you.'

The colonel smiled. 'We are not exactly the same. For instance, you are in my country, and I am not in yours.'

'He committed crimes in my country, too. Crimes far worse than the tableau in the warehouse.'

'But he is here now. As are you.'

'Is that all you have to tell me?'

'Oh, I thought I would see how you were doing. One lawkeeper checking on the welfare of another. Also,' the colonel said, 'I was wondering if you might like to demonstrate how you use that silly stick of yours.'

The lucidor knew that it was a test he couldn't afford to lose, but the invitation pinked his pride. 'Why not?' he said, pushing away his dish of porridge. 'I'm not going to be able to finish this.'

They ascended half a dozen floors in a small elevator to a gymnasium with a sprung wooden floor and mirrorlight slanting through tall windows. With the help of an aide, the colonel changed into white pyjamas tied with a broad red belt; the lucidor refused the offer of a similar costume, shrugging off his leather coat and saying that he usually fought in ordinary clothes.

'Whatever makes you comfortable,' the colonel said, testing the flex of his fencing foil. 'Though I recommend you wear a mask. I don't want to put out one of your eyes by accident.'

'You won't get the chance,' the lucidor said.

He drew his staff and the colonel took up a position, right knee bent, foil extended in front of him with the other hand raised for balance, and came at him in a quick blur of motion. The lucidor stood his ground and leaned backwards to avoid the colonel's thrust and knocked the foil out of his grip with a twisting strike.

'Not bad for an old man,' the colonel said and shook his stung knuckles and picked up the foil and came at the lucidor again.

The lucidor countered three thrusts and pitched the colonel to the floor with a judicious kick to his knee and stood over him with the iron-shod end of the staff a finger's width from his eye.

'Tricky,' the colonel said, with a thin smile, and got to his feet and tested his knee by flexing it in several directions.

'You didn't explain the rules,' the lucidor said. 'So I assumed that there weren't any.'

'Street rules,' the colonel said.

'Do everything you have to do to win.'

'Exactly so.'

The colonel pushed back a stray curl of black hair and waved away the aide, who had stepped towards him with a towel draped over his arm. He raised his foil vertically before his face and suddenly was in motion again, thrusting left and right, high and low. The lucidor deflected his blows and retreated slowly, counting his steps, letting the colonel exhaust himself. When he knew that he was three paces from the wall, he countered a jabbing strike and slid the staff to the foil's cupped guard, forcing it up and stepping close, numbing the colonel's wrist with a swift rap and sweeping his legs from under him.

For a few moments, the colonel lay where he had fallen, breathing hard, arms outspread. When he pushed to his feet, he said, 'That stick of yours isn't bad for close fighting. But not much use, I think, against small arms and long guns.'

'We make it hard to obtain pistols in our country. And as long as lawkeepers don't carry them criminals don't need to either.'

'I am familiar with the concept of escalation,' the colonel said. 'But it's a hopeless ideal in a city that's the staging post for a war.'

The lucidor smiled. 'Even so, it's comforting to have a familiar companion at your side when you are travelling in a strange place.'

Someone else said, 'I think you will find that the actual war is a very different country.'

It was the governor, dressed in a black silk coat and loose black trousers, coming across the wooden floor of the gymnasium with Orjen and Cyf following, and the lucidor knew then that he had passed his final test.

28

War Train

The expedition left the Twin Cities for the old capital, Ymr, in a carriage tacked to the rear of a troop train that in the grey hour before arcrise drew out of Delos-Chimr's Grand Terminal and passed through a flatland of apartment houses, manufactories, roads and canals, crossing the river on a castellated stone bridge and heading north and east. The carriage was the personal transport of the general who had conspired with the governor to win permission for the expedition, one half given over to stalls for horses, the other appointed in some luxury. Carpets, leather swivelling chairs, a cabinet stocked with finger foods and liquor, a tiled washroom. There were seven passengers. The lucidor and Cyf, Orjen and Lyra, and three mercenaries with experience of infiltrating alter women territory, including a scrier, Angustyn, a scrappy, scornful young man who had fronted up to the lucidor when they had first met, telling him he needed to turn off or at least dial down his gift.

'That's not how it works,' the lucidor had said.

'I can look away from people I've glommed onto,' Angustyn had said. 'So why can't you look away from me?'

'If you want to do your thing, all you have to do is keep your distance.'

'How about you keep your distance? Like maybe ride in another carriage,' Angustyn had said, and Veca, the briskly professional woman who fronted the mercenaries, had stepped in, telling the scrier that if he had a problem he could go and sit in hard class with the meatgrinder fodder. Angustyn had shut up, but now and then shot a sullen glance at the lucidor, while Veca frowningly worked through a folder of large-scale maps, licking her thumb before turning each page, and the third mercenary, Surmal Neas, dozed slump-spined in one of the chairs.

Officially, the expedition was a quick and dirty scouting mission, following up on a recent report about the strange behaviour of alter women around a frontline nest near an abandoned fishing village. The coast was infested by aquatic monsters and the general had been unable to wrangle a support ship, so after reaching Ymr the expedition would have to trek across some fifty leagues of what the army called disputed territory without attracting the attention of alter women or other creatures of the invasion. It would observe the nest and scout the immediate area, and if Remfrey He had set up camp nearby and was conducting field experiments the general would decide whether to initiate contact and try to negotiate his surrender, or to send in troops to capture him.

The lucidor believed that Remfrey He might have made contact already: that report, no more than a brief unsigned note attached to a daily operational memo from one of the frontline brigades, might have been planted by some proxy Remfrey He had cozened with his gift. When the lucidor had shared this concern with Orjen, she'd told him that the only thing that mattered was whether or not the man's work was of any use. If he really had found how to manipulate the behaviour of alter women and gain control of their nests, they had to be prepared to strike a bargain with him and concede to any reasonable demands. It could be a turning point in the war. It might even be the beginning of the end.

'She still doesn't understand that there's no reasoning with the man,' the lucidor had said to Cyf afterwards. 'But I will have to go along with it for now, because it's the best chance of finding him.'

'It's also the Patuan army's best chance to get rid of a major embarrassment. Use you as bait to put him in the sights of a sniper.'

'That's how I see it too. Look, Cyf, I'm willing to risk my life if that's the only way of stopping Remfrey He, but there's no reason why you should.'

'And what about all your fine talk about bringing him to justice?'

'As you already pointed out, the Patuans are unlikely to let him go back to the Free State. Especially if he has something they want.'

'The Patuans think that you're just an old man with some quaint notions about lawkeeping and a little skill in the art of the staff. An old man who's useful only because of his history with Remfrey He. Someone they can dispose of when they're done with him, because the department and the Free State government won't make any fuss. But I know better. I'm the only one here who understands you. I know that once you get an idea into your head you don't let go. And I know that you'll risk my life and everyone else's for the smallest chance of capturing Remfrey He. That's how you are, Thorn. And I also know that Remfrey He will most likely give you that chance, because that's how he is. I could ask you to swear that you don't have some kind of crazy plan, such as ignoring orders and trying to bust in and take down the man on your own, but I know you wouldn't tell me if you did. So I'm coming along on this expedition, and I aim to be at your side every moment of every day. And when this is over, whether or not we capture Remfrey He, no matter what the governor and the army decide to do with him if we do, you're coming home with me.'

It was the longest speech the lucidor had ever heard Cyf make, and he thought that dropping in his birth name was a nice touch.

'I give you my word that I won't do anything foolish,' he had told Cyf. 'That's the best I can do. And much as I like Orjen, she is young and eager and ambitious. If we're not careful she'll do something that will put her life at risk, and ours too. So I'm glad you have my back.'

Now, as the train sped past glimpses of tidy whitewashed villas and the walled estates of castellated manors at the edge of the city, Cyf was sleeping or pretending to be asleep, and the lucidor watched the landscape flow past the carriage window. A broad floodplain gave way to ranges of hills covered in thick forest where the railway wound through steep-sided cuttings and crossed small swift rivers on stone bridges, the forest opening out and falling back, yielding to yellow grasses and thorn bushes and bare stretches of gritstone and baserock where soil had been washed out or blown away. This was the sourlands, once the larder of Ymr, now a niggardly scrubland depleted and ruined by more than a thousand years of intensive farming, stretching away to a flashing line of reflected mirrorlight that must be the sea. Not the pinched channel of the Horned Strait, but the wild unbound vastness of the World Ocean. Thousands of leagues of rolling waves stretching away north and east and west towards neighbouring maps so unreachably distant that most were little more than scraps of half-remembered stories. And somewhere out there, too, was the origin of the invasion, which had crossed that immense desert of water and taken root here for a purpose that no one yet knew or understood, or perhaps for no other purpose than to grow and spread. A different kind of life: vital, transformative, protean. A power that Remfrey He wanted to grasp and use to further his fell schemes.

Presently, the lucidor realised that the railway was running through the vast ruins on the outskirts of Ymr. Founded when godlings had walked the world, it had once been the largest and oldest city on the map, and although it had shrunk to an irreducible core after a centuries-long decline it had been the seat of Patua's government and the home of its monarch until the invasion had forced both government and Queen to move south. At first there were low ridges imposing a sketchy geometry on the piebald scrub, then stretches of broken walls, and then ruined buildings, league after league of them. Roofless manufactories, burned and blackened row houses, the shattered frames of apartment blocks. Roads grown over with grass and scrub. A canal choked with debris. A freight yard where abandoned strings of carriages and wagons stood amongst gardens of dead weeds. A lake penned by earth banks, wind-driven fleets of stiff white clods of foam sailing its surface and foul water pouring into it from the maw of an enormous pipe.

At last, the train began to slow and the spires and towers of the city's heart appeared ahead, gleaming gold and silver in mirrorlight. Orjen set down her tablet and turned her chair to the window and watched them drift past, telling the lucidor that she had worked for two years in Ymr's university, explaining that the invasion had gradually made ordinary life impossible. Red tides had thickened along the shore and rotted and choked the air with sulphurous fumes. A flock of things a little like flittermice, tens of thousands of them, had roosted amongst the spires of the High Temple, their noxious dung defiling the tombs of monarchs, viziers and commanders-in-chief. There had been water shortages. Martial law. And at last, just three years ago, a tailswallower plague spread by rats had killed more than ten thousand people. Ymr's northern precincts had been razed to contain the contagion, there had been a mandatory evacuation of all remaining civilians, and the army had taken control of what was left of the city.

Cyf wanted to know where the front was. He'd woken up and like everyone else (except Surmal, who slept on heroically) was watching the towers drift past.

'It's not much further,' Orjen said. 'And getting closer every day.'

'Strictly speaking, there isn't a front as such,' Veca said. 'There are pockets of invasion stuff scattered through the ruins and sourlands. Monsters in the sea. In the waterways, too. Those flittermice. And birds, or things like birds.'

'And bugs,' Angustyn said. 'Don't forget the damn bugs.'

'Animals follow the roads and railway tracks,' Veca said. 'It's best to stay off them, at night.'

'A creeping tide of new life,' Orjen said.

'That sounds like something Remfrey He would say,' the lucidor told her.

'It's the title of a talk I gave at a conference on the natural history of the invasion,' Orjen said.

The lucidor and Cyf shared a look, and the lucidor knew they'd had the same thought. That where they were going would not be amenable to the theories of scholars and philosophers, and if Orjen believed otherwise they were in more danger than they had first believed.

The train clattered through the gleaming delta of a big junction, taking a line that curved east of the heart of the city, towards the docks. Passing strings of carriages and wagons parked in sidings, passing paved yards where military wagons and vehicles were drawn up in gleaming rows, passing paddocks crowded with horses and draught oxen, rattling across a bowstring bridge above a waterway lined with merchant ships. The lucidor spotted chain guns, belt armour and other modifications, presumably for defence against sea monsters, and then the train passed the far end of the bridge and entered the maw of a huge station under a glass canopy, where troop trains and freight trains loaded with armaments were drawn up alongside twenty or thirty platforms.

Angustyn was the first out of the carriage, walking away towards the end of the long platform while Veca and Surmal oversaw the unloading of their equipment and their horses – ordinary horses, a nimble, shaggy-maned breed – and the troops who had ridden in the rest of the train were marshalled into lines that one after the other marched off deeper into the cavernous station. Officers wearing plumed helmets chatted in groups or walked up and down the rows of recruits. A string of warhorses went past, each led by a uniformed groom.

'Most of those troops won't see any fighting,' Veca told the lucidor and Cyf. 'They'll be assigned to clean-up squads or unloading at the docks, or to back office work. The army likes paperwork more than it likes fighting. It gives High Command the illusion that it's imposing some kind of order on a situation where there isn't any order at all. Meanwhile, the invasion keeps spreading regardless. This station is about to be abandoned in place. The army is building a new mobilisation centre thirty leagues to the west, though I won't give it more than a year or two before they have to abandon that, too.'

'We don't need to be reminded that we're heading into a bad place,' Cyf said.

'Don't let any of this fool you into thinking there is any semblance of control here is all I'm saying,' Veca said. 'It's mostly futile busywork. And your princess, over there?'

The three of them looked at Orjen and Lyra, who were checking the straps of boxes slung either side of their pack horse.

'She might think she knows a little about the invasion,' Veca said. 'But we're heading into alter women territory, and it takes a special kind of crazy to survive out there. The kind of crazy me and Surmal and Angustyn have. So listen to what we say and do exactly what we tell you to do, no more and no less.'

'What worries me most,' the lucidor said to Cyf, after Veca had sloped off to check her mount, 'is that she seems to think that alter women are the worst thing we face.'

'What worries me,' Cyf said, 'is that you think that you and Remfrey He have some kind of special bond.'

'Let's hope that Remfrey He thinks so. It will make finding him much easier.'

The lucidor was feverish with anticipation, thinking of the hostile territory beyond the city, infested with alter women and other monsters, where Remfrey He waited like some orb spider squatting at the confluence of a fan of threads, monitoring the tugs and tiny displacements that signalled the presence of potential prey. The mercenaries were armed with pistols and crossbows and fat-barrelled long guns; explosive and gas grenades hung like ripe fruit from their bandoliers. Angustyn had several thin-bladed throwing knives sheathed at his belt. Surmal carried a double-headed axe. Veca had an ivory-handled blazer holstered at her hip. The lucidor did not doubt that they were adept at taking down ordinary monsters, but their arsenal would be of little use against the kind of traps and tricks Remfrey He liked to deploy.

Angustyn came back from the end of the platform and made a big deal about how distance and the usual static meant that he hadn't been able to acquire their target.

'Kid's trying to prove he's the expedition's only true scrier,' Cyf told the lucidor. 'He knows fine well he won't be able to pick up any trace of Remfrey He until we get much closer.'

'You'll let me know as soon as you do get a sense of him,' the lucidor said.

'I intend to let everyone know.'

They saddled up and rode out, Cyf and the lucidor behind Orjen, Lyra and their pack horse, the three mercenaries in their boiled leather armour riding at point as they trotted down a cobbled road between brick-built warehouses. Huge ships loomed above flat roofs: the hulks of arks that had once carried people and cargo across the World Ocean to other maps on voyages that lasted years, the paintwork of their hulls and superstructure mostly gone, their control towers empty shells with shattered windows, the stacks of decks where crops had been cultivated on the long voyages overgrown with weeds and hung with shrouds of ivy and red-leaved vines. Cranes reared above one ship and people were working on its deck and in cradles hung alongside its hull; Orjen dropped back and told the lucidor and Cyf that it was the *First Pilgrim*, the smallest and oldest of the arks, built three centuries ago to circumnavigate the map and chart its reefs and coastline on a voyage that had lasted two decades, now being modified to serve as a command base.

'After she's been commissioned, I hope to spend some time on her and extend my work on sea monsters,' Orjen said. 'Not the little monsters I was collecting in the Horned Strait, but true leviathans. Creatures so big that only a ship the size of the *First Pilgrim* can trawl for them.'

'Perhaps they would be better left in the sea,' the lucidor said.

'Knowledge drives out fear,' Orjen said serenely. 'That's why we are here.'

They rode past a long stretch of demolished warehouses, with a view across slumps of brick rubble towards the wreck of an ark that lay on its side, revealing its keel and splayed ranks of propellers. The seawall of the harbour loomed in the distance, with the white pillar of the great lighthouse marking its entrance: the tallest building in the map, crowned by iron bowls where fires fed by forests of pitch pine burned, visible for a hundred leagues at night.

They were riding now through a grid of blasted streets. Scarcely a wall left intact. Shell holes. A tank washing a swale of rubble with long arcs of blue flame. Troops moving in a line across a field gone to scrub. Troops sitting in the lee of a broken wall, dirty faces lifting to watch the party ride past. Trash fires in the streets and the taste of smoke and burned plastic in the air. A manufactory standing in a desert of rubble, its brickwork pock-marked by shrapnel.

This dead zone gave way to marshes that had overtaken the city's eastern outskirts centuries before. The road ran on top of an embankment raised above long stretches of reeds and reaches of black water. It reminded the lucidor of the Land, and he wouldn't have been surprised to see Alcnos and Doros part the reeds and clamber up the steep side of the embankment, eager to join the expedition. But apart from brushstrokes of smoke leaning at the western horizon there was no sign of human life anywhere. No sound but wind rustling in reeds, the plash of water, the lonely cry of some unseen bird, the clop of their horses' hooves on the road's stone paving. And then the road curved along the inner edge of a bay, and for the first time in his life the lucidor had a proper sight of the World Ocean.

Late afternoon mirrorlight sparked on the waters of the bay, glinted on long parallel white lines where waves that had rolled across ten thousand leagues of open water broke on the adamantine reefs the creator gods had raised around the coast of the map. Beyond, a desert plain of iron-coloured water stretched to a haze that hid the joint between water and sky. Mountainous ranges of cloud hung in the sky out there, so far off that they seemed level with the lucidor as he sat on his horse and took in the view. A clean wind blew from the ocean and things like giant naked birds, their long jaws crowded with needle teeth, hung on the wind above the bay, now and then stooping down and skimming the waves with hook-clawed feet and snatching up a fish.

Beyond the bay, the road ran straight across another stretch of marsh, and a clot of figures in the far distance slowly resolved into a small band of soldiers. Some mounted, some on foot, all of them bedraggled and battle-worn. A man lay on a travois dragged behind a warhorse, bloody bandages wrapped around his bare chest. Three bodies were draped over the back of another warhorse, their heads and feet jostling limply as it went past.

Veca reined in her mount and talked with the leader of the band, a sturdy woman who took off her leather helmet to reveal close-trimmed blond hair and a square-jawed pugnacious face. She turned to point over her shoulder, shook her head when Veca asked her a question, and spoke at some length before slapping palms with the mercenary and riding on after her troops.

The expedition dismounted and let the horses graze along the edge of the embankment. Lyra handed out pocket breads stuffed with diced vegetables and soft cheese, and Veca explained that the soldiers had been ambushed by alter women while manning a watch post on the coast, about six leagues ahead. They had been overrun, lost five people as they fought their way clear, and had to leave two bodies behind because the alters kept coming.

'If it was on the coast it won't be anywhere near our route,' Orjen said.

'That's true,' Veca said. 'But we might have to change our plans if we run into the same bunch, or another like it.'

'And no one bothered to warn us,' Angustyn said, around a mouthful of food.

'It might be a splinter group, looking to set up a new nest,' Orjen said. 'The nests further east are three or four years old now, well established and no doubt ready for division. It's bad luck for the soldiers, but it shouldn't affect us as long as you make sure that we know where the alters are before they find us.'

She was overtopped by the three mercenaries but had a determined commanding air. Lyra stood behind her, arms folded across her denim work shirt, fists resting in the crooks of her elbows.

'I can spot any that get close,' Angustyn said, looking at the lucidor, 'as long as this walking blank spot keeps away from me.'

The lucidor stared back until the scrier looked away.

'You and Surmal ride point,' Veca told Angustyn. 'The rest of you stick close to me. Saddle up and stay sharp.'

As they mounted their horses, Cyf said to the lucidor, 'Do you think these irregulars know what they are doing?'

'I'd trust Veca in a fight. But I also know that plans don't often survive contact with the enemy.'

'Don't hope to take advantage of any confusion. Whatever happens, I'm sticking right by your side.'

They rode on, the mirror arc sinking behind them. The lucidor was alert and apprehensive, watching for movement in the marsh's reaches of black water and stands of reeds. The human bustle of the railway station and the hulks of the arks and ruins of the great city seemed a long way behind.

The marsh gave out and in the incarnadine flame of the setting mirrors they rode on through a bald scrubland. Low rounded hills gouged with slumps and pockmarked with shell holes. Scant grass and brush burned to char and ash.

At last, Angustyn and Surmal halted beside a pair of posts crookedly crowned with wagon wheels, disturbing a handful of large black birds that flapped heavily into the air and circled high above, calling hoarsely each to each. When the lucidor and the others caught up they saw child-sized bodies had been lashed to the wheels. Alter women, gone mostly to leather and bone, broken legs and arms threaded through spokes.

'These weren't here the last time we came through,' Angustyn said.

'Are they supposed to be a warning to other alters?' Cyf said.

'More likely a warning to travellers like us,' Lyra said. She was sitting straight in her saddle, scanning the land around them, one hand on the hilt of the knife slung from her bandolier.

'Any live ones about?' Veca said.

'Sure,' Angustyn said. 'Before your man there rode up and shut me down it was like a thousand tiny snakes were hissing in my head. Same as it always is out here.'

'I mean close at hand,' Veca said.

'None I could tell.'

'It'll be dark soon. Gus, you and me will go on up the road to where it tops that rise and take a look around.'

'I already told you it's clear.'

'And I want to be sure. Surmal, you take our guests up there,' Veca said, pointing to a group of standing stones on the crest of a distant hill. 'Long as it's safe, that's where we'll make camp.'

'I'd like to go with you,' Cyf said.

'I don't need any help,' Angustyn said.

'I've been riding close to Thorn all day,' Cyf said. 'I'm curious about this interference the alter women are supposed to put out.'

Veca studied him for a moment, said she didn't see why not. 'Take the rest of 'em up there, S. Keep 'em close.'

They were big, the stones. Roughly squared pillars three times the height of a person, set in a circle. Two pairs were still joined by crosspieces; others fallen long ago were half-sunk in the ground. Soldiers and mercenaries had painted their unit or company signs on several of the stones, and left the blackened circle of a big camp fire. Surmal sifted ashes, said that it could be days or weeks old, and walked off to the edge of the circle to keep watch as Veca, Cyf and Angustyn rode towards the crest of the road.

'This is a temple from the first days, built by the so-called Primitive Folk,' Orjen told the lucidor. 'Some say that the godlings hunted them like animals, others that they rode them like they rode the First People. Anyway, they're gone now. All that remains of them are places like this and a few traits from their life maps, preserved in ours. It seems that, after the godlings left, the First People enslaved some of the Primitive Folk's women and had children by them, which means that they must have been more closely related to us than the old scriptures claim. Some say it's those fragments that confer gifts, rather than direct descent from those ridden by godlings, but I am not aware of any study that shows a direct correlation.'

The lucidor said, 'If this was a temple when godlings walked the world, what kind of worship was practised here?'

'No one knows,' Orjen said. 'But there are stories that feral tribes of the First People took over these circles and performed human sacrifices inside them.'

'What's up?' Lyra said to the lucidor. 'You look like you've seen a ghost.'

'In a place like this, it wouldn't be surprising,' the lucidor said.

The shatterling had been absent for so long that he had let the stark cold reality of his link with it slip to the edges of his mind. But now he felt, faint but clear, its presence at his back again, and remembered the vision it had spun at the City of the Copper Mountain. The ranks of whitewashed captives. The ceremonial decapitation. The shatterling had told him that the industrial slaughter had marked the fabric of the world, and he wondered if that fabric had been likewise marked here, wondered if that was why the shatterling had been able to reach out to him from its pit. A chilly thought. If it found it easier to contact him in those places where the world had been stained by murder, what did that say about its nature?

Surmal was coming towards them, grim-faced, telling them to quit their chattering and look sharp.

'Are we in trouble?' Lyra said.

'Don't know yet,' Surmal said. 'But Veca and the others are coming back in an awful hurry.'

29

Foraging Party

Veca said that they had spotted alters moving across the top of a hill about two leagues away. 'Five or six workers, most likely a foraging party. They won't be a problem as long as they keep heading south, so I reckon we will be safe enough hunkering down here for the night.'

'If it is a foraging party, it's a long way from any nest,' Orjen said.

'They have to range far and wide these days,' Veca said. 'If we move on now we could run into more alters. And there are other things just as bad out there, too, and some of them like to hunt at night. Gus, you take first watch. Keep an eye on that little party, let me know at once if it changes direction.'

'I'd rather not have to set up a ways from the old guy,' Angustyn said. 'Maybe he should set up his own bivouac a ways from us.'

'If you're scared of the dark, I can keep track of that party for you,' Cyf said.

'You and your friend can best make yourselves useful by scouting up kindling,' Veca said. 'We'll cook some food, boil up a pail of chai. Everything will seem better once we get things civilised around here.'

They hobbled their horses inside the stone circle while Angustyn walked out into the dusk and took up position behind the shelter of a stone fallen some way from the circle. Tiu stood bright and blood-red above the largest of the stones and Surmal said that it was a good omen: the wanderer was the sign and symbol for war and warriors.

'I would be happier to see the star for a safe journey,' Cyf said. 'If there is one such.'

'Some say that Tiu is the remnant of the world of the Ur Men,' Orjen said. 'Whether or not that is true, we do know that it appears to be a body of stone and is much smaller than our world – if you could peel it like a pippin and lay its skin on the World Ocean it would be larger than Gea but smaller than most of the other maps. Small though it is, it has an envelope of air, and seas and polar ice caps, and perhaps even some kind of life. And it shines so brightly because it is lit by mirrors. Recently, the skywatcher Albus Starstrider was able to split their light into its component colours, confirming the claims of certain old texts it is identical to the light of our own mirrors, and therefore must have the same source, namely the Heartsun.'

'People once rode through the air and went to war against Tiu,' Veca said. 'So I read in one of those old texts, anyway. But who's to say what they tell true and what is fantasy got up to scare children?'

They were all sitting around a fire pit, eating fish and rice cakes Lyra had cooked on a griddlestone.

'We can test ideas with the tools and methods of practical philosophy,' Orjen said. 'Such as Albus Starstrider's experiments in splitting the light of Tiu's mirrors using a telescope and a prism. Or calculating Tiu's mass from the radius and period of its orbit around our world, and its density from its mass and volume. As for your story about a war of the worlds, anything thrown hard enough into the sky would either keep falling around the world or escape it entirely, so flying to Tiu, or anywhere else in the sky beyond, is not as impossible as it might seem. That's what the creator gods did, and the Ur Men in time's dawn. Perhaps we will be able to do it one day, and find out if there are people like us on Tiu.'

'Not too much like us, I hope,' Veca said. 'The present war is enough for me. I don't need to go looking for another.'

After a short silence, the lucidor asked Cyf if scrying the alters had been very different from scrying people.

Cyf brooded on the question and said, 'You ever go to the Founding Day fair?'

'Once or twice.'

With friends, when he hadn't been much older than Panap, and later with his wife, but he wasn't going to tell Cyf about that.

'Then perhaps you remember there was a tent where you walked through a kind of corridor of mirrors.'

'The ones that were all bent and warped?'

'They gave back your reflection as a fat dwarf or a skinny giant, gave you two heads, and so on. It was a little like that with the alters, except the mirrors were reflecting each other. I can't think of any better way to describe it. They weren't human, they weren't like animals, and it was hard to tell one from another. For once, I'm glad to be sitting inside your cone of silence. Glad I don't have to worry about having them inside my head.'

Lyra looked at them across the fire pit. 'Way I see it, the soldiers took a hit for us. Alter foraging parties don't search for anything in particular. They wander randomly until they stumble over something tasty or useful, and draw others to the spot. So if those alters hadn't found the soldiers, they might have found us instead.'

'We have certainly been lucky so far,' Orjen said.

'Don't count on luck to see us through,' Veca said. 'Stick together and stay sharp. See trouble before trouble sees you.'

'And if trouble finds us, stay out of the way when I start swinging,' Surmal said, patting the axe on the ground beside him.

They slept, or tried to. The lucidor lay a little way from the others, looking up at the red tides of stars and frozen billows of star stuff, wondering again why Remfrey He had put himself in danger by heading out into alter women territory. Not to help the army or end the war, that was certain. And the man wasn't interested acquiring knowledge for knowledge's sake, either. He was a pragmatist, only interested in devices and ideas that he could use to assert his authority, to manipulate or humiliate and hurt other people, to make mischief. To amuse himself. That most of all. He had once asked the lucidor if he had ever, as a child, poked a hole in the side of a white ant castle. If he had watched the insects boil out, swarming everywhere, looking for something to fight and failing to find it because they could not understand what had happened. Could not grasp the nature of their human enemy, let alone his motive.

'And why does the child torment them?' Remfrey He had said. 'Out of curiosity, perhaps. Or boredom, or malice. Or simply, like some capricious godling, because he can. And if you have ever been that boy, you might have felt a little like me.'

The lucidor thought again of a spider waiting for its prey, remembered the time he had found, in the garden of his childhood home, a golden ball hung at the centre of a web. Which, when he'd touched it, had split into a hundred spiderlings that scattered in every direction. Suppose something like that happened if they reached the alter nest and triggered one of Remfrey He's traps . . .

At some point he must have fallen asleep, for he was rising above the standing stones, the fire pit shrinking to a tiny star below, vanishing into the dark land. Slowly, slowly, an asymmetrical lace of faint lines developed, radiating from bright nodes scattered along the ragged edge of the coast, and the nodes also extended long threads out into the World Ocean, converging and knitting into a single strand that shot away over the horizon.

The lucidor hung above all this, a calm all-seeing eye watching without fear or wonder the slow pulse of the nodes and the shifting patterns of the web laid across the land, its fine faint threads shrinking or growing, angling this way or that, breaking connections and making new ones. He knew that he was dreaming and wondered if it was his dream or the shatterling's, and with that thought his point of view began to fall, the ragged little star of the fire pit reappeared, and he woke up.

It was still dark. A faint sense of grey light at the east illuminated nothing more than the division between earth and sky. Everyone else asleep except for Veca, sitting up on one of the lintel stones that lay across the tops of two uprights, looking out into the darkness beyond the notional safety of the stone circle.

The lucidor propped himself up on an elbow, staring into the pulsing embers of the fire, trying to puzzle out the meaning of the dream. Which had been no ordinary dream. He had no doubt about that. No, the shatterling had reached into his sleeping mind to tell or show him something. If he had it right, those bright nodes were alter women nests, each connected to each and all of them connected to something or somewhere beyond the horizon of the

World Ocean. The place where they had been made or created, perhaps, or a map they had conquered before making landfall here. That much seemed obvious enough, but what it meant, how he was supposed to make use of it, was much less clear.

So far the shatterling had not objected to, or at least had not yet interfered with, the lucidor's mission, but he knew that it would not hesitate to intercede if his pursuit of Remfrey He conflicted with its own plans and desires. He had to be ready for that, even though he had as yet no idea how he could outwit the shatterling. And if it could use the godspeaker link to reach into his dreams, perhaps it could also reach into his thoughts . . .

He knew that he wouldn't be able to go back to sleep and shucked his blanket and walked across the stone circle to Veca's perch. She looked around as he scrambled up the trimmed branch she'd used as a ladder, and told him, 'All's well. Nothing's moving out there. Nothing I can see, anyway.'

'I could spell you for a while, if you like.'

'I have pills if I need 'em, but just being out here is enough of a kick. Keeps the heart pumping strong, the brain alert.'

'I know that feeling,' the lucidor said, and eased down beside her.

Veca said, 'I'm guessing your line of work is much like mine. Long stretches of boredom punctuated by moments of acute terror.'

'Something like that. There was also a lot of paperwork.'

'Add polishing or painting anything that doesn't move, and you have life in the army.'

'You were in the army?'

'Sixteen years. Had just gone back to civilian life when this blew up. I had comrades who became mercenaries and I thought, why not? The pay is good, and you see plenty of action. The army holds the line; we go outside it, where you can have yourself some real fun.'

'It seems both of us are old campaigners, seeking the thrills of our misspent youths.'

'Maybe some people aren't fit for civilisation, either by inclination or by circumstance.'

224

'Yet here you are, defending it.'

'My first stretch as a mercenary, I was sent to help put down the rebellion in the south. The government says it's an armed insurrection whose leaders want to overthrow the monarchy and the established order, but most of the so-called rebels I fought were ordinary folk. Farmers, farriers, shopkeepers . . . People who didn't have much to begin with and lost most of what they had to tithes raised to pay for the war against the invasion. None of them had ever been more than a couple of leagues from where they had been born, and they were mostly armed with farm implements or the tools of their trade. Scythes and machetes. Axes and hammers. If they had guns, it was old muzzle-loaders used for hunting, or pistols they'd taken off landlords and landlords' overseers, and they used stones instead of roundshot and gravel instead of scattershot because stones and gravel were all they had. Any iron they could find, from jewellery to fetters, they beat into swords and spearpoints.'

'I know the kind of people you mean,' the lucidor said, thinking of Alcnos and Doros and the rest of the landers.

'They fought hard,' Veca said. 'We took back villages and towns house by house, street by street, and we didn't take any prisoners. People we caught, people who surrendered, we'd line them up and shoot them. Same for anyone we thought had helped 'em. As a warning to others. Those were our orders. And still they fought, and they are fighting still. Long before the end of my contract I'd had enough of it. And dumb as I am, without any other thought of what I might do, I signed up to fight alter women instead. And that's what I've been doing until this little job landed in my lap.'

'Remfrey He is the exact opposite of your rebels. They were fighting to protect and save their families and their way of life. He likes to break things, for the sheer fun of it.'

'I've met more than a few mercenaries like that, and I know it's hard to make them change their ways. Impossible, oft-times, short of killing them. So how are you going to convince Remfrey He to surrender?'

'Orjen thinks she can lure him back with the promise of better toys. If that doesn't work, we will have to think of something else.'

Best not to mention his belief that the army and Orjen's father would prefer that Remfrey He was killed rather than captured. If Veca had been given that task he knew that he would have to do his best to stop her, and she probably knew that too.

After a short silence, he said, 'Going up against the alters as you do, you must have learned a lot about them.'

'If you're wondering how they fight, or how to fight them, I can maybe tell you a thing or two.'

'I was wondering about their nests. Whether they are linked together somehow.'

'Why do you ask?'

'I'm about to get close to one of them, so I reckon I need to know as much as I can.'

'I don't know if this answers your question, but there was this one time I was part of a crew that tried to take down a nest. We sneaked in by sea, aiming to plant explosive charges around the foundations of the spires, but we were spotted before we were done. Six of us were killed, and the alters drove the rest of us back and cut or quenched the fuses we'd managed to light. That was that. Next crew that tried the same tactic, targeting a different nest, warriors swarmed them as soon as they got in amongst the spires.'

'You mean the nest you attacked told the others,' the lucidor said, realising with a sudden plunge of dismay the implications of the shatterling's vision.

'I don't know the workings of it,' Veca said. 'Whether there are connections we don't know about, or it's just a word-of-mouth kind of thing. But it seems that when alters in one nest develop a new way of fighting, it quickly spreads to all the others.'

'So if Remfrey He can interfere with the behaviour of one nest, if he can take control of it, he might be able to take control of all the others.'

'Is that why you can't sleep, worrying about things like that?'

'I'm beginning to realise what we might be up against.'

'One thing in our favour. If your man Remfrey He tried to poke the alters in the wrong way, if he got on their bad side, well, there have been plenty of people who didn't survive that kind of

226

mistake. Got themselves killed and drug off to a fungus garden, like the alters do their own dead.'

'I don't think we can count on that. He's crazy, but he's also smarter than just about anyone I've ever met.'

'It sounds as if you admire him,' Veca said.

'I've learned the hard way that you should never underestimate him,' the lucidor said.

They sat side by side with their legs dangling over the edge of the lintel stone, watching the horizon brighten in the east. Crests of low hills developing out of the dark, sketched in shadow and shades of grey. Scattered clumps of trees in stark silhouette. Nothing moving anywhere until there was a scrape behind them and Angustyn came up the makeshift ladder, saying quietly, 'They're out there again. And this time they're heading towards us.'

30

Last Stand

By the time the first alters appeared at the top of the rise to the north-east, everyone was awake and packing up the camp. Veca and the lucidor stepped outside the circle of standing stones and used their spyglasses to study the small figures silhouetted against the brightening sky.

'See how some are bulkier?' the mercenary said. 'There are warriors mixed in with workers.'

'Angustyn said they were coming from the west, as well.'

'I know you don't have much liking for him, but when it comes to doing what he does he's not often wrong.'

The lucidor thought about that and said, 'It's as if they're trying to outflank us.'

'Reckon so. Could your man Remfrey He be behind it?'

'If he is, he'll be somewhere close by. He wouldn't want to miss the fun. But I don't think we should wait to see if he turns up.'

'Neither do I.'

They walked back to the others and Veca told Orjen that if she still wanted to make it to the coast they were going to have to punch through the line of alters heading towards them.

'They'll most likely try to follow us, because that's what they do, but we can easily outpace them on horseback. They should give up the chase once we're out of sight, and then we can cut towards that nest of yours, as planned.'

'What if they don't give up?' Orjen said. 'Or suppose we run into more of them?'

'There's a place we've used before, not that far from where we have to get to,' Veca said. 'A pele tower built by one of the march lords who had charge of these lands a couple of centuries ago, back when the Pirate Queens were raiding this coast. If those alters are bent on pursuing us we can hole up there and think about our next move. Worst case, we can get on the godspeaker and call in reinforcements.'

'If we do, we will not get another chance to find Remfrey He. The army will most likely bring in a battle cruiser and pound that nest flat. That's what they wanted to do before my father and I persuaded them otherwise.'

'I'll only ask you to do it if there's no other way out. And I reckon we still have a good chance of shaking off this bunch of alters and reaching the nest as planned.'

'And if we do not go forward we will have to go back.'

'Yes, ma'am. And there's alters circling behind us, so whatever we do we're going to have to deal with them. It's your call, and you need to make it now. They aren't going to wait.'

'I am not ready to go back,' Orjen said.

'Long as we ride fast and stick together, we'll knife right through 'em,' Veca said.

As he rode with the others out of the stone circle the lucidor felt a familiar hollowness in his belly, a sharpening of focus. The alters were coming up the hill now, a line of small dark figures wading through waist-high dry grass with a quick, swivelling gait, as if their knees had been welded together.

Cyf drew his horse close, a borrowed pistol in one hand, told the lucidor that all he needed to do was stay in the saddle. 'The mercenaries will try to pick off any alters that come too close, and I'll take care of any they miss. You just do your best to keep up, old man.'

'Don't worry about me,' the lucidor said, and reached behind his head and drew his staff. 'Look after yourself.'

The alters flanking the riders on either side began to close in. Veca and Surmal raised their long guns and two alters dropped into the grass as the sound of the shots echoed off the hillside, then two more. Veca stood in her saddle and pointed at the gap she and Surmal had made and spurred her horse. The lucidor's mount quickened its pace of its own accord, jolting him as it moved from canter into full gallop, charging down the hillside after the rest of the party. He raised his staff and yelled in defiance, and alters were suddenly on either side of him, none of them close enough to strike, he heard the pop-pop-pop of Cyf's pistol behind him, and then they were past.

When the riders reached the crest of the next hill the lucidor looked back and saw that the alters had turned around and were coming after them, moving at the same steady pace. There was a singing in his blood, and the glimpse he'd had of the alters as he galloped past was at the front of his mind. Most of them had been workers, small and skinny as starveling children, but there had been a couple of warriors too, with barrel chests and mouthfuls of crooked fangs and long arms reaching for him, fingers tipped with stout black thorns. None of them had made any sound. That was the most unsettling thing about them: the silence of their common intent.

The expedition rode on, down the hill and up the next, the horses blowing hard and trotting now, descending to the floor of a broad valley filled edge to edge with wild wheat, and climbing the steep slope at the far side. They halted at the top and looked back. Saw a straggling line of tiny figures coming down the slope at the far end of the valley, and turned their horses and rode on.

After a couple of hours they had left the hills behind and were riding along the edge of a high plateau where wind blew across a trackless heath scarred with wandering pavements of gritrock. They had long ago outpaced the alters, and when they reached the ruin of a solitary building, little more than a ragged arch and a flooded cistern, Veca called for a rest stop.

The lucidor was grateful for the respite. He had seen something other than the ruin from afar: a square white shrine with a domed roof, and statues of cat-headed women standing either side of its square entrance. This vision growing as unstable as a mirage as he drew nearer, collapsing into the reality of the ruin and leaving a needling headache behind his eyes and the puzzle of what the shatterling had been trying to convey by this glimpse of the past.

While the horses drank from the cistern their riders filled their water bottles and shared a late breakfast of oatcakes and dried figs. Lyra kindled a small fire, saying that she reckoned they had time for a brew, and Angustyn and Surmal mounted their horses and trotted off to scout the way they had come, to check if the alters were still following.

The lucidor asked Cyf if he wanted to scry for alters, too; Cyf shrugged and said that Angustyn could do it well enough.

'Reaching out to those things isn't pleasant, and he can scry through the damned static better than I can.'

'He's had practice.'

'It's like a rainstorm of white noise. Or the ringing you get in your ears after someone lands a good punch to your head in a boxing match,' Cyf said. 'Once again, I'm grateful that your gift has muted it.'

'And I'm glad to hear I'm still of some use.'

Cyf studied him. 'You seem to be enjoying yourself.'

'It is a little like the old days, back when I was hunting for bandits along the border.'

'Only now we're the ones being hunted.'

'Hardly a new feeling, as far as I'm concerned,' the lucidor said.

Lyra handed out cups of the bitter green chai favoured by the citizens of Delos-Chimr, saying that there was nothing like a good brew to steady the nerves. They stood in a circle, warming their hands on the cups, sipping cautiously. Cyf told Orjen that he had been expecting to see monsters out here.

'This is alter women territory,' Orjen said. 'They catch and eat most animals along the coast, and drive away the rest. You want monsters, go inland, or further north. Mutable bears, shriek hogs, twitch birds, trooper hornets – you will find all kinds there, if they don't find you first. Some interesting diseases, too.'

'But aren't they all creatures of the invasion?' Cyf said.

'You have mistaken it for a conventional army,' Orjen said.

Her eyes were smudged, her lips pressed in a thin straight line. She was feeling the strain of being chased by the alter women more than anyone else. Everything she had invested in this expedition had been put at risk.

Cyf wasn't about to give up, saying, 'But the monsters and the alter women and all the rest were all created by the same thing, so why don't they share a common purpose?'

'Did you not pay any attention to my briefings? There is no common purpose here. No plan or strategy. No alliance. Just a metamorphic plague spreading as best it can.'

'But it's a kind of war, all the same.'

'That's what the army thinks. I do not,' Orjen said, and stalked off to the edge of the cistern.

'She's a bit on edge,' Lyra said. 'And what she meant to say is something like how leopards and goats were quickened by the creator gods, but they don't lie together. Life preys on life to live, the same as everywhere else. It's just that it's a bit more lively here.'

'Life preys on life,' Cyf said. 'Does that mean the different alter women nests go to war against each other, the way ants do?'

'They aren't like ants,' Veca said.

'I know that,' Cyf said. 'I scried them, remember? I was wondering if we could lead the ones following us into the territory of another nest, slip away while the two sides fought it out.'

'It might work, if nests fought each other,' Veca said. 'If you insist on mistaking them for ants, think of their territory as one big nest.'

'Except they aren't ants.'

'There you go.'

The lucidor put a hand on Cyf's shoulder, asked him if he had killed any alter women with that borrowed pistol.

Cyf, caught unawares, had to think for a moment. 'Maybe one. She fell down, anyway. I didn't have time to see if she got back up.'

'Use your staff next time. You'll know then.'

'Stick to what I know, is that what you're telling me?'

'I think it's a good idea, considering we know so little,' the lucidor said, and walked over to Orjen, who was standing at the edge of the cistern's square of black water and looking out at the territory they still had to cross.

'Cyf didn't mean anything,' the lucidor told her. 'It's just his manner.'

'I didn't expect to encounter alters so soon.'

'I think we got the better of them.'

'All I did was cling onto the reins and let the horse take me where it would.'

232

'Leave the fighting to Veca and her boys. That's why they're here.'

'And you? Did you kill any?'

'I don't know why I drew my staff. Like you, I was mostly holding onto the reins.'

'But you could, if you had to.'

'It's surprising what you find you can do, if you have to. But let's hope it doesn't come to that.'

Orjen hunched her shoulders. She was wearing a long quilted coat, its fur-trimmed hood thrown back. Her black hair stirring in the cold wind blowing out of the north, across the flat heath.

She said, 'There are thousands more out there. Tens of thousands. If they have taken to roaming far from their nests we are bound to run into more of them.'

'Can I ask you a question?'

'As long as you don't question my answer.'

'It's something I was discussing with Veca. Whether or not the nests can communicate with each other. She told me a story about how, after an attempt to blow up one nest, all the others seemed to have learned about it.'

'I have heard stories like that.'

'And are they true?'

'I don't know. Even if there's some truth to them, stories aren't the same as experimental evidence. They are single observations that are not representative of the whole, they cannot be properly tested, and just because one thing happens after another doesn't mean there is a causal relationship. They might point to something that is worth investigating, but it doesn't mean that what they suggest is true. So, yes, it is possible that alters can pass information from one nest to another, but they also exhibit a wide variety of habitual behaviours, such as macerating plant material for their fungus gardens, or raising their young. Things they do the same way every time they do them. Our observations are far from complete, so we can't tell if an apparently new kind of behaviour is something the alters have recently learned or a habitual response that hasn't been observed before.'

'I was wondering if Remfrey He might be able to take control of all the nests.'

'Alters don't have anything resembling a traditional command structure, so it's unlikely. But not impossible.'

'He could be trying to forge a command structure. To put himself at the centre. To turn the alters into an army.'

'What would he do with an army?'

'Pretty much anything he wanted to do. Nothing good.'

'We did not come here to confront him, or try to subvert his plans. We will locate and observe him, and the army will decide what action to take, based on our findings and my recommendations.'

'I haven't forgotten that.'

'I will be sure to remind you,' Orjen said, 'if it ever seems that you have.'

Angustyn and Surmal came back at a swift trot and without dismounting the scrier told Veca that they had gained some distance on the alters, but they were still coming on.

'How many?'

'If we wait for them to catch up I could tell you,' Angustyn said. 'Right now they're too far off.'

'Perhaps they lost sight of us and are returning to their nest,' Orjen said.

'We'll soon find out,' Veca said. 'We'll keep heading north, for the pele tower. If they aren't following us they'll turn towards the coast soon enough.'

As they rode on, the lucidor saw that a boulder half-buried amongst the coarse grass was the weathered remnant of a carved head, with cat's ears and an enigmatic smile. He thought of the brief vision of the shrine, and thought of his dream, if that was what it had been. The faint lines connecting nests, the lines cast across the World Ocean knitting together into a glowing braid that stretched away beyond the horizon . . .

The feeling that something was at his back had gone, but he spoke to the shatterling anyway, telling it very quietly that he knew it had shown him a true picture of the shrine as it once had been. 'Was the dream a true vision, too? That braid shooting off across the ocean, where was it aimed? Did it point towards the origin of the invasion?'

He half-hoped, half-dreaded that he would be shown something else, but there was no reply.

A little further on they cut west to skirt a small village of low, rough-stone buildings, tile roofs mostly fallen in, gardens lost to weeds, grass and bushes growing in the single street. The lucidor wondered if its people had been caught up in the changes caused by the invasion or if they had managed to flee. He thought of people falling ill all at once, men and children lapsing into deathly comas, women changing, bodies and minds distorting as their life maps were rewritten by the invasion's tailswallowers. Giving birth to litters of strange babies that grew into monsters at unnatural speed.

Grim speculations in the bright windy mirrorlight.

Beyond the far edge of the village they struck a track sunk between high banks where bushes grew in dense masses of dark green leaves and white, saucer-sized blooms that filled the air with a strong deep musky scent. Veca was riding point some way ahead of the others, Surmal and Angustyn bringing up the rear, when her horse shied and an alter rose up from a scrape under one of the bushes, white petals showering around its shoulders. Veca shouted and tried to bring her carbine to bear as the alter swivelled down the short slope, and her horse reared and she fell backwards. She landed hard, blindly groping for her carbine, kicking out when the alter caught hold of one of her legs. The lucidor urged his horse forward and drew his staff and swung it in a single motion, striking the alter with a ringing blow as he went past. It would have shattered the skull of any ordinary person, but the alter shook its head and started towards him as he hauled hard on the reins, trying to turn his horse, and Surmal rode up and slammed his axe into the back of the alter's head.

The alter had clawed through Veca's leather britches and gouged her calf with three parallel gashes. She winced when Lyra blotted away blood and poured a clear liquid over the wounds, told her to hurry up as she knotted a bandage.

'I'm sorry, boss,' Angustyn said. He was standing over the alter's body, pale and shaken. 'I should have ridden ahead.'

'And I should have squared the damn thing away before it had a chance to go at me,' Veca said.

'I was too busy looking for our followers,' Angustyn said. 'Hanging back so the old man there didn't block me.'

'It isn't anyone's fault, Gus,' Veca said. Surmal helped her to her feet and she pulled up her britches and buckled her belt, said that they needed to get going in case the alter had any friends nearby.

'I won't let one get past me again. I swear it,' Angustyn said, and kicked the alter again.

It lay on its back, the dirt under its head black and wet with blood, a white petal stuck to one of its round black eyes, its belly swollen by a pouch stuffed with leaves and grass chewed to pulp. Orjen said that it was perhaps no more than a stray scavenger that had stumbled across them by chance.

'Let's hope you're not wrong,' Veca said.

The lucidor was holding the bridle of her horse. After she swung stiff-legged into the saddle she gave him a thin smile, said that his stick was handier than she'd thought, but he would find it harder work if he ever came up against a warrior.

'Are you all right?'

'A tad shaken is all. Lyra said that salve of hers will prevent any infection. It better had, because it stung hard enough,' Veca said, and raised her voice and told the others to quit gawping and get on.

They had hardly ridden half a league when Veca folded in her saddle, and would have fallen from her horse if Surmal hadn't cut close and caught hold of her. He and the lucidor eased her down, laid her out. She was only partly conscious, pale around the lips and eyes, sweating hard. Lyra briefly examined her, said that she might be suffering from a reaction to some kind of toxin, and needed rest and bleeding.

'She's already bled enough,' Surmal said.

'A little more, properly controlled, will reduce the toxin load,' Lyra said. 'I can make up an antipyretic to reduce her fever, too, but with the alters coming on behind I don't think it will be safe to treat her here.'

Surmal stood up and told Orjen, 'It's the pele tower then. Veca needs treatment, and this isn't any kind of place to make a stand.'

'When we get there, we will talk about what to do next,' Orjen said.

'First we get Veca fixed up,' Surmal said. 'Then we'll talk.'

Surmal and Angustyn draped Veca over the saddle of her horse and Surmal tied its reins to his saddle and they rode on. After a little while, Cyf rode up beside the lucidor and said, 'If you have a plan, you had better tell me about it. Because you know I'm not going to let you try to find Remfrey He on your own.'

'I might not need to. If he set these alters on us, they could be driving us towards that tower. And if they are, he will be waiting there.'

'I can see why you hope that's true, but it's a tad heavy on ifs and mights, and light on facts.'

'I would rather meet him on my own terms,' the lucidor said. 'People caught up in his games tend not to survive them. But if he found out how to control the alters, it's exactly the kind of thing he would do.'

'I guess we'll find out soon enough,' Cyf said, 'since that tower seems to be our best and only chance.'

Angustyn took point as they rode on, splashing through a bog patched with hummocks of bright green moss and stands of cotton grass flying white flags in the wind, following a small river that, running swiftly around and between big boulders, tumbled into a ravine. Trees stood stark and naked on steep slopes either side. Stripped of their leaves by foraging alters, according to Orjen, after she dismounted to examine small footprints trampled in soft dirt amongst a litter of torn and broken branches.

They struck a path that crossed the river on a bridge built from stone slabs, and climbed through a press of leafless trees that gave out to scree slopes rising to the crest of a high ridge. On the far side, cliffs fell straight and sheer to a long lake of black water, and a track ran along the edge of the drop, winding towards a kind of buttress or crown of rock on which the pele tower stood: a foursquare stone building rising into the windy sky, one wall shrouded in red vines from top to bottom, a splinterstone roof tented above crenellated battlements. The lucidor studied it through his spyglass, saw that the track approached the tower through pinch points between big boulders and outcrops, at one point passing through a short tunnel cut into the flank of the buttress. There was a gate at the far end of the tunnel, Surmal said, and another path that was also gated, a back door that led to the valley beyond the lake.

The lucidor glassed the tower's battlements and slit windows and saw no sign of movement; Angustyn rode a little way up the track and came back and said the damn static was too much for him, he would have to get much closer to check out the place.

'I'll come with you,' Surmal said. 'Everyone else set down here. Don't move until we call you forward.'

Lyra and the lucidor lifted Veca from her horse and made her as comfortable as they could in a grassy hollow which gave some small shelter from the wind. She was still unconscious, and her skin was hot and dry. Lyra checked the gashes in her leg and retied the bandage and said that she was in a bad way.

The lucidor said, 'Do alters have poison claws?'

'Not that I know,' Lyra said. 'But I'm no kind of expert.'

'I was wondering if it might be some design of Remfrey He's.'

'The two map readers he took with him were amongst the best the army had,' Orjen said. 'But even they wouldn't have had time to breed up that kind of trait.'

'He could have brewed some kind of poison and smeared it on their claws,' the lucidor said.

'We can ask him about that when he's in custody,' Orjen said.

Cyf was standing at the rim of the hollow, watching the two mercenaries approach the tower; now he called out, said something was up. The lucidor pulled out his spyglass again. Under the shadow of the buttress Angustyn and Surmal were sawing their horses around as small dark figures emerged from crevices and fissures in the rock face. Alters, at least fifty, maybe more. Half a dozen swarmed around Angustyn's horse and pulled him from his saddle; Surmal turned back to help, slashing left and right as more alters ran at him.

Cyf tugged the lucidor's sleeve, pointed to movement far below. Alters were leaving the cover of the leafless trees alongside the river, scrambling up the steep slope like a crowd of malignant and horribly deformed children. Orjen snatched the blazer from Veca's belt, and before the lucidor could tell her that the alters were too far away she raised it in a two-handed grip and fired. The beam was a bright crease in the air, setting fire to a tree, blinking out. Orjen fired again and the beam glanced past two alters. One fell, smoking; the other dropped to one knee and pushed up and limped on. When Orjen squeezed the blazer's trigger a third time it drily clicked; the weapon's charge was exhausted, and the alters were coming on unchecked as flames and smoke began to spread through the trees behind them.

Cyf emptied his pistol and missed every time, and shots sounded small and sharp from the direction of the pele tower as Surmal broke free of a crowd of alters and galloped away down the track with Angustyn's riderless horse cantering behind. The lucidor jacked Veca's single-shot carbine from the saddle of her horse and took aim and fired, knocking shards from a rock in front of the alters climbing the slope. Lyra stripped off Veca's bandolier and thumbed a greasy cartridge from one of the loops and tossed it to the lucidor. He worked the carbine's lever to eject the spent shell, inserted the cartridge and racked the lever forward to close the breech and took a breath and centred his aim, telling himself that the alters were the invasion's foot soldiers, and squeezed the trigger. The butt of the carbine kicked him in the shoulder and the shot punched an alter in the chest and it dropped face down and slid backwards in a cascade of small stones. The other alters stepped around it and came on. Lyra handed the lucidor another cartridge and he dropped a warrior with a clean shot to the head.

'How do you know about guns?' Cyf said.

'I had to use them now and then when I rode border patrol,' the lucidor said, and took aim and held his breath and fired a shot that tore off an alter's arm at the elbow.

'Not bad,' Cyf said, 'but it might be quicker to get down there and clear them out with our staffs.'

'Let's thin them out a little and wait for them come to us,' the lucidor said.

He killed two more and wounded another, but the rest were still climbing the slope, more were emerging from the trees, and a pack of them were coming along the spine of the ridge as Surmal cantered up, breathless and grim, and told everyone to get moving before their line of retreat was cut off.

The lucidor said, 'Did you see Remfrey He out there?'

'I saw things coming out of the rocks, I saw Gus go down, and that's all I saw. Saddle up, quick as you can.'

Lyra and Cyf hoisted Veca onto her horse and Surmal hitched its reins to his saddle and took the lead, the rest following as best they could down a steep slant of sliding stones. The lucidor gripped his reins with one hand and the horn of his saddle with the other, nearly pitched over his mount's head when she lost her footing and bucked to an abrupt halt. He steadied himself and caught his breath and urged her on.

Cyf was a little way ahead of him, Surmal, Lyra and Orjen had almost reached the trees, and the alters were very close now, scrambling along the slant of the slope under a thickening reef of smoke. A skinny worker lurched towards Cyf. He swung his staff and knocked it down, and cut his horse around the flank of a flat-topped boulder. The lucidor saw a twitch of movement, shouted a warning, and Cyf glanced back as an alter rose up and leaped from the boulder, striking him square and knocking him from his saddle.

The lucidor's horse baulked and spraddled. He kicked her hard to get her moving, and chopped the alter across the back of its head with a short hard blow, struck it square in the face with the follow-through. It coughed a spray of blood and fell backwards and rolled away in a clatter of stones, and the lucidor pulled his horse hard around and jumped down.

Cyf tried and failed to stand, looking at the lucidor with a woozy unfocused gaze, blood running freely from a gash in his forehead. 'I'll be all right in a minute,' he said. 'I just need to get my breath.'

'We don't have a minute,' the lucidor said, and clipped him on the jaw, just hard enough to put him out, and caught his horse and with some effort lifted him up and slung him over the saddle. The other riders had disappeared into the trees and the alters were moving relentlessly along the slope and more of them were pouring down from the crest. The lucidor swung into his saddle and grabbed the reins of Cyf's horse and coaxed his own horse into a fast trot, riding down an alter and sending it spinning away, knocking down another with a one-handed head strike that shocked his arm to the shoulder, glimpsing more of them lurching towards him as he clattered through the bare trees.

The pack horse had fallen close to the bridge, was struggling to rise as alters swarmed over it. A second horse, riderless, reins trailing, trotted away downstream, barging past an alter that tried to claw it down, disappearing into a haze of smoke, and Lyra stood at bay in the shallows at the river's edge, her back against a boulder as she straight-armed a pistol. She shot an alter as it waded towards her, shot at another and missed and fired again. The round snapped the alter's head back and it collapsed into the water, but two more were already splashing past it.

Surmal sat on his horse a little way upstream, using his long gun to pick off alters coming out of the trees, and Orjen was trying to calm her mount as it stepped about behind him. The lucidor slapped the rump of Cyf's horse with his staff, sending it at a canter towards Surmal and Orjen, and curbed his own horse and urged it into the river, chopping down alters as they turned towards him. Lyra saw him coming and fired a last shot and threw her spent pistol at an alter and caught the lucidor's arm and swung into the saddle behind him.

'I lost Veca,' she said breathlessly. 'Her horse bolted. Mine too.'

There were alters on either side of the bridge now. The pack horse had vanished under a jostling crowd, and others were wading towards the lucidor and Lyra. Several lost their footing when they stepped into deep pools, and vanished beneath the surface or were swept away, but the rest came on with heedless persistence. The lucidor urged his horse across the stream, ignoring Lyra's protests as it mounted the far bank, kicking it into a gallop up the steep path beyond.

31

Ordinary Beetles

The lucidor reined in his horse at the top of the slope and turned to look back at the path he had just climbed. Lyra sat behind him, arms around his chest; the horse was blowing hard, heat rising from her. Trees were on fire all along the stream now, and alters were coming up the slope, three warriors stumping along in the lead. Others were splashing upstream, chasing Surmal, Orjen and Cyf, and a small crowd was dismantling the pack horse, and blood running into the water fed a widening muddy red plume.

'We have to help the others,' Lyra said.

'We have to get closer to the nest,' the lucidor said. 'The others will find us there.'

'Or you could go back down there and do the right thing,' Lyra said, and crooked an arm around the lucidor's neck. The lucidor glimpsed the flash of her knife, slammed the back of his head into her face and jabbed her in the belly with the butt of his staff and shouldered her from the saddle.

'Try to find the others if you like,' he told her as she sat up, winded, her nose bleeding. 'But I didn't come this far to turn back.'

He kicked the horse into a trot and rode off downhill without waiting to see what Lyra would do. The land fell in a broad sweep towards the sea. To the east, about three leagues off, was the curved indent of a bay and a cluster of dark spires at the sea's edge, small as thorns and sharp and clear in the bright mirrorlight.

When he reached a stretch of grassland patchworked with drystack walls he reined in the horse and turned in his saddle and saw Lyra some way above, scrambling down the bare slope ahead of a ragged line of alters. Thunderheads of smoke were boiling into the blue sky beyond the crest, no doubt visible for leagues around. So much for the expedition's plan to make a stealthy approach and covert observations.

The lucidor rode on, crossing fields long abandoned and over-grown with scrub and pioneer saplings. Urging the horse to jump walls or finding gaps in them, skirting several fields blanketed with red creeper that threw up tall spires of intertwined vines, halting in front of an abandoned croft with grass grown up around its stone walls and weeds in the rotten thatch of its roof.

Lyra had reached the far edge of the patch of red creeper. Half a league behind her, the alters were crabbing towards the bottom of the slope, the three warriors still out in front.

The lucidor had kept hold of Veca's carbine, but had no way of picking off the pursuers because the bandolier of cartridges had gone south with Cyf and the others. He sat on his horse in the shade, waiting as Lyra slogged around the perimeter of the fields. She was out of breath and sweating hard when at last she reached the lucidor, saying, 'You're a damn crazy fool. I don't know why I'm following you.'

'I imagine it's because you want to stay alive.'

Lyra blotted sweat from her face and neck with her sleeve. 'Are you sure the others will find us?'

'I hope Orjen will. If you want to ride the rest of the way, you will have to hand over that knife you tried to stick me with.'

'Maybe I'd rather walk.'

'Then those alters will most likely overtake you. They aren't going to give up, and they're fresh to the chase.'

'You didn't rescue me out of kindness, did you? It was an excuse to break away from the others.'

'I didn't need any excuse, and I could have escaped more easily had I not stopped to help. Do not give me cause to regret it. Hand up your knife or start walking. And if you choose to walk, I won't wait for you to catch up a second time.'

'I'm surprised you stopped at all,' Lyra said, and stepped forward and held out her knife, hilt first.

They rode on, following the rim of a bluff, descending through a gully crammed with evergreen trees, and turning east. When they crossed a stream the lucidor stopped to let the horse drink, and he and Lyra drank too. The afternoon was growing hot. The land around was silent and still.

Lyra scrubbed dried blood from her face and sat back on her haunches. 'Do you think they lost us?'

'No, I don't. But they might give up the chase when they realise where we are going.'

'Are they really controlled by Remfrey He?'

'I very much doubt that they chose to hide out at the tower.'

'If he is in command of that nest, you are probably going to get us killed.'

'He won't kill us right away. He'll want to show off what he's done first.'

They rode on through meadows gone to scrub, skirted a cluster of small baserock spires that thrust from the ground like a buried giant's fingers. The lucidor felt the shatterling's attention push through the link for a moment. A red pulse in his eyes, an unscratchable itch inside his skull, there and gone.

A rise off to their left – the lucidor reckoned it was the headland above the abandoned fishing village – cut off the view of the sea, and a parcel of woods stretched across their path. Some of the trees were draped in red vine from root to crown; others had fallen under masses of vines that sprawled away in every direction. There was a strong pungent medicinal odour and the big, hand-shaped leaves of the vines faintly rustled in the moveless air, like someone whispering unfathomable secrets. It was the only sound apart from the steady thump of the horse's hooves. There were no birds. No insects. Once, the lucidor glimpsed a pair of alters caught in a distant splash of mirrorlight as they plucked leaves from the lower reaches of a vine-clad tree, but they were too absorbed in their work to notice the horse and its riders pass by.

The far side of the woods had been stripped bare. No foliage, no vines. Only stark skeletons of trees, trunks glistening white where bark had been peeled away, and a desert of bald rock and clay sloping towards the bay.

The alter women's nest stood at the end of a short promontory: a cluster of tall skinny spires conjured from underlying baserock by some unfathomably strange gift. The lucidor had been shown drawings and diagrams of alter nests at briefings before the expedition had set out, but the sight of the spires, soaring into the sky behind concentric arcs of earthworks, chilled his blood. If alters could reshape the fundamental material of the world like a potter squeezing clay, what else could they do?

Lyra leaned at his shoulder, pointed to movement in a path that cut through the earthworks. A thin but steady traffic of alters was heading out into the countryside, passing groups of alters moving in the other direction, towards the nest.

'No sign of anything strange or unusual,' she said. 'Just your commonplace, everyday scavenging behaviour.'

'The ambush at the tower wasn't commonplace. Remfrey He enticed us here with that note. He's expecting us, might even be watching us. We'll lay up in the village, scope things out, and wait for him to show his hand.'

'And wait for the others to catch up with us.'

'That too.'

They turned away from the nest, struck a road that ran through a shallow cutting and sharply bent to reveal the southern end of the bay, where four or five streets of terraced houses rose behind charred and smoke-blackened remains of tanks, granaries and godowns and the curve of a quay. A seawall of piled stones enclosed a small harbour and slicks of red weed floated on the still water, climbed the masts of a small ship sunk at anchor and grew up the stone wall of the quay, spreading across cobbles in a froth of bladders and feathery fronds.

The nest loomed on the far side of the bay's shallow horseshoe. Relatively small and only a few years old, according to the briefings. They were close enough now to see the webs of walkways and cables strung between its spires. The lucidor reckoned that the biggest stood at more than a hundred spans, taller than the dome of the People's Palace in Liberty City.

Lyra said, 'If Remfrey He is waiting for us, he's playing hard to get.'

'Let's check out the rest of this place,' the lucidor said.

They rode up streets where houses stood still and silent as tombs, windows shuttered, dead sticks in flowerpots beside doors painted in primary colours. Apart from the burned-out buildings around the harbour there was no sign of violence or panicky flight, and no answer when the lucidor called out Remfrey He's name. Only a loose window shutter clapping to and fro in the breeze.

The door to one of the houses stood ajar. The lucidor caught a whiff of a sharp acrid stench when he pushed it open, and something rippled across the far wall, like a curtain drawing back: tens of thousands of black beetles clung there, packed tightly, dropping away where the wedge of light falling through the doorway struck them, some crawling in random directions across the floor, others taking wing with a sizzling buzz.

Ordinary beetles, according to Lyra. The invasion had not only introduced monsters of every size but had also perturbed the subtle checks and balances of ordinary life.

The neighbouring house was crawling with beetles too; so was the next. The lucidor and Lyra gave up on their search and led the horse back to the harbour, found a perch on an empty cart near the edge of the sprawl of dark red weed. The skeleton of a bullock lay between the shafts of the cart, picked clean and white.

The expedition's supplies had been lost with the pack horse. The lucidor shared with Lyra a scant meal of oat biscuits and dry figs he'd filched from the train carriage's buffet, and they drank from their water bottles and studied the nest. Late afternoon mirrorlight shimmered on the calm waters of the bay, flashed from the nest's needles and spires. Through his spyglass, the lucidor could make out small figures moving stiffly along walkways and nets strung between the spires or climbing in and out of pods that clung to the sides of the spires. He saw a swarm of alters moving across the promontory, vanishing into the shadows at the bases of the spires, and wondered if it was the gang which had ambushed them.

The activity across the bay was rendered harmless by distance, and the quiet of the abandoned harbour was broken only by the distant smash of waves on the far side of the seawall and the random crepitation of weed bladders spraying little spurts of seawater. Troops of small red crabs with scorpion tails curled over the backs of their shells skittered through the miniature jungle of fronds and bladders. Once, something like a leathery ball two or three spans across skipped along the irregular backbone of the seawall and splashed into the water and did not resurface.

'The others should have found us by now,' Lyra said, after a while.

'Perhaps Remfrey He found them first. Or perhaps Orjen decided to do the sensible thing, and headed back to Ymr.'

Lyra shook her head. 'She'd come here if she could, try to redeem something from this shambles. And since she hasn't, we should go look for her.'

'Better to wait here.'

'She might have got herself into trouble. And we can't wait for ever. Alters will find us. Either the ones that were following us, or a scavenging party from the nest.'

'I don't think any alters been here recently. They would have harvested those beetles. And the weed, and the crabs.'

They sat quietly for a little while. At last, Lyra looked sideways at the lucidor and said, 'What will you do if Remfrey He comes looking for us?'

'Find out what he wants. Why he wanted me to come here. Overmaster him if I can.'

'You aren't much interested in what he might have been doing here, are you? And I don't reckon you are planning to take him back to Delos-Chimr, either.'

'He was sent here because of a secret agreement made without due process. He needs to go back to where he belongs.'

'I don't know about your country, but in mine people who uncover secrets that might embarrass anyone in authority usually end up in prison, or are disappeared.'

'Yet here we are.'

'I'm here because my boss is about as stubborn as you are,' Lyra said. 'Everyone thinks she's this rich kid, playing at reading the life maps of monsters. But she isn't playing. She has a real gift for it, and real dedication, and she gave up a lot for her career.'

'You have worked with her for a long time.'

'From the beginning.'

'I have known Remfrey He for a long time, too. I know what he is, and what he can do. He may have been sent here to help your army, but that wasn't ever in his plans.'

'As far as I understand it, he did some good work before he took off. That's why we need to know why he came here. What he's discovered.'

'How's that going?'

'I can't help noticing you haven't had much success in that department either.'

'I'm where he wants me to be,' the lucidor said. 'He will be along when he's good and ready.'

But the mirror arc slanted towards the rim of the hills above the fishing village and shadows grew and flowed together across the quay and there was still no sign of the other survivors of the expedition, or of Remfrey He. For the first time, the lucidor hoped that the shatterling would make an appearance. A little star. A hooded figure. Something that would point the way to Remfrey He and help to capture him. He walked to the end of the quay and talked to the shatterling as he sometimes talked to his wife, but there was no reply. Not that he'd expected one. Either it would help him or it wouldn't. He had no control over it, or the link that bound him to it.

Lyra grew restless too. Standing on the back of the cart and shading her eyes with her forearm as she stared at the nest. Prowling along the quay, studying the burned-out granaries and godowns. Squatting at the edge of the sprawl of weed, telling the lucidor that the crabs seemed to be organised into packs or tribes.

'When two tribes meet they draw up opposing battle lines, but they don't fight. There's a lot of frantic signalling with claws and stingers, and then they all go their separate ways. We could learn a lot about avoiding conflict from them.'

At last, after the mirrors had set and the first stars were beginning to pop out in the sky above the ocean, the lucidor suggested that they should light a fire to signal their presence.

'If your boss and the others are holed up somewhere close they need to know where we are.'

'She isn't the only one you hope will see the fire, is she?' Lyra said.

'That's why, after I light it, you should find a good place to hide. If the others come, they will need to know what happened. And if they don't, you can make your way back to Ymr and tell the army.'

'And meanwhile you ride off with Remfrey He. I don't think so. Besides, if he's been watching this place, he'll know you didn't come here alone.'

'Then we will have to try something else,' the lucidor said, and drew Lyra's knife from his belt.

Lyra gave him a hard look. 'If you have to use a knife to win an argument, I don't reckon you have right on your side.'

'If I wanted to force you to do something, I wouldn't use a knife,' the lucidor said, and started to carve letters into the top board of the cart's load bed.

The horse, tethered to one of the tall wheels, began to step about. Lyra stroked its neck and spoke to it softly until it settled. 'Nice and succinct,' she said, when the lucidor had finished his work, 'but I think Orjen might have other ideas.'

'This isn't for her. It's for Cyf and Surmal. We should find some kindling before it gets too dark.'

Lyra followed him along the quay. 'What's your plan if it draws alters to us?'

'They haven't found us yet.'

'We haven't lit a fire yet.'

'Take this,' the lucidor said, and tossed the knife to her.

Lyra deftly caught it and said, 'I wish I could say it made me feel safer.'

'If it comes to it, we'll jump on the horse and make a run for it,' the lucidor said. 'The weed at the far end of this patch has dried out. It will make good kindling.'

They built a small pyre with dry weed fronds and shards from a crate the lucidor smashed with his staff, and Lyra used her flint to set light to it. The fire caught quickly, weed bladders popping, flames and sparks whirling up into the dusky air. The lucidor broke up another crate and he and Lyra sat by the fire and fed it as darkness settled around them.

At last, a small shadow detached from the base of the nest and started across the bay. The lucidor studied it through his spyglass. A boat very like the crabber of the two smugglers, painted blood-red by the lurid afterglow dying back from the western horizon. The burly figure of an alter warrior standing behind the wheel-house, and at the prow, posed like a figurehead, a tall slender man with arms folded across his chest and long white hair blowing in the warm breeze. Remfrey He, come at last to meet his visitors.

32

Vanity

During one of their conversations after his arrest Remfrey He had told the lucidor that at the very beginning of his career he had recruited a trio of map readers and fed them drugs to enhance their gifts, and in the short time before the drugs drove them insane they had rewritten the life maps of certain cells of his body, giving him immunity from common diseases and halting the biological and physiological changes associated with ageing.

'It also turned my hair white,' he said. 'A side effect my map readers failed to anticipate, although I prefer to think of it as a happy accident. The indelible mark of my uncommon genius and my rebirth as something more than human.'

The only thing that could be certain about Remfrey He was that nothing could be certain. He loved to embellish his notoriety, had a long history of laying false trails and concocting elaborate fictions about himself and what he called his little amusements. Still, seeing him for the first time since his sentence and exile, the lucidor wondered if there might be something to his claim that he had found a way to stop the ordinary ageing process, for he seemed utterly unchanged: a tall, lean, sharp-featured man, his white hair parted down the middle of his scalp and combed in two wings that flowed over his shoulders. His bushy white eyebrows, ends waxed in neat points, overhung sharp yellow eyes, their colour another modification of his life map. His coat of ten thousand nails was unfastened, displaying an unblemished white shirt and blush-pink corded trousers belted with a scarlet sash; some of the scales of his coat were enamelled in the same shade of scarlet, like random drops of blood.

As the boat motored out of the harbour towards the nest, he told the lucidor that the signal fire had been a foolish and unnecessary provocation that might have attracted stray alters. 'I knew you were there all along, and I was hoping that Orjen Starbreaker would join you. At least two of your friends were killed when you stirred up the alters at the pele tower, and please do not try to tell me otherwise. The alters brought parts of their bodies to the nest, mixed up with parts of a horse. I do hope that young Orjen wasn't a victim of that butchery. I was looking forward to meeting her.'

'By now she should be halfway back to Ymr,' the lucidor said. 'And reinforcements will be coming out to meet her, and deal with you and your alter friends.'

'Oh, I don't think that she will have run very far. Or that she has called for reinforcements. She has a small talent for map reading, and will be eager to see what I have achieved. You won't be able to appreciate it, but I know she will.'

'I don't see anything to appreciate, Remfrey. Judging by that jackpot at the pele tower, your attempt to gain control of the alters has been a complete failure.'

They were standing at the prow of the boat, Remfrey He balancing like a dancer, the lucidor clutching a stay, trying to ignore the alter warrior that stood behind him. Lyra was in the wheelhouse, with one of the map readers Remfrey He had turned and brought with him at the helm.

'I suppose things may have got a little out of hand at the tower,' Remfrey He said. 'I led several warriors there and set them in place with a simple chemical cue. The idea was to frighten you off should you decide to hole up there instead of coming to me directly. But the warriors attracted a small crowd of scavenging workers that must have come to believe that the tower was their nest, and when you came along they defended it with their customary vigour. That's how I lost one of my assistants, after an early experiment went a little too far. But once you have tricked the alters into accepting you as one of their own, as I have, you can come and go as you please, and shape and guide their communal gestalt by selecting and encouraging subtle idiosyncrasies in their behaviour. It's a mistake to think that every alter in a particular caste, worker, warrior, whatever, is identical to all the others. Far from it. What appears to be a rigidly monolithic culture harbours a marvellously subtle complexity that mitigates stagnation and enables the alters to survive and adapt to challenges and adversity. And only I hold the keys to controlling and exploiting it.'

Remfrey He's preachiness, his need to appear to be the master of every situation: that had not changed either.

'You lost control of the alters at the tower,' the lucidor said, 'one of the people you kidnapped has been killed, and now my little fire has forced your hand. I came here to rescue you, and it seems that I am just in time.'

'I am in no need of rescue, and certainly don't need the help of someone whose principles are based on simple-minded binary oppositions. Good and evil. Life and death. Truth and lies. Crime and punishment. It's the morality of a dull-witted child who clings to the comfort of the nursery because it refuses to confront or accept the buzzing blooming complexity of the real.'

'And yet I was able to force you into a situation where the only way to avoid arrest was to surrender yourself.'

They had last met more than eight years ago, but were already needling each other with easy familiarity. It sounds like an old married couple bickering about who was to blame after some trivial domestic upset, his wife had said, after the lucidor had described one of his interrogation sessions with Remfrey He, and she hadn't been far off the mark.

The man saying now, 'If that is what you still tell yourself, then you have learned nothing at all. In any case, my incarceration was only a temporary inconvenience. As I always knew it would be. Did you ever get any of my messages, by the way?'

'They were passed on, but I didn't bother to read them. After you were sent into exile your boasts and threats no longer mattered.'

'Then perhaps you did not receive my thanks for giving me the time and space to plan out my next hundred years or so,' Remfrey He said. 'So I will thank you now, and we can move on.'

'You will be measuring your life in days or hours unless you turn this boat towards Ymr.'

'You will change your mind after I have shown you what I have been up to,' Remfrey He said. 'You won't be able to understand much of it, of course, but Orjen Starbreaker's steward might be of some help. I imagine you saved her life, fought off numerous alters, and so on. The usual tedious heroics.'

'I couldn't leave her behind, if that's what you mean.'

'Ah yes. Your sentimentality. Another weakness. Do you know why I allowed you to catch me, all those years ago?'

'Don't bother telling me that it was part of your masterwork. I have already heard it, and you know I know it isn't true.'

'You lack any real intelligence or insight, but your single-minded stubbornness almost makes up for that. Plodding on as you do, bullheaded and relentless, long after most others would have given up. I made good use of it back then, and I knew I could rely on it now. Knew that you would follow me.'

'And I knew that you knew,' the lucidor said.

'But you came anyway. Because how could you not? And here we are. Welcome to my latest work of art,' Remfrey He said, posing with one hand on his hip and raising the other in an elegant flourish as the boat's motor cut out and they glided into a dark void beneath the outer edge of the alter women's nest.

The lucidor was glad that his old enemy hadn't lost his liking for the grand gesture, either. If he could cultivate and exploit the man's vanity, he just might be able to survive this.

33

Nest Scent

After the boat docked at an old stone-built jetty tucked between the wave-washed foundations of two of the nest's spires, Remfrey He produced a small bottle of darkly tinted glass. Holding it up between thumb and forefinger, telling the lucidor, 'Possession of the correct smell is the first stage of gaining acceptance. My little cocktail reproduces that essential nest scent – the chemical signature shared by its alters.'

The oily liquid had a sharp fruity odour. The lucidor and Lyra dabbed their faces and wrists with it, and Remfrey He's assistant, a gaunt young woman with a puff of curly black hair, kindled a lantern and led them down the jetty.

'It's like she's drugged,' Lyra told the lucidor. 'I couldn't get any sense of what they've been doing here. All she wanted to do was praise her master.'

'That's what Remfrey He does, when he turns people. Makes them believe that he is their god. As long as you stick close to me he won't be able to do the same to you.'

They climbed a short flight of slimy stone steps and followed Remfrey He and his assistant in single file down a narrow passage, with the alter warrior bringing up the rear, and emerged into twilight and a foul hot stink, part charnel house, part sewer, underlain by deep notes of fungal rot. The spires of the nest soared all around, rooted in mounds of compost, tapering towards points a hundred spans or more above. Helical ramps spiralled around them to platforms and spars and bulging outgrowths like giant galls, they were linked by a web of ropeways and nets and delicate arches of baserock, and a roof of taut black sails stretched between their tops. Dabs of green phosphorescence shone everywhere, and the whole dim shadowy structure was filled with a rustling murmur of activity that reminded the lucidor of doves roosting in the gum trees that grew around the oasis pools of his childhood home.

Remfrey He's assistant led the way through the midden covering the nest's floor to the old watchtower at the centre of the nest. Porters staggered along beneath toppling loads of leaves and grass and broken branches; workers spread fresh mulch across mounds of rotting vegetation or harvested mushrooms from oozing slopes or piles of rotting wood. One worker, emaciated and half-dead, stumbled across their path, dragging the corpse of another by its legs.

'The oldest and weakest workers spend their last days as fungus gardeners,' Remfrey He said. 'And when they reach the end of their short lives their bodies are quickly recycled. That will be your fate if you harm even the feeblest corpse carrier. My compound lends you the stink of the nest, but you must avoid every kind of confrontation.'

He waved a hand above his head, turning completely around. 'Isn't it wonderful? The purest expression of human social organisation imaginable. A great family in which every member ceaselessly labours for the good of the whole. The things I have learned!'

'I don't see anything human here,' the lucidor said.

It was like opening a file in the department's stacks and finding white ants swarming in the tunnels they had eaten through its pages.

'Oh, but it is all too human,' Remfrey He said. 'My research suggests that this is not the expression of alien traits introduced by the invasion. Instead, the invasion uncovered an archipelago of hidden traits baked into our life maps when the gods created us. A gift that will allow our children's children's children to survive in an ailing and much depleted world. Imagine nests like this spaced equally across our map, each nest in harmony with its neighbours, each harvesting a tithe from forests and grasslands. A utopia in which everyone knows their place and works for the common good, without war or strife, crime or hate.'

'And without freedom or love or individuality,' the lucidor said.

'By then, everyone who ever cared about any of that will be long dead,' Remfrey He said. 'Everyone but me, of course. I will have to find a role. Perhaps I will chronicle the alters' slow green thoughts and philosophies. Perhaps I will become their god emperor, and guide them to some presently unimaginable endpoint where their collective intelligence evolves into a new kind of being. That's why, when with my help the invasion is brought under control, some of these nests must be preserved. They contain the key to taking control of our destiny.'

'It sounds like one of your soma dreams,' the lucidor said.

'Oh, I gave that up before I escaped. When I was ready to embark on this gloriously new and wonderful project, and no longer needed the help of drugs to deal with dull, irritating people who believed that they could control me with their petty rules.'

'That's right. You killed them.'

Remfrey He ignored that. 'My work has been more successful than even I dared hope. And it is just the beginning. After finding the key to controlling the alters, I will discover the true nature of the invasion, and how to prevent it from laying waste to the entire map.'

'You need to talk to my boss,' Lyra said. 'She can give you all the resources you need.'

'If you came to offer me help, why did you bring my old friend with you?'

'He came along as an adviser,' Lyra said. 'No more, no less. And he won't have any say in what happens when we get you safely back to the Twin Cities.'

'But I am quite safe here,' Remfrey He said. 'I have discovered how to live amongst the alters, and how to communicate with them, too. Scent and pheromones play important roles, but the alters also have a language. Some might say it is rudimentary; I believe that it would be more accurate to say that it has been stripped to an essential core. Alarm calls. Calls to gather others to investigate something, or to help with a task. A tongue clicking sound of reassurance, shared by alters engaged in a mutual task.'

He stopped again, tilting his head and cupping a hand around one ear. The foul heat of the midden seemed to have invigorated him.

'Listen. Do you hear that background hum? It's the sum of a thousand tongue clicks. The sound of happiness and fulfilment. And then there are command phrases used by older workers to organise younger ones. Lift this, take that there, and so on. Like this,' Remfrey He said, and lifted a small metal tube to his lips and blew, then pointed at the lucidor.

The warrior moved like a striking snake, so quick the lucidor didn't have time to reach for his staff before he was seized and pinioned against the ridged carapace of the creature's chest.

'Don't worry,' Remfrey He said. 'It meant no more than "Take hold". As long as you stop struggling you won't be harmed. You have my word.'

The warrior held the lucidor in an unbreakable grip while Remfrey He's assistant unpinned his barrette and went through his pockets, confiscating his spyglass and folding knife, and took his staff and handed it to her master.

Remfrey He tried and failed to break the staff over his knee and gave it back to the assistant and told her to get rid of it. 'You need no badge of office here,' he told the lucidor, 'because you have no power over me or anyone else.'

The lucidor gave him his best stony stare, trying not to glance away as the assistant scurried off. He had been given that staff when he'd sworn his oath of office. Had carried it for more years than he cared to count. Practised with it almost every day. He had only used it when there had been no other choice, but even so it had saved his life many times over. It was as much a part of him as his hands or his heart, and now it was likely that he would never see it again.

'He is possessed by the foolish belief that he is my nemesis,' Remfrey He told Lyra. 'It blinds him to everything else. I can help you understand the true nature of the invasion and show you how to defeat it, but he thinks that I do not deserve to be walking up and down in the world. He would let everything burn, so long it satisfied his foolish ideas about justice and punishment.'

'Don't listen to him,' the lucidor said. 'Don't trust him. Don't believe anything he says.'

'I will show you such wonders,' Remfrey He told Lyra, and blew on his little whistle again, three quick shrill notes.

The warrior heaved the lucidor off his feet and marched across a carpet of mulch and mushrooms to the watchtower, climbing a spiral stair to a small room at the top, throwing him to the floor and stepping back and slamming the door with swift precision.

There was no handle or lock on the door, no furniture in the small square room, and the single slit window gave only a pinched view of the midden heaps. The lucidor sat on his folded coat with his back against a cold stone wall and reviewed his options, such as they were. Even if he could break out of his prison, he would still be stranded in the middle of a nest of alters controlled by Remfrey He, and couldn't count on Lyra's help. By now Remfrey He would have rendered her docile as his wretched assistant. He supposed that he was being kept prisoner because he might have some use as a hostage or as a go-between with the Patuan authorities, and because Remfrey He wanted to have some fun. Wanted to brag about his achievements and plans, gloat about his old enemy's humiliation. All the lucidor had to do was keep the man talking and wait for a moment of carelessness or inattention. Turn the tables and take him hostage. And if that didn't work out, then perhaps Cyf, Orjen and Surmal would find and act on the four words he had carved into the side of the cart.

In nest.
Call army.

34

Gestalt

It had been a long exhausting day. Despite his resolution to stay alert, the lucidor fell into a fitful doze, dreamed that he had somehow escaped from his cell and was rising bodiless through a dense weave of luminous threads shimmering between the stark shadows of the nest's spires. It was exquisitely complex, bustling with enigmatic activity. Little lights pulsing with common purpose shuttled along threads or clustered at knotty intersections, and the general glow flared and dimmed as bright waves of activity passed through it, clashing and merging and fading as patches of threads unravelled and reknotted. For a moment it seemed that the shifting constellations of lights and the waves and pulses and restless shimmer were about to resolve into something comprehensible, but then, like a flung stone that had reached the peak of its arc, the lucidor began to fall, plunging down through threads and lights towards a star that burned all alone in a black bubble, and jerked awake a moment before impact.

The cell was quiet and dark, and he was no longer alone.

'I know you're here,' he said. 'But I don't think it's like before, at places whose histories left imprints on the world. This time you're tapping into the activity of the nest. Into the – what did Remfrey He call it? Into the gestalt.'

There was no reply, but the lucidor kept talking, telling the shatterling that Remfrey He had taken him prisoner and now would be a good time to show him what it could do. Telling it about the ambush at the pele tower, his flight with Lyra to the abandoned fishing village, everything Remfrey He had said to him before he had been pitched into this cell.

'It looks like I am safely locked away,' he said, 'but I'm old and cunning and know more about Remfrey He than anyone else. He can't use his gift to turn me, so he has to find some other way of asserting his superiority. And when he comes back to taunt and humiliate me, I'll find something I can use against him. Some opening. Some slip. His vanity was his downfall before, and will be again. And if you don't help me, if I have to get out of this by myself, we will be done, you and I. You'll have to find someone else to help you save the world.'

The shatterling did not reply or show itself, and at last the lucidor, all talked out, fell into another restless doze, and woke to thin grey dawn light falling through the narrow window. He plaited his hair into a loose pigtail and began a thorough inspection of the walls of his little prison, and at last discovered a small stone that shifted slightly under his fingertips. He snapped a button from his coat in two, started to chip at the mortar around the stone with the point of one of the halves. It took him several hours; his fingers were bruised and his fingernails broken when at last he eased it from the wall. It was roughly triangular, about half the size of his hand. He was sharpening an edge on one of the floor's flagstones when he heard footsteps and voices, and tucked the stone under his folded coat just before the door swung back.

The alter warrior, or another exactly like it, stepped inside, followed by Cyf, who set two bowls on the floor. Crudely woven from grass and glazed with some kind of thick clear resin or hardened slime, one contained a slippery mess of limp mushrooms, the other a shallow puddle of water. The lucidor hadn't had anything to drink since his capture. He imagined the first cool sweet sip bathing his parched tongue, knew he couldn't risk it.

Cyf retreated to the doorway and said, 'If you want to eat and drink do it now. I have to take them away when I leave.'

'Did you surrender, or did he catch you?' the lucidor said.

Cyf wouldn't meet the lucidor's gaze. He was stooped and unshaven and his mouth worked silently for a moment before he said, spitting out the words as if they were poisoned seeds, 'You're the prisoner. I'm his guest.'

The lucidor was pierced by a pang of sorrow and pity. 'And the others – Orjen and Surmal. Are they also Remfrey He's guests?'

'Orjen is talking with Remfrey. Technical stuff about the alters I don't really understand.'

'And Surmal?'

'We saw your fire, in the fishing village. We came looking for you, and found a gang of alter warriors instead. They had killed your horse and eaten part of it, and when they came towards us Surmal didn't understand that they wanted to help. Wanted to bring us to their master. He killed two before the rest got him.'

Remfrey He had set a trap. Of course he had.

The lucidor said, 'Did you see the message I left? Did Orjen call the army?'

Cyf's mouth twitched and made shapes, then he said in a rush, 'I drew my staff and told her to run. But they knocked me down and caught her, and brought us here.'

'You may think you're a guest, Cyf, but you're just as much a prisoner as me. We need to help each other,' the lucidor said.

'Remfrey He told us what he has been doing here. What he knows. He wants to go back to Delos-Chimr. Wants to share what he has discovered. Wants to do more work. But on his terms.'

'Were you alone with him, when he told you this? It may have been in a dark room, with a candle burning between him and you. Do you remember something like that? Do you remember his voice, and what he said? Think, Cyf. Think. You have been turned, but it can be undone.'

'I know what he can do. I have training. If he tried to make me to do things, I'd know.'

'One of his best and most dangerous tricks is to convince people that the things he wants them to do are their own idea,' the lucidor said, the last of his hope ravelling away. 'Think, man. Try to remember what he told you. Try to remember what we came here to do.'

It was no good. Cyf's mouth made more shapes, and he said in a sudden rush, 'He showed us everything. The brood queens and the nurseries. Workers turned into water barrels, with bellies swollen so huge the skin is transparent. And the alates – alters who leave the nest and mate and found a new nest, something no one has seen before. It turns out that there are alter men, but they are small small small, and attached to their alate brides. And the brides are swimmers. That's why the nests are by the sea. The brides swim to a new location, and baserock spires begin to grow up through the ground while the brides are raising the first litter of workers. Remfrey doesn't yet know how they manipulate the baserock, but he knows much else. He knows where they came from. Where the invasion started. We're taking him back to Delos-Chimr so he can help the army.'

'I see. And what of his plans for me?'

'He says that it's time you faced up to everything you have done. Time to take your punishment. And he told me to tell you that he's going to give a demonstration. Before we leave. A demonstration of what he can do. As long as we can use what he's found to destroy the alters and push back the invasion, save tens of thousands of lives, save civilisation here on this map and maybe others, does it matter what he wants in return?'

'And the people he killed to get here,' the lucidor said. 'Did he persuade you to forget them?'

'If you don't want to eat or drink I'll take it away,' Cyf said.

'If the water isn't poisoned it's probably drugged. Remember how Remfrey He used to treat his followers back in the day? A light dose of soporific to keep them docile. And those mushrooms are grown on corpses, just like Remfrey He's ideas and his so-called reputation. Tell him that, Cyf. And tell him that if he wants me to know what he knows, he should come and talk to me himself.'

When he was alone again, the lucidor sat down and began to sharpen the stone he'd prised from the wall against the stone flags of the floor. Working methodically until at last he had a serviceable edge.

Then there was nothing left to do but wait.

35

His Idea of Fun

It began just before arcset. A discordant symphony of short shrill whistles from near and far that brought the lucidor to the slit window. In the reddening light he saw little figures running and dancing across the midden heaps. No, not dancing. Fighting. Alters fighting alters. Wrestling, bludgeoning, biting. Two warriors slashing at each other tirelessly, drenched in blood. Another warrior toppled beneath a frantic swarm of workers. High above, a warrior charged down a walkway slung between two of the nearest spires, knocking smaller figures out into the air. Higher still, two figures tumbled from a net, struggling with each other all the way to the ground.

The lucidor's first thought was that the nest was under attack from one of its neighbours; then he remembered that the shatterling had shown him how every nest was linked to all the others, like neighbourhoods in a city stretched along the coast, and remembered Orjen telling Cyf that it was best to think of alter women territory as one big nest. No, this mass slaughter was no attack. Somehow, Remfrey He had turned the nest against itself. A demonstration of his mastery. His idea of fun.

The narrow shafts of mirrorlight slicing between the sails of the nest's roof grew redder and dimmer, the demented whistling calls grew fewer and fainter, and the fighting began to die back. The lucidor counted more than twenty bodies in his limited field of view, could see several wounded alters on their backs or bellies, feebly kicking. A warrior that had been smashing its head against the flank of a spire with obstinate persistence, perhaps because it could find no other enemy but itself, stepped back and shivered in a full-body fit and keeled over. Two workers locked head to head in a meadow of trampled mushrooms waltzed in slow circles like a pair of weary drunks. They were still at it when darkness fell and Remfrey He at last came for the lucidor.

He carried a stick that glowed with the same green phosphorescence as the myriad little dabs that outlined the nest's spires. It gave him the look of a corpse animated by malicious good humour and glistened on the ridged chest plate of the alter warrior standing in the doorway and set two green stars in the unfathomable pools of its eyes.

'I see that you didn't manage to kill all of them,' the lucidor said.

'The warrior belongs to me, not to the nest. I hope you enjoyed the entertainment.'

'Not especially.'

'Well, it wasn't meant for you. It was for young Orjen. A proof of concept. And now that she has seen what I can do, I can return to Delos-Chimr, and deserved acclamation. You, on the other hand, will die here, while trying to escape. Killed by one of the last survivors of this little civil war because the nest scent I gave you wore off. Such a shame. Such a pity. I shall miss you, but only a little, and not for very long.'

'If that's what you are going to tell Orjen, she may well not believe you.'

'Ah, but she does. You see, I have already told her about your demise.'

'You turned her, I suppose. Like you turned Cyf.'

'As a matter of fact I didn't. I have no doubt that the army will test her when she gets back to Delos-Chimr and tells her story. They will find no trace of my influence, and know she is telling the truth.'

'Then she'll find out that you lied. Just as she will find out that you have lied to her about your ability to control the alters.'

'How can you doubt me, after you have just seen for yourself what I can do? I suppose your obsession with me, your trite and immutable judgement of my character, prevents you from seeing the truth. It's funny, isn't it? You're a good man who has done some questionable things to further what you believe to be a just and noble cause, and I have found a way of saving the world even though my motives were, shall we say, sometimes less than pure. How does your childish binary morality account for that?'

'I'd say that you spoil everything you touch. That in your hands everything fair becomes foul.'

'I'm sure you saw the fields that once fed Ymr, on your way here. Just like those fields, the whole world and everything in it is used up and dying. The creator gods, and the fragmentary aspects of those gods who rode the first of us for the pleasure of being incarnate once more, are long gone. The old laws, forged in the echo of their departure in a vain attempt to preserve the world as it once was, no longer have any meaning. Fair is foul and foul is fair, and we are free to do as we will.'

'We have talked about this before. I wasn't persuaded or impressed by your nihilism then, and I'm not now.'

'Your belief in justice led you to this. My so-called nihilism, on the other hand, has lent me the discipline and will to overcome all obstacles in my quest to understand the alters. You will be forgotten. And I will be rightly celebrated as the man who turned back the invasion and took the war against it to its root.'

'The alter nests are linked to each other, but they are also linked to something else. Something across the World Ocean, to the north and west. Is that where you want to go?'

'Did your former colleague tell you that?' Remfrey He said. 'I suppose I may have let slip something or other along those lines to him.'

'I knew it before I came here,' the lucidor said. 'Tell me why you want to go there. Tell me what you want to find.'

'Have you not yet learned that you cannot trick me with your silly mind games? How amusing it was, after I let myself be arrested, to watch you try to understand me, and brush off your feeble attempts to trap me into revealing more than I intended to reveal. I didn't fall for that then and I won't fall for it now. I have other kinds of fun to look forward to.'

Remfrey He flourished a small metal tube, blew three notes on it, pointed. The warrior shouldered past him, and the lucidor stepped inside the spread of its arms and jammed the sharpened stone into its eye. The warrior shrilled and reared backwards, clawing at its face, and the lucidor grabbed Remfrey He and dragged him out of the cell and kicked the door shut.

'I won't plead with you,' Remfrey He said calmly, as the lucidor pushed him down the steep spiral of the stairs. 'But I want you to think of the consequences. Not for me, or for you, but for the Free State. Because if the invasion is not checked it will spread there, too, and everywhere else. Assuming, of course, that it has not already conquered other maps. Think of that. All the other maps in the world may have already fallen to the new flesh. We might be the last people, fighting the last battle. Would you really put that in peril to assuage your hypertrophied sense of justice? Do you not think that you might be wrong?'

'You said that you weren't going to plead, but that sounds exactly like pleading to me,' the lucidor said.

He was holding the luminous stick high, ready for some kind of ambush. A warrior, a mob of workers, Cyf. His escape had been too easy. Remfrey He wasn't finished with him, would have some kind of backup plan. He always did.

'Even if you do manage to get me all the way back to the Free State,' Remfrey He said, 'I am too important to be kept in prison. The Patuan army and government will do everything they can to win my return, and when it realises what is at stake the government of the Free State will swiftly accede. But if you let me go, I can strike a deal with the Patuans, make sure that you won't be sent back to the Free State and arrest and disgrace. I can even help you find work.'

'I am doing what needs to be done. I don't need your help.'

They were near the bottom of the steps now.

'There is one small thing I should have warned you about,' Remfrey He said. 'An accident I didn't have time to clear up.'

The lucidor hustled him through the doorway and saw two people sprawled close by. Cyf, and Remfrey He's assistant. The assistant lay on her back, a look of surprise not yet faded from her dead face. Cyf was lying face down in a puddle of blood, blood that looked black in the green light of the luminous stick, a pistol close to his hand. The bodies of a warrior and three workers lay a little way beyond.

'Your colleague tried to free you in the confusion of my demonstration,' Remfrey He said. 'He shot my assistant, as you can see, and that attracted a small pack of feral alters.'

'I don't think so. Cyf wasn't carrying that pistol when he visited me, and he had used up all his ammunition when the alters attacked us at the pele tower.'

The lucidor was looking all around, but in the dim green glow could see nothing moving amongst mounds of detritus or the walkways and nets strung between the spires.

'Then perhaps you killed him,' Remfrey He said. 'You tried to stop him. There was a fight, a struggle for that pistol . . .'

The lucidor pulled the man close, forearm braced across his throat, thumb against his left eye. 'I don't need a stone to blind you, or a weapon to kill you. Where are Orjen and Lyra?'

'Still very much alive. I need young Orjen, and she needs me.'

The lucidor pressed a little harder. He could feel the ball of Remfrey He's eye moving under its lid. 'Where?'

'I asked them to wait by my boat while I tidied up after my little demonstration.'

'They had better be there. Lead the way.'

'Of course. I am very interested to see how this will turn out.'

The spires and their faint constellations reared silent and still above the midden. Child-sized bodies curled up here and there, carbon shadows in the green glow. No movement anywhere but the slow waltz of two workers locked head to head and feebly clawing at each other's backs, ignoring the lucidor and Remfrey He as they went past.

The lucidor held Remfrey He's luminous stick like a truncheon and pushed the man ahead of him, hustling him down the narrow passage that led to the sea-washed vault under the nest. When they emerged at the far end, a bright light flared and pinned them, and figures moved behind the glare. Human figures coming forward, three, four, five of them, aiming pistols and long guns. The lucidor stood his ground and called Orjen's name, was answered by a command to surrender.

Remfrey He casually raised his hands, saying, 'I quite forgot in the excitement. Orjen used her godspeaker to call the army before my warriors caught her, and the army sent a ship. It arrived just before I came to visit you. I know what they want from me, but what, I wonder, will they do with you?'

PART THREE
New Maps

36

Open Sentence

Loya Heaventree had been born into a prosperous mercantile family which lost its home and its livelihood after it was displaced by the invasion; she was living with her parents, grandmother and three sisters in two rented rooms in a tower block in Delos when a routine test uncovered her gift for reading and rewriting life maps. She spent a year in an accelerated apprenticeship, joined the army's research and development division, and shortly afterwards was assigned to the team detailed to support Remfrey He's research. When she died in the alter nest Remfrey He had infiltrated, she was just twenty years old.

The lucidor learned of her name after he was brought back to Delos-Chimr and formally arrested. The army's investigative team accepted Remfrey He's claim that Annor Skychild, the other map reader he'd turned, had been killed by alters during an early experiment, but the lucidor had to stand before a military tribunal to answer for the deaths of Loya Heaventree and Lucidor Cyf.

The trial was held in camera. Three senior army officers presiding. There were no witnesses for the defence and the lucidor was not called to speak. Nor did he ask to. There was no point. Everything had been decided before the tribunal had been convened; nothing he could say would alter the outcome. The proceedings marched forward with crisp precision, concluding that Loya Heaventree had been killed when the lucidor and Cyf had attempted to escape during Remfrey He's demonstration of his absolute control over the alter nest, and while it wasn't clear whether Cyf or the lucidor was responsible for her death, both were deemed equally culpable. The tribunal refused the Free State ambassador's request for extradition, the senior presiding officer told the lucidor that the usual death penalty would be waived and he would instead serve an open sentence, to be reviewed once a year, and that was that.

He was imprisoned in a villa in the hills to the west of Delos-Chimr, within the bounds of an army base. There were always six soldiers on watch, and a veteran coronet, Kasian Lightborn, accompanied the lucidor on the walks he took around the perimeter of the villa's grounds and while he worked in his little vegetable garden, and drip-fed him news of the decimation of alter nests along the north-east coast and the progress in fitting out the *First Pilgrim*, the small ark which had been commandeered for an expedition to the nearest neighbouring map, Simud, identified by Remfrey He as the origin of the invasion.

Kasian Lightborn was a portly, balding man in his middle years, with an impressive white moustache and a dry sense of humour. He was also a widower, like the lucidor, and the lucidor didn't think it was a coincidence, reckoned the man was an intelligence officer charged with befriending him and extracting any information he might have withheld. As he had. For although he had given his interrogators a detailed account of his conversations with Remfrey He, and the army had followed up his suggestion that the man had left at least one informant behind after he escaped (it turned out that a clerk in the Shadow Service had committed suicide on the day the expedition left for Ymr and points north: there was no hard proof that Remfrey had turned her, but the coincidence was suggestive), the lucidor had carefully edited the story about how he made his way across Patua to Delos-Chimr, omitting the help that the landers had given him and the help he'd given them, and his encounter with the shatterling and the link it had forged and the visions it had shown him.

The shatterling hadn't reached out to him since the alter nest. Perhaps it had lost interest in him after his arrest and incarceration, or perhaps it was busy elsewhere, especially if it had found a way to tap into the alter nest network. Or perhaps nothing of any significance had ever happened on the site of this small, shabby villa at the edge of the Twin Cities; there was no imprint it could use to conjure up visions and phantoms. In any case, the lucidor welcomed the silence. He'd had enough of being haunted and treated like a puppet. Was glad to be relieved of the burden of the shatterling's ambition.

He believed that the Patuans were holding him because they might need his help if Remfrey He tried to trick them again. As he almost certainly would, for deceit and a liking for grandiose mayhem were indelibly printed in the man's psyche. There was some small chance that the lucidor's thraldom might then be of some use, even though the shatterling's revelations about the connections between alter nests and something far across the World Ocean had been pre-empted by Remfrey He, who claimed to have observed and translated so-called compass dances inside the nests. Meanwhile, the lucidor was guardedly cautious in his conversations with his guards and especially with Kasian Lightborn. Even so, the lucidor and Kasian grew to understand and like each other, and shared a little of their experiences of loss and grief. Kasian's wife, also a coronet, had been badly injured by a roadside bomb while fighting rebels in the south. She had been strong, Kasian told the lucidor, had lasted two weeks before she succumbed to her injuries. Although he had since remarried and had two young daughters, he still thought of her every day.

In turn, the lucidor told Kasian about the disaster in which his wife, Deme, had been killed. She was a civil engineer specialising in water conservation and had been sent upriver into the mountains to supervise remedial work on an old dam. It should have been a routine project, but winter rains had been earlier and heavier than usual, and Deme and eight other engineers were swept away when a pulse of floodwater overtopped the dam and caused it to collapse. The lucidor had seen the devastation afterwards. Had insisted on going there. The flood had churned downstream for a dozen leagues, overwhelming a farming village and burying fields and orchards in mud and boulders; a river was still running in full spate through the remains of the dam and the gorge beyond when the lucidor arrived. More than a hundred people were missing. Most of them, including Deme and the other engineers, were never found.

'It must have been hard to come to terms with that,' Kasian said. 'I was lucky, if you can call it luck. I was given compassionate leave so I could be with my wife. But when there's not even a body . . .'

'I knew she was dead, but for a long time I couldn't believe it,' the lucidor said. 'I put her favourite tablet and a sheaf of her sketches and drawings in an urn, and interred it in her family's vault in Liberty City's old cemetery. I would go there sometimes, and talk to her.'

His wife's urn had been set next to the urn containing the ashes of their daughter, but he wasn't going to tell Kasian that, or tell him that Deme had nearly died when their daughter had been stillborn, and the operation which had saved her life had left her unable to have another child.

Kasian nodded. 'I did that, too. Told her what was happening, how I was.'

'It's a peaceful place, the old cemetery. Gave me space to think about things. To come to terms with the idea that she wasn't coming back.'

Deme had haunted their apartment. When he had returned from the devastated dam, her clothes and tablets had still been there, just as she'd left them. The furniture they'd bought. The bedroom she'd painted in cool shades of blue. The lucidor had slept in a chair in the parlour, or up on the flat roof of the apartment house. Never in the bed they had shared. And then he'd had to leave, because the apartment was too big for one person and others had need of it, and he had sold most of what he still thought of as their possessions, and moved into the Number Eighteen Hostel for Single Men.

He had resigned from the department the year before, had been working in the docks, supervising the loading and unloading of river barges. He was working there still, six years later, when his old boss reached out and told him that Remfrey He had been sent to Patua. He'd visited the vault and told Deme about his plans before he left, knowing that he was really trying to justify the mission to himself, knowing that if she had still been alive she would have done her best to talk him out of it.

'I believed then that Remfrey He was too dangerous to be allowed to walk up and down in the world,' he told Kasian. 'And I believe it still.'

'You needn't worry. The army has him under strict supervision now.'

'That didn't do much good the last time, did it?' the lucidor said.

The *First Pilgrim*, with Remfrey He and a small menagerie of alter women to guide the way with their compass dances, set sail for Simud a little over five hundred days after the lucidor's trial and incarceration. A hundred and eighty days later, less than halfway to its destination, the ark reported the sighting of the coast of an uncharted island or map; three days after that it sent a brief message saying that it had run aground and discovered an alter woman nest, and then fell silent.

When Kasian Lightborn gave him the news, the lucidor asked the man to pass a message to Orjen Starbreaker. Army interrogators came to the villa instead, asking the same questions they had asked before the lucidor's trial, asking him if he remembered anything new about his conversations with Remfrey He, going through the old transcripts word by word, looking for hidden meanings.

'I warned you that something like this might happen,' the lucidor said. 'It gives me no pleasure to say that you should have listened to me.'

'We have no proof that Remfrey He had anything to do with the loss of communication,' the senior interrogator said.

'But you think it likely. That's why you're here.'

'We are investigating every possibility,' the interrogator said. 'Two hundred souls sailed with the *First Pilgrim*. If you know something that might help us understand what happened to them, it would be noted at the next review of your sentence. You might even be allowed to return to the Free State.'

'I'll give it some thought,' the lucidor said, reckoning that the interrogators would return with better terms if they really needed his help. Instead, Orjen came to the villa ten days later, turning up unannounced, telling him that she had tried to see him long before everything blew up, but the army had turned down her requests.

'You have cut your hair,' she said.

'The army shaved it off after I was sentenced. I've grown it out since then.'

The lucidor had brushed it back and tied it in a short ponytail, was dressed in army issue denim shirt and trousers.

'Why don't we take a stroll around the grounds,' he said. 'I can show you my vegetable garden, and you can tell me about the deal you've brought. I mean, that is why the army allowed you to come here, isn't it?'

He picked a handful of pea pods and shared them with Orjen as they walked down the long slope of parched lawn, and she told him that if he knew anything that would help to recapture Remfrey He the army would agree to commute his sentence and allow him to return to the Free State.

'Where I will be arrested for conspiracy,' the lucidor said. 'It doesn't seem to be any kind of bargain.'

'I'm told that you will have to stand trial, but you will receive a minimal prison term. Three years, less time already served here. It's shorter than the sentences given to the Free State politicians who agreed to let Remfrey He help us.'

'For acting against the will of the people. My friend told me about it,' the lucidor said, glancing at Kasian Lightborn, who was walking a few paces behind. 'If the army is planning to capture Remfrey He, it must also be planning a second voyage. Is there another seaworthy ark? Or have you rediscovered the secret of flying machines?'

'There's no secret to building a flying machine,' Orjen said, 'only problems to be solved. Philosophers and mechanics working for the army's Dark Research Unit are developing a prototype right now, and are also trying to recreate the ancient ballistic machines that could shoot out of the atmosphere and come down thousands of leagues away . . . What's so funny?'

'The importance you and Remfrey He place in those old stories and legends about the magic of the First People.'

'It only seems like magic because we have fallen so far from what we once were,' Orjen said. 'The Dark Research Unit has also built a new kind of cargo ship that can evade or resist the attacks of sea monsters. It's called the *Resolute Mind*, it's small and fast and mostly powered by mirrorlight, and there's a plan to use it to search for the *First Pilgrim* and Remfrey He.'

'How long will this wonder of practical philosophy take to reach the *First Pilgrim*?'

'About seventy days, if all goes well. If it isn't attacked by some monster or swamped or sunk by a freak wave, or a storm. There are huge waves in the open ocean, and huge storms. That's why the arks that travelled between maps were so big, and the *Resolute Mind* is about the size of a coastal cutter.'

'But you want to go, all the same.'

'When Remfrey He made his deal with the army, a deal my father and I helped to broker, he insisted that I should not be allowed to have anything to do with planning and preparations for the *First Pilgrim*'s expedition. I was refused a place on it, too, and Remfrey He made sure that I knew he'd had a hand in that.'

'The man has a long history of abusing those who have given him any kind of help. It's his way of maintaining the fiction that he is beholden to no one. Don't take it personally.'

'I tried not to. Fortunately, I found other work of equal importance: supervising production of the pheromones we have been using to destroy alter nests. Remfrey He didn't lie about any of that. And if he didn't lie about the source of the invasion, we might be able to find a way of putting an end to the rest of its manifestations. The *First Pilgrim* may not have reached Simud, but it found something out there. Something strange and unexpected. A mystery that needs to be properly unriddled. So to answer your question, yes, of course I want to go. I want it more than anything I have ever wanted.'

Orjen didn't seem to have been much changed by their adventures. Still the same ardent single-minded passion for philosophical inquiry, the same bold frankness. She was dressed in a long white shirt that hung to the knees of her yellow trousers, and her face was shaded by a wide-brimmed straw hat.

'Remfrey He lies as easily as he breathes, but even he sometimes finds the truth useful,' the lucidor said. 'And telling the truth about his work with the alters certainly got him what he wanted.

It turned what could have been a grave embarrassment to your army and government into something they could call a success. The human cost of that, the people he murdered, the lives he ruined, was forgiven and forgotten. Swept aside. But the people he killed are still dead, and the people he turned will never be the same again. There has to be an accounting for that.'

'If we find him, and if he was responsible for what happened to the *First Pilgrim*, he will definitely have to answer for everything he has done,' Orjen said. 'The problem is, we aren't certain if that message had any truth to it. We don't know anything about this mysterious island, and we don't know if the *First Pilgrim* really ran aground, or how badly it was damaged if it did. None of the old charts show an island there; some believe that there is no island at all. We can't even be certain that the *First Pilgrim* is where it is supposed to be. Godspeakers enable instant communication across any distance, so there is no way of telling how far away it was when that last message was sent, or from which direction it came. It's possible that Remfrey He took over the ship and changed course and headed for some other destination. That's why, if you want him found and brought to justice, you must take the army's deal, and give up everything you know about him but haven't yet told us.'

They walked a little way in silence, Kasian Lightborn padding behind them. The drowsy air under the close ranks of sugar pines was packed with late summer heat. Soft carpets of fallen needles. Clumps of ferns growing on and around the decaying trunks of fallen trees. A distant crackle of gunfire from the base's firing range.

The lucidor said, 'If I help you, I don't want to be sent back to the Free State. I want to go with you, on this ship of yours.'

'I hardly think the army will allow it.'

'I think you can persuade them. You and your father and your father's friend the general, and all his other influential friends and allies. Do I have your word that you will try your best?'

'It depends on what you know.'

'It's not just what I know,' the lucidor said. 'Will you swear to do all you can to help me?'

'On my life,' Orjen said.

The lucidor stopped walking and turned to Kasian, asked him if he had heard that.

'Every word,' the coronet said.

'And you will be a witness, if a witness is needed.'

'It's what I'm paid for.'

The lucidor walked on, with Orjen and Kasian following. When the villa came in sight beyond the edge of the pine wood, he said, 'To begin with, I know that Remfrey He sent that last message. That little tease about an alter nest is an unmistakable signature. He found something out there, he wants an audience for his work, as we know only too well, and he almost certainly knows about this new ship of yours. Knows that the army will send a rescue party.'

'That's good to know, but it might not be enough to get you a berth,' Orjen said.

'I also know that Remfrey He didn't lie about the origin of the alters and the rest of the invasion. Or at least, the direction it lies in. He worked it out from the alters' compass dance, or had some other way of calculating it. And I, out of stupid pride, I confirmed it when I was his prisoner in the nest.'

'How could you have confirmed it?' Orjen said. 'How could you have known?'

'Because I was shown it directly,' the lucidor said, and began to explain how he had first encountered the shatterling, deep in its pit under an old abandoned city on an island off the southern shore of the Big Island.

Orjen said, 'I know the place. A branch of my family, on my mother's side, has title to it.'

'Was their sigil three peacocks set in a triangle?'

Orjen nodded.

'They should have taken better care of their people,' the lucidor said.

'I suppose it must be a coincidence. Strange, but not impossible. The world is very large, but our map, especially the habitable part of it, is very small.'

'I hope it is,' the lucidor said. 'For otherwise I have had far less agency in this story than I believed.'

It took a little while to tell the rest. How he had helped the landers overcome the diggers. How the shatterling had established a permanent link with him, and what it had shown him. Its claim that it wanted to put an end to the invasion. By the time he was done, he and Orjen and Kasian were sitting in the shade of the villa's veranda.

'You should have told me this before,' Orjen said.

'You would have thought me crazy.'

'I am not certain that you aren't.'

'There are ways of proving that everything I have told you is true.'

'I hope there are, because I will need some hard evidence in order to sell it to the army.'

'The landers will tell you about the diggers, and what they were trying to dig up,' the lucidor said.

He knew that he was betraying Alcnos and her people, but told himself that it was for a higher cause and hoped that they would understand why it was necessary.

'I want you to promise that whoever you send to question them treats them as kindly as they treated me,' he told Orjen. 'Also, assuming that Mirim ap Mirim didn't steal it, you should be able to find a traveller's account of the shatterling's activity in the Imperial Library, here in Delos-Chimr. And perhaps your family knows a thing or two about it, too.'

'It's one thing to prove that this shatterling exists,' Orjen said. 'Quite another to show that it is linked to you.'

'I will submit to any tests the army's doctors want to make,' the lucidor said.

Kasian said, 'I know someone who can organise that.'

'The shatterling hasn't reached out to me for a while, but if the tests don't get its attention, I know something that will,' the lucidor said.

Alcnos and the other landers wouldn't be happy about it, and he didn't like to think about how the shatterling might react, but couldn't think of any other way of forcing it to cooperate.

Orjen said, 'Even if it's true, the army still might not let you join the rescue expedition.'

'I'm relying on you to keep your word. Remind them that I captured Remfrey He for them, and can easily do it again.'

'He claimed that he was planning to surrender.'

'Maybe so. But I made sure that he did.'

37

World Wanderers

The *Resolute Mind* quickly outstripped its escort after leaving port, passed through the outer reef into the open ocean an hour later, and by the morning of the next day was out of sight of land. The lucidor scarcely noticed. He spent the first five days of the voyage horribly seasick, mostly confined to the bunk in his tiny cabin as the ship heaved and shuddered through an endless succession of waves rolling out of the north like an army of hills on the march.

When he could manage it, he hauled himself along a ropeway strung in the shifting, bucking passageway to the mess, what they called the roundtable, shared by the petty officers and marines. He was able to keep down a few bites from discs of edible plastic, or hardtack, made palatable by dipping in water or green chai, but everything else came back up again. He was exhausted by his nausea but found it hard to sleep. He would doze off and be woken by something shifting or rattling in his cabin, or a loose door banging somewhere outside, or shouts and the tramp of feet in the passageway, and lay awake for hours as his bunk rocked to and fro and his stomach bumped against his throat, listening to the battering smash of water against the ship's hull and the vibration of the ship's motors, relentless as his heartbeat.

And then one day he woke and found that the movement beneath him was smoother and gentler, the floor of the cabin was more or less horizontal, and his incapacitating nausea had faded to a faint queasiness. Hollowed out by exhaustion, it took him a good while longer than it should have to shave with the army issue razor and fingercomb his hair and fasten his ponytail with the leather barrette he'd bought when Kasian Lightborn and Orjen had taken him shopping for clothes and necessaries, and he had to sit on the edge of his bunk for a minute or so before he was ready to pull on some clothes and try the round door of his cabin.

He had been squared away in the crew quarters at the stern, to minimise the effects of his gift on the expeditionary company's map readers and pair of scriers, who were quartered with the ship's officers in the front, or bow. The bare passageway drummed with the vibration of the motors and squares of light shifted to and fro on its white-planked floor – the companionways to the deck above had been opened. The lucidor unsteadily hauled himself up a short ladder into blinding mirrorlight, had to blink away tears before he could see, beyond the hump of the propeller shroud and the flying bridge mounted above it, that almost everyone on board seemed to be up on the foredeck. Civilians strolling about, sailors using long-handled mops to clean salt from the black panels that rose in tiers on either side, two officers taking some kind of sighting at the bow.

The *Resolute Mind*'s streamlined spindle-shaped hull was constructed from planks of pressure-formed ironwood. Originally, it had been driven by a radial propeller revolving around its waist, but that had proved to throw up too much spray and create excessive drag, and now the ship was fitted with conventional screws mounted on a pair of stern shafts, and its radial propeller was used only for close manoeuvres. Powered by over a thousand motors that had been scavenged from runabouts and which used electricity generated by arrays of light-collecting panels, the stern screws churned up a V-shaped wake as they pushed the ship faster than any built in centuries: at top speed it could cover fifteen leagues every hour. All around, the ocean stretched out towards a hazy horizon that seemed by some trick of the eye to circle above the ship, as if it was a toy crossing the bottom of a gigantic saucer. Here was proof that the great globe spun by the creator gods around the Heartsun really was an ocean world, dotted here and there by insignificant clusters of stone and dirt.

Some heretics claimed that the creator gods had made human beings as an afterthought; that their favoured creatures were the leviathans which mostly lived in the frigid seas around the floating caps of ice in the north and south, sieving the smallest animals from seawater or hunting monsters in the canyons of the deepest parts of the ocean. Some were so large and lived at such a slow pace that vegetation brought by the feet of seabirds grew on their backs while they slumbered on the surface of the ocean, and sailors had been known to mistake them for islands and anchor beside them and go ashore, only to find the ground sinking beneath their feet when the leviathan, disturbed by their tread or stung by their campfires, stirred awake and dived, and with a casual flip of its tail smashed their ship to flinders and left them to drown.

As yet there was no sign of any of those fabled giants, or of any monsters quickened by the invasion. The ocean all around the *Resolute Mind* was an empty desert of water under the pure deep blue of the sky, with just a hint of cloud directly ahead, and the arc of mirrors burning in the western quarter.

The lucidor walked to the stern, feeling the deck shift under his feet like the muscles of a restless animal, and looked out at the spreading V of the wake and the two huge white birds hung above it, bigger than any he'd ever seen before, their narrow wings easily a dozen spans across and beating slowly and steadily as the birds matched the ship's speed.

A little later, Orjen and Lyra climbed out of one of the companionways and joined him. Lyra was pale around the eyes and as unsteady as the lucidor, but Orjen claimed that she suffered more from being confined to quarters than from seasickness, and explained that they were presently crossing one of the bands of quieter water over one of the ocean's deep troughs.

'The old charts claim that it is more than four thousand leagues wide, and as much as two leagues deep. Imagine what it must look like on the inner side of the world – a huge mountain range, or a map as big as any on the outside.'

'And more rolling water and misery on the far side,' Lyra said. She was wearing her usual denim jacket, and had clipped her hair close to her scalp.

'We won't reach the far side for days and days,' Orjen said, and gave the lucidor a serious appraising look. 'Now you are recovered, do you have any sense of our destination, or of the shatterling?'

'Not yet. What's the latest news about the engineers?'

'The same as yesterday. I am told they are due to depart for the Land any day now.'

Orjen had discovered the old traveller's tale that had set Mirim ap Mirim on her quest, and several documents in her family's archives that corroborated it; an army investigative team dispatched to the Land had interviewed Alcnos and other landers, confirming that a crew of bandits had been digging up something ancient and active buried deep under an ancient temple; and army doctors had charted patterns of what they called significant anomalous activity in the lucidor's brain, similar to patterns recorded centuries past in the brains of certain saints who had claimed close relationships with shatterlings and other revenants. This evidence, and the influence of Orjen's family, had won the lucidor his berth, but the shatterling had not responded to any of the doctors' tests, the investigators had discovered that the landers had filled the shaft under the Temple of the Well of the World with dirt and rubble, and there had been grievous delays in organising and dispatching the engineering corps charged with excavating it.

'At this rate, we'll find Remfrey He and his mysterious island before they have unpacked their spades and drills,' the lucidor said. 'And it might be better if we did. I wouldn't have to fear the consequences of the shatterling's wrath, or worry about how the landers will react when they realise what the army intends to do.'

'If the shatterling really does want to learn all it can about the invasion, there won't be any need to threaten it,' Orjen said. 'Once it knows where you are and where you are going it will be eager to help.'

'I hope you're right,' the lucidor said, although he suspected that nothing concerning the shatterling would ever be easy or straightforward. It might already know where he was and where he was going, might have its own plans for him when the *Resolute Mind* found the *First Pilgrim*. He changed the subject, asked if the birds following the ship meant that it had not yet reached the true open ocean.

'Oh, we left behind the seabirds that hug the coasts days ago,' Orjen said. She was dressed in a padded cotton longcoat and was brimming with delight, like a child surveying her presents on Independence Day. 'Our companions are the true inhabitants of the ocean. The world wanderers. They sail the winds above the water and from birth to death never touch land. They mate on the wing and give birth on the wing. Their young crawl into pouches where they live, feeding on oily secretions and regurgitated fish and shrimp until they are fully fledged and ready to take up the life of endless flight themselves.'

'People used to catch them from the decks of arks,' Lyra said, 'boil the oil from their flesh and eat them. Can't say I fancy it.'

The three of them looked up at the pair of giant birds. Narrow white wings rowing the air with steady powerful strokes. Flattened saucer-shaped bodies, long necks and tiny heads. Crooked black beaks furnished with rows of tiny serrated teeth.

'It would be a crime to harm them,' Orjen said. 'According to one of the early natural histories, they live for a very long time. Centuries. Long enough to circumnavigate the world at least once.'

'You can find all kinds of stories in tablets,' the lucidor said. 'Some of them are even true.'

'We will be writing some new ones soon enough,' Orjen said.

'Or finding out that we should have taken more notice of the old ones,' Lyra said.

38

Red Line

It was Orjen's idea to introduce the lucidor to Captain Saphor Godshorse.

'He's a scion of one of the oldest of the High Families,' she said. 'His mother is a distant cousin of the Queen, and his aunt is First Lady of the Flowers of the Inner Bedchamber. A nice young man with good manners, and I think a little shy. I also think it's time he knew who you are and why you are here. Var Stonebuilder has been trying to win him over, so we need to assert ourselves and remind him that this voyage isn't just about trawling for monsters.'

Captain Godshorse was a last-minute replacement for the *Resolute Mind*'s original master and commander, Odo Anile Heaventree, who had been badly injured in an accident during a dry-dock inspection. The lucidor hadn't been privy to any briefings involving the new captain, had first seen him after boarding the *Resolute Mind* with Orjen and Lyra in the bustling confusion of pallets of supplies and equipment swinging from the dock to the aft deck of the ship on ropeways, labourers trudging up gangways bent under improbably huge loads held fast by bands around their foreheads, departing workmen carrying the tools of their trade, sailors hurrying to and fro. Orjen had pointed out the captain, a slender straight-backed figure amongst a small group of officers up on the bridge, and then they had been intercepted by a harassed junior lieutenant who had marked their names on a checklist and told them to stay below until the ship was under way. By the time the lucidor had helped Orjen and Lyra locate their belongings amongst the luggage and crates piled on deck and everything had been squared away and they had snatched a meal in the officers' mess, the *Resolute Mind* had cleared the reef and begun to smash through the endless waves beyond, and seasickness had dispatched the lucidor to his bunk.

Now he followed Orjen and Lyra along the spine of the bridge, crossing over the fat hump of the radial propeller's shroud. The helmsman stood at the wheel in the shade of a taut sheet of white canvas and Captain Saphor Godshorse was out on the right hand or starboard bridge wing, in discussion with two officers. Turning when Orjen hailed him, a look of surprise hardening to patrician distaste.

'Forgive me, madam,' he said to Orjen, 'but I don't recall inviting you up here.'

'I thought you should meet my good friend Thorn,' Orjen said blithely. 'Formerly a lucidor in the Free State, a guest of our government, and an important member of our expedition.'

Saphor Godshorse stared at the lucidor down the length of his narrow nose, as if down a gunsight. His grey uniform was immaculately pressed, its high collar buttoned tight under his chin; his black hair was brushed from his forehead and tied at the back of his neck with a white ribbon.

'I know exactly who he is,' he said. 'The Freestater who claims to be possessed by some sort of revenant.'

'It would be more accurate to say that we have a kind of understanding,' the lucidor said.

'May I ask it a question?'

'Ask what you like, but don't expect an answer. It has been quiet recently.'

'Of course it has.'

'I can tell you that you are heading in the right direction.'

'I need no help from you in matters of navigation or anything else,' Saphor Godshorse said, and turned to Orjen. 'Aside from his fantastical story, is there any reason why this man is on board my ship? Can you assure me that he is a servant or agent of his government?'

'My work led to the arrest of Remfrey He in the Free State,' the lucidor said, before Orjen could answer. 'And I found him and handed him over to the army after he escaped from their supervision in Patua. I'll happily do it again if necessary.'

'You won't be arresting anyone,' Saphor Godshorse said. 'You have no authority here.'

When he'd been a callow rookie, the lucidor had several times been punished for some minor transgression by a couple of swift stripes from the staffs of one or another of his tutors, and he had likewise straightened out rookies in his care. This arrogant young captain clearly had not benefited from that kind of discipline, and for the hundredth time or so the lucidor wished that he had his staff to hand. The army had failed to find it when they had searched the alter nest, and they hadn't found Cyf's staff either. Buried in some midden most likely, or thrown into the sea. Something else he would hold Remfrey He to account for, when he met him again.

'You are responsible for him, madam, but I am responsible for the ship,' Saphor Godshorse said to Orjen. 'Allow me to tell you that I won't have this otherlander trespassing on my bridge, or on the command bridge, the officers' quarters, or anywhere else where it is necessary to cross a red line, such as the one painted on the third step of the aft stair. If you have been too busy or too preoccupied to read the standing orders regarding such lines, perhaps you could spare a moment to study them now.'

Orjen stood her ground, saying, 'If this is an inappropriate time for introductions, we can return when it is more convenient.'

'Lieutenant Paleflower will escort your guest and your steward off the bridge. You, of course, are quite welcome to stay if you wish, but I'm afraid that I can't spare any time for small talk. I have business with the officer on watch,' Saphor Godshorse said, and turned and stalked back to the bridge wing.

'I don't feel the need to meet the captain again,' the lucidor said, after they had returned to the aft deck. 'And I'm sure that he feels the same.'

'He's a jumped-up little prig who overreacted when you fronted up to him,' Lyra said.

'I embarrassed him,' Orjen said. 'I will apologise to him at dinner, and when all is made smooth I'll do my best to change his opinion of you. Which may well have been coloured by the poison Var Stonebuilder has been dripping in his ear.'

As far as she was concerned the upset was no more than a matter of etiquette, but the lucidor wasn't so sure. Captain Godshorse clearly misliked and mistrusted him, and he wasn't much reassured when the ship's first officer, Jy Solon, found him the next day.

'You have to remember that the ship is a floating kingdom,' Jy Solon said, 'and the captain is its absolute monarch, and expects his every word and whim to be obeyed. I suppose that must seem strange to someone like you, being from the Free State where everyone is the equal of everyone else, but there it is.'

'What seems strange is that every sailor on board is a man,' the lucidor said.

'It didn't use to be that way. But after the Pirate Queens were defeated, the king at the time ruled that no woman should ever again be given command of a ship, and the army took it somewhat further.'

'You might find it easier if there were women in the crew,' the lucidor said. 'They don't have the same obsession with hierarchy as men.'

'We must work with what we have, not what we would like to have,' Jy Solon said. He was a stocky middle-aged man with quick dark eyes and a brisk cheerful manner. 'Captain Godshorse has replaced a much liked and highly experienced officer, and it's his first command. Given that, and the importance of this expedition, he's cleaving so close to the regulations he might as well be wearing them, wants them carried out to the last word and full stop, and comes down hard on any petty infractions. And given who she is, I have no doubt your friend the governor's daughter expects to get her own way, so we shouldn't be surprised when one clashes with the other. The nub of it being, if you could ask her to temper that expectation it would greatly help to smooth the running of the ship.'

'You could ask her yourself.'

'Oh, I don't think she would listen to someone who rose up through the ranks from humble beginnings. Would you care to stroll with me? I need to inspect the aft cargo hold. We've a problem with roaches getting in the flour bins.'

'I'm surprised that a ship as new as this has any kind of vermin.'

'Roaches are found on every ship, and everywhere that ships go,' Jy Solon said, as they clattered down a ladder. 'Them and rats. The gods may have had some purpose in mind when they created them, but in all my years at sea I have yet to discover what it might be.'

He unlocked a door at the bottom of a second ladder and switched on the lights as they stepped inside. They were in the cavernous aft hold, one half of it given over to crates and barrels of supplies, the other converted to a dormitory that could accommodate survivors from the *First Pilgrim*. Dim electric lamps strung along the high walls, tiers of bed bunks, each with a pillow and folded blankets and sheets squared neatly on a ticking mattress, the constant whisper of water brushing the hull.

As Jy Solon prowled down a row of storage bins, unlatching lids and peering inside, shining a small torch behind them, he told the lucidor that he was the fifth and youngest child of a farming family in the Eastlands, had signed up for service because there wasn't enough work for him at home and he didn't want to marry into another family and be forever obligated to them. He had crewed on merchant ships for ten years, but the war had been the making of him. After joining the army's fleet, he had quickly worked his way from second mate to commissioned officer seasoned in combat, and had volunteered for this voyage because the bonus would enable him to buy a farm of his own. Something to set by for his retirement.

'It no doubt seems a chancy way to win a secure berth,' he said, 'but men like us can't afford to turn down an opportunity as rare as this. And besides, I reckon we're pretty well set up. The ship's new and set out for parts and dangers unknown, but fundamentally sound. Punching through that patch of lumpy water was the proving of it, and the proving of the crew, too. And while our captain may be a trifle young and somewhat unseasoned, he isn't stupid, and knows he can rely on the advice of old salts like me. I expect that's how it is with you and the governor's daughter, eh?'

'She has her skills, and I have mine. I suppose you could say we complement each other,' the lucidor said.

He liked the first officer, but didn't entirely trust him. There was a calculating slyness tucked inside his cheerful candour, and the lucidor was waiting for him to get around to why they had come down there, out of sight and earshot of everyone else on the ship.

'That's what I mean. Let the top brass think they're in charge, and get the work done despite them,' Jy Solon said, and stowed his torch in a pocket and dusted his hands. 'No sign of our roach friends that I can see, but I'll have someone set out some glue traps. Now you have your sea legs, be sure to let me know if you need any help settling in.'

'I have already learned I should know my place,' the lucidor said.

'You shouldn't take it personally. The captain mislikes and mistrusts all Freestaters. His brother was a centenary in the Third Foot Lancers. Killed while serving on the border between our country and yours.'

'I know that border. I served there myself, when I was much younger than I am now. It's a hard land.'

'Aye, and the captain's brother had a hard death. He was wounded and captured by Freestater bandits while out on patrol. After they tried and failed to ransom him, they skinned him alive and sent back the only survivor of the patrol to let the army know what they did to any they caught trespassing on what they considered to be their territory.'

'I'm sorry to hear of his loss,' the lucidor said. It sounded inadequate, as it always did. 'I trust that the bandits were hunted down. As far as the Free State was concerned, they were no longer citizens of the Free State. Anyone who turns to border reiving loses all rights, for it demonstrates that they no longer have any regard for law or nationality.'

'Maybe so, but it'll be of no use telling that to the captain.'

'I suppose it won't.'

'That's why he came down on you, and will again, if you cross him,' Jy Solon said. 'So if you or your boss are in want of anything, I'm the one to ask.'

There it was.

'I'll remember that,' the lucidor said, reckoning that he couldn't afford to repay any favour he owed the man.

Lyra had her own opinion about Orjen's rank and privilege. 'You have to remember that the boss doesn't have to make use of her gift, let alone put her life at risk in service of it. In fact, she isn't supposed to use it, being who she is. But she never has much cared for what other people think.'

'She's stubborn,' the lucidor said.

'She can be,' Lyra said. 'And I know she can seem arrogant, too. But the main thing is, she's dedicated her life to her work, and she's given up a lot for it. She didn't have her father hire someone to tutor her in the use of her gift. Instead, she apprenticed to the temples, like every other map reader, and swept the floors and emptied the commodes and worked in the kitchens and gardens while she learned how to meditate and empty her mind so the impressions of life maps can come clear. Two years of that, and years more on her own, honing her craft, when she could have been playing at lords and ladies. It didn't come easy, and she's worked twice as hard as anyone else ever since because she knows that, being who she is, she has to prove that she is not just a dabbler.'

'I respect that,' the lucidor said.

'As you should,' Lyra said.

'But she still has the privilege she was born to, and all the rest. How does that sit with you?'

'How I started working for her, I was hired by her father when she was just a scamp with a passion for collecting beetles. You have to imagine us out in the woods or up some mountainside. Young Orjen with her killing jar and her net, her little knife for digging bugs out of bark or rotting wood. Me with a pistol and a godspeaker – to call in the backup team, if things went sideways. I didn't know anything about natural history back then, but I soon learned that there are more kinds of beetles than there are people in the entire kingdom. The creator gods had a particular liking for them, it seems. As did Orjen,' Lyra said, with a rare smile.

'Did you study with her, at the temples?'

'Do I look like the kind of woman who would sit motionless for two days straight, trying to think about nothing at all? No, I lost sight of her then, but she got in touch a few years later, asked if I wanted to help out. And here we are. I've picked up bits and pieces of natural history along the way, but I'm mostly her fixer. There's a problem, I do my best to sort it out. We've roughed it in swamps and forests, stayed in back-country villages that haven't seen a stranger since the godlings departed, were once stuck for twenty days in a shepherd's hut halfway up a mountain when a snowstorm cut us off, and she took all of it in her stride. But I don't deny that her being who she is makes things easier. We have the best equipment and the best people, and we generally get to go where we want. Sometimes, though, she can push things a little too far. Which is how we ended up like we did, trespassing on the bridge and getting the short end of the captain's temper. And she's sorry for getting you in trouble. She really is.'

'The captain had formed his opinion of me long before I set foot in his realm,' the lucidor said, and told Lyra the story that Jy Solon had told him.

'That would harden anyone's mind,' Lyra said, 'but the boss will do her best to find his good side. You wait and see.'

The lucidor was quartered with the sailors, petty officers and a squad of marines, but custom and tradition forbade him from entering the sailors' commons and the senior petty officer made it clear that he was not especially welcome in their roundtable. So in the calm, balmy days as the ship sailed the doldrums he most often took his meals alone, up on deck. He didn't mind the solitude, and loved to watch the pair of world wanderers rowing the air beyond the stern rail. Every now and then one or the other would break away and rise in a wide circle and abruptly plunge into the sea, folding its wings so that it entered the water with barely a splash, emerging after a minute or so and beating back into the air with a fish caught in its toothed beak.

The lucidor admired the precision of these dives. The calculation and graceful execution. The way the birds sprang up from the sea, shedding water from the edges of their long wings. Sometimes, at twilight, they would trawl just above the edge of the ship's wake, scooping up tiny squid that came to the surface to feed at night and were caught in the churn of the stern propellers. Orjen said that in open water they would sit on the surface and spread their wings wide and spin in circles to create a vortex that gathered the squid at its centre; they liked to follow the ship because its propellers did all the work for them.

'Then these birds really must be long-lived, or pass on traditions from generation to generation,' the lucidor said. 'Given that this is only the second ship to have sailed these waters in several centuries.'

'Sometimes a steady wind blowing across the surface of the water will set up parallel rows of rotating currents,' Orjen said. 'Each current rotates in the opposite direction to its neighbours, so that material drawn to the surface is trapped in the troughs between. The propellers create a similar effect, and knowing of one the world wanderers can make use of the other.'

'Being able to make sense of the world like that, seeing the laws built into it by the creator gods, must be enormously satisfying.'

'It isn't much different to the way you work,' Orjen said. 'Making careful observations. Teasing out patterns and correspondences, making deductions.'

The lucidor glanced towards the flying bridge, where Captain Saphor Godshorse stood with his back turned to them.

'You have an advantage,' he said. 'Unlike people, animals don't pretend that they are other than what they really are.'

39

Zig Zag

The expedition's crew of map readers, technicians and assistants was commanded by Var Stonebuilder, a dour, formidable woman who made it clear that she thought the lucidor's presence was a foolish mistake and the search for Remfrey He a distraction from the important work of discovering the origin of the invasion and cataloguing the variety of its monsters and teasing out their relationships with each other.

She and her crew spent most of their time raking through fish and other creatures they caught in purse net trawls, drawing, dissecting and life-mapping specimens, and bottling them in heart-of-wine. Once, they brought up a school of tiny black squid that hopped around the deck like agitated spiders and mostly escaped back into the sea. Another time they caught a fish that was entirely transparent except for the silvery backing of its eyes; even its blood was as clear as water. But although the *Resolute Mind* was heading on a straight course towards what Remfrey He claimed to be the origin of the invasion, everything caught in the trawls, no matter how strange, lacked any sign of the invasion's taint in their life maps, and at last Var Stonebuilder persuaded Saphor Godshorse to widen the search by cutting away from their plotted course, angling sixty leagues west and then crossing back a hundred and twenty leagues east.

She tried again the next day, and the day after that, making trawls at the end of every zig and zag but still failing to find any trace of the invasion's influence. When the nets were hauled in after the last trawl her crew raked through the meagre catch and found nothing new or unusual and tipped everything over the side without bothering to take specimens. One after the other, the pair of world wanderers gracefully swooped to the surface and snatched up this bounty, and settled behind the ship as it turned back to its original course.

Lyra told the lucidor that Orjen and Var Stonebuilder had gone head-to-head when the crew chief had claimed that Remfrey He had either been mistaken or had lied about the location of the invasion's origin. Orjen had pointed out that it had been confirmed by the lucidor's observations; Var Stonebuilder had said that neither man could be trusted. They were both from the Free State, might be part of the same conspiracy. And besides, how could Orjen know, really, absolutely know, that Remfrey He hadn't at some point used his silvertongue gift to persuade her that he was telling the truth?

'After that, it got properly ugly,' Lyra said. 'Orjen accused Var Stonebuilder of looking for evidence to support her prejudices, rather than trying to understand what the evidence meant. If you want to insult a philosopher, that's absolutely the best way to go about it. And Var Stonebuilder doubled down, said that the boss was a privileged dabbler who had never done any real work in her life. The woman's poison.'

'We'll see who's right when we get where we're going,' the lucidor said.

'Let's hope so. Meanwhile, the two of them aren't speaking to each other, and Stonebuilder still has the ear of the captain.'

A few days later, Orjen told the lucidor that the army's engineering corps had at last set up at the Temple of the Well of the World and started to excavate the shaft. 'The landers caused some trouble when the ship carrying the equipment arrived, but it was only a minor delay. I understand that the work is proceeding well, and the engineers have the equipment to drill through the baserock at the bottom of the shaft, if necessary. Hopefully, they won't have to.'

'What did the landers do? Was anyone hurt?'

'They tried to blockade the harbour, but the army arrested the ringleaders and dispersed the rest.'

The lucidor thought of Alcnos and Doras. Told himself that the landers' attempt to stop the excavation may have been right and necessary by their lights, but making contact with the shatterling was more important.

He said, 'They should be set free once the work is finished.'

'I'm sure they will be,' Orjen said, and asked if the shatterling had tried to reach out to him.

'Not yet. I confess that I'm not looking forward to renewing my acquaintance with it. I had no control over it before. It rode me like a godling.'

'This time it will be different.'

'As long as there is nothing it can draw on out here, if all it can do is talk, I reckon I can deal with it. But if it tries to harm me, if it gives me dreadful visions or fits, or worse, I want you to make sure that the ship's sawbones will knock me out with a stiff dose of easing powder.'

'I will stick you full of the stuff myself, if it comes to it,' Orjen said. 'But I am certain that it won't. The shatterling wants to know what we want to know.'

'So it said.'

'You don't trust anyone, do you? Not even a servant of the creator gods.'

'Call it caution born of long experience.'

The lucidor had taken to going up on the aft deck first thing every day and working through a series of simple exercises with a fighting stick he had borrowed from one of the marines. It was half the length of his staff, but he worked up some nice moves. One morning three of the marines asked if they could join him, and he spent a satisfying couple of hours teaching them an assortment of direct attacks and flanking moves.

The marines were barely a third of his age, but hardened by combat. The lucidor shared lunch with them and they told him stories of the campaigns against the invasion and he told them stories about his work and the day passed in pleasant camaraderie, but early the next morning the sergeant found the lucidor and apologised and said that Captain Godshorse had forbidden his men to have any further fraternisation with him.

The lucidor told the sergeant that there was no need to apologise and asked if he should return the borrowed fighting stick.

'Oh, I reckon you can keep it, seeing as the captain made no mention of it,' the sergeant said.

'When he remedies that oversight, I will say that I took it without permission,' the lucidor said. 'No need for you and your men to take any of the blame.'

The next day, Lyra came up on the aft deck while the lucidor was exercising, and after watching him for a little while asked him if he could teach her some moves.

'I don't want to get you into trouble with the captain.'

'I'm not under his command, so there's not much he can do about it.'

'Because of Orjen.'

'Like I said, privilege sometimes has its uses. How about it?'

They exercised together every morning after that, and talked about their different lives and the differences between their two countries. The lucidor told Lyra about his adventures on the way to Delos-Chimr; she told him about expeditions she and Orjen had made to obscure parts of Patua.

'What do you think strangest about our country?' she asked him one day. 'I don't mean revenants like the shatterling, or monsters like the leeches. I mean something we Patuans think ordinary, but you think freakishly bizarre.'

'I can't understand how some people can be abandoned by everyone else,' the lucidor said, and told Lyra about his first encounter with beggars in Tinkers Market.

'It's always how it's been,' she said. 'There are those who have nothing and those who have everything, and the majority in between, who strive to better themselves. As they can, with hard work and a little luck. After all, the fortunes of some of the High Families have very humble beginnings.'

'In the Free State no one is higher or lower than anyone else. Every life has equal value, and everyone has the opportunity to live the life they deserve. Why is it so hard for Patuans to understand that it is the right way to live?'

'Perhaps because you can't choose what you want to be. You don't have the freedom we have. You have to serve as the government sees fit.'

'The House of the People acts according to the people's will. It does not oppress or persecute them, let alone go to war with those who disagree with it. And because my country is not as rich in resources as yours we must make the best use of what we have, including the talents and skills of our people.'

'You never wanted to be anything else?'

'I haven't always been a lawkeeper,' the lucidor said. 'I resigned my post some years ago, and took up work in the river docks instead. We have the freedom to refuse our calling, although most don't. It isn't a crime, but most think it selfish. A serious breach of social custom and common trust.'

'But you didn't give up lawkeeping entirely. For here you are.'

'Which proves, perhaps, the worth of our labour allocation process.'

'So the Free State has the best way of living, even though everyone is as poor as everyone else.'

'Of the two systems I have experienced, I know which is better than the other.'

'Yet your desert paradise still needs people like you to keep the rest in line.'

'We don't police the people. We serve them, and keep them safe from those who want to exploit or hurt others. From what I have seen, people are the same mix of good and bad in both our countries, but the Free State does all it can to promote the better side of human nature.'

So it went until one morning the lucidor came up on deck and found two of Var Stonebuilder's assistants launching a small plastic dinghy off the point of the stern, floating backwards and paying out the line that kept them attached to the ship. At first, he thought that they were preparing for another trawl, but then he saw Var Stonebuilder was standing on one of the wings of the flying bridge, accompanied by a man armed with a long gun.

The lucidor broke into a run as the sharpshooter took aim and fired. As usual, the pair of world wanderers were floating in the wind behind the ship, one high, one low. The shot hit the highest one square and its wings folded around it and it fell, and the lucidor took the stairs two at a time and charged down the bridge, halting when Saphor Godshorse stepped forward and said loudly, 'Enough, sir.'

'Tell me why,' the lucidor said. He was out of breath, glaring past the captain at the marksman and Var Stonebuilder.

'I don't have to explain myself to you,' the captain said. His hands were bunched into fists, and two stocky sailors and a junior officer stood at his back. 'I warned you of the consequences the first time you crossed the line. Now you will suffer them.'

The lucidor stared at Var Stonebuilder as he let the sailors take hold of his arms, putting some force into it, letting her know what he thought. As he was hustled down the stair to the aft deck, he saw that one of the assistants was hauling the dinghy back to the ship by pulling on the mooring rope hand over hand while the other stood behind him, holding the boathook that secured the dead bird. It floated behind the dinghy with its wings spread wide, flexing on the white water of the wake as if in flight, and its mate circled high above, calling harshly in distress.

40

Luckbreaker

The lucidor spent eight days locked in the ship's brig, a windowless closet so small he had to sleep on the hard floor with his knees tucked against his chest. Not that he got much sleep, because the brig was close to the thunderous roar of the engine room and lit day and night by a bare bulb that glared behind a thick plastic shield. Jy Solon was waiting for him when he was let out, took him to the petty officers' roundtable and gave him a plate of tomato and rice stew with a side of fried plantain.

'The captain didn't ought to have locked you up,' Jy said, watching the lucidor eat. 'But at least you don't seem much harmed by it.'

'I learned how to tough out punishment from an early age.'

'Were you something of a bad boy before you turned lawkeeper? I've heard that isn't uncommon in your line of work.'

'It was more that I had a problem with unearned authority.'

'I can see why you might have a problem with the captain.'

'It wasn't about him. It was what he allowed.'

'Well, we're in agreement about that. There's some who sympathise with what you did because they think it bad luck to kill one of those big birds.'

'Do you believe that?'

'I believe you let your temper get the better of you. Luckily, you're a passenger. If you were crew, the captain would have had you flogged, and the stripes washed with seawater.'

'I meant about the bad luck.'

'It hasn't done much for the crew's morale. Most of them are volunteers, picked for their experience. If the captain had more

304

prudence he would show them some proper respect. Instead, against all custom and common sense, he allowed Stonebuilder to kill that bird. We've already had more than our share of snags and shakedown problems, what with the ship lacking a proper sea trial before it set out, and a slew of the kind of little problems that try a crew's good humour. We had to clean out one of the water tanks because the water was tainted, for instance, so if we don't get a good amount of rain we might have to start rationing. Food might become a little tight, too. A round ten dozen cases of jarred preserves spoiled because the seals cracked. Not to mention that the jakes in the crew quarters keeps flooding, and it turns out that the roach problem is worse than I feared. Little things in themselves, but they add up. Result is, the men aren't working as well or as carefully as they should. And the sea has a way of punishing carelessness. Sooner or later someone will make a mistake that will get them hurt or killed, and now the men have a reason to blame it on the captain.'

'Because he let Stonebuilder kill that bird.'

'Because those who claim there'll be a reckoning for it will think themselves vindicated. They're already calling her "Luckbreaker".'

'Why are you telling me this?'

Even though they were alone in the roundtable, Jy Solon leaned closer, spoke softly.

'If things get ugly and the captain fails to get on top of it, I might have to step in. I'm going to do my best to make sure it doesn't come to that, but if it does, I reckon you'd be a good man to have at my back. There's no need to agree to it now, but I'd be grateful if you'd think about it. Meanwhile, if you're done with that stew, you might want to go up top. Your friend the governor's daughter is waiting to see you. And don't be crossing any more lines.'

The sky beyond the ship's stern was empty. Orjen told the lucidor that after its mate was shot the surviving world wanderer had circled the ship for the rest of the day before flying off at arcset. And although Var Stonebuilder claimed that she had killed the bird because it might have scooped up small monsters her trawls had missed, its crop had contained only the remains of ordinary squid.

'It had a point as far as the captain was concerned,' the lucidor said. 'I lost my temper and handed him an excuse to assert his authority over me. I won't make that mistake again.'

'I have some other news,' Orjen said. 'While you were locked away, the engineers reached the bottom of the shatterling's shaft.'

The lucidor felt an electric sting in his blood. 'Before you ask,' he said, 'it still hasn't reached out to me.'

They were leaning at the aft rail in bright mirrorlight and a stiff clean breeze. The empty ocean stretched blue and sparkling out to the haze that hid the far horizon. Orjen looked sideways at the lucidor and said, 'Are you certain?'

'When was this?'

'Two days ago. You didn't feel or hear anything?'

'Not a thing.'

'No strange dreams?'

'None that I recall.'

'It definitely reached out to the engineers. There was a ground tremor the night after they reached bottom. A big one. And one of the crew went mad, and killed three and injured six more before she was shot.'

'Was this crew accompanied by a muzzler, as I suggested?'

'By two of them,' Orjen said. 'The woman who went mad, she was one.'

'My own gift didn't do much to mute it, either, but I hoped they might do some good,' the lucidor said. 'What are they doing now? Have they tried to make contact with it?'

'They left their equipment in place and withdrew. At this moment they are back on their ship, waiting for High Command to decide what to do next. That may take a while. But at least they have direct proof that there is an active revenant down there,' Orjen said. 'And they found two bodies at the bottom of the shaft, too. A man on the floor and a woman wedged inside a kind of well, exactly as you described. So the army knows now that your story is true.'

'The shatterling may not have reached out to me because it didn't know that the engineers had anything to with me. As far as it was concerned they might have been another gang of treasure hunters, like the diggers. A minor inconvenience, swiftly dealt with. They need to get back down there and finish their work.'

But for days and days nothing much happened. The engineers set up a perimeter around the Temple of the Well of the World, and volunteers dropped small explosive charges and other noise-makers into the shaft and played an amplified recording of the lucidor's voice, but the shatterling did not seem to take any notice. Meanwhile, as the *Resolute Mind* ploughed on across the ocean, the mirror arcs traced lower and shorter paths across the sky and the nights grew longer and the weather cooler. When the lucidor wondered if the ship might at last sail into permanent darkness, Orjen said that he would see soon enough why that wouldn't happen, but wouldn't explain what she meant.

At last, they crossed the far edge of the deeps and, as Lyra had predicted, struck another band of high waves running over shallower water. The lucidor was incapacitated by bouts of seasickness until at last the violent pitching slowly eased off. He slept deeply, woke to a preternatural silence. The motors had been switched off. For the first time since it had left port the *Resolute Mind* had stopped dead in the water.

The lucidor dressed and went up to the aft deck and saw calm water stretching away into mist in every direction, with the glow of an arc of mirrors low in the mist astern and the glow of a second arc ahead, somewhat lower in the sky. In this eerie light sailors were climbing into the ship's two boats, which floated against the stern amongst slicks of some kind of red weed. Jy Solon and another officer were leaning at the aft rail, directing the activity; on the foredeck Var Stonebuilder's crew were combing through clumps of weed they had pulled on board.

Lyra found the lucidor and told him that the ship had run into a mass of the stuff, and it had jammed the propellers. 'Mr Solon reckons it will take all day to clear it, and maybe all night too. They're going to drag a knotted line under the hull, and if that doesn't work, they'll send down divers with air lines and masks.'

'Will it ever be night again, now we have new mirrors in the sky?'

'I wondered if you had noticed that.'

'I see now why Orjen didn't want to spoil the surprise.'

'As I understand it, the world is so big that any one spot needs several mirror arcs to light it. For if there was only one, travelling around the world at the accustomed speed, the usual stretch of daylight would be followed by days and days of darkness. And if it travelled fast enough to return inside a day, it would sweep from horizon to horizon in a couple of hours. So the creator gods gave us a chain of arcs instead, each rising and setting in turn until the first comes around again.'

'That's how I understand it too. But why can we see two arcs now?'

'Again, because the world is so big. If there was only one chain of arcs, most of it would be in darkness. Instead, there are several chains, one circling the world's waist and others circling above and below it, bringing light and heat to every part of the world except for its top and bottom, which are in permanent darkness and covered with floating maps of sea ice. Are you with me so far?'

'I think I am.'

'I hope so, because there's a further twist,' Lyra said. 'We're agreed the world is a ball.'

'Of course.'

'And being as it's a ball, the distance around it grows less as you travel above or below its waist. We're used to seeing five different mirror arcs, one following the next with intervals of night between until after five days the first appears again. As we sail further north, the track of those familiar arcs will fall behind us until they disappear below the horizon. And the track of the new arcs will rise ever higher ahead of us, and according to Orjen there are only four of them.'

'Because they have less distance to travel in the same time.'

'We'll make a philosopher of you yet.'

'The creator gods didn't stint, when they made the world.'

'They might have made a lot less of this damned weed.'

'Did the creator gods make it, or is it invasion stuff?'

'We don't know yet, although there are some odd-looking little crabs and shrimp riding along with it. Var Stonebuilder seems happy, for once. As is the boss. I'd better go forward and tell her you've recovered. If you want something to eat, you'll have to fend for yourself. It's all hands to deck until the weed's cleared and we can be on our way.'

The lucidor found a pot of manioc porridge in the petty officers' roundtable, and filled a cup with strong black chai from the urn and stirred three spoonfuls of sugar into it. He ate as much as his tender stomach could stand, and refilled his cup and went back up on deck. The two boats had rowed down the length of the ship and now were rowing back, moving slowly, ropes stretching from their bows and dipping under the hull, officers walking on either side of the foredeck to keep them aligned.

The lucidor was leaning at the starboard rail, sipping chai and trying to make out from the diffuse glow how many mirrors were in the new arc, when he saw a faint movement deep in the mist. There and gone. At first he thought that it was a trick of the light or a premonition of one of the shatterling's visions, but then he heard a faint splash, and a moment later something big and round and red rolled out of the skirts of the mist.

He threw his cup aside and shouted a warning and ran to the small pile of tools by the aft rail and found a boathook. The big ball was rolling steadily towards the ship, trailed by a flock of smaller balls that skipped along in its wake like a flock of ducklings following their mother. Sailors were leaning at the rail and officers were shouting at the men in the boats, and Jy Solon was running across the foredeck towards the bridge, with half a dozen marines chasing after him.

The big ball slewed sideways and rolled past the ship's bow, but the flock of smaller balls came straight on, hopping and skipping over slicks of weed as if animated by a common baleful glee. They threw themselves high on the last bounce, splitting into two clumps that arced fore and aft. When the lucidor struck one with a blunt swing of the boathook its taut red rind turned out to be no thicker than the skin of a child's handball, for the thing split open and instantly deflated. The lucidor ducked as a second flew at his head and batted away a third with a backhanded blow, sending it rolling into the scuppers, where a sailor stomped it flat. Another sailor lashed two balls out of the air with the end of a rope; dozens more bounced across the deck and skimmed over the port rail. Marines lined along the bridge fired a volley as the balls skipped away. There were quick flares of light as balls struck by bullets blew apart, and the rest vanished into the mist before the marines could reload.

A sailor was missing after he had been knocked from one of the boats, and two of Var Stonebuilder's crew had been injured, one with a serious concussion, another with a broken arm. Captain Godshorse put the crew back to clearing weed, stationed pairs of marines on the flying bridge and at the stern and bow, and told Var Stonebuilder to take such samples as she needed from the remains of the balls that the lucidor and others had struck down, and throw everything else overboard.

The mirror arc ahead of them set, followed two hours later by the one behind, and the work of clearing the red weed from the propellers was finished in the glare of lamps hung along the rails. Saphor Godshorse wanted to make way as soon as possible, but Jy Solon persuaded him to wait until the sailors had held a ceremony for their lost comrade.

It was a strange and touching affair. Sailors, marines and passengers gathered on the foredeck and Saphor Godshorse gave a short, stiff speech littered with clichés about duty and sacrifice before yielding to Jy Solon, who talked briefly about the lost sailor. His qualities, the bone flute he liked to play, the family he had left behind.

'He was a good shipmate, and we aren't going to leave his spirit here, in a place where the creator gods forgot what they were about. Look lively now. Give him the send-off he deserves.'

Sailors stepped to the rail and cast brightly coloured paper flowers into the water, and Jy Solon lit a candle in the basket of a paper balloon, which rose on the candle flame's breath like an infant mirror, vanishing into the mist and taking with it the spirit of the missing man into whatever sky lay beyond.

41

Where No Island Should Be

The ship went forward slowly, running on battery power in the dim light, pushing through mist and a fine rain that had begun to fall through it. Everyone was subdued. Oppressed by streaming blankness that reduced the world to a hazy space scarcely longer than the ship. Wondering what other monsters might be lurking out there.

Orjen told the lucidor that the red weed and the red balls were definitely products of the invasion, with traces of the invasion's tailswallower pathogens embedded in their life maps. The balls, derived from a species of jellyfish, had been inflated by hydrogen gas, which was why the ones struck by the marines' gunfire had exploded; their inner surfaces were covered with a fluffy white rind that had given sailors who had touched it a bad rash.

'Each ball has a tiny muscular pore,' she said. 'I think that they feed by deflating themselves and everting part of their inner rind through it – the rind contains stinging cells very similar to those of ordinary jellyfish.'

'Then we are on the right track,' the lucidor said. 'Heading in the right direction.'

'Var Stonebuilder thinks so. And for once I agree with her.'

It was too cold and wet for the lucidor to take his meals on deck. Returning to his cabin from the petty officers' roundtable one night, he saw two sailors in conversation at the foot of the ladder, their backs to him. The first saying that they wouldn't have been a sitting target if the captain had known enough to slow down when the ship had hit the weed patch; the second agreeing, adding that someone who fouled up like that was going to foul up again sooner rather than later. Both falling silent, staring sullenly at the lucidor as he pushed past.

He thought about reporting it to Jy Solon, decided that it wasn't his place. Still, it was unsettling to realise that the first officer had been right in thinking that the crew had little love or respect for their captain.

At last, the mist began to break up and thin, and a few hours later the *Resolute Mind* was running at full speed through open water under a vast blue sky flecked here and there with shoals of white cloud. Only the mirrors ahead of them were visible now. New light on new territory, Orjen said.

They ran for more than twenty days through calm water and fine weather. One day Orjen reported that the army engineers had begun to dig a new, lateral shaft some distance from the temple mound, but it would be a long and laborious undertaking.

'We might well reach the *First Pilgrim* before they are halfway to reaching the shatterling,' she said.

'If the shatterling doesn't reach out to them first,' the lucidor said.

'It still hasn't tried to contact you?'

'Not yet.'

Without sufficient rain to replenish the tainted water tank, water had to be rationed, and although there was as yet no shortage of hardtack and salt pork, preserved vegetables and fruit were also in short supply, and after two jars of apricots were discovered in a sailor's locker Captain Godshorse had him flogged as an example to the others.

It was a sombre, sullen affair. All hands and passengers lined the foredeck and the captain and his senior officers watched from the bridge as the man was stripped of his shirt and bound to a timber brace and gagged with a knot of rope. Jy Solon read out the charge and counted every one of the fifty lashes. When it was done and he was untied the man stood as straight as he could, gasping but not crying out when his bloody wounds were rinsed with salt water, and the lucidor saw that several of the men whispered reassurances to him as he was led away to be treated by the sawbones.

Soon after that, islands of brittle lace began to appear, rising and falling on the ocean's slow breath. Study of samples showed that it was another kind of red weed: feathery fronds armoured in sheaths of some kind of chalky secretion, knitting into lacy mats that pushed up in crackling ridges on either side of the ship as it nosed forward at quarter speed. Patches of ordinary red weed grew on the mats, and crabs, glass eels, bristle worms and other creatures skittered and slithered across them. Clouds of tiny shrimp flicked up with a seething crackle like frying oil. Worms sheathed in the same chalky material as the mats extruded fans of tentacles, like flesh flowers scattered across snowy meadows.

Orjen was delighted by the unexpected fecundity, and dismissed the lucidor's speculation that this might be the kind of stuff which had stranded the *First Pilgrim*, saying airily that they were still more than four thousand leagues from the ship's last reported position.

At last, the *Resolute Mind* entered a broad open channel between two vast shoals of chalkweed, and followed its wandering path for the rest of the day. In the last light of dusk, the lookout posted at the bow sighted land ahead: an island rising in a smooth shallow cone against the darkening sky. Half a league from this uncharted shore, they hove to. Waves broke on submerged shoals that skirted its rim; its pale bare slopes showed no sign of animal life or human habitation.

No such island was marked on the old charts, and the *First Pilgrim* had not reported sighting it or the shoals of chalkweed floating all around. Yet there it was, an island where no island should be. A solid black silhouette against the starry sky.

The next morning, Var Stonebuilder and half her crew packed themselves and their equipment into one of the ship's boats and set out for the island's shore. Orjen, Lyra and the lucidor followed in the second boat, accompanying a party of marines and sailors sent by the captain to look for fresh water. The boatswains picked a way through channels between offshore shoals to the shallow lagoon that circled the island, with a white sand floor where small red crabs skittered on unfathomable errands, and anchored the boats in the shelter of a low cliff at the rim of the island.

When the lucidor and others clambered ashore Var Stonebuilder's crew was already at work, half of them assembling a drilling rig, the rest scattered across the slope, collecting stones and specimens of lichens and thornbush. The small party of marines set off to scout for streams or springs of fresh water, and Orjen led Lyra and the lucidor up the long slope towards the island's summit. Friable chalk crunched underfoot and white dust puffed knee-high at each step. A dry taste in the air. Pale feathers of dust blowing off ridges.

As they climbed higher, they discovered orange and black lichens patching boulders and bare ridges, and the shafts of small sinkholes that dropped straight down to water rising and falling at the bottom. When Orjen kicked a stone into one of the sinkholes it bobbed up to the surface of the water and floated there in a scum of dust, thirty or forty spans below.

'As I thought,' she said. 'The ocean is deep here, and unless there's a submerged peak of baserock unmarked on any chart it's likely that this island is floating on the surface, like that pebble. The shoals we passed through are the upturned rim of a submerged shelf that extends around it, which is why there is a sudden transition from deep ocean water to shallow lagoon. And if it's slowly drifting on the ocean currents, it would explain why the *First Pilgrim* didn't report it.'

'Because it wasn't here when they passed by,' the lucidor said. He was sweating inside his leather coat, and the trek up the slope had set off his trick ankle.

'Exactly. I have all kinds of questions,' Orjen said, an eager shine in her gaze, that keen mind of hers no doubt whirring away like the *Resolute Mind*'s engine room. 'How old is it? And if it is built from submerged layers of chalkweed, how was its mass pushed up in this shallow cone? Was it shaped by storms and wind, or is it built from a different kind of chalkweed, one which can grow in air rather that seawater?'

'Isn't the important question whether or not it was created by the invasion?' the lucidor said.

'If it's made from chalkweed stuff, I reckon there's no argument that it was,' Lyra said. 'I'm wondering about the lichens. There are at least eight kinds by my reckoning, and some of them are so big, have to be at least a century old.'

'If they grow at the usual rate,' Orjen said.

'Point is, it's likely the island grows from below. Otherwise those lichens would have been buried long ago.'

'I'm wondering about their morphology.'

'You think there might be some sort of red weed in them?'

'We need to take some back. You said eight kinds?'

'Maybe more. I'm not so good at telling one from another.'

'Let's get samples of them all.'

The lucidor sat on a flat-topped lump of chalk and massaged his ankle while the two women quartered the ground around about, measuring lichen patches, cutting off samples and dropping them in glass bottles. All the while continuing their animated discussion about the island's structure and growth. There was no other sound but the wind. No birds. No insects. Bare white slopes shimmering with reflected light and heat, mirrorlight burning off the glassy water that circled the island. The *Resolute Mind* floated small and trim beyond the white dashes of waves breaking over marginal shoals, and the ocean stretched away under the blue sky to the haze of the far horizon.

They had been sailing for more than sixty days now. The World Ocean was so vast that it was impossible to imagine that anything could change it, that it wasn't anything other than it had been when the creator gods had made the world, yet it was infected by red weed and feral red balls, and shoals of chalkweed teeming with strange life. And now this floating island fabricated by something outwith the designs of the creator gods. A stain spreading across the world, turning life into its own kind of life . . .

The lucidor jerked awake with a start: in the warmth and quiet he had drowsed off for a few seconds, like the old man he was. He pushed to his feet, walked a little way up the slope. There were tiny stars embedded in the general glare, facets of chalk stuff reflecting mirrorlight directly into his eyes, and now the stars began to move, rising to different heights in the air, circling each other in tight orbits like a toy galaxy, and at their centre a watchful presence turned its attention towards him, and a voice spoke in his head.

'Here is a new thing in the world, made by something very old.'

It was scarcely louder than the hiss of blood in his ears, the whisper of the wind and scratch of wind-blown dust, the murmur of Orjen and Lyra and the chink of their tools and sample bottles, but the lucidor felt a cold squeeze in his heart, an electric tingling in his scalp.

He said, 'I'm glad you are here.'

'I am where I have always been since I fell. Did you send the people who are trying to dig me up?'

'You have been silent a long time. I didn't know how else to get in touch with you.'

'Do you really think that you can threaten me?'

'I wanted only to get your attention,' the lucidor said. The squeeze around his heart had tightened and he felt as if a cold wind was blowing through him. 'There's much we need to talk about.'

'You have had as much of my attention as you deserved. I made contact with you now and then, after you quit the alter nest. Watching through your eyes. Listening through your ears. You were in the same house or the same garden every time. Nowhere near alter women's nests or any other place modified by the invasion.'

'I was a prisoner, then. Now I'm following the transmissions from the alter nests to their source, and that's why I want to talk to you. We can help each other find out how the invasion started. Where it came from. The seed from which it grew.'

'You misunderstand the nature of our relationship. This has only ever been about whether or not you can be useful to me. For a long time you were not. But now . . . Now you may be, in a small way.'

'You said this island was a new thing made by something very old. Is that a kind of riddle?'

'I infiltrated the network that links the alter nests,' the shatterling said. 'And learned much, before it was degraded by your army. To begin with, I discovered the point of origin of the invasion.'

'Is it somewhere on Simud, or on the island where the *First Pilgrim* ran aground? Are any of its crew still alive?'

316

'They are no longer its crew.'

'What about Remfrey He?'

'He has been a disappointment.'

'You spoke with him, didn't you? Back in the alter nest.'

'He was useful, until he was not.'

'Remfrey He is clever, but he's also insane. And interested in helping no one but himself. But we can help each other, and put an end to the invasion. Perhaps you could begin by telling me what you have found out about its origin.'

'You may be able to provide some small help when you reach it. We will talk then.'

'What about Remfrey He? Do you know where he is? Do you know what he is doing now?'

'You are in danger. You need to wake up.'

The lucidor discovered that he was still sitting on the lump of chalk. He hadn't moved at all. And Lyra was standing behind him, gripping his shoulder and gently shaking him, telling him that they had to go.

'The idiots have disturbed something,' she said. She had drawn her knife, was pointing its blade towards Var Stonebuilder's drill site.

There was a scuffle of movement around it, people scrambling away as some kind of thick red fluid spread from their rig. And all across the slope black whips were lashing up from sinkholes, contracting and stiffening as things like a cross between spiders and crabs levered themselves out. Small misshapen bodies thatched with coarse red hair perched tall and tottering on whips that stiffened into wiry legs, lurching into jerky motion. Some fell and jacked themselves up and whirled on; two collided in a flurry of legs that instantly transformed back to whips, striking out in a blind frenzy inside a spreading fog of dust.

The lucidor was on his feet now. Watching as Var Stonebuilder's crew and the party of marines and sailors converged on the boats, swerving this way and that to avoid skittering spider crabs. The marines halted and aimed their long guns and fired, took down two spider crabs, started to run again. One of Var Stonebuilder's people wasn't quick enough: a spider crab seized her in two coiling legs and swung her high into the air and dashed her to the ground, snapping up her broken body and smashing it down again like a child abusing a toy. Blood on white dust, darker than the scarlet stuff spilling downhill from the drill site.

Lyra shouted a warning. The lucidor turned, saw more spider crabs emerging along the top of the slope, etched small and sharp against the sky.

'We can't stay here,' Orjen said.

'We'll have to be quick,' Lyra said.

The boatswains had backed their boats away from the shore and men and women were jumping into the water and swimming out to them.

'I'll lead the way,' the lucidor said and pulled his borrowed fighting stick from his belt and started down the slope. He was afraid, but it was a small and neatly parcelled fear, and his blood thrilled with an exhilaration he hadn't felt for a long time. Pinched between two sets of enemies, outnumbered, with a poor chance of success – this was the kind of danger he could understand. The kind he could deal with.

He half ran, half slid, his ankle stabbing him with every step. A little crowd of spider crabs jostled around the body of the woman, and others were whirling in tight circles around the two downed by the marines. It left a good number patrolling back and forth along the shore, but the lucidor reckoned that if he could outrun the ones coming down the slope behind him he had a good chance of reaching the water.

The red stuff which had boiled out of the drill hole turned out to be a fluid mass of smaller crabs. Hand-sized things with claws snapping like scissor blades and a kind of red fur covering their shells, scuttling and stalking sideways through the chalky dust. They didn't take any notice of the lucidor and the two women until Lyra stamped on one that threatened to climb her leg. That attracted every crab nearby, and when the lucidor put on some speed to get past them his ankle gave out and he stumbled and fell headlong.

Almost at once, one of the crabs was on his chest. The sharp points of its claws pricking through his shirt, its pincers clicking

318

a bare finger-length from his face, a nightmare parody of a face tucked under the rim of its shell. Red eyes bulging on stiff stalks. A mouth that was all flaps and jointed claws. It pinched his finger as he knocked it away, and then Orjen and Lyra were hauling him to his feet. He had cut his shin, blood was seeping into the white dust that coated his loose trews, but he was able to limp after the women.

There were fewer crabs around them now; most were jostling in a kind of feeding frenzy around the one Lyra had stamped flat, and a spider crab was tottering towards the spot too. It gave the lucidor an idea: he smashed a crab with his stick and limped a few steps and smashed another. Orjen and Lyra caught on immediately and stamped on several more, leaving a trail that attracted crabs and spider crabs and allowed them to reach the abandoned drill site unhindered. Orjen armed herself with a shovel; the lucidor picked up a coil of rope and threw one end to Lyra and pointed to the monsters strung along the water's edge and said breathlessly, 'If we bring down one of the big ones.'

'The rest will come running,' Orjen said.

'And we dodge through any gap they leave. Jump in the water.'

'Let's hope they can't swim,' Lyra said.

They picked out a spider crab and ran at it. The lucidor and Lyra hauling the rope taut, Orjen holding the shovel like an axe as she chased after them. The spider crab spun around at the last moment. The lucidor ducked as one of its legs lashed at him; the rope burned his palms as it tangled around two more and he was jerked off his feet as the spider crab slewed and crashed backwards in a huge cloud of white dust. Orjen ran past him and chopped at the creature's body until Lyra pulled her away. Several spider crabs were already turning towards the spot, and the lucidor picked himself up and ran after Orjen and Lyra towards the edge of the cliff, and trod in a pothole brimful with white dust and went sprawling.

He rolled over, holding his bad ankle, saw red crabs coming at him from both sides and a spider crab towering above, and there was a flash of brilliant light that bleached colour out of everything and the spider crab twisted away. The crabs had all frozen on the spot, claws raised, but started forward again when the lucidor pushed to his feet, shrugging off his leather coat and stumbling to the edge of the cliff and more or less rolling over it.

He hit the water hard, sinking to the bottom in a caul of bubbles, frog-kicking to the surface. In the distance, one of the boats was running the tide through one of the channels, but the second had turned towards him, its flank suddenly looming above, Lyra and one of the marines leaning over the side and grabbing him and hauling him aboard.

42

Infection

The lucidor was placed in quarantine as soon as he returned to the ship. Confined to his cabin with a sailor stationed outside the door. It was only a precaution, Jy Solon told him. Nothing serious.

'Your sawbones took a sample of my blood when he bandaged my hand,' the lucidor said. 'Was that also a precaution?'

'Standing orders. One of the marines was badly mauled by one of those monster crabs, and two others were nipped or bitten, along with one of Stonebuilder's crew, and they are all being treated in the exact same way. Sit tight, do your time, and you will be out and about in a few days.'

The enforced isolation gave the lucidor plenty of time to think about his encounter with the shatterling. If that was what it had been. He had dozed off and thought that he'd woken up before the shatterling spoke to him, but then he had woken again, so it could have been nothing but a dream, got up from his need to re-establish contact. He had his doubts about the flash of light which appeared to have driven off the spider crab, too. No one else seemed to have seen it; rather than an intervention by the shatterling, it was possible that the spider crab had been struck by a stray round when it had pounced on him and the flash had been nothing more than mirrorlight reflected from a cleaved rock, or some kind of hallucination – after all, he'd banged his head when he had fallen over.

He turned it over and around in his mind, but couldn't resolve it one way or the other. The shatterling had told him that it needed his help, so if he hadn't conjured the entire conversation from fancy and dream stuff, if it really had reached out to him, it would reach out again. And it seemed that it had tried to involve Remfrey He in its plans, too – perhaps it had made contact with him through the alter network, and Remfrey He, in his arrogance, had tried to trick or double-cross it. The lucidor hoped so. Hoped that the shatterling would have a good reason to want to help him take the man down.

His sleep was restless and intermittent. Time and again he surfaced from dreams patched from fragments of the day's horrors, and every time he woke he woke alone.

Orjen visited him the next morning, wearing her white coat and thin plastic gloves, a cotton mask tied over her mouth and nose. She examined his bruised hand and the cut on his shin, took his pulse and temperature, and asked him how he felt.

'I feel like I'm back in the brig. How long is this quarantine going to last?'

'Have you had any headaches, night sweats, nausea?'

'My ankle still hurts, but otherwise I feel fine.'

'Digestive upsets, cramps?'

'What's this about?'

'There's no other way of telling this than telling you straight,' Orjen said. She looked as if she hadn't slept since their misadventure. Smudges under her eyes, lank hair unbrushed. 'I mapped the sample of blood the ship's doctor took from you. The plain fact is that you are infected with the invasion's tailswallowers.'

'Are you sure?'

'One of Var Stonebuilder's map readers confirmed it. The others who were bitten are also infected.'

'You said that crabs and other creatures couldn't infect people.'

'It seems that these crabs can,' Orjen said.

The lucidor felt numb. The same ringing numbness he'd felt when he had been told of his wife's death. The aftershock of a moment when a life is violently divided into before and after.

He said, 'It was no more than a nip. It hardly broke the skin.'

'I'm sorry.'

'What now?'

'All we can do is wait and see.'

'Wait until it kills me, or until it turns me into some kind of monster?'

'You are thinking of the infection carried by the red tides. This isn't that.'

'What is it then?'

'We don't know. It's similar to the tailswallower plague spread by rats in Ymr. Similar, but not identical.'

'The plague that killed ten thousand people.'

'Some survived after they were infected. They weren't ever cured, but the disease became dormant,' Orjen said, and told him that although the technician who had been bitten by a crab had developed a high fever and a badly swollen leg, the two marines who had been likewise bitten were so far, like him, unaffected.

'What about the other marine? The one who tangled with a spider crab?'

'He died in the night, but as far as we can tell he died from complications caused by his injuries, not from his infection.'

'I wish I could feel comforted by that.'

'You aren't showing any obvious symptoms. That's a good sign. Also, you are a stubborn man. If anyone can beat this, it's you. And I promise,' Orjen said with fierce avowal, 'that I will do everything I can to make sure that you do.'

'And if I don't, how long will I have?'

'Why don't we wait and see how it goes?'

'I would like to know the worst case as well as the best.'

'The best case is that it remains dormant, and you get to live a normal life. More or less normal, anyway. But if it does progress, and if it progresses in the same way as the tailswallower plague, then somewhere between thirty and a hundred days.'

'Thank you for answering honestly.'

Orjen looked puzzled. 'What other kind of answer should I give?'

Like any true philosopher it hadn't occurred to her to give him comfort with a lie. The lucidor should have reciprocated, should have told her about the shatterling's manifestation, but after a moment's hesitation knew that he couldn't. Not only because he wasn't certain if it had been real, but also because he didn't yet know what it meant.

'You're taking this very calmly,' Lyra said, when she came to visit a little later. 'If I were you, I would be raging at the sky right now. Calling on the creator gods to account for themselves.'

'This tailswallower disease wasn't made by the creator gods.'

'They could have done a better job of making us, so we weren't so damn vulnerable to it.'

'It is what it is,' the lucidor said.

He was still gripped by a cool numbness, as if he was set at a slight angle to the rest of the world, but knew from his experience of dealing with his wife's death that numbness would give way to anger if he let it, and anger to futile appeals for an intercession by the creator gods. What would it have cost them to turn back time, or to have given him one more day with Deme? He would have offered up his life for that, for just one day, as it once had been, but in time he had learned that, like anger, his futile yearning had been a stage in reconnecting with the world as it was, not as he had wanted it to be. In coming to terms with the stark fact that everything had been forever changed. He didn't have time for any of that now, and besides, he told himself, he had already offered up his life when he'd set out in pursuit of Remfrey He. Had already anticipated a reckoning such as this.

'It's unfair, is what it is,' Lyra said. 'But I think, you being a tough old door kicker, you're going to beat this thing.'

'All I ask is that I have enough time to get where we're going, and find Remfrey He,' the lucidor said. 'And when we do, I hope I will have enough life left in me to be able to do the right thing.'

43

Change of Command

The sea was calm, red weed and chalkweed shoals grew ever more widely scattered, and the ship made good headway. Orjen visited the lucidor every day, taking a blood sample and telling him that he was doing well, telling him about her work. Partly to distract him, partly because, being who she was, she couldn't not. The lichen specimens she and Lyra had collected had been lost in the scramble to escape from the island, she said, but she had been collaborating with Var Stonebuilder's crew, and it appeared that although the small crabs from the shoals looked identical, they were from at least three different species, and both the red weed and chalkweed were patchworks of different species which all had the same appearance and growth habit. The current hypothesis was that the invasion's tailswallowers silenced life-map patterns that created differences between species, driving them back to earlier, common forms, and then in directions never before taken.

'Remfrey He told me that alter women were our future,' the lucidor said. 'The inescapable destiny of our descendants.'

'He told me that too, at interminable length,' Orjen said. 'And he was wrong in every respect.'

The lucidor was amused by her acid disdain. 'How do you know?'

'He cannot read life maps, and I can. I know the field, and he doesn't. Alter women are not a possible future for our descendants, but for the distant ancestors used as a template by the creator gods when they made the First People. A path not taken until people were infected by the red tide's tailswallowers, just like the crabs and chalkweed. There's a good, sound way of testing that idea. We could infect closely related species of crab or fish, and if we are right, their offspring will all develop in the same way. And then, once we have established how tailswallower infections work, we can begin to find out how to stop them.'

'Does this mean you are closer to finding a cure?'

'We are closer to finding the beginning of a path that may lead to a cure, but I'm afraid that any cure is still a long way off. At least you still show no symptoms, and the tailswallower load in your blood has levelled off,' Orjen said brightly. 'As long as that lasts, there's still hope.'

'Yes, I know that I should count myself fortunate,' the lucidor said, 'given what happened to the others.'

Lyra had told him that the technician had not survived an operation to amputate her leg after it had developed gangrene, and both of the marines had been struck down by high fevers. One was coughing up blood; the other had developed chalky nodules under his skin. Despite Orjen's reassurances, and his resolution to last long enough to find Remfrey He, the lucidor had a deep-rooted feeling that his own prognosis would be little better. Horrible to think about; impossible not to, when every little twinge or ache might be the onset of something terminal.

Impossible, too, to dismiss the nagging hope that the shatterling might somehow intercede. After all, it was a servant of the creator gods: perhaps, if the lucidor could find some place imprinted with the requisite emotional energy, it could work some kind of miracle. It was a small hope, but all the hope he had, and all the more reason to find Remfrey He, and the root of the invasion.

At last, the fifteenth day of his quarantine, Orjen told the lucidor that a hint of land had appeared at the horizon. Like the island they had visited, this strange coast was not recorded on any of the old charts, and according to her last message the *First Pilgrim* was shipwrecked somewhere along it.

'Saphor Godshorse has been consulting with his superiors back home about how to proceed,' Orjen said. 'And he has told Mr Solon to start to make preparations for a landing party.'

'You should remind the captain that he will need me soon,' the lucidor said.

'I don't think that will do any good.'

'Then perhaps I should talk to Mr Solon.'

'I am not going to be allowed ashore either,' Orjen said. 'We have been told that there will be no time for research until the *First Pilgrim* is found and any survivors are rescued. And perhaps not even then, if it may put the ship in danger. It's stupidly short-sighted, but the captain won't listen to reason. He prefers to take the advice of people who have no knowledge of or interest in what we can learn about the invasion.'

'I wasn't planning on doing any research,' the lucidor said. 'Tell Jy I have been missing his company.'

Orjen promised that she would pass on the message, but apart from the sailor who delivered his evening meal the lucidor had no other visitors that day, and early the next morning the ship hove to. The lucidor wondered if it had sighted the *First Pilgrim* or if it was sending an exploratory party ashore, but a little over an hour later the vibration and muffled roar of the motors started up again.

No one brought him breakfast, the time for Orjen's usual visit came and went, and around midday he heard the distant but unmistakable sound of gunfire. A small fusillade followed by several spaced shots; a faint swell of distant shouts. The lucidor pounded on the ironwood shield of the door but there was no response. Soon afterwards, the ship slowed and stopped again. Dead in the water. Wallowing gently to and fro.

The lucidor had worn his hair loose ever since he had been confined to the cabin; now he gathered it up into a ponytail and pinned it with the barrette, and sat on the edge of his bunk and waited for something to happen. He knew how to wait. He'd spent hours and days watching back-country shacks and caves, floating lodges in the marshes, houses and godowns in Freetown or in dusty little desert towns, and all the other places where suspects lived or were supposed to be hiding, and he had spent at least as much time waiting outside offices to obtain warrants from magistrates or to explain to his superiors what he needed to do or what he had done. Waiting had been a significant part of his work and he had long ago learned how to be patient. To endure the passing of time without becoming annoyed or upset or restless. A state of being without doing.

Darkness fell outside the cabin's small round window. The lucidor didn't switch on the light, wasn't surprised when, like his breakfast and lunch, his evening meal didn't arrive. At last he heard the faint sound of voices outside, a muffled scuffle. It wasn't monsters, then. That was one of the scenarios he had been entertaining: giant crabs or alter women swarming aboard the ship and killing everyone except for him. But it wasn't monsters. It was people. He hoped it was a gang come to take him to Remfrey He, because it would save him the trouble of searching for the man, and he moved to one side of the door, ready to take them down.

The door slammed back and sailors crowded into the small cabin in a disorganised rush, getting in each other's way. Faces half-masked with kerchiefs, wearing leather gauntlets or elbow-length rubber gloves, some armed with staves, others with hammers and knives. The first one through the door had a pistol. The lucidor smashed it from his hand and grabbed the next man and was trying to use him as a shield when someone struck him hard on the back of the head. He was seized and slammed to the floor, rolled into a cocoon of blankets that was cinched tight around his chest and hips and feet, and dragged out of the cabin and hauled up a ladder. The bindings around the blankets were pulled away, and when he managed to free himself he discovered that he was inside a square cage bolted to the aft deck. He was bleeding from a cut in his scalp and was bruised all over, but had suffered no serious injury.

The beam of one of the spotlights up on the flying bridge transfixed him as he used the bars of the cage to pull himself to his knees. He couldn't stand because the cage was too small. The crowd parted and two figures stepped forward, backlit by the spotlight's glare. Jy Solon and one of the petty officers, Jy telling the lucidor that the new arrangement was a necessary precaution.

'The two marines who were bitten, like you? One of them is like a living skeleton armoured in chalk plate. The other died yesterday. Growths in his belly squeezed his bowels shut, he died in agony, and he was thrown into the sea like a side of spoiled beef. Some of the men wanted to do the same with you. I convinced them that you will help us to find Remfrey He, but they didn't want you below decks, breathing the same air as everyone else. This cage, it's a compromise. Not ideal, I know, but better than drowning.'

'What happened here, Jy? Where's the captain?'

'Captain Godshorse is, you might say, indisposed,' Jy said.

'Locked in his cabin along with others who objected to the change in command,' the petty officer said.

He was the stout middle-aged man, Effra Ro, who had objected to the lucidor eating at the petty officers' roundtable. He stood with his arms folded across his chest, trying and failing to stare down the lucidor.

'Then who is in charge now?' the lucidor said.

'You might say I'm the captain, acting at the pleasure of the crew,' Jy said.

'Acting under advisement,' Effra Ro said.

'Exactly so.'

'The crew mutinied, and you went along with it,' the lucidor said.

'Mutiny is a contentious word,' Effra Ro said.

'I don't know what else to call it,' the lucidor said.

'It's a change of command, as Mr Ro said,' Jy told him.

'Dictated by the circumstances. And you're lucky Mr Solon came over to our side, because if he hadn't I have no doubt you would be sleeping with the fishes now,' Effra Ro said. 'Or with what passes for fishes, out here.'

'We're still on course to find the *First Pilgrim*,' Jy Solon said. 'And we still aim to capture Remfrey He and rescue any of the crew who might be alive. As long as you keep quiet and don't cause trouble, and give such help as we might need, you'll do all right.'

'You had better be as useful as Mr Solon claims,' Effra Ro said, and turned his back on the lucidor and told the sailors it was done, they had all earned a tot.

After the spotlight had been switched off and the mob had dispersed below decks, the lucidor ripped a corner from one of the blankets with his teeth and used it to staunch the cut in his

329

scalp. The cage was bolted securely to the deck, its walls and roof were lattices of ironwood bars, and its door was secured with an iron padlock as big as his fist. An heirloom centuries old, recently greased. The lucidor examined it by touch, then stretched out along the cage's diagonal, wrapped in the blankets.

The night sky was clear and cloudless. A long, low, ragged line silhouetted against the clash of stars to the right, to starboard, had to be the coast that Orjen had told him about. He hoped that she and Lyra were safe. Locked up with the rest of the expeditionary company in their cabins, or in one of the cargo holds.

Although the ship was still aimed towards the *First Pilgrim*, that might quickly change. The mob was in control, and in the lucidor's experience mobs were fickle, flighty creatures. Jy Solon was like a rider on a maddened warhorse, holding the reins but utterly unable to check its headlong flight. And even if they did find the *First Pilgrim* and rescue its crew, where could they go afterwards? If they returned to Patua and tried to surrender to the army, no story that Jy might concoct would save him and the crew from execution for mutiny, and if they abandoned ship and tried to trek overland to the Free State they wouldn't be accepted as political refugees because it would violate every treaty. Their best chance, the lucidor decided, would be to join one of the rebel groups, and ransom Remfrey He and any crew they could rescue.

It wasn't the outcome the lucidor had promised to deliver when he had set out from the Free State, and the lucidor doubted that he would be allowed to return to Patua, for all Jy's fine words – if the mob had its way he wouldn't live long enough to be killed by his infection – but there was no point in trying to do anything about that until the ship reached the *First Pilgrim* and he could see how things were going to shake out.

He lay on his back, staring up at the eternal spectacle of the night sky, trying not to think about worst-case outcomes, what might or might not happen. Although the ship had left the familiar mirror arcs far behind, the washes of stars and gas that spanned the sky from horizon to horizon were still much the same. The world was large, but the sky was larger still. An ancient arena of gods and godlings, indifferent to the plight of ordinary people.

It would not matter to the stars if the *Resolute Mind* succeeded in finding the heart of the invasion and a way of putting an end to it, or if the invasion pushed across Patua into the Free State, and overwrote the gods' creation there and on all the other maps. No, the stars would continue to shine as they always had, long after the petty struggles of men and women had passed away.

The wanderer, Tiu, stood high and bright to the east. The lucidor remembered that Surmal had said it was the star of war and warriors, and he hoped it was a good omen, although he knew that there was only a slender chance that this adventure would have a better ending than the affair of the alter nest.

He woke at first light, his shirt and blankets cold and clammy, his chest greasy with perspiration, and felt a deep plangent pang of dismay: night sweats were one of the symptoms Orjen had asked about. But he didn't feel feverish, told himself that the sweating and bone-deep aches in his arms and legs were no more than the aftermath of his struggle to escape the mob of sailors. Told himself that he didn't have time to fall ill. Not now. Not when he was so close to his quarry.

The ship was on the move, running parallel to the distant coast. He shed his blankets, let the warm breeze dry him. A little later, a sailor poked a tray through the bars and turned away without answering the lucidor's greeting. Breakfast was a cardboard cup of water and a heel of stale bread. More a statement of contempt than a meal. The lucidor soaked the bread to make it palatable, took stock as he slowly chewed. Jy Solon and Effra Ro were up on the bridge, open sea stretched away under a cloudless sky to port, and to starboard dashes of white water broke on reefs and a low smudged line of land ran west and east, too far away to make out any detail.

After finishing his breakfast, the lucidor urinated in a corner of his cage and exercised as best he could, then sat cross-legged with a blanket hooded around his shoulders and head against the growing glare and heat of the mirrors, watching the distant shore slide past, waiting for the next thing to happen.

Early in the afternoon he was roused by a disturbance on the foredeck. Sailors were crowding along the port rail, and on the flying wing of the bridge Jy Solon had fitted a brass spyglass to one eye and was scanning the water close to the ship's port side. The lucidor pushed up to a crouch, saw long smooth shadows in the green swell. Three, four, five of them moving parallel to the ship and matching its speed. They were big, half the ship's length, standing off by three hundred or so spans. Leviathans, or something very like them.

After half an hour or so, the creatures arched up one after the other, smooth black backs breaking the water before vanishing in swirls of foam. A little later, Orjen and a sailor came up onto the aft deck. The lucidor felt his heart turn at the sight of her. She told him that Jy Solon had sent her to collect a sample of his blood to check the progress of his infection, said that she hadn't been harmed. The first officer had locked her in her cabin when the trouble had started.

'I'm sure you will be safe,' the lucidor said. 'Being who you are, you're a valuable hostage.'

'As safe as I can be, on a ship full of men unconstrained by authority. You look terrible, by the way.'

'I tried to put up a fight before they wrestled me into this cage. It looks worse than it is.'

'Mr Solon told me that Var Stonebuilder is locked up with the captain and most of the other officers. Lyra is in the brig,' Orjen said. 'Sailors beat her when she tried to stop them throwing the equipment and specimens overboard.'

'What about Stonebuilder's people?'

'I don't know,' Orjen said. 'I think most of them went over to the crew's side.'

She gave him a brief account of the mutiny. Shortly after the marine died and his body had been unceremoniously shot over the side, a pod of leviathans had appeared and some of the sailors had panicked, mistaking them for monsters.

'I saw them myself just now,' the lucidor said.

'The sailors thought that they were going to attack the ship,' Orjen said. 'They broke into the armoury and started to shoot at them. The captain was seized when he tried to intervene, and everything went bad very quickly.'

The sailor escorting her told her to get on with it. The lucidor extended his arm through the lattice of the cage and Orjen pricked his finger and squeezed out a drop of blood that she smeared on a slide. As she worked, she said quietly, 'I am going to tell Mr Solon there are fewer tailswallowers in your blood. That you appear to be getting better.'

'Even if he believes you, he can't set me free. It wasn't his decision to put me here.'

Orjen ignored that. 'I will tell him I need to examine you, to find out why you are throwing off the infection. And when I get you out of this stupid cage we can work out how to free Lyra.'

But she didn't return that day, and the next morning Jy Solon brought the lucidor's breakfast and told him that they were about a day away from the *First Pilgrim*, so he had better start thinking about how he could help them secure Remfrey He.

'I can tell you one thing,' the lucidor said. 'You won't find him anywhere near the ark.'

'How do you know that?'

'Long experience of the man. He doesn't play well with others.'

'If you know where he might be and what he might be doing, it would be best if you told me now.'

They were crouching head to head, separated by the cage's bars. The lucidor could smell heart-of-wine on the first officer's breath.

'You once told me that you hoped I could help you enforce discipline if Captain Godshorse lost control,' the lucidor said. 'It's too late for that, but I can still help you, and I think you know it. It's why you persuaded the crew to let me live.'

'I can only keep you alive if you agree to cooperate.'

'We can find Remfrey He together. We don't need anyone else.'

Jy Solon hesitated for a moment, glancing over his shoulder at the bridge, where Effra Ro was talking with several sailors. 'Your friend the governor's daughter tried to convince me that you are throwing off your infection,' he said. 'But one of Stonebuilder's map readers double-checked the blood sample and found no difference. If the two of you are planning something, I advise you to give it up. I can keep her safe so long as you cooperate. Her servant too. I give you my word on that. But if you don't do everything that's asked of you, or if you try to escape, I can't say what will happen.'

'Your life hangs on the whim of the mob as much as mine does,' the lucidor said, as Jy Solon pushed to his feet. 'That's why we should work together.'

It would be useful to have the man's help, if only because he knew how to handle a boat, but it wasn't essential. Orjen and Lyra had been puttering up and down the coast of the Horned Strait when the lucidor had first met them, and they were both resourceful and fiercely committed. He believed that he had more than enough time to work out what he needed to do, but then the leviathans returned, and everything was thrown at hazard.

44

Little Leviathans

There were just two leviathans this time, appearing late in the afternoon, standing off from the ship as before and accompanied by half a dozen smaller versions, man-sized, swift and fierce, each armed with a single tusk as long as their bodies. These little leviathans swam on either side of the wave ploughed up by the ship's bow, sometimes launching themselves into the air with muscular shimmies and arching back into the sea with precise elegance.

The lucidor, watching inside his cage, suddenly felt that someone was standing at his shoulder, and knew that the shatterling had opened their connection. Knew, with a fizzing mix of apprehension and excitement that reminded him of all the times he'd waited for a raid to kick off, that something was about to happen.

Sailors standing at the bow's guard rails started to take pot shots at the little leviathans, ignoring Jy Solon when he shouted at them to cease fire. As the first officer bustled down the steps from the bridge to the foredeck there was a series of sharp thumps along the starboard side of the ship as some of the little leviathans began to ram the hull. Sailors fired their long guns straight down into the water and for a few minutes it seemed that the creatures had been driven back, but then a shout went up and the lucidor glimpsed the sleek shape of one of the big leviathans pushing up a foaming wave as it powered towards the ship.

Jy Solon ran back towards the bridge, the lucidor braced himself against the cage's bars, and the ship slewed around and heeled over as the leviathan slammed into it. A wave of green water washed over the bow and smashed into the racks of light-collectors. Sailors grabbed at rails and stanchions or lost their footing and fell. Two of them were knocked overboard, splashing helplessly in the choppy water, and the shadow of a little leviathan rose beneath one of them and he was struck and briefly lifted up, clutching the end of the tusk which had spiked him through his back and belly, before vanishing in a welter of foam.

Up on the bridge, Jy Solon and Effra Ro were standing toe to toe, shouting at each other. The sailors regrouped along the starboard guard rail, two of them throwing a rope to the surviving man in the water and hauling him aboard, others aiming their long guns here and there. No one was paying any attention to the lucidor as he pulled the barrette from his ponytail and shucked the two ironwood pins from its leather patch.

The original barrette, the one he'd lost in the alter nest controlled by Remfrey He, had also possessed two pins, each with a cap that when unscrewed revealed an iron spike. They could have been used as weapons, in a pinch, or as lock picks. The lucidor hoped that the simple ironwood pins of his new barrette would serve just as well.

He slammed into the side of the cage and fell to his knees as the ship heeled under a second impact, and as it rocked back he scrambled to the door and inserted the pins in the big iron padlock, and in less than a minute had raked its pegs and unsnapped it.

The ship was making a sharp turn towards the shore: Jy Solon must be aiming for a channel in the reefs, hoping to run into shallower water where the big leviathans couldn't follow. The lucidor shouldered through the cage door and ran for the nearest companionway, was clambering down its ladder when another smashing impact rocked the ship. He lost his footing and fell heavily, hurting his bad ankle, picked himself up, and limped towards the narrow gangway that ran through the ship's waist. The ship was listing now, and there was a constant tattoo of thuds and bangs against the hull. The lucidor scrambled through the gangway in the massed roar of the motors, checked the passageway beyond and saw no one, and headed towards the officers' quarters.

The door of Orjen's cabin was bolted on the outside. She sprang at him when he opened it, a scalpel dropping from her hand when he caught and twisted her wrist.

'I suppose you expect me to go with you,' she said, after the lucidor had told her what was happening and what he planned to do.

'I don't expect that you want to stay here. And we must make haste. The leviathans are keeping the crew busy, but sooner or later someone will notice that I have escaped, and they'll come looking for me.'

'There is no point in escaping if I am unable to do my work,' Orjen said. She was packing leatherbound notebooks, sample jars and tubes, vials of chemicals, a magnifying loupe and other necessaries of her trade into a canvas bag. 'We must find Lyra, and free Saphor Godshorse and the other officers. We can't leave them to the mercy of the mutineers, and they can help us.'

'I doubt that,' the lucidor said, but before he could explain what he meant Orjen had slung the bag over her shoulder and pushed past him.

He followed her to the captain's cabin, at the far end of the passageway; when she opened the door, a familiar foul stink rolled out. The lucidor told Orjen to stay where she was and ducked through. There they were, the captain and the sawbones, the second and third officers, Var Stonebuilder and three of her crew. Seated around a table, lashed to their chairs, heads lolling. They had been badly beaten and cut, and other things had been done to Saphor Godshorse; the lucidor didn't care to look too closely.

Papers and broken glass and crockery covered the floor and the captain's bedroom had been looted, but the lucidor found a bottle of heart-of-wine under a heap of clothes. Orjen gave him a pale grim look, said, 'Lyra is in the brig. Down on the lower deck.'

'I remember where it is.' The lucidor didn't need to tell her that, despite Jy Solon's promise, the mutineers might also have killed her steward. He could see it in her face. He said, 'We need to do something else first. It will only take a moment.'

The ship's boats were kept in cradles that retracted into the hull on either side of the bow. The lucidor led Orjen to the boat on the port side, climbed into it and found an axe in its emergency kit, and started to chop a hole in its planking.

'So the mutineers can't follow us,' Orjen said.

'Exactly,' the lucidor said. He had to pause and brace himself when a dull thunder boomed through the ship and everything tipped sideways and slowly righted, and finished his work and climbed out.

'Those leviathans aren't going to give up until the ship is at the bottom of the sea,' he said, as they made their way towards the brig.

'Do you think Remfrey He directed them to attack us?'

'More likely we strayed onto their territory. Bad luck for the mutineers; good luck for us.'

'If they sink this ship, and the *First Pilgrim* is too badly damaged to be repairable, how will we get home?'

'Let's worry about one thing at a time.'

Ankle-deep water sloshed in the storage lockers on the bottom deck and the air was filled with the noise of the ship's motors: the lucidor didn't hear the sailor approaching, almost bumped into the man as he rounded the corner of a narrow passageway between two walls of crates. The sailor dropped the stack of cardboard boxes he was carrying and reached for the pistol at his hip, and the lucidor clouted his head with flat of the axe blade, kicked his legs from under him, and handed the pistol to Orjen.

The key to the brig's door was hung on a hook beside it. Lyra crouched at the back of the tiny room, fists raised, breaking into a smile when she saw the lucidor and Orjen. Her nose was swollen and skewed to one side and both eyes were blacked. She nodded when the lucidor told him that they were getting off the ship, said, 'What about Stonebuilder and her crew?'

'Stonebuilder's dead,' the lucidor said. 'As for her crew, those who weren't killed went over to the mutineers. Give me a hand. Find anything that will burn.'

'How will we get back to Patua if you sink this ship?' Orjen said.

The lucidor did not believe that he had any chance of going home, but he didn't want to get into that.

'Let's hope that the *First Pilgrim* is still seaworthy,' he said. 'Because this ship is in the hands of the mutineer, and I want to make sure that they won't be able to follow us.'

'He's right,' Lyra said. 'We have no chance of taking it back, and it will give that mob of murderers the advantage if we don't do something about it.'

The lucidor searched the pockets of the unconscious sailor, found a tobacco pouch and a packet of lucifers. While Lyra and Orjen poured cooking oil over the crates, he opened the bottle he'd taken from the captain's cabin and wet a rag with heart-of-wine and twisted it in the bottle's neck. The lucifers were soaked and wouldn't catch, so he used the axe to chop the cabling between a pair of light globes and brushed the cut ends of the wires together. Sparks spat, kindling flames in the twist of rag, and he hurled the bottle at the bulkhead above the oil-soaked crates. It smashed in a bloom of blue fire that spread in a quick flood across the crates and dripped onto the surface of the water and set fire to floating pools of oil.

The lucidor, Orjen and Lyra beat a hasty retreat, dragging the sailor with them, propping him against a stair for his friends to find. Smoke chased them as they made their way to the starboard side of the bow; the lucidor heard something explode with a dull thump, and distant shouts of alarm, as he and Lyra cranked the hatch open. The boat swung out as the hatch angled up, swaying from two davits, and they clambered into it and worked the ropes and pulleys that lowered it, dropping past the hull and smacking into the water.

Orjen and the lucidor unhitched the ropes and Lyra started the motor and turned the boat in a tight arc, aiming it towards a distant line of trees on the far side of a reach of shallow water. No one saw them go. Sailors were lined along the rail on the other side of the ship, firing ragged fusillades: the *Resolute Mind* had escaped the big leviathans by slipping through a channel in the outer reef, but it was still being harried by their little companions, and now the fire blossomed through one of the hatches in the foredeck, shooting a tumble of flames and smoke into the air.

'That'll keep 'em busy,' Lyra said.

'The only way is forward,' Orjen said.

'Straight on to the end,' the lucidor said.

45

Threads

As the stricken ship dwindled astern, partially obscured by the smoke of its burning, one of the little leviathans caught up with the boat and swam alongside it. The creature's broad muscular back was spotted like a sand leopard and there was a cap of tangled red threads on the bulge of its forehead, behind the root of its spiral horn.

Orjen looked at lucidor and said, 'Do you remember when I told you about the rats that spread the tailswallower plague in Ymr?'

'Vividly.'

'Some of them were also infected by a fungal pathogen that grew in a kind of caul over their heads and infiltrated their brains. Exterminators found nests of them, all knotted together.'

'She has a theory,' Lyra said. She sat sideways at the stern, gripping the tiller with her left hand as she guided the boat through a maze of tabletop reefs, running parallel to the trees that lined the edge of the water.

'The fungus that infected those rats had tailswallower patterns in its life map,' Orjen said. 'The cauls it produced were blood-red, like the cap our escort is wearing, and the threads we saw covering the shells of crabs and spider crabs of the floating island. I still regret that we weren't able to take specimens.'

'As I recall, we had other things to think about,' the lucidor said.

'I wonder what we might find if we dissected our companion,' Orjen said. 'Whether those threads grow down into its brain, as in the rats.'

The little leviathan dropped back as the boat slid through a narrow channel between two reefs, catching up with a flick of its flukes once they were past.

'Its friends saw the ship as a threat, but we seem to pass,' the lucidor said, misliking this talk of infection and dissection, wondering if Orjen would treat him like any other specimen if he succumbed to his tailswallower infection. 'Best not to even think of doing anything that might change that. Especially as the first and only thing we need to do is find out what happened to the *First Pilgrim*.'

'I would not be surprised if the fungus and its tailswallowers have something to do with it,' Orjen said.

When the boat crossed a stretch of open water the little leviathan sheered away, turning back towards the *Resolute Mind*, and soon afterwards the ship disappeared behind a bend in the shore. The lucidor, sitting in the bow with the axe laid across his lap, felt a little lift in his heart. The shatterling's brief contact had vanished, unnoticed, sometime during their escape. He was heading into the unknown with no guide, little in the way of resources and tailswallowers swarming in his blood, but at last he was free to put an end to Remfrey He and his mischief.

They drove on through a seemingly endless archipelago of tabletop reefs, keeping close to the fringe of trees. They grew close together, the trees, naked trunks standing on arched knots of roots and curving up to untidy mops of red ribbons. According to Orjen they weren't trees at all, but what she called homologous structures most likely derived from some kind of kelp. Their roots were really holdfasts, their trunks were stipes, and the ribbons that crowned them were blades, dripping a continuous rain of salt water.

The reefs appeared to be built of layers of chalkweed. Patches of sea grasses, long red tresses combed by currents, grew between them. Red crabs scuttled across stretches of white sand; schools of red fish glided above their shadows; scarlet jellyfish pulsed like errant hearts. Larger crabs lurked inside the knotted holdfasts of kelp trees, and a small troop of things like leathery black bags limberly swung through the treetops on writhing tentacles, calling each to each with high-pitched fluting whistles. Perhaps they had once been octopuses, Orjen said. Or squid. She was brimming with enthusiasm, trying to look everywhere at once, trying to catalogue every strange wonder, pointing out that the tree octopuses were patched with red threads, saying that this new map had been raised up from the seabed, so everything living on it was most likely derived from marine life. The invasion made use of everything it infected with its tailswallowers, altering plants and animals by blind selection or by design.

'Hold tight,' Lyra told the lucidor. 'When she starts on a train of thought like this you never know where it will end up.'

'All I can do is speculate,' Orjen said. 'I don't have the tools or the time to begin to properly unravel this mystery. And even if I could, it's likely that no one else will ever know. We set fire to the ship that was supposed to take us home, and we don't even have a godspeaker.'

'The *Resolute Mind* wasn't going to take us home,' the lucidor said. 'Not after the mutiny. As for a godspeaker, it's likely that Remfrey He didn't destroy all of the ones carried by the *First Pilgrim*. At some point he will want to boast about what he's done.'

'It wouldn't surprise me if he still had followers back home, keeping him in touch,' Lyra said. 'He might be expecting us.'

'Then he will be gravely disappointed when we turn up without a ship,' Orjen said.

'I plan to disappoint him as much as possible,' the lucidor said.

At last, with the mirrors sinking behind them, the coast turned sharply and they saw that they had rounded the point of a peninsula, with the mouth of what looked like a river beyond. A small island covered with red vines sat in the centre of the river mouth and kelp trees fringed it on either side, with rounded hills rising in the east. Black water, dark blue sky, everything else in shades of pink and red, softly glowing in the red light of the setting mirrors.

The lucidor scarcely noticed the panorama. He was looking towards the eastern horizon, and a thread of pale fire slanting up into the sky. And the shatterling was looking at it too, eager and hungry and fierce, sweeping through the lucidor and carrying him off, helpless as a leaf on a flood tide.

46

Never Get Off the Ship

He woke in a hammock slung from ceiling hooks in some kind of kitchen or galley, with pots and pans hanging from hooks above griddlestones and clay ovens, worktables topped with white stone, a double sink cluttered with unwashed crockery. Floor and tables and sinks all at a sideways tilt, everything starkly agleam in the clinical light of electric lanterns.

He had bitten his tongue and the insides of his cheeks and there was a cloudy shadow in the left side of his vision, a presence that slyly moved away when he moved his head towards it. When he sat up, gripping both sides of the swaying hammock, Orjen rose from a chair behind him and helped him swing around and plant his bare feet on the floor. She told him that he had suffered a full-blown fit and lapsed into unconsciousness, but she and Lyra had managed to reach the wreck of the *First Pilgrim* and get help from the last man left aboard.

'The last man? Where is everyone else?'

Orjen handed him a glass of water. 'It seems that they abandoned ship.'

'Including Remfrey He?'

'Including Remfrey He.'

'Where did they go?'

'We don't yet know.'

The lucidor couldn't tell if the shadow at the edge of his vision was a manifestation of the shatterling or an after-effect of his seizure. There was an obscure weakness in his left arm, a faint tremor in his left hand. Even though he was holding the glass in both hands he had trouble guiding it to his mouth.

343

He took a sip of warm flat water, asked how long he'd been unconscious.

'Almost a day.' Orjen hesitated, then said, 'I took a reading on a sample of your blood after we got you settled. I'm afraid it isn't good news.'

'The infection isn't dormant any more, is it?'

He was not surprised or especially upset. He had been expecting it ever since his diagnosis.

'The number of tailswallowers in your blood has increased,' Orjen said. 'And because of your fit they may be active in your brain, too.'

'How long do I have?'

'I don't know. Truly. It seems to progress in different people at different rates. Wait. I'm not sure that's wise. You need to rest.'

Blood thumped hard in the lucidor's head and he spilled half the water left in the glass when he stood up, but he managed to take several steps along the slanting floor.

'I have already rested,' he told Orjen. 'Show me what you've found.'

The big ship was resting on its side at around twenty degrees to the horizontal; a system of ropes helped to navigate the tilted corridors and companionways. The climb left the lucidor light-headed and breathless; he clung to the skewed frame of the companionway for a few moments, sweating hard, before he followed Orjen onto the deck. He wasn't so much tired as hollowed out, and his bones ached and his left leg was loose and uncooperative.

The bridge loomed above, a square tower with platforms and balconies jutting at different levels and an observation deck with wraparound windows in its upper storey. It was partly overgrown by a thick weave of red vines, and cast a long shadow across the slope of the foredeck, where ranks of light solar collectors were half-submerged in a sea of vines.

'I remember seeing an island in the river,' the lucidor said. 'I didn't realise it was the *First Pilgrim*.'

Low, rounded hills spread away in late afternoon mirrorlight. He found that he could look at the pillar of what looked like smoke or fog that stood in the distance. A thin white scratch climbing into the sky and bending into a tail that spread westward.

'A pillar of cloud by day, and of fire by night,' Orjen said. 'Just as in the *First Pilgrim*'s last report. This way. It's only a short climb. Can you manage?'

The lucidor refused Orjen's offer of help, hauled himself, sweating and aching, up the sloping deck. The sole remaining member of the ship's crew, Sub-Lieutenant Romar Skywatcher, was sitting with Lyra on a small platform got up from scrap wood and wedged between the starboard rail and the slant of deck behind the bridge. He greeted the lucidor affably, offered him a glass of lemonade. 'It's quite tasty. Spiked with a little jenever.'

'By a little he means a lot,' Lyra said.

'Savoury sips throughout the day help me to maintain a proper attitude to the situation,' the sub-lieutenant said.

He was a lean young man with a spade-shaped beard, dressed in a grubby but neatly pressed uniform. A pistol was holstered at his hip, a machete lay on a small table beside him, next to a spyglass and a sweating pitcher of iced lemonade, and a long gun with a telescopic sight leaned against the rail.

'I need to keep a clear head,' the lucidor said, and carefully lowered himself into one of the canvas chairs. He saw Orjen and Lyra exchange a look, and knew that Lyra knew about his infection.

A rope ladder lashed to the rail ran down the tilted flank of the hull to the stolen boat, anchored in muddy water some thirty spans below. Most of the hull was covered in scrambling vines, but the lucidor could make out several small holes punched below what had been the waterline before the ship had grounded at a tilt, and a ragged wound that exposed two internal decks.

'What exactly happened here?' he said to Sub-Lieutenant Skywatcher. 'And where did everyone go?'

'They broke the first rule,' the sub-lieutenant said, refilling his glass with narrow concentration. 'Which is what, Mistress Gurnek?'

'Never get off the ship,' Lyra said.

'Exactly,' the sub-lieutenant said and raised his glass of lemonade in salute and drank half of it down with a grimace of pleasure. 'Rule number one: never get off the ship. Rule number two: maintain the perimeter. That's all there is to it. That's why I'm still here.'

He told the lucidor that he had fallen ill with a fever shortly after the *First Pilgrim* had sighted the coast of this new map, had woken hungry and thirsty, and discovered that the *First Pilgrim* had run aground and he was quite alone. Everyone else, the rest of the crew and the passengers, including Remfrey He's troupe of alter women, had abandoned ship.

'If you go to the bow and look straight ahead you'll see the boats drawn up on the shore. Mostly covered in vines now, but you can still make them out.'

'Why did they leave?'

'Someone must have broken the first rule. Went ashore, got themselves infected, spread it to everyone else when they came back on board. Sickness, madness, compulsion. Call it what you will. Everyone took to the boats and left, and I don't know what happened to them after that.'

'And Remfrey He went with them?'

'No one was left behind. No one but me,' the sub-lieutenant said. 'Frankly? I hope they're dead. If they aren't, what might have happened to them, what they might have become, it doesn't bear thinking about.'

He wasn't surprised or especially upset that the ship sent to rescue the *First Pilgrim*'s passengers and crew had run into trouble. As far as he was concerned the worst had already happened, and everything that followed was mere confirmation of his plight. He told the lucidor that he had never left the ship. Said that he had no reason to leave. There was plenty of food in the ship's stores, the light-collecting panels generated more than enough power, and he caught rainwater in a system of tarpaulins that channelled it into one of the ship's tanks. He made regular observations of the shore and river. He catalogued creatures he saw and noted their behaviour. He patrolled the decks, cutting back vines where they grew too thickly and searching out and eliminating crabs.

'You have to get them before they start to make nests in the vines or get inside the ship. It's the gods' own task to get rid of them if you don't. But crabs are the least of it. There are the things that come at night. Things from the sea. Luckily, most of them can't climb the hull, but if even one of them gets on board it's one more than I can deal with. I have to barricade myself below-decks while they smash around, wait until they leave. And then there are the watchers. Have you been told about the watchers?'

'Not yet,' the lucidor said.

'They gather every evening. More and more of them each night. You'll see soon enough,' the sub-lieutenant told the lucidor, and took a sip of lemonade.

'It's like animals that come to a waterhole at night,' Lyra said. 'Except they aren't here to drink. All they do is stare at the ship. The ones with eyes, anyhow. It's unnerving.'

'I think they are using the crabs as scouts,' Sub-Lieutenant Skywatcher said. 'To test me. To find weak spots in my defences. That's why it's important to maintain the perimeter. Never get off the ship. Never deviate from your routines. That's all there is to it. That's why I'm still here.'

He told the lucidor that he didn't know what was at the root of the pillar of cloud and fire, didn't know if that was where everyone else had gone, didn't know if Remfrey He had led them there.

'I had nothing to do with the fellow. I'm an electrical engineer. Helped to run the engines. He came down to the engine room once, but I wasn't introduced. It was First Lieutenant Leck who showed him around. Taklor "Greybeard" Leck. Good man to work under. Helped design your ship. The variable cranks in the motor array? They are his. Anyway, he showed Remfrey He around, and that was as close as I ever got to him. He didn't seem dangerous to me, although standing orders were never to find yourself alone with him. On account of his gift. His silvertongue. That's why, when he visited us, he was escorted by a muzzler. He was curious about everything. Wanted to know how it all worked. Was a very quick study, Mr Leck told me. A unique mind.'

'Where did he spend most of his time?' the lucidor said.

'Have you seen his workshop yet?'

'Not yet.'

'Oh, but you must. It's a cabinet of marvels.'

347

'Perhaps later,' the lucidor said. 'Are you quite certain that you never spoke with him?'

'I've told you what I remember,' Sub-Lieutenant Skywatcher said, and drained his glass of lemonade and picked up the machete and pushed to his feet. 'Day's in its last quarter. Time for my patrol. One last go around the perimeter, and then we will need to take ourselves below.'

'I'll come with you,' Lyra said, and stood up too.

'Don't forget to look at the workshop,' the sub-lieutenant told the lucidor. 'Remfrey He had a unique mind. I promise that you will be amazed by what he dreamed up.'

'The poor fellow talks about maintaining the perimeter,' Orjen told the lucidor, as they descended the sloping deck towards the companionway, 'but the ship is infested with crabs, and he is losing the battle to stop the vines overgrowing it. They are some kind of modified kelp, by the way.'

'Like the trees.'

'Exactly so. Everything here comes from the sea. And it's relentless. Mr Skywatcher has already lost the battle, but still he carries on, pretending that the expedition isn't completely lost.'

'It isn't lost,' the lucidor said. 'We found the *First Pilgrim*. All we need to do now is find its crew.'

He had to stop to catch his breath at the bottom of the companionway's ladder.

Orjen said, 'How are you holding up?'

'I can do what needs to be done.'

'I see you haven't lost any of your bullheaded singlemindedness.'

'It got me this far. Do you believe Mr Skywatcher's story about waking up alone?'

'I wondered if you had seen through that.'

'I'm a little feverish, but my mind is clear,' the lucidor said, trying to ignore the ghostly shadow hovering at the edge of his vision. 'What really happened?'

'Mr Skywatcher was unconscious for several days, but not because of a fever. I found his bunk, in the sick bay. He had been fed nutrients through a vein. Drugs too. Specifically, a derivative of soma.'

'He was kept asleep.'

'It seems so.'

'"Never get off the ship." That isn't Mr Skywatcher's rule. It's Remfrey He's. To make sure Mr Skywatcher stayed here, ready to receive us when we arrived, and tell us his story.'

'He talked to Mr Skywatcher before he was put to sleep, didn't he?' Orjen said.

'Or while he was asleep. Remfrey He liked to whisper in the ears of his followers while they nodded out on soma. He can charm people while they were awake, like anyone with the silvertongue gift, but when they are in a soma daze he can give them compulsions that they'll carry out days or weeks later, with no memory of being told what to do.'

Remfrey He had used a variety of drugs to control the members of his cult. They had habitually smoked kush to keep them mildly sedated and suggestible, and had taken small measures of a psychotropic that gave them transcendental visions that Remfrey He spun into stories of power and prophesy. He had given larger doses of the same psychotropic to new followers, as part of a programme to break their will, and to followers who had transgressed or shown any kind of resistance, humiliating them in front of the rest of the cult while they raved, steering their hallucinations into nightmares that some had never escaped.

'As soon as we came aboard, Mr Skywatcher tried to take us to Remfrey He's workshop,' Orjen said. 'He was very impatient, dancing around while Lyra and I were getting you settled. That was when I began to realise that he wasn't quite right in the head. There are things he wants to talk about, and things he doesn't. Things he refuses to acknowledge. Like the bodies Lyra found in one of the cold storage lockers. Twenty-three of them. Shot, stabbed, beaten. Mostly officers.'

'Including the captain?'

Orjen gave a tight nod. 'I think that they discovered that Remfrey He was up to something, but they were too late and too few.'

'It looks like they put up a fight,' the lucidor said. 'The small holes in the hull, below the waterline, were punched through from the outside. Probably by the same kind of leviathans that attacked the *Resolute Mind*. But the big hole was made by some kind of explosion inside the ship. What does Mr Skywatcher have to say about that? Was he part of the fight? And if he was, which side was he on?'

'He claims that he doesn't remember anything about a fight for control of the ship.'

'He also said that he had barely met Remfrey He, but twice mentioned He's unique mind,' the lucidor said. 'He's only weakness is his vanity. That's how I caught him, the first time. And that's how I'll catch him again.'

Remfrey He had liked to leave cryptic taunts at the scenes of his crimes. Towards the end, when the lucidor had broken up his network of stooges and accomplices, confiscated his assets and uncovered his lairs and spiderholes, the last of his followers began to paste up posters across the city. Boasts about his achievements. Threats to civic order. Rewards for the deaths of the lucidor and other lawkeepers. The lucidor had identified the men and women responsible for the posters and had them watched, and at last one had led him to Remfrey He. Although the man had escaped when the lucidor had led a raid on his hideout, he'd been wounded in the leg and had run out of resources, and had surrendered before the lucidor could find him again. Afterwards, of course, he had claimed that it had all been part of his plan.

'I left clues that you were supposed to unpick, but you were too dull and slow to understand them, so I had to lay a cruder, more obvious trail. Why? The plain truth is that my followers had grown too needy. As if they were pups and I was their mother. They would have sucked me dry if they could. A prison cell will give me peace and quiet. Time to think. To regroup. To make new plans. I have many years of work still to do.'

At the time, the lucidor had thought that this was nothing more than boastful bluster. A fantasy the man had spun to rationalise his defeat. But now, after Remfrey He had escaped from exile and the Patuan army's supervision, and turned his surrender at the alter nest to his advantage, he wasn't so sure.

Orjen said, 'He left Mr Skywatcher behind, and he left some of his work, too. How is your stomach?'

'I have seen what he can do.'

'This is something new,' Orjen said.

'You're going to show me rather than tell me?'

'It's the kind of thing that has to be seen to be believed.'

The workshop was near the bow and three decks down. More ladders. More ropes strung along slanting passageways. Orjen said that the ropeways were another reason why she and Lyra had realised that something was wrong.

'Mr Skywatcher was very insistent that we look at the workshop, he had woven this elaborate system of ropeways, but wouldn't go with us. We had to look. How could we not? We checked every step of the way, mindful of what Remfrey He had left behind in his workshop in Chimr, but this time he hadn't set any booby traps.'

'Remfrey He doesn't want to kill us,' the lucidor said. 'He needs the world to know what he has done.'

'He's certainly been very busy,' Orjen said.

The double doors of the workshop were propped open; the lucidor felt a chill stab of apprehension as he hauled himself inside. It was a long room, much like the galley where he had woken up, cluttered with the usual cabinets and workbenches. Everything that hadn't been fixed to the floor had rolled down its slope and lay in a heap along the footing of one bulkhead. The caged wall lights had been smashed, and spotlights had been trained on what Remfrey He had left behind.

Two tall glass cylinders, similar to those recovered from He's workshop in Delos-Chimr, and off to one side a smaller jar sitting inside a basket fixed to a workbench. In one cylinder tube a naked woman hung in clear liquid, skin flayed from her head and neck and shoulders, part of her skull removed to give a window onto her brain. In the other was what looked like a person-shaped vine, some stems pinkish-red, others bleached white. A pair of forked roots grew from a skinny trunk with fine short branches spaced on either side and two longer branches braided from a dozen long fibres, the whole grotesquely topped by a naked brain, complete with two eyes gone milky in the preservative fluid.

'It's a whole-body dissection of a human nervous system,' Orjen said. 'A beautiful piece of work that shows the full extent of the fungal infection. How the parasitic fibres are fully intertwined with the brain and spine, and the long nerves which control the limbs.'

They were leaning side by side against a workbench. The pitch of the floor and the darkness outside the focused glare of the spotlights, the thought that the same fungus might be growing inside him, invading his thoughts, gave the lucidor the sense of toppling into a void.

He said, 'Did he get this fungus from the alter nest he took over?'

'Nothing like it was ever found in any alters. In rats, yes. But as far as I recall their infection ate into their brains. This is something else. More refined. I don't believe that Remfrey He has the skill or knowledge to instruct map readers to create it; it's more likely that he went ashore and brought it back. From crabs, or some other creature. He infected the crew and left these specimens to show us what he had done.'

'It wouldn't take much to infect them, as I very well know.'

'I don't know if this is the same as your infection.'

'But it may be similar.'

'There's a lot I don't know yet.'

Orjen had a grim drawn look but her eyes were as bright as a hunter's. The lucidor thought that she was holding up pretty well, considering.

He said, 'Were they aware? Did they know what had been done to them, how they were changing?'

The loyalty of Remfrey He's followers had seemed fiercely genuine, and in almost every case that loyalty had not faded in the years after Remfrey He's arrest and the breakup of his cult. But sometimes, while questioning them, the lucidor had seen a flicker in their gaze and wondered if they knew, at some deep level, that they had been tricked into living a lie. And now he had to wonder if he was being changed, too.

'The fungal infection seems to have infiltrated the frontal lobes of the brain,' Orjen said. 'The throne of consciousness, according to the old texts. It's possible that its victims had little or any awareness left after they were turned into puppets. There is a good deal of growth around the dharma node, too. You can see it here.'

She slid along the workbench to the jar in its wicker cage; the lucidor followed, his left leg dragging. The jar contained half a brain, sliced vertically to show the folded helmet of the frontal and parietal lobes, the leafy cerebellum tucked behind the rope of nerves that gathered to run down the spine, and a grape-sized node enclosed by a fine network of red threads.

'The godlings spoke to the minds of the First People through their dharma nodes,' Orjen said. 'I think it likely that those infected by the fungus could communicate in much the same fashion.'

The lucidor had a bad thought and said, 'Is Sub-Lieutenant Skywatcher infected?'

'I don't know. There's no way to find out short of operating on him.'

'If he is, he could be relaying everything he sees and hears to Remfrey He. We should be careful what we say in his presence.'

The lucidor was gripped by a kind of clammy dismay. Remfrey He still possessed a full measure of his maniacal energy and inventiveness, while he was tired and mortally ill, at the outer edge of his endurance. A wanderer whose single-minded pursuit of his enemy had marooned him in a strange and hostile land far from home, bereft of authority and resources. And now the shadow at the corner of his sight was darkly pulsing, and he wasn't surprised when the shatterling stepped around the bench and looked at him. It was cloaked and cowled, as before. Stars for eyes. Orjen and the spotlit horrors and everything else in the room fell away.

'This is new and interesting,' the shatterling said, its voice soft as the slither of silk on silk.

'You didn't know about it?'

'He made it after I lost contact with him.'

'You told me before that you talked to him. You came to an agreement, I suppose, and he broke it.'

'You seem to think that I owe you an explanation.'

'As a matter of fact, you do,' the lucidor said, putting into it all the force and confidence that he could muster and looking straight at the two stars floating in the unfathomable darkness inside the figure's cowl. 'You no longer have Remfrey He's help, so I reckon that you need mine.'

'Do not think you can bargain with me. Especially as you are ill, and therefore of limited use.'

'So you know about that. I wondered if you did.'

'Assume that I know everything I need to know.'

'I caught Remfrey He before, and a little infirmity won't stop me from catching him again.'

The lucidor hesitated, knowing that it was weak, knowing that it was the kind of impossible bargain he had tried to make with the world after his wife's death, but he couldn't help himself. Saying, 'I would be more useful to you if you could fix me up.'

'I might be able to cure you. When this is over, and you have done all I ask of you.'

The lucidor was attuned by years of experience of spotting evasions and lies in the testimonies of wrongdoers and scofflaws, and knew then that the shatterling could not or would not help him. And knew too that the old cautionary tales about what happened to ordinary people who tried to enlist the help of revenants had it right, knew that he should not trust it.

He said, 'You told Remfrey He about this place, didn't you?'

'How did you guess?'

'You showed me that the alter network extended across the ocean. And if you thought Remfrey He could help you make use of it, you would have shown him too. After he surrendered to the Patuan army, he made up some story about alter compass dances to cover the truth, and persuaded the army to allow him to take alter women with him. He said that they would point the way, but I think he used them to keep in contact with you. And killed them, no doubt, when he had no more use for your help.'

'I was able to get inside the alter nest network when you carried our connection inside it,' the shatterling said. 'I found out how to access the link across the ocean, and followed it to its far end. And found something that was instantly and comprehensively belligerent. We fought such a battle that has not been seen on this world since the godlings departed. Intricate, furiously fierce, and over in less than a second. I was forced to retreat and wall myself off, but I knew where my enemy was, and understood the nature and limits of its powers. I knew that I could defeat it if I could confront it directly, outside of the network it had created, and needed a proxy to travel to its lair. And because Remfrey He had taken you prisoner and seemed to satisfy your flattering description I reached out to him through one of the alters, and we came to an agreement.'

'You could have freed me,' the lucidor said.

'If you had been of any use, you would have freed yourself.'

'I very nearly did.'

'But Remfrey He tricked you.'

'Tricking people is what he does. He also lied to the army, and betrayed your trust.'

'Yet his work here is of great interest. I believe that he had some help.'

'He had made contact with this thing you fought, hadn't he? Made some kind of arrangement with it, and betrayed you.'

'It may have recruited him.'

'You have to tell me what it is if we are going to work together. What I will have to confront, and anything that might help to overcome it.'

'That is as yet unclear.'

'Whatever it is, it's at the root of that pillar of smoke and fire, isn't it?'

'Something fell there,' the shatterling said, and dissolved into the spotlights' glare. The twin stars inside its hood were the last to disappear, and the lucidor found himself on the floor with Orjen kneeling over him.

'Lie still,' she said, when he started to get up. 'You had another fit.'

'I'm all right now,' the lucidor said. 'We should find Lyra. There's something we need to discuss.'

47

Watchers

As he followed Orjen out of the companionway onto the aft deck
the lucidor heard the crack of a gunshot, and someone, it sounded
like Lyra, let out a whoop of wild delight. The last mirrorlight
was fading in the west, stars were brightening overhead, the
contours of the land were limned in faint green foxfire, and the
pillar of smoke was now a pillar of fire, bright yellow-white at its
base, dimming to shades of scarlet and rose as it leaned across
the vault of the sky.

As he looked up at it, the lucidor felt a plangent tug in the deep
core of his self. A yearning that reminded him of coming back from
the mountains with the cactus herds, rounding the bare broken
spire of Outlook Pinnacle and seeing, far below, the familiar huddle
of houses and the green splash of the oasis. He wondered if it was
an echo from the shatterling, an imperfect translation of some
inhuman emotion or thought bleeding through their connection.
Something had fallen there, the shatterling had said. Something
powerful. Something dangerous. Something Remfrey He might be
trying to use. Something that might be using him . . .

Orjen wanted to know if he was all right.

It took an effort to look away from the streak of light etched
across the darkening firmament. The ghost at the edge of his
vision was back and the lucidor was certain now that it was a
manifestation of the shatterling, not a symptom of his illness.

He said, 'What are they shooting at?'

'The watchers must have arrived.'

Lyra and Sub-Lieutenant Skywatcher were on the little platform, leaning side by side at the rail. The sub-lieutenant studying

the shore through a spyglass, telling Lyra, 'There's a group of what I call rolling horrors off to the left.'

'Those wheel things?' Lyra said. The sub-lieutenant's long gun was butted firmly against her shoulder, and she was squinting through the telescopic sight. 'Are you sure they aren't in range?'

'They won't be. Even so, don't aim at them. Try for the very edge of the shore. Knock up some mud to show them they can't come any closer.'

'On it,' Lyra said cheerfully, and twitched the long gun a couple of degrees to the right and fired a single shot.

'Not bad,' the sub-lieutenant said, and without lowering the spyglass groped for the tumbler of lemonade on the table behind him.

'We're having a little target practice,' Lyra said, as the lucidor and Orjen approached.

'Maintaining the perimeter,' Sub-Lieutenant Skywatcher said, and with a slightly cross-eyed smile offered the spyglass to the lucidor.

The watchers were scattered across a meadow of tall crimson grasses that slanted towards the river. A picket of monsters. A cluster of things that must be the sub-lieutenant's rolling horrors: fat quilted discs standing upright and slowly pulsing. Giant segmented snakes, their blunt eyeless heads raised above the coils of their bodies. Red crabs big as horses, enormous claws raised like boxers' fists. Bloated bags squatting on clusters of restless tentacles. Bell-shaped translucent jellies. Something very tall and very thin inside a flutter of red veils. Balls got up from armour plates, teetering on spiky tripods. Child-sized things that appeared to be wearing their internal organs on the outside . . . And all of them, from rolling horrors to inside-out children, sported patches of red threads.

'They start to gather at dusk,' the sub-lieutenant said, as the lucidor handed the spyglass to Orjen. 'There will be more and more of them as the night wears on. I used to play them music. Hooked a gramophone to the ship's public address system, blasted out High Spirit cylinders one of my crewmates had brought along. I hoped it might fool the watchers into thinking that there were more people here than just me. I rigged up lights too. On the decks, behind portholes. Set them up with circuit breakers that switched them on and off at random, to give the impression of activity. Of people moving about. All it did was attract more crabs, more things from the sea. Meanwhile, the watchers just stand there, and watch.'

He freshened his glass with lemonade and raised it towards the gathering on the shore and drank.

'I salute the troops who tirelessly defend their land against the invaders from the map across the ocean. And your generals. Your invisible commanders. I salute you too.'

He more or less fell into his chair, covering his glass with his hand as lemonade sloshed, smiling tipsily.

'Don't mind me. A little mindless defiance in the face of the inevitable.'

Orjen said, 'They all seem to be derived from marine species. Worms, eels, octopuses, crabs . . . And they have something else in common. Did you spot it?'

'They are all infected with red threads,' the lucidor said. 'It's possible that something is controlling them. Giving them a shared purpose.'

'It might not be an army commanded by a general, but something more democratic,' Orjen said. 'We think that the natural order of things is a hierarchy, with the creator gods at the apex, and then the Queen and the first families, and the government that serves them, and so on. All the way down to the least spider-sweeper and guttersnipe. As with society, so with armies, and even our bodies, with the brain commanding the other organs. But perhaps the creatures of invasion are organised differently. Horizontally instead of vertically. A single intelligence distributed across many bodies.'

'Sounds like a description of a mob,' Lyra said.

'I have this terrible idea,' the sub-lieutenant said. 'One night the watchers will gather as usual. And my crewmates will be standing amongst them.'

'I saw the workshop,' the lucidor said. 'And what was in it.'

The sub-lieutenant's sombre mood switched at once to boyish enthusiasm. 'I told you. Didn't I tell you? Man's a genius. Unique mind.'

'It seems that he has used his genius to turn people into monsters, exactly as you fear. What else did he do?'

'I was asleep,' the sub-lieutenant said, and drank from his glass, holding it in both hands like a toddler. 'I woke up. And, poof! Everyone was gone.'

'And you never thought to find out where they went or what happened to them.'

'First rule. Never get off the ship. Very important.'

It was hopeless. The poor man's mind had been broken and rebuilt by Remfrey He's drugs and silvertongue gift. No doubt he drank not only to numb his fear of the monsters that nightly came to lay siege to the ship, but also to forget what had been done to him.

The lucidor turned to Orjen and Lyra, said, 'We need to discuss how we are going to break that rule.'

'I wondered when we would get around to your obsession with Remfrey He,' Lyra said.

'It's something more than that,' the lucidor said, and looked at Orjen. 'The fit I had in his workshop? It wasn't exactly a fit.'

48

High-Angle Shots

After the lucidor had explained about the shatterling's visitation, what it wanted him to do and what he needed to do, Orjen and Lyra sitting quiet and still while he talked, and Sub-Lieutenant Skywatcher uncharacteristically quiet too, watching the watchers on the shore through his spyglass and sipping from his tumbler of lemonade, Orjen said, 'as "Something fell." The shatterling didn't tell you any more than that?'

'All I know is that it is hostile, and seemingly stronger and smarter than the shatterling.'

'You thought that the invasion might have been brought here by a starfall,' Lyra said to Orjen. 'Looks like you were right.'

'Starfalls are mostly stone or iron.' Orjen said. 'They might carry seeds of life, but I don't think that they could create that pillar of fire.'

'I didn't say it was an ordinary starfall,' Lyra said.

'This is not so much about what it is but what it can do,' the lucidor said. 'And whether Remfrey He has found a use for it, or it has found a use for him.'

'Him, and the ship's crew,' Lyra said.

'The pillar marks where it fell,' the lucidor said, turning to look at the livid stroke burning in the darkening sky. 'Whatever it is. I doubt the *First Pilgrim* stumbled on it by accident. The shatterling admitted that it told Remfrey He about this new map, and Remfrey He lied when he said it was further north, in Simud. Because he thought it would give him an advantage, or because he thought that the army was more likely to send an expeditionary force against an old enemy than to an apparently empty spot in the middle of the World Ocean. Or simply because that's what he likes to do.'

'Can we trust the shatterling any more than we can trust him?' Orjen said.

'That's a good question.'

'Does that mean you don't know,' Lyra said, 'or does it mean that you know, but you can't say?'

'I mean we will know more when we find the root of the pillar,' the lucidor said.

'I'd like to know more before we set out,' Lyra said. 'Maybe you could have another word with your friend.'

'Unfortunately, that isn't how it works,' the lucidor said.

The sub-lieutenant stood up, startling them. 'It's dark,' he said. 'Time to go below. The perimeter has been maintained, but it won't stop things coming up from the sea.'

Back down in the galley, over a meal of canned fish and beans, and canned apricots sprinkled with hot paprika in the Patuan style, the lucidor eating only a few mouthfuls because the smell of food made him nauseous, they made their plans, such as they were. Take the boat and head around the coast, get as close to the pillar of cloud and fire as possible. A scouting mission to assess the situation, Orjen said firmly. Nothing more.

'The shatterling has to understand that its interests and ours may not coincide.'

'It wants to put an end to the invasion, and so do you,' the lucidor said. 'And I haven't given up on Remfrey He.'

'Who has the crew of the *First Pilgrim* at his back, and might be controlling the watchers and other horrors too,' Lyra said.

'We will know more tomorrow,' Orjen said. 'And then we can decide what to do next.'

The lucidor agreed, although he suspected that Orjen knew that he had other ideas. He didn't have much time left now that his infection had kicked in, and had nothing to lose. And as he lay in his hammock, making his own plans, he could feel the shatterling's attention aimed at the pillar of fire like a scrier's planchette quivering at a surveillance target. It would help him only because it needed his help. It would let him get close to the pillar's root only because it needed to get close. He could only hope that it would be close enough to deal with Remfrey He, or at least to find out if he had been changed beyond recourse or remedy . . .

He woke to the glare of the galley's lights, and Orjen leaning over him. He was drenched in sweat and was gripped by a bone-deep chill, and his body ached all over, as if he had been beaten with tiny hammers wielded by a crew of experts. Orjen had to explain twice over before he understood. The *Resolute Mind* had found them and Lyra and Sub-Lieutenant Skywatcher were up on deck, keeping watch on their visitor and trying to work out what to do about it.

The lucidor found it hard to climb out of his hammock; harder still, after spending a bad ten minutes in the head and drinking several glasses of water to slake his feverish thirst, to haul himself along slanting passageways and clamber up ladders to the aft deck. It was some way past dawn. A faint rain was drifting through the air, blowing across the river and the mud flats and stands of kelp trees, and two orange mirrors sat just above the hazy horizon, the rest of the arc still below it. The watchers had quit the meadow, and the *Resolute Mind* sat about a league off, beyond the river's mouth.

It had arrived an hour ago, Lyra said. Rounding the western point of the river mouth and dropping anchor. As the lucidor leaned at the canted rail, studying it through Sub-Lieutenant Skywatcher's spyglass, the distant ship sparkled with a brief stutter of light.

'It's been doing that on and off,' Lyra said. 'If I knew army code I could tell you what it's trying to say.'

'Mr Skywatcher should know,' the lucidor said. 'Where is he?'

'Patrolling for crabs on the foredeck. The perimeter must be maintained, and all that.'

'You had better find him before he is minded to reply to that signal and invite them on board,' the lucidor said.

'Why would he do that?' Lyra said.

'Because he was left here to wait for visitors and tell them all about his master's genius.'

After Lyra left to find the sub-lieutenant, Orjen said, 'We are lucky that they haven't come any closer.'

'For all they know, the captain and crew are still aboard, and have received news of the mutiny. Or the ship might have been taken over by alter women or some other kind of monster. So they are standing off and keeping close watch, and sending messages that are no doubt asking for a parlay. Sooner or later, if they get no reply, they'll get up the nerve to investigate.'

The lucidor was using the spyglass again, doing his best to ignore the shadow in the corner of his eye. The *Resolute Mind*'s bow was wrapped in canvas sheeting, there were patches of new timber in its hull, and two rakes of light-collecting panels were missing from the port side of the foredeck.

Orjen said, 'If you have some idea about what to do, you should share it.'

'First, I need to ask Mr Skywatcher a few questions.'

Lyra was carrying a tray of food when she returned with Sub-Lieutenant Skywatcher, saying that there was no point in skipping breakfast on account of their visitors. While she and Orjen ate gruel laced with black treacle, the lucidor questioned the sub-lieutenant and learned that in addition to the pair of breech-loading heavy cannons in the iron-clad turret at the bow there were several dozen light cannons and carronades behind hatches in the lower decks, and racks of mortars amidships. The sub-lieutenant claimed that he didn't know if the mortars had been sabotaged, he was just a humble sparks, so they all went forward, following a path he had cleared through banks of red vines to the mortars on the starboard side.

There were four of them, stout ironwood tubes reinforced with iron bands and set on simple swivels, much like the siege mortars the lucidor had once used to put a hole in the mudbrick walls of an old border fort commandeered by bandits. The sub-lieutenant led Lyra to the armoury, and after they returned, carrying a heavy case between them, Lyra helped the lucidor to load the mortars with shaped charges and iron-cased explosive shells, and they puzzled out how to aim and angle the tubes and lock them in place.

'If we accidentally sink the *Resolute Mind*, it's a long swim home,' Lyra said, as she fitted the friction fuses.

'All we can do is point them away from the ship and fire high-angle shots and hope for the best,' the lucidor said.

He counted backwards from three, Lyra pulled the lanyards of the fuses, and a pair of mortars fired with a sharp double bang that echoed back from the shore. For several seconds nothing happened; then two water spouts shot up in front of the *Resolute Mind*, somewhat closer than the lucidor had expected.

Orjen, watching the ship through the spyglass, reported that it was signalling again.

'Do you know code?' the lucidor said to the sub-lieutenant.

'Not really.' The man tipped his glass to drain it, ice cubes rattling against his teeth and meltwater running down his beard.

'Because you're just a sparks.'

'I really am,' the sub-lieutenant said amiably, with a look of childish candour.

'Let's see if they understand this,' Lyra said, and fired the second pair of mortars.

They were reloading the mortars when the *Resolute Mind* began to move, turning in a neat circle amid plumes of spray as it engaged its radial propeller, slowly making way towards the eastern point of the river mouth.

'They'll be back,' Lyra said. 'Probably wait until night, and try to sneak aboard.'

'If they do, the things from the sea might get them,' the sub-lieutenant said.

'We can't count on sea monsters,' Orjen said.

'They might not come back at all,' the lucidor said. 'Especially if they reach the pillar before we do.'

49

Caretaker

The sub-lieutenant leaned at the rail, watching anxiously as Orjen and Lyra helped the lucidor clamber down the rope ladder to the boat. He'd told them that he strongly disapproved of their mission and wouldn't let them board when they returned, if they returned, but had also said, with sudden childlike rapture, that they would see such wonders.

They were still planning to find the root of the pillar of cloud and fire, but because there was a risk that the *Resolute Mind*'s mutinous crew might ambush them if they followed the coastline in the boat, the lucidor and Orjen were going to head across country instead. It was more or less a straight shot to the west, a little over four leagues, according to the sub-lieutenant, who had abruptly volunteered the information but had been unable to explain how he knew. Another hint planted by Remfrey He, no doubt. Lyra had volunteered to go with the lucidor, but Orjen had instructed her to babysit the sub-lieutenant and the ship, search for a functioning godspeaker, and do her best to fend off the *Resolute Mind* if it came back.

'And if you don't come back after two days, I'll come and look for you,' Lyra had said.

'No, you won't. Not under any circumstances,' Orjen had said. 'I mean it, Lyra. If we don't come back, assume the worst, and parley with the mutineers. Jy Solon will no doubt want to take you back to Patua so that he can ransom you. Take my notebooks, keep them safe, and hand them over to someone who can make good use of them. Make sure our work does not go to waste.'

'You should have hired a silvertongue,' Lyra had said. 'I'll probably talk myself into an execution.'

Now, she drove the boat across the river's brown flood in a long curve and beached it at the edge of a mud flat covered with vines. The *First Pilgrim*'s boats were a row of humps in the red carpet. Orjen and Lyra embraced and wished each other good luck, and Lyra clasped hands with the lucidor and drew him close and said quietly, 'I know what you want to do. And I don't care, just as long as you don't involve the boss.'

'It doesn't have anything to do with her.'

'It better not. Else I'll come and find you, and there will be a reckoning.'

'Prime those mortars, keep a look out for the *Resolute Mind*, and keep the sub-lieutenant close, too. He seems harmless, but we don't know what Remfrey He has put inside his head.'

'Him I can take care of. But I'm not too happy at the prospect of facing down the mutineers on my own.'

'You will be fine. And there is something you can do for me, when you get home. I would like you to reach out to my old boss, Lucidor Pyn. He gave me this task, and deserves to know how it played out.'

'You can tell him yourself.'

'Tell him everything,' the lucidor said. 'As straight as you can.'

They shared a look, part embarrassment, part mutual comprehension, and Lyra pushed the boat back into the water and the lucidor and Orjen picked their way over the carpet of vines and set off across country. They tried to keep the pillar of cloud directly ahead of them, the lucidor gimping along with the aid of a staff Lyra had found in the *First Pilgrim*'s armoury. Orjen had given him a flask of milk of poppy and heart-of-wine she had mixed up in the ship's pharmacy, telling him to use it only when he felt it was absolutely necessary. He had taken a draught before climbing into the boat, and topped it up with cautious sips each time he needed to stop and catch his breath. Even though Orjen's paregoric displaced the ache in his bones with a pleasantly numb warmth, he had to ask for a moment's rest more often than he liked, and each time summoned up his resolve and

366

what remained of his strength and forged on. He was too close now to even think of giving up.

The land rose in a gentle slope, covered with a pinkish grass that grew in dense interlocking spirals, like the diagram of a vast machine. Several large crabs were grazing in the middle distance, scissoring grass with their claws and feeding it to their mouths with mechanical regularity. They didn't seem to take any notice of Orjen and the lucidor, but he wondered if the thread network had registered their presence, and what its response might be.

Quite soon they came across an irregular scattered trail of discarded possessions. Cutlery and cups and plates. Ration packs. Books. Tools and coils of rope. Clothing. Shoes.

'Now we know where the crew went,' Orjen said, as they followed it.

'We always knew,' the lucidor said, thinking of Remfrey He leading a long line of men and women gripped by a common infection and a collective mania. Shedding everything they had brought with them. Shedding their lives, and everything that made them human. The death march of his last cult.

The pillar rose in the misty distance, white vapour boiling up in a muscular column whose top was lost in the low cloud. Thin rain tickled the lucidor's face and beaded on his eyelashes as he limped after Orjen, leaning on the staff, sweating inside the stiff carapace of his oilskin slicker. His left leg was stiffly strapped from thigh to ankle and he was floating on a warm sea of paregoric. Orjen had pulled the hood of her slicker over her head and her canvas bag of necessaries bumped at her hip, weighted by the wheel gun Lyra had insisted she carry.

They took another rest break at the crest of the slope and studied the hills saddling away under low cloud and rain, and after the lucidor had regained his breath and taken another sip of paregoric they went on. They saw several spider crabs grazing amongst a stand of kelp trees that grew along a muddy slough, and when they splashed across a saltwater creek dozens of bristling worms as thick as the lucidor's wrist recoiled into their burrows. Something like a giant millipede, black and glistening and several dozen spans long, scuttled away downslope and poured itself into a pond. Another pond was packed edge to edge with circles of pink and purple arm-sized tentacles, tips held erect above the water like strange fleshy reeds.

There were no birds, and no insects. No sounds but plashing footfalls on the sodden ground, the harsh engine of the lucidor's breathlessness. Unmoored by fatigue and the numbness of the paregoric, he wondered what might happen to his body if it was interred under the red grasses and chalky soil of this strange land, what kind of flowers might grow from his grave, and told himself that there was no use wondering what would happen afterwards. He hadn't given it much thought when he had set out from the Free State, and he had no time to think about it now.

He was still mostly pain-free, but was growing tired. Stumbling and lame-footed and sluggish, as if he was growing heavier with every step. Chilled to the bone, permanently out of breath. Several times Orjen drew a good way ahead of him, and waited without comment for him to catch up. At last, they climbed a long shallow slope pockmarked with the scars of what appeared to be old shell holes overgrown by grass and vine, and found at the top a hollow about half a league across. It was circled by a strip of hard white material and a double wire fence, and a clutch of small buildings squatted at the centre of its flat floor of close-cropped red grass like eggs in a nest. Blunt cylinders fabricated from tough white seamless plastic, each propped on three pairs of sturdy struts.

The lucidor and Orjen found a gap in the fence where something had trampled it down and they sat on wet turf and studied the buildings for a while. They glistened in the gentle rain as if freshly laid. There were no paths or tracks, no vehicles, no sign of graves, no sign of the *First Pilgrim*'s crew or any inhabitants.

Orjen said that the scene reminded her of illustrations in antique tablets from the dawn of the world, but nothing on this map, unmarked on any charts made when arks still plied the World Ocean, could be anywhere as old as that.

'The only thing that matters is that they prove that we are not the first to find this place,' the lucidor said.

He had taken out the flask of paregoric but had not yet unscrewed its top, and after a few moments put it away. They were close to the centre of the mystery now. He needed a clear head.

'Who built them, what they did here and when they left: all of that matters too,' Orjen said, with a familiar shine in her gaze.

The lucidor smiled. 'You want to go down there, don't you?'

'Their builders may have left behind some clues about the nature of this place.'

'Suppose the ship's crew, or whatever they turned into, are hiding inside?'

The lucidor imagined them waiting in ambush, or cocooned like insect larvae, ready to emerge after undergoing some unimaginable and terrible transformation.

'You can wait here if you like,' Orjen said. 'I promise that I won't be long.'

She was up and walking down the slope towards the buildings before the lucidor could react. He used the staff to push to his feet and limped after her, feeling the first little knives of pain working in his hips and knees and ankles, telling himself that pain was good, it would help to keep him sharp. Trying not to think about the soothing warmth of the paregoric.

Orjen had climbed a short ladder to the round door set in the blunt end of one of the buildings, was feeling around the door's seam for a catch or lock, running her fingers over its surface. She paused, as if she had found something, then punched the door in its centre. It swung in, and before the lucidor could say anything she had swarmed through it.

A light came on inside; someone spoke. The lucidor hauled himself up the ladder, tossed the staff through the door and tumbled in after it. Orjen stood alone in the middle of an empty space lit by a pearlescent glow, listening as a soft precise voice neither male nor female spoke out of the air, several brief sentences in a language the lucidor didn't recognise.

Orjen told him that it was trade pidgin, dating back to the time when Patua had still been trading with the neighbouring maps. After a brief conversation with the voice, she said that the buildings had been brought here by people from Simud;

the caretaker didn't know exactly when because it had lost its calendar function.

'The caretaker?' the lucidor said. He was sitting on the floor by the door, propping himself up with the staff and trying to ignore the knives stabbing at the paregoric's cottonwool cocoon.

'That is what it calls itself,' Orjen said. 'As I understand it, the houses share a common mind that inhabits their machinery. It has been looking after them ever since the Simudanese left. It says that it has been able to keep most of the native creatures away, although I cannot quite understand how it did. Something to do with the white strip, and sound and electricity.'

The house spoke again, and again Orjen translated.

'It has been waiting for its people to return,' she told the lucidor. 'It does not know if they will. And it asked if we are hungry, and apologised because it has no food. It is lonely, I think. If a machine can be lonely.'

The lucidor said, 'What happened to the Simudanese? Did they die here or did they return home?'

The floor had softened beneath him and become nicely warm, was absorbing the water dripping from him. It would be lovely to sit there and never have to move again.

Orjen asked a question; the voice answered.

'They were here and they were gone,' Orjen said. 'The caretaker says they flew away in little houses with long arms, but it does not know where they went.'

'They flew?'

'Perhaps the Simudanese did not forget how to use their flying machines. Do you know the story of the Little Duke and the *Lucky Goose*?'

'This isn't the time for fables.'

'It is a true story. About how, in a time so long ago that a few of the First People were still alive, the Duke of the White Towers – that's a citadel that once stood on the coast east of Delos-Chimr – ordered his craftsmen to build him a special flying machine. It was very light, and had wings that were a hundred spans long and covered in the light-collectors that powered its engines, and he named it the *Lucky Goose*. He was a dwarf, which is why he was called the Little Duke, so needed less space than ordinary people, and fewer supplies. He flew away across the World Ocean and although he was a brave and skilful pilot he was gone for so long that people believed him dead. But one day a different flying machine appeared in the sky and circled the White Towers and landed, and the Little Duke emerged. He had reached Simud, but its high plateau, with its deserts of red sand and bare mountains and deep valleys, had been covered from edge to edge with a huge dust storm, and the Little Duke had crashed after the engines of the *Lucky Goose* had become choked with dust. Fortunately, he was not injured, and one of the wandering towns of the Simudanese had found him before he ran out of food and water. I wonder,' Orjen said, 'if these buildings might not be modelled on the walking houses of those towns. I should have thought of it sooner.'

'It is a nice story, I suppose, but I don't see how it is relevant.'

'After the Simudanese saved his life, the Little Duke taught them how to build flying machines, and returned to Patua in one they built for him. And for several centuries the two maps traded in goods flown across the World Ocean, until the war between Patua and Simud ended the connection. The point being, if the caretaker is telling the truth, and the Simudanese still possess flying machines, they would find it easy to reach this new map by air.'

'Does this caretaker know why they left?'

Orjen had a short conversation with the voice, and said, 'I was trying to find out if the Simudanese knew of a cure for infection by tailswallowers, or if they learned how to use them, and turn other species into monsters. But it says that it doesn't know.'

'Why would they want to make monsters?'

'As weapons, of course.'

'To make war on us?'

'On us, on other maps . . . A war of the maps, yes, why not? It's possible that the invasion was not quickened by a skyfall after all, but is an accident caused by misuse of applied philosophy.'

'It is here and the Simudanese are not. The rest is speculation. If this machine can't tell you anything useful, we should move on,' the lucidor said.

It took him a long time to get to his feet; in the end Orjen had to help him.

'You are running a fever,' she said. 'And when did these appear?'

She was prodding a scatter of hard little nodules under the skin on the back of his right hand.

'I don't know,' the lucidor said. 'They don't hurt.'

He had discovered similar nodules on his hips and back after waking. Rashes of hard little bumps. He hadn't told anyone about them in case Orjen decided that he was unfit for the long trek.

'The tailswallowers are redistributing the calcium in your body.' Orjen said. 'Your bones will become increasingly brittle, and judging by the way you have been limping, I think you are already having problems with your joints.'

'I can manage.'

'Perhaps you should rest here while I scout the origin of the pillar. I will only be a little while. We are close now.'

The lucidor shook free of her grip and tottered to the door and held onto its frame: the knives in his joints had turned to ground glass. He said, 'Ask the caretaker one more question.'

'What do you have in mind?'

'If the white strip around these buildings can still fend off crabs and other monsters, what keeps the grass cropped short inside it?'

50

Hole in the World

Orjen was helping the lucidor climb down the ladder when the small machine puttered up to the house, rolling on two pairs of triangular tracks, a sharp-edged disc fastened to its belly. The caretaker had told Orjen that once there had been three of these grass-cutters, and even though this was the only one still functional it would gladly lend it to them for as long as they needed it. And so the lucidor made his final procession perched on a small uncomfortable saddle fixed to the motor casing of what amounted to a mechanical goat. There were levers that could steer the machine by varying the power to the tracks, but Orjen gave it a command in trade pidgin and it obediently followed her, carrying the lucidor through the broken fence and across the hilltop, halting at the edge of a sudden steep slope.

The rain was easing off and a wedge of light split the clouds and lit up the overgrown ruins of a small town or settlement that spread around the curve of a bay. The *Resolute Mind* was anchored off the western point of the bay, but the lucidor barely glanced at it, fixing instead on a small island that stood a little way offshore. A shallow, roughly circular cone topped by a thick stream of white vapour that roiled up from a hole or vent and bent into the sky, throwing a long shadow across a patchwork of reefs.

The lucidor felt the shatterling lean in, heard the silken whisper of its voice telling him that he was close but needed to get closer. 'And then, I promise, all will be made well,' it said, and he was lying on his back with rain faintly kissing his face and Orjen was kneeling beside him, saying that he had been seized by a small fit.

'It was the shatterling,' he said, as she helped him sit up.

'Did it talk to you? What did it tell you?'

'We have to get closer. I suppose it means that island.' The lucidor turned to look towards the bay again. The ruins and the island sitting offshore under the pillar of cloud. 'That's quite a sight.'

Orjen aimed the spyglass she had borrowed from Sub-Lieutenant Skywatcher at the island and the reefs around it.

'Something fell, all right,' she said. 'And it may have punched through the shell of the world, or at least drilled a good way into it. All the way to the inner shell would be my guess. That pillar is most likely fed by water boiled by the Heartsun's heat. But if its impact released enough energy to pierce baserock, it should have left a much bigger hole . . .'

'There's only way to find out what made it,' the lucidor said. 'And we have to get there before the mutineers do.'

Orjen helped him to get to his feet and regain his perch on the grass-cutting machine. When he was settled, she handed him the spyglass and told him that the mutineers might be the least of their problems. 'Look there, on the shore close to the island.'

He turned the spyglass to where she was pointing, saw the spires of an alter nest, half rooted in land, half in water.

'Now I know where I can find Remfrey He,' he said, and shut the spyglass and handed it back to Orjen. 'You should stay here. Find out everything you can about this place, and the source of the invasion. Its first cause. Its strengths and its weaknesses. That's why you came here, and I know there's no one better suited to the task. You might even find a way of stopping it. But dealing with Remfrey He – that's my job. That's on me.'

'It doesn't matter what I find out if I can't tell anyone about it,' Orjen said. 'And I have no way of calling home, let alone returning.'

'Someone as clever and determined as you will find a way.'

'I can't let you go down there on your own.'

'I'll be all right once I have rested for a little while longer.'

'This is not something you can outrest.'

'When I first set out from Liberty City I knew I had only a small chance of success. And knew that even if I found Remfrey

374

He and brought him back, I would be arrested and tried and imprisoned. But it was the right thing do, and so is this. I probably won't succeed, but it is better to go out trying than to give in. And who knows? Perhaps the shatterling has been telling the truth all along. Perhaps it really can end the invasion and save the world.'

'I know that it will promise anything to get you to go down there.'

'It doesn't need to. I am going anyway.'

'I suppose that if I told the grass-cutter that it shouldn't go any further, you would try to walk there.'

'You know that I'd try to get there any way I can.'

'I want to go a little further anyway,' Orjen said. 'There is something interesting at the bottom of the hill. But we need to apply a little protection first.'

She rummaged in the clutter of her pack and extracted a handful of vials and sorted through them. Choosing one and dropping the rest in the pocket of her coat, snapping the vial's seal and shaking a few drops of liquid into the palm of her hand and rubbing it into her hair.

'I reverse-engineered the pheromones Remfrey He dabbed on me,' she said. 'The so-called nest scent. An apothecary helped me to work out how to synthesise them, and I remapped little makers to turn them into pheromone factories. Don't worry. It has been tested, and works exactly like his mixture.'

'The alters down there might not be like the ones he tamed,' the lucidor said, but bent his head so that Orjen could anoint him.

The oily liquid smelled of mushrooms and decaying flowers.

'Hopefully we will not need to find out if they are,' she said. 'Let me help you get back in the saddle.'

Orjen gave the lucidor's mount another command and walked alongside it as it bucked and slewed and skidded down the hillside, smashing down wet red grass, finding a path between clusters of dripping kelp trees. The lucidor clinging to it grimly, glass grinding in his spine and hips and joints with every jolt. When they reached the bottom, Orjen cut away across a long flat strip of concrete towards mounds of red vine; as he rode after her, bumping over potholes and churning through puddles, the lucidor saw that the vines had swamped machines with boat-like hulls and long slender wings. One was riddled with bullet holes, another was half-burned and belly down in a scorched scar in the landing strip, but two others seemed to be intact, angled on wheeled struts.

Orjen reached the first of the machines ahead of the lucidor, used the creepers that hung from the edge of one of the wings to scramble onto it and looked down at him as he puttered up on the grass-cutter. 'Flying machines!' she said, grinning with delight. 'A flock of flying machines! Aren't they amazing?'

'So the caretaker was telling the truth.'

'I never doubted it,' Orjen said, and trod carefully along the wing towards the hull, testing every footstep.

The lucidor rolled the grass-cutter back so he could keep watch, glimpsed a stutter of multicoloured light inside a glass blister on top of the hull, heard a voice exactly like the voice of the caretaker.

'It's alive!' Orjen called out, and bent to look inside the blister and spoke to the machine in trade pidgin, listened attentively to its reply.

'What does it have to say for itself?' the lucidor said.

'That it has been waiting a long time, and needs repairs,' Orjen said, and abruptly straightened up and looked past the lucidor, shading her eyes with her wrist.

The lucidor hitched around in his seat and saw movement in the tall red grass at the edge of the strip of concrete, was reaching for his staff as Jy Solon and four men armed with long guns and pistols stepped out.

51
Red Caps

'When we tried to parley with the *First Pilgrim* it fired on us and drove us off,' Jy Solon told the lucidor and Orjen. 'So we followed the coast north and west, looking for a place where we could make proper repairs to our ship, and when we saw the houses and the harbour we believed our luck was beginning to turn for the better. We anchored at a prudent distance and came ashore hoping to find supplies, but almost immediately were attacked by alters. The civilians and crew led by Effra Ro were overwhelmed; my little group managed to escape by heading inland.

'We were waiting for things to quieten down when we spotted you. Standing against the sky at the top of that hill as if you didn't care who saw you. I have no doubt that you reached the *First Pilgrim* before we did, and turned its crew against us. And borrowed that little cart you're riding from them, too. I suppose you need it because your infection has taken a turn for the worse, and I can't say I have any sympathy. Not after you tried to burn our ship to the waterline, and then incited the *Pilgrim*'s crew to try to sink it with shell fire.'

'We scavenged the grass-cutter from a place nearby,' the lucidor said, 'and saw you off ourselves. The only crew member left aboard the *First Pilgrim* is a somewhat addled sub-lieutenant. The rest went over to Remfrey He, or were killed.'

'All of them?'

'As far as we know.'

'Were the alters that attacked you wearing red caps?' Orjen said.

'So what if they were?' Jy Solon said.

'It means that they may be under Remfrey He's control,' the lucidor said. 'If so, we'll find him and the *First Pilgrim*'s crew in their nest. And if you and your men help me to capture him and return him to Patua, it will guarantee you a hero's welcome.'

Jy Solon thought about that for a few moments, loosely aiming his pistol at his two prisoners, his men standing at his back. His black curls were bushed up by a bandage wrapped around his head and he had a haunted, dishevelled, desperate look. The lucidor's staff and Orjen's bag were slung over one shoulder, and he had stuck Orjen's wheel gun in his belt.

'There aren't enough of us to go up against those alters,' he said. 'Especially if your man is leading them.'

'It would give you some satisfaction for the deaths of your friends,' the lucidor told him. 'And we can help you if you help us.'

Jy Solon had taken the wrong path when he had joined the mutineers, but the lucidor hoped that he could be persuaded to try to set things right. He was prepared to tell the first officer about the shatterling and share Orjen's nest scent with him and his men, prepared to do anything to put an end to Remfrey He and his plans, but Jy was shaking his head.

'Revenge is a fool's game,' he said, 'and we have more pressing concerns. It looks like the *Pilgrim* is pretty much stuck fast, so the *Resolute Mind* is our best and only chance of getting home. We managed to patch up the damage to its hull, but as yet it's by no means seaworthy. We need ironwood planks and timbers to make it good, and there's enough on the *Pilgrim* to rebuild *Resolute Mind* a dozen times over. So what you will do, if you want to see out this day, is forget about Remfrey He and put your best efforts into parleying with whoever is left on board and making them understand the situation.'

'My steward has instructions to fire on you again if you try to take the *First Pilgrim* by force,' Orjen said. 'But if we can reach an agreement to help each other I will ask her to stand down.'

'If she has only that addled sub-lieutenant for company, I hope that she'll see sense and stand down as soon as she learns that you're my prisoner,' Jy said. 'And I also hope that you understand why I can't take your word that they are all we have to deal with.'

'Do what you will with the *First Pilgrim*, fix your ship and go wherever you want,' the lucidor said. 'It doesn't matter to me so long as you let me do what I came here to do.'

'And you can let me go too,' Orjen said. 'I have no quarrel with you, and my friend needs my help.'

'Ah, but you I do need,' Jy Solon said. 'And not only to convince your steward and anyone else aboard the *Pilgrim* to surrender. There's no going back on what we did, so we must all stick together somewhere on the far side of the law, as we well knew when we took command. And I have every hope that we can ransom you for enough money to set us up in shipshape fashion.'

'You overestimate the value of my life,' Orjen said.

'I know it is worth enough to be the saving of mine,' Jy said. 'Now get moving, both of you. I don't aim to overstay my welcome in this ghastly place.'

'If you turn me loose now, I can be of some small help with that,' the lucidor said. 'I'll distract Remfrey He and the alters, and you'll be able to escape back to your ship.'

'And just how long do you think you could distract them? Effra and his men were overwhelmed in a matter of minutes, and they were armed to the teeth. Despite that fancy cart, I don't see how you can do any better.'

'Remfrey He won't kill me,' the lucidor said. 'At least, not right away. Not until he has shown off his work. If you let me go right now I'll be the distraction that will give you a clear path to your boat.'

'Don't test my patience, old man. Right now you're the least of my concerns.'

The four sailors took the lead, moving cautiously from one piece of cover to the next, long guns held ready, following an overgrown street at the edge of the Simudanese settlement towards the western end of the bay and the boat they had been forced to abandon. The street was surfaced with some kind of seamless ceramic, pockmarked with the craters of old explosions in some places, buried under drifts of sandy soil or sprawls of red vine in others. Cylindrical houses stood along one side, some cracked open or burned to the stumps of their legs, almost all of them overgrown by red vine. Everything quiet and still. No sign of alters or any other creature.

Jy Solon walked on one side of the grass-cutter as it ground along, with Orjen on the other, and the lucidor could feel a third presence at his back, the shatterling leaning into his eyes and ears, whispering inside his head, telling him that all he needed to do was find the source and it would do the rest.

'I was driven away on first contact,' it said, 'but learned much from it and know how to take control now. I have infiltrated the local network and even as we speak I am using customised tools to probe the edges of its defences and plant a stealth army of weaponised clones. Once you are close enough to the root of the network, I can use our connection to mount a full-scale attack.'

'So you still need me.'

'You will go there whether I want you to or not, because you want to find Remfrey He.'

'I don't care what you do as long as you let me take him down,' the lucidor whispered back.

Silk rustled on silk. 'Why not? You are merely the vessel for the connection. Once you have delivered it to the right place, it does not matter if you are killed afterwards.'

'Then we have an understanding.'

There was no reply. As usual, the shatterling had told him what it thought he needed to know, and no more.

They hadn't travelled very far when the sailors halted at the end of a row of overgrown but mostly intact houses. There was a big crater half-filled with water beyond, and a spider crab stood in the middle of it, languorously grazing on the crimson froth of some kind of waterweed. One of the sailors, a skinny lad who had been an assistant to the ship's engineer, was aiming his long gun at the creature, and Jy Solon caught the barrel and pushed it skyward and said that a shot might bring others running.

'Remember what I told you. We can't fight our way out of this. Let's move forward nice and quiet. If that one spots us it might call up its friends.'

The spider crab seemed to take no notice as the sailors and Jy Solon and Orjen trod cautiously and bent-backed past vine-covered mounds of rubble at the edge of the crater. The lucidor followed on the grass-cutter, steering it with the manual controls as it ground over the fractured road, clattering loudly over unevenly tilted ceramic shards. The spider crab raised itself up, weed dripping from its mouthparts, and he felt the weight of its attention as he drove on towards where the others were waiting.

'Make any more trouble like that and you can walk the rest of the way,' Jy told him. The sailors were aiming their weapons at the spider crab, which had resumed its placid grazing.

'Or you could leave me here,' the lucidor said. 'Let me find my own way.'

'You don't give up, do you?' Jy said.

'I don't plan to.'

'It might be best to leave him,' one of the sailors said. 'He's already slowing us down.'

'Your man has a point,' the lucidor said.

'Like it or not you are going to come back with me, and help deal with the *First Pilgrim*,' Jy said.

'Or we could just shoot you,' the sailor said.

'No more killing,' Jy said. 'We're done with that.'

As they walked on, Orjen asked him why he had gone over to the side of the mutineers.

'What choice did I have?'

'You could have stood by the captain.'

'It was the captain who got us into this mess. He was high-handed and bloody-minded, showed no fairness or respect to the men, and wouldn't take my advice, because I was the son of a farmer and he had the blood of First People in his veins. When the pinch came, he lost the last shreds of his authority and the men turned against him, as I warned him they would. Bad things happened,' Jy said. 'Bad decisions were made. Some of them by me. Don't think that I don't know it. But I did my best to keep you and your friends safe from the mob, and despite all the trouble you caused instead of thanking me for it, I reckon I've saved you again.'

'Did it look like we needed rescuing?' the lucidor said.

'Matter of fact it did.'

The little party halted at an intersection with another road, waiting while Jy crossed it and looked right and left before beckoning the rest forward.

'He has to repair the *Resolute Mind* before it can leave,' Orjen said. 'We will have time to work on him, or to find a way of sneaking off.'

'I don't have any more time,' the lucidor said. 'But that spider crab had a patch of threads on its shell, just like every other creature here, and that gave me an idea.'

'You hope that it might have been linked to the alters. That's why you made so much noise when you crossed in front of it.'

'It didn't seem to take much notice, but you never know. And if the alters don't find us soon, all we have to do is get the attention of some other creature infected by those threads, and they should come running. Your nest scent should protect us, and with luck we will be able to slip away.'

'While they kill Mr Solon and his men.'

'Would you have a problem, if it came to that?'

'They want to ransom me, and they mutinied and murdered Saphor Godshorse and the others,' Orjen said with a hard look. 'They would hang for that, if they were caught.'

'If we do manage to escape, you should head back to the *First Pilgrim*. I'll stay here, and do what needs to be done.'

'With the help of your friend the shatterling, I suppose. I noticed you whispering something to it just before we encountered that spider crab.'

'I am not certain that its plans coincide with mine, but I trust it more than Mr Solon. We should be ready to take our chance when we can, without any thought for what might happen to him and his men.'

'What have we become?' Orjen said.

'What we have always been,' the lucidor said. 'But now we're pared to the core.'

Jy Solon was waiting for them to catch up. 'No more talking,' he said. 'We're getting close now.'

The little party crossed another stretch of ruins, halting when a spider crab was spotted tottering through a distant scatter of kelp trees, moving on again when it had gone past. Still no sign of any alters, or any of the crew Remfrey He had turned. The lucidor gripped the sides of the grass-cutter's engine casing as the sturdy machine bumped over the uneven ground, sweating hard, little knives grinding in every joint. He knew that a shot of paregoric would ease the pain, but he needed to stay sharp, and endured the discomfort as best he could.

They passed between two smashed houses and halted at the edge of the road beyond. A row of big domes, with plastic skin stretched over arched supports, some peeling or partly flayed but otherwise intact, others burned or broken, was strung along the far side of a wasteland of rubble and red vines, with glimpses of the sea between them. Storehouses, according to Jy Solon.

'We landed a little way beyond them. As long as the alters have dispersed, we can find the boat and be back on board the *Resolute Mind* inside an hour,' Jy said, and sent two of the sailors to scout the way ahead.

The island and the root of the column of cloud were less than a league to the east, edged with the golden light of the mirrors shining in clear sky offshore, and there was a low vibration in the air and a fine rain was blowing here and there. The lucidor was staring at it with a kind of hungry frustration, the shatterling close at his back, when Orjen said that something was wrong.

The scouts had stopped a little way from the domed storehouse. After a moment, the lucidor saw a stir of movement, and figures stepped from rips in the hem of the dome's plastic skin. Alters. Warriors and workers. The scouts fired a quick volley of shots and turned and ran, and more alters rose from their hiding places amongst tangles of vines and took them down.

Jy Solon and the two remaining sailors fired a frantic fusillade as the alters began to move across the wasteland, but wherever one fell another stepped up to take its place. Orjen gripped the lucidor's shoulder and told him that they would be safe so long as they stayed still, and he reached up and clasped her hand as the alters closed in. Jy dropped his spent pistol and pulled Orjen's wheel gun from his belt; the young engineer's assistant lost his nerve and tried to run, and a warrior smashed him to the ground and tore at him in a frenzy while the rest swarmed past. Jy Solon emptied the wheel gun with five rapid shots and threw it at a warrior, struck at another with the staff he had taken from the lucidor, and turned and ran, chased by the remaining sailor. The alters followed them remorselessly, flowing past the lucidor and Orjen. A shot, an angry cry suddenly cut off, and it was over. The alters turned back towards the storehouses, passing men and women in ragged and filthy uniforms or civilian clothes, heads capped with snug tangles of red threads, armed with long guns and pistols, crossbows and lances. They lined up along the road, confronting the lucidor and Orjen, and a man stepped out between them.

It was Remfrey He, dressed in a ragged white coat, a red cap on his head. Showing all of his teeth in a parody of a smile, saying, 'You made it!'

52

Omphalos

Remfrey He slung Orjen's bag over his shoulder and appropriated the lucidor's staff, twirling it overhead as he walked beside the grass-cutter, feinting at imaginary opponents, asking the lucidor and Orjen if they had enjoyed and understood the little display he had left behind after taking advantage of what he called the fluid situation when the *First Pilgrim* had run aground. Telling them that they shouldn't expect any more help from the *Resolute Mind* because he had sent a small party to deal with what was left of its crew, and expressing false sympathy for the lucidor's plight.

'My people captured Effra Ro before the alters could have their way with him, and after a few words from me he was my new best friend. Told me everything he knew about your voyage, including how you became infected after you were bitten by a crab. I hope you will forgive me for finding that base indignity amusing. Such a pity that you have so little time left. We could have had some fine fun together.'

The man had lost none of his false, quick-witted charm, still prattled on as if giving voice to everything that flitted through his mind, but every now and then he paused and cocked his head as if looking at something that wasn't there, hearing something only he could hear. Most likely listening to the commands of the thing that rode him: the lucidor didn't doubt that the man was a servant of the invasion, despite his explanation that the red threads rooted in his skull weren't like those which had infected the alters and his acolytes but were derived from a series of experiments and careful tweaks. His mind had not been destroyed, he said. No, it had been augmented, giving him access to the local network, a good deal of control over the alters, and direct contact with what he called the omphalos, which was very interested in meeting the lucidor.

'Or rather, with the shatterling you are linked to. Oh yes, I know about your sly little liaison. We had a very interesting conversation, the shatterling and I, back in the nest.'

'I heard that you promised to help it, and broke that promise when you found a better ally,' the lucidor said.

'Did it tell you about that? How, after it gave up on you and put its trust in me, I tricked an ancient and powerful servant of the gods into giving away its secrets? The things I can do! I hope you were suitably impressed and amazed,' Remfrey He said. 'What did it offer you, by the way? What did it say it would give you, in exchange for your help?'

'A throne where I could sit and act as its mouthpiece, after it put an end to the invasion and saved the world. I wasn't interested in any of that, but it also offered to help me to catch you.'

'And how has that worked out?'

'Well, here we are.'

'It isn't quite what you expected, is it?'

'I would say it's too early to tell.'

'Oh, I think I know exactly how it is going to work out,' Remfrey He said. 'The shatterling made all kinds of promises to me, too. Told me that it was becoming a god, and would raise me up, so on, so forth. All of it nonsense, of course. Bluster and boasts and outright lies.'

'About which you know more than a little.'

'And in my expert opinion, you would be even more of a fool than you appear to be if you think the shatterling will give you any help. It rebelled against the creator gods, and to justify that rebellion it believes that it is destined to become more powerful than they ever were, and can use its powers to save the world. When in truth it cares about nothing but saving itself. It has never been and never will be anything more than an unfaithful and untrustworthy servant, and will kill you in an instant if it thinks it will help its plans. Such as they are. Best to leave it in its pit, brooding over its failures and betrayals. My new friend is so much older, so much stranger, so much stronger. The shatterling managed to break contact and escape the first time it tried to overmaster the omphalos, but it won't be able to escape when it tries again. Does it have anything to say about that? No? Well, I suppose you wouldn't tell me if it had, and in any case it doesn't matter.'

The omphalos was the source of the invasion, but Remfrey He wouldn't or couldn't say exactly what it was, where it had come from and what it wanted. Telling the lucidor and Orjen that they would find out soon enough, telling them now about the history of the ruined settlement.

'As I understand it, some members of the first Simudanese expedition became infected, fought and killed the rest, and gave birth to the first generation of alters. The second expedition was more careful. They bombarded the original alter nest, killed the breeders outright, picked off stray warriors, workers and porters, and fortified their camp against crabs and other animals. For most of the time they stayed inside their magic circle, using machines like the one you are riding to probe the omphalos. But the machines were clumsy and easily disabled or subverted, and the siege by creatures linked to the omphalos's network was relentless. Very soon, the Simudanese abandoned their camp and went home. Meanwhile, a few alter workers who had escaped the massacre converted to breeders and began to procreate parthenogenetically in scrape nests, and raised a new generation that rebuilt the original nest.'

'When was this?' Orjen said. 'How long ago?'

She was walking on the other side of the grass-cutter, and a party of men and women and alter warriors were shambling behind it. Some of them carrying the bodies of Jy Solon and the four sailors.

'Oh, not very,' Remfrey He said carelessly. 'I suppose the first expedition might have arrived thirty or forty years ago. It's hard to be precise. The alters don't reckon time like we do. In fact, they don't reckon time at all. Every day is day zero as far as they are concerned. As for the omphalos, it thinks big. Big time. Big distances. Big plans. Marvellous mindbendingly big plans. You'll see.'

'I'm looking forward to it,' the lucidor said.

'Don't think that your secret sharer can save you. It can't. And it won't be able to save itself, either.'

'Is that your threat or your master's?'

Remfrey He ran his hand over the stout red threads rooted amongst what was left of his hair. 'Unlike you, I am more than I once was. So much more. While you, my dear old friend, are so much less.'

'You like to fool people. Now, I think, you are fooling yourself. Telling a comforting story to patch over the truth. You are as much a servant as any alter worker.'

'I thought about bringing you with me on the *First Pilgrim*, you know. I even raised it with the people who supposedly had oversight of my work – what a joke that was, by the way. The kind of people I had to deal with! They rejected the idea, of course. Given your conviction, and so on. I suppose I could have changed their minds by telling them about your link with the shatterling, but I decided that should be our little secret.'

'You couldn't tell them about the shatterling because that would have exposed your lie about being able to access the alter network,' the lucidor said. 'You didn't unriddle alter compass dances to find out where the infection came from. The shatterling told you.'

Remfrey He ignored that. 'It has all worked out, as I rather expected it would, thanks to the pathological fascination – you might even call it a perverse kind of love – that drove you to follow me to Patua, and now all the way to this marvellous new map, and the omphalos. I don't believe in fate, but I must say that this strongly tests my lack of belief.'

'Fate had nothing to do with it,' the lucidor said.

Remfrey He's laugh was a kind of soft dry hack, like someone in the final stages of sand lung. 'I suppose that you still think that you are the hero of our mutual adventure. After all this time, after all that has happened, everything you have seen of my work, you haven't learned anything. It would be amazing if it wasn't so pitiful.'

'I know one thing,' the lucidor said. 'I know that I have been changed. And you have been changed too, more so than me. You

388

may think that you are still who you once were, but ask yourself this: are those thoughts really yours?'

Remfrey He spun the staff over his head, three times dexter, twice widdershins. 'That's profound. For you, at any rate. Let me see. If I think my thoughts are my own, does it make any difference if they are or not? If a fake is a perfect copy, is it a fake? And so on. But let me turn it around: do you think you have come here to bring me to what you like to call justice, or are you here because the shatterling wanted you to come here?'

'I'm here,' the lucidor said. 'That is the one thing we can agree on. That is all that matters.'

'You are not a map reader,' Orjen said to Remfrey He.

'My gift is more powerful and much more useful. It helps people like you understand what kind of fun you would have, working for me. As you will. I am going to infect you. Do not doubt that I won't. But it might be interesting to find out how your little gift can be augmented and put to use, so perhaps I will infect you with the same remapped threads that transformed me. You will still be you, or think that you are, but you will be under my command. The things we are going to do together!'

Orjen ignored that, saying, 'And since you are not a map reader, you may not know about suicide ants.'

'If you are working up some kind of analogy between ants and alters, it pains me to remind you that alters are not ants. Pains me because I should not need to remind a map reader of so basic a fact.'

'This is about ants and a fungus,' Orjen said doggedly. 'The fungus infects ants, and grows through and around their nervous system. It becomes a kind of parallel nervous system, in fact. Does that sound familiar?'

Remfrey He twirled the staff, almost dropped it, and swiped with a careless one-handed lunge at a curtain of red vines that hung from the ruin of a cylindrical house that something, long ago, had sliced neatly in two. He said, 'I think I know where you are going, but carry on.'

'When the fungus inside it matures,' Orjen said, 'the infected ant exhibits a very specific kind of behaviour never seen in

389

ordinary ants. It climbs a tree or bush and walks along a twig and clings upside down to the very tip. And there it stays and there it dies, as the fungus develops a fruiting body that grows out of the ant's body and ripens and scatters spores into the air. And that is why the ant climbs somewhere high: to make sure that the spores will be carried as far as possible on the breeze before they fall. It gives them a better chance of finding new ant colonies.'

'The infection in this case is not a fungus. And I am not an ant.'

'Ever since I learned about the ant and the fungus I have always wondered what thoughts the ant might be thinking, at the end,' Orjen said. 'As it climbed the tree. As it hung from the end of the twig, above the abyss. Was it thinking its own thoughts, or the thoughts of the fungus? And if it was thinking the fungus's thoughts, did it believe them to be its own?'

'Perhaps they were the thoughts of neither ant nor fungus, but of something new that shared the best qualities of both,' Remfrey He said.

'Or perhaps you are ill, Mr He. Perhaps you are gripped by a fever dream, and are unable to tell what is real and what isn't. You don't know what the omphalos is or what it wants,' Orjen said. 'You only think that you do. It is a fantasy got up from fragments and scraps to comfort what is left of you.'

Remfrey He turned and thrust the staff at Orjen, its point quivering a span from her face, tracing small slow circles.

'I could drop you into the pit,' he said quietly, showing all his teeth, his gaze bright. 'You would have a few moments to understand what's real and what isn't before you burned up like a moth in a candle flame.'

Orjen did not flinch, staring at Remfrey He with weaponised disdain, and after a few moments the man gave his dry imitation of a laugh and raised the staff and turned on his heel, and the procession went on. They were close to the nest, now. Its spires of naked baserock rearing against the sky, webs and walkways strung between them busy with alters, a thin traffic streaming away from its base, passing alters returning with swollen bellies or carrying bales of grass and kelp twice their size. All of them were capped with red threads, as were the shells of the handful of spider crabs that stepped daintily amongst them.

Orjen said, 'Would you say that you are a warrior or a worker, Mr He?'

'I have made myself into something new,' Remfrey He said. 'The Simudanese failed to understand what this is, and fled from it, but I have embraced it. I rejoice in it. The maps are dying. Will die, if nothing is done. But with my help they will be renewed, and all will be changed. It is the culmination of my life's project. Not one I had foreseen, I grant you, but one far greater than I ever imagined.'

'If you mean that you have finally embraced your insanity, I can't disagree,' the lucidor said.

'If there is any part of you that's still aware of what you really are, it isn't too late to give it up and come back with me,' Orjen said. 'My family has all the resources and influence you will ever need.'

Remfrey He laughed. 'Do you really think that you can stop me with a paltry bribe? Soon I will take everything your family has. Everything on the entire map. And that's just the beginning.'

'I am not trying to stop anything,' Orjen said. 'I am trying to save whatever fraction of humanity is left inside you.'

The lucidor knew that she was really trying to save herself, and was pierced by sorrow and guilt. He hadn't imagined ending up in a place like this when he'd set out, yet he had come here all the same, step by step, and he had come willingly. But Orjen did not deserve this. She did not deserve any of it.

'To become something more than human you have to give up everything you once were. I have been giving it up all my life,' Remfrey He said. 'And at last I have arrived at where I was always meant to be.'

53

Sparks in Everything

Unchallenged by the hulking warriors who guarded the busy path, they followed the irregular procession of alter workers into the nest. Stinking mounds of fungus gardens were spread around the bases of slender black spires, beneath an aerial maze of nets and platforms and ropeways. The scratch and hum of the alters' unceasing activity filled the hot close air. A narrow gap between two spires framed a glimpse of the sea and the island squatting at the base of the pillar of cloud.

The lucidor felt a curious calm. Intricate filigrees glimmered through the shadowy air like dewy cobwebs, reminding him of the bright threads that had linked the nests along the coast of Patua and shot out across the World Ocean, bending towards each other, knitting into a cord that curved away beyond the horizon. This was the end point of that common cord. His final destination. And because he could see the shifting patterns of the alter network he knew that the shatterling was with him, watching through the connection it had built inside his head.

Bodies were strewn along the slope of one of the mounds: crew and passengers of the *Resolute Mind*, torn and mutilated, arms outflung, dead faces turned up to a patch of sky between the spires. The lucidor recognised young Lieutenant Paleflower, several others. Alters and red-capped men and women stepped forward and carelessly dropped the bodies of Jy Solon and the four sailors amongst them, and Remfrey He caught hold of Orjen and drew her close, said that she smelled of something very familiar and bent his face to her hair and snuffled up a long draught of air.

'That's not a bad copy,' he said. 'But pheromones won't keep you safe here. Only I can do that.'

He pointed to a cluster of wicker cages slung high above, told Orjen that she would spend time in one of them while she was being transformed into his servant, and began to explain how he had taken control of everything in the nest. Boasting and bragging as he always did, stitching every random encounter, every accident and coincidence, into a seamless narrative in which he was the hero, never failing, always right, endlessly triumphant, talking talking talking.

When the lucidor had come home after interrogation sessions with Remfrey He, his wife had sometimes told him that he needed to run a few errands or take a walk around the neighbourhood so that he could shake the man from his back and find himself again. Some lawbreakers could read him pretty well and know how to needle him, but they were trifling annoyances compared to Remfrey He. He was something else. Every time the lucidor talked with the man it was as if his very essence was in contention, yet he'd kept at it with stubborn resolve, for although Remfrey He had confessed to enough murder and mayhem to keep him in prison for the rest of his life there were unaccounted victims in the long list of charges and the lucidor felt that he had to speak for them. Discover everything that Remfrey He had done and put it on record for all to see. Every day he tried his best to convince the man to do the right thing and every day he failed. Failed to make any impression, failed to find any flaw or purchase in the man's sardonic demeanour, failed to find out anything other than what the man wanted him to know. As far as Remfrey He was concerned, murders he had committed out of spite or momentary irritation or some species of ghastly whim, crimes which did nothing to burnish his image or contribute to his grand and gaudy self-mythos, were of no account. As trivial as squashing bugs, or trimming a hangnail. It was a battle of wills, and the lucidor was losing and knew that he was losing, yet he refused to back down or walk away.

His wife had once told him that you could only fix what could be fixed and had to let the rest go, or else failure would mark you for the rest of your life. He missed her clear way of seeing the world exactly as it was, thought once again that if he had listened to her advice he might not now be trying to square up to ending his life in such dire and dreadful circumstances. On the other hand, he wouldn't have won this chance to overturn Remfrey He's schemes, and perhaps, just perhaps, help the shatterling to put an end to the source of the invasion. If that was what it intended. If its earnest assurances and promises were not, as he had long suspected, some trick got up to convince him to satisfy some secret plan. For here he was, exactly where it wanted him to be, and it still hadn't explained what it planned to do.

Remfrey He was telling him that it was too bad that he didn't have long to live, because it would have been a lot of fun to cage him and watch as the threads took away everything he knew and was. 'Never mind. I will get to find out what happens to you when the omphalos eats the mind of your secret sharer. Which will be even more fun than turning you into a brainless puppet.'

'And I'm going to enjoy finding out what happens to you when you are proven wrong.'

'You can't admit that you picked the wrong side, can you?'

'Neither can you. That's why you're thinking of sticking me in a cage, so you won't have to put everything you have at risk.'

'It's good to see that you still have a little spirit left. It will make your final downfall all the more enjoyable.'

'I don't have much time left, Remfrey. If you want to have your fun, you need to put up or shut up right now.'

Remfrey He regarded him for a moment, his gaze brightening. 'I have seen many people in their last moments. Only a few died unknowingly, for imminent death often brings clarity to the most clouded mind. Some went happily, understanding that it was the final fulfilment of their service to me, but most died in a state of impotent desperation, denying what I told them was about to happen, or trying to bargain with me. And quite often, when they realised that denial or bargaining could do no good, they would become angry and defiant. A few would even dare me to do it, as if they reckoned that they could somehow call my bluff. As if they reckoned that I was neither willing nor able to make an end to them. You are at that stage now.'

'You mistake speaking the plain truth for defiance. I don't have long left, and I have come to terms with it. As much as anyone can. If we are going to do this thing, then let's do it. Let's see who is right and who is wrong. Otherwise you'll miss your chance, and I'll go down into darkness with the warm thought that I called your bluff.'

'You should know by now that I never bluff. Can you walk?'

'I would rather not try.'

'Use your chariot to follow me, then, or I will have you carried.' Remfrey He looked at Orjen and told her, 'You can come too. I wouldn't want you to miss the fun.'

Orjen saw that the lucidor was having trouble operating the grass-cutter, and spoke to it in trade pidgin.

'Don't try any tricks,' Remfrey He said, 'or I will have the threads consume your forebrain instead of turning you into my servant.'

'I asked it to follow you,' she said. 'As you can see.'

Several warriors and a single spider crab fell in behind them as they crossed the nest, threading between the bases of the spires and heaps of rotting vegetation, coming out into mirrorlight and a salt breeze. A causeway ran on top of a low embankment that ribboned away towards the island. Remfrey He led them across it, telling them about the hard labour necessary for its construction, and how many alters and members of the *First Pilgrim*'s crew had died in the course of it.

The lucidor scarcely noticed. The causeway and the island and the encircling sea glittered with brilliant splinters and flakes of light, billowing drifts of fine rain sparkled like diamond dust, and the column of cloud continuously unpacking into the sky shone like a crystalline fracture in reality. The shatterling had told one thing true, at least: the world was underwritten by a fine-grained ghost of everything ever done in it. Somewhere in that luminous, lovely sea of memory the ordinary life he and his wife had made together might still live on. Some part of them might still share a common space, infinitely small and infinitely precious.

He blinked back foolish tears and said to Orjen, 'Do you see?'

'See what?'

'Sparks. Sparks in everything.'

The causeway ran above wave-washed gardens of chalky pillows and fans of delicate lace and clusters of stubby red spikes to the edge of the island and a long slope rising towards the base of the column of cloud. The ground trembled faintly and constantly and light burned in the roiling vapour and threads of light shone like streaks of molten iron inside the chalky stones and dust of the slope. Light was leaking through everywhere the lucidor looked, as if Afram Auspex's prophecies had come true and the Heartsun had reignited and its fires were about to crack the world open, like a chick hatching from an egg.

Remfrey He was using the staff to poke along through the glitter and glare of holy light, the grass-cutter slid and slipped and skewed as it gamely did its best to keep up, and Orjen and the alter warriors and the spider crab followed behind. Two of the warriors seemed to have forgotten their orders, one walking back along the causeway and the other standing knee-deep at the edge of the sea, but Remfrey He either hadn't noticed or didn't care about their defection.

The slope topped out on a broad flat rim that circled the vent. It was big enough to swallow the *First Pilgrim* entire. Gouts of vapour blasted up from it and unpacked into the towering column of cloud; its walls stepped down in steep terraces and gushes of seawater arched out from the terraces and fell in streams and curtains that were blown apart and turned to steam by hot winds blowing from the depths, where something burned too brightly to look at directly. The lucidor blinked back green and purple after-images. Everything was vividly lit by the vent's stark glare, drenched by gusts of warm mist and spray, trembling and shuddering in the industrial roar of falling water and boiling vapour.

Remfrey He gestured grandly, as if he was the sole author of this spectacle, and said, raising his voice to be heard, 'The cradle of a new creation!'

He led the lucidor and Orjen and their escort along a path through a litter of chalk stones and boulders, following the rim of the vent to a figure revealed and obscured by sheets and scarves of mist blowing in the hot winds. As they drew near, the lucidor saw that it was the chief petty officer, Effra Ro, standing with his back to a sheer drop, drenched and bedraggled but coming to attention as Remfrey He stepped towards him.

'This man killed the captain and most of the officers of the *Resolute Mind*,' Remfrey He said. 'Had he caught you, he would have killed you too, my dear lucidor. And ransomed Orjen after despoiling her in the filthiest of ways. But he's under my command now, and ready to pay for his crimes.'

'You don't have to do anything you don't want to do,' the lucidor shouted to Effra Ro. 'Remember why I was kept apart from the map readers and scriers. As long as I'm here, his words are only words.'

'Oh, I hadn't forgotten about your gift. That's why I prepared him in advance,' Remfrey He said, and put a hand on Effra Ro's head and told him to do it.

The man lifted his arms like wings and took two steps backward and toppled over the edge, vanishing into mist and glare.

For a bare moment the lucidor was wiped clean by shock; then anger rushed in, strengthening his resolve.

Remfrey He walked over to a cluster of red spikes and gestured to the lucidor and Orjen, leaning on the staff amongst wisps of vapour like a spellbinder from one of the old stories.

'This is where the omphalos fell,' he told them, when they had stepped close enough to hear him above the constant roar. 'It is more powerful than any shatterling, and much older. It began its fall far away and long ago, long before the creator gods smashed the worlds of the star of the Ur Men, built a flimsy globe around the star's iron corpse and flooded it with the meltwater of comets, and populated maps of long-lost worlds with imitations of their ancestors.

'Did they create our world as an act of reverence, or was it a moment of caprice? Who knows? Who cares? We only know that the avatars of the creator gods played out their old stories for a little while, and when they'd had their fun they quit the world they had made and went elsewhere, without a moment's thought for its fate. And now another kind of god has arrived.

A god older and more powerful than the gods that created us. So much time has passed since the universe hatched from the cosmic egg that countless races have been able to bootstrap themselves to godhood. Every star in our galaxy, every world, has been visited, used or changed by some kind of god. Everything that was familiar to the creatures we imitate has been lost, or changed beyond all recognition. Even the galaxy is no longer the galaxy they knew . . .'

The lucidor didn't hear what else Remfrey He had to say, because a familiar hooded figure was floating in the wind-torn mist, the twin stars of its eyes as bright as the light burning up from the pit.

'There is no god down there,' the shatterling said. 'Merely another servant that lost its way.'

'Can you really put an end to it?'

'My clones are interrogating the network it grew here, searching for subtle paths to its heart. All you have to do is cooperate with the man, Remfrey He, until I am ready to finish this.'

'I think the omphalos wants to use me as a way of reaching out to you.'

'It tried to find me before, and I have fixed that vulnerability. Wait. Wait.' The figure was speaking to someone else. 'Wait, don't interfere—'

The lucidor returned to himself with a jolt, as if he'd fallen from a great height, his heart leaping madly in the cage of his ribs, sweat starting all over his body. He was lying on the ground, rain kissing his face as he looked up at the great column of vapour jetting into the sky.

Remfrey He stepped back, glint of a needle in his hand, and told Orjen that the shot had better be nothing more than adrenalin. 'You'll suffer for it if he's benumbed or rendered insensible. He has to be fully conscious to the very end.'

'I can't guarantee he won't have another fit,' Orjen said, and helped the lucidor to sit up.

'That wasn't a fit. It was a visitation,' Remfrey He said. He flicked the needle into the void and looked down at the lucidor. 'I know that the shatterling is trying to take control of the omphalos. And

I know that it won't succeed. The omphalos will defeat it and absorb it, and everything it knows. Including the key.'

The lucidor's heart was pounding in his chest and his mouth was dry. He had to suck up spit before he could speak. 'The key to what?'

'The omphalos collided with a mirror in the final moments of its fall, and a fragment of that mirror is still down there, transmitting a small fraction of the heat and light of the Heartsun through a link to the inner surface of the world. And it is not a one-way link. No, it is a gate that allows passage in both directions. The omphalos needs to unlock the way to the interior, and shatterlings possess the key. Once the omphalos has absorbed your secret sharer, it will be able to slip inside, to the space where the controls to the world lie.'

Orjen laughed. 'Is that the story you tell yourself?'

'It's no story, as you'll soon see.'

'Something fell,' Orjen said. 'And it infected ordinary life, and changed it. But imagining that you are helping something to take control of the world – that's pure fantasy.'

'No,' the lucidor said, remembering that the shatterling had been trying to dig down to the inner rind of the world's shell. 'No, I don't think it is.'

'The shatterling told you some version of the truth, I suppose,' Remfrey He said, as he walked back to the cluster of red spikes. 'But did it tell you about this?'

He struck the ground with the footing of the staff and the cluster of spikes split apart, throwing out a thousand threads that extended and grew into each other, forming the sketch of a bed or couch, with a shock of threads curving up at one end.

'You will lie on the couch,' Remfrey He told the lucidor, 'and the threads will penetrate your skull and brain and take control of the connection with the shatterling. The omphalos will absorb everything it knows. And perhaps it will absorb you, too. Perhaps you will live on, in some fashion. Endlessly tormented by the knowledge that you failed.'

'There's something you have overlooked,' Orjen said.

Remfrey He and the lucidor turned to her. The warriors which had been standing behind her were walking away down the slope. Only the spider crab remained.

Orjen held up a hand, displaying a small spray bottle nestled in her palm. 'The nest scent wasn't the only pheromone I made. This is a distress signal I got up. It triggers a fear-and-flight response in alters. They move away from the source. Scatter and go into hiding.'

'Very clever, and very pointless,' Remfrey He said. 'I could call them back if I wanted to, but I have no need of protection here. Give me a hand with your friend. Help me carry him to his dying bed.'

Orjen folded her arms across her chest and stared at him with grim defiance, saying, 'Bring back the warriors if you need help. Or show me what that spider crab can do.'

'You wouldn't like it if I did,' Remfrey He said.

The lucidor pushed to his feet. He was a loose bag of blood and flesh stretched over a scaffolding of broken glass that stabbed and sliced him with every movement, but the shot of adrenalin had pushed the pain into the background and he was calling up every last reserve of strength and resolve in a final and desperate effort. Remfrey He swiped the staff at him as he staggered forward, and the lucidor leaned away as the end swung past his face and caught it and tried to shove Remfrey He backwards, towards the edge of the vent. But he was too weak, too unsteady; the man snatched the staff from his grip and struck his left hip, a hard chop that sent him sprawling. Remfrey He loomed above him, raising the staff to strike again, the lucidor lifted a hand to protect his face, and the staff struck the ground close by, sending chalky fragments flying.

'I don't need you, but I do need what's inside your head,' Remfrey He said, and gestured towards the spider crab.

Nothing happened.

Remfrey He gestured again, swiping the staff through the luminous air, and for a bare moment the light blazing up from the vent blinked out. Remfrey He screamed and clutched at his head, the spider crab tottered and pitched over the edge of the drop, and Orjen shouted a command and the grass-cutter lurched forward. Remfrey He turned, tried to fend off the machine with the staff, and it struck him and bore him backwards and they were gone.

When the lucidor tried to stand up, he found that he was paralysed from toes to fingertips. The shatterling's voice whispered in his head. Silk ravelling across silk. Sand blowing across sand.

'I am inside the so-called omphalos now. Be still while I finish downloading myself, and then I will be everywhere.'

The lucidor blanked out again, jerked awake. His pulse pounding in his chest; his heart heaving against the cage of his ribs. Orjen was cradling his head in one hand, holding a needle in the other. She helped him sit up. Despite the second shot of adrenalin, pain was universal.

He said, 'Dealing with Remfrey He. That was my job.'

'All I did was finish what you started.'

'The caretaker will be upset. How will it keep its grass trimmed now?'

The staff lay at the rim of the steep drop. The lucidor asked Orjen to hand it to him, and with her help was able to use it to lever himself to his feet. Light and vapour shot up past them. Hot air battered them.

Orjen said, anxiety in her gaze and her voice, 'If you can walk just a little way, down to the shore, I can find Mr Solon's boat and get you back to the *First Pilgrim*.'

'I have one more thing to do. One last thing. The shatterling is using the connection inside my head to take control of the omphalos and the mirror fragment. And I have to put a stop to that because Remfrey He had it right. The one true thing he ever told straight. If we let it, the shatterling will become the worst kind of god. It might be able to save the world, but it will also force everyone in every map to bend their knee, for all time to come.'

'How can we stop it?'

'All you have to do is step aside. Let me do what needs to be done.'

Orjen understood at once. 'I won't. I won't let you kill yourself.'

There was no time. The shatterling was coming back. Fluttering at the edge of his vision. Pushing past the temporary bulwark of the adrenalin shot.

The lucidor swung the staff in a short, calculated jab, coming down on his front foot and pushing his weight through the staff as it struck Orjen beneath her sternum, square in her solar plexus. She doubled over, gasping for breath, and the lucidor dropped the staff. He didn't need it any more. He didn't need anything. The shatterling was inside his head now, raving and furious, but it was too late. He took two short steps and gave himself to the air, and a moment of light and heat burned everything away.

54

Legacy

'If I've got this right,' Lyra said to her boss, after she had come aboard the wreck of the *First Pilgrim* and persuaded Orjen to sit down and tell her story from one end to the other, 'the old man killed himself because it was the only way to destroy his connection with the shatterling, and stop the shatterling taking control of the omphalos.'

'That's what he said.'

'And this was after you pushed Remfrey He over the edge of the long drop with some kind of lawnmower.'

'In the heat of the moment,' Orjen said. 'I can't help thinking that I should have let him live. There was so much I could have learned from him.'

'He would have turned your brain into a fungus garden. Made you into his slave. The man was a legitimate monster,' Lyra said, thinking that before they had been dragged into this mess her boss would never have dreamed of killing someone, even by remote control. She had been through the fire. They both had.

'Well, he is gone,' Orjen said. 'And Thorn is gone too, and it is up to us to decide what to do next.'

She was haggard and raggedy and her eyes were bruised, but there was a familiar gleam in her gaze. Lyra had seen it too many times before and it was especially alarming to see it now, in this strange map, so very far from home and everything she knew.

'You've already done some figuring out, haven't you?' she said. 'Pulling one of your all-nighters, by the look of you.'

'I found some wake-up pills,' Orjen admitted. 'And while I was keeping watch for alters or worse, I tried to work out how things have changed. Or even if anything has changed. The pillar is still there, same as it ever was.'

Both of them looked across the bay to the column of cloud climbing up from the island and bending north, high above the sea.

Lyra said, 'All it means is that the omphalos's mirror fragment is still doing its thing.'

'It means that we can't be certain that Thorn succeeded. For all we know the shatterling might have taken control before he sacrificed himself.'

'He was a straight-ahead stand-up kind of fellow,' Lyra said. 'Always ready to do the right thing when the right thing needed doing. If he said he was going to stop the shatterling then that's what he did.'

Seeing the old man the only way she could see him now, in the mind's eye of memory. His sharp blue eyes. His creased face, skin several shades darker than her own. That stupid ponytail he'd been trying to grow ever since the army had forcibly cut his hair. He had always been neatly turned out. Alert and limber. Even when his infection had started to grip, he'd held himself as steadily and straight-backed as he could. He'd had his own agenda, had been stubbornly faithful to the damned code of honour which some might say had killed him in the end, but he was also the kind of capable, cool-headed man who would always have your back when things went sideways.

She said, 'I know he made some kind of difference. Knew it before I got off the ship and headed here. Knew it when the watchers didn't turn up along the shore, and the things from the sea didn't lay siege in the night.'

Orjen, as stubborn in her own way as the old man, said that she didn't yet have enough data to discount other explanations, said that the absence of the watchers and the things from the sea might mean that the shatterling, if it was now in control of the omphalos, had no use for them. 'Or it might have called them off to lure you here.'

'I would have come anyway,' Lyra said.

She'd set out at first light, had spent more than half the day following the coast north and west, scared the whole time that the mutineers or a little leviathan or something even worse might ambush her, at last rounding the point of the bay and spotting the ruins of the Simudanese settlement, and turning towards the *Resolute Mind* when Orjen fired a flare that scrawled a trail of smoke across the sky and burst in a brief bright red flower.

In the aftermath of the final confrontation between the old man and Remfrey He, Orjen had found the boat Jy Solon and the others had used to go ashore, and lit out for the nearest safe place. The *Resolute Mind* appeared to have been attacked by leviathans again: its hull was holed in several places and it had settled in shallow water above a chalk reef, flooding the engine room and the holds. Orjen had scavenged potable water and canned food from the galley, found Captain Godshorse's godspeaker in his cabin, where Effra Ro appeared to have taken up residence, and spent the night on the aft deck, keeping watch on the island and activity in the alter nest and the ruins of the Simudanese settlement.

'You weren't supposed to come here and you didn't need to,' she told Lyra. 'I have Mr Solon's boat, and could have found my own way back to the *First Pilgrim* on my own.'

'Like you know how to pilot a boat all of a sudden. And here's another bit of data. Do you think that the shatterling, if it had won control, would have let you escape from that island and walk through the alter nest and take the boat?'

'We shouldn't discount the protective effect of my pheromone mixtures,' Orjen said.

Yes, she was still as stubborn as ever, still refusing to accept what ordinary folk believed to be common sense. That need to question every assumption, married to her razor-sharp focus, was why she was so good at what she did, but sometimes Lyra wondered how she had put up with her boss's contrary ways for so long.

Well, you know why, she told herself. And it isn't just because no one else is able or willing to do it.

'Your pheromones might have protected you from the alters,' she said, 'but I don't know that they would have had any effect on the poor fellows Remfrey He recruited. Not to mention those spider crabs. And if that doesn't convince you that the old man put an end to the shatterling's plan, it looks like we'll have plenty of time to gather more evidence. There's no way we can patch up this wreck by ourselves, and Sub-Lieutenant Skywatcher isn't going to be of any help. When I left him, he was up on his observation post, with his long gun and his jug of lemonade, keeping watch for enemies that aren't going to come any more. Man's firmly wedded to his routines, shrugged me off when I asked him if he wanted to come along with me. We should get back to the *First Pilgrim*, and after you've rested we can return and take a proper look around. And maybe you can use that godspeaker you found to tell the army what happened. The sooner they know, the sooner they can make a start on a rescue plan.'

'I have already talked to the army, and to my father,' Orjen said. 'They are discussing how to proceed, but everything turns on the launch and outfitting of the *Resolute Mind*'s sister ship. Even if the work is expedited, it won't be ready to sail for at least a hundred days.'

'Then we'll just have to tough it out here for a while.'

'Perhaps not,' Orjen said. 'Let's go ashore. There's something I haven't told you about yet because it's best if you see it for yourself.'

'I don't know, boss. It's awfully late in the day. Maybe you could tell me about this little surprise of yours on the way back to the *First Pilgrim*, and we'll go see it tomorrow.'

'We can spend the night in the settlement built by the second Simudanese expedition,' Orjen said. 'It's close by the thing I want to show you, and its caretaker will be happy to look after us.'

They took Lyra's boat straight across the bay, and Orjen recounted what she knew of the history of the two Simudanese settlements as they walked up through the ruins. The mirror arc was dropping towards the horizon and shadows were lengthening everywhere. A woman with a red cap covering most of her head turned to look at them as they went past. Lyra jacked up the long gun she'd brought along, but after a few moments the poor creature went back to gathering armfuls of red weed, as innocent as a child picking flowers.

'We came here to find an enemy,' Orjen said. 'Something we could defeat or destroy. And we found the omphalos, but I am not certain, now, if it ever was any kind of enemy. It fell here and grew defences around itself, recruited animals which had been changed by its tailswallowers, and got up alter women from the survivors of the first Simudanese expedition. And here it stayed, at the edge of the new map it had created, indifferent to the rest of the world.'

'But it changed our map too. I mean, this is the root of the invasion.'

'Its tailswallowers were most likely lofted on that plume of cloud, blowing on the wind, settling on the ocean, changing sea creatures and weed that drifted to land on tides and currents . . . It's as I have always contended. There was an invasion, but no enemy, no plan. Just a new kind of life struggling like any other to pass its life maps from one generation to the next.'

'For all we know it might have infected the whole wide world. If that's not an invasion I don't know what is.'

'I don't know about the rest of the maps, but I think it likely that the tailswallowers reached Simud. The Simudanese came here to find the source, just as we did. They ran foul of the omphalos and its defences, and were absorbed or defeated, but they left behind something we can use. It isn't far now.'

The two women climbed an overgrown slope beyond the far edge of the ruins and Orjen led Lyra along the long paved strip towards the flying machines squatting under their shrouds of red vine, and explained what they were.

'Do you really think that any of these wrecks could still work?' Lyra said.

'One of them woke up and spoke to me after I climbed onto it. They haven't been here long, the vines have protected them from the worst of the weather, and it seems that they are powered by the light-collecting panels which cover their wings. We can patch up at least one with parts from the others, and if we can't find everything we need here there's a machine shop on the *First Pilgrim*. The caretaker of the second settlement may be able to help us, too.'

'Even if we manage to repair one, it's a long way home. Can any of these things really fly that far?'

'The Simudanese flew here in machines like this,' Orjen said. 'And since we are roughly halfway between Simud and Patua, I have every confidence that we can use them to return home. They have boat-shaped hulls, so they can settle on the ocean whenever necessary, and we should aim to fix up and fly two of them, so if one fails we will still have the other. We will get back to Patua long before any rescue mission can set sail, and I will use what I have learned here to help the army deal with the invasion. I doubt that we can completely destroy it. It has spread too far and it is too sly, and so very quick to adapt. But I believe that we can halt its advance and contain it, and then we can think about returning here, and think about moving on to Simud, too. It's clear that the Simudanese know a lot about machines. Much more than we do. But I think it likely that they do not know very much about reading and rewriting life maps. If they did, they would have worked out how to control the alters and the other creatures of the invasion. We can help them with that, and they can help us. Two nations that were once at war united in a common cause.'

There was that gleam in her gaze again, feverishly bright. Once, during one of their expeditions in the mountains in the south, Lyra had found the pugmarks of a dire wolf freshly printed in the mud by a stream, and she felt the same little fizz of fear and caution now.

Something must have shown in her face, because Orjen smiled and said, 'Don't worry. I was always close to Thorn, protected by his muzzling gift. Remfrey He didn't ever get the chance to silvertongue me. He was a bad man. No doubt about that. Even so, and even though he lied as easily as breathing, and many of his ideas were crazy and his methods were questionable, he had a unique mind.'

'Which he sorely misused,' Lyra said.

'He knew how to think big,' Orjen said. 'And if we are to understand what happened here and what it means we need to think big too. Remfrey He said that the mirror fragment is a gateway, and the shatterling possessed the key to it. Thorn may have put an end to the shatterling's plans, but he did not destroy it. It is still squatting under the ruins of Pythos. If we can wrest the key from it, or deduce its nature from first principles, we can slip through the fragment to the interior of the world's shell, and perhaps we can find out how to fix and renew it. And that may only be the beginning. The shatterling wanted to be a god, and Thorn gave up his life to thwart it, but his true legacy may be far greater than that. Look there, at Tiu,' she said and flung out an arm.

Lyra turned, saw the wanderer's blood-red lamp glimmering low in the darkening sky to the east, then stepped forward and caught Orjen as she swayed uncertainly, helped her to sit down.

'It's been a long day,' Lyra said. 'We'll rest a bit, and then we'll get on to this other settlement.'

'If we can use the mirror fragment as a door to the world's interior, we can also use it to reach the mirrors around Tiu,' Orjen said. 'And perhaps find gateways to other worlds. In time, we might even find where the creator gods have gone, and hold them to account. Think about it, Lyra! Thorn may have helped us make the first step on the path that will help us to escape our past and discover our full potential, and do everything we could ever want or need to do.'

Lyra touched her boss's forehead with the back of her hand. 'You're tired, and overthinking things. And you're running a bit of a fever, too.'

She hoped that was all there was to it, but remembered the miserable, anxious hours she'd spent as Remfrey He's prisoner in the alter nest, listening to him boast about his achievements and plans. Afterwards, the head doctors who had examined her said there was no evidence that she had been affected by the man's silvertongue gift, but she had never quite shaken off the notion that Remfrey He had planted some kind of malign seed inside her head, and knew she would carry that uncertainty until the end of her days. A good part of the reason why she had agreed to stay behind on the *First Pilgrim* was that she hadn't wanted to confront the man ever again, and now she was worried that he had managed, somehow, to use his gift to plant a legacy in

Orjen's mind. Crazy ideas that could as easily destroy the world as save it.

First thing she'd do when they got back to civilisation was have her boss looked at by the best head doctors she could find. Meanwhile, there were more pressing considerations. She asked Orjen where this other settlement was, said they ought to reach it before nightfall.

'It isn't far,' Orjen said. 'Just over the top of the rise. But perhaps I should sit here for a minute or two first.'

'I'll brew a pot of chai,' Lyra said. 'We'll both feel the benefit.'

She opened her day bag and set up the little spirit burner and an ironwood pot, stirred in two pinches of leaf powder when the water had boiled, and poured the chai into two cups and handed one to Orjen. The familiar routine had given her a little space to strengthen her resolve, to make her confession sooner rather than later.

'I got to know Thorn pretty well on the voyage,' she said. 'While you were busy with your work on the invasion's flora and fauna. We had some interesting conversations about the different ways our countries are run. He helped me see things from another angle, question what I'd thought to be the natural order of things. Such as the way power and money are so unequally distributed in Patua. How laws benefit the few, not the many.'

'It sounds like the kind of nonsense put out by the rebels,' Orjen said.

'The old man had some sympathy with them. Understood why they are still fighting, even though they must know it's hardly likely that they will win. How he put it, when you start out with nothing you have nothing to lose and everything to win. Do you remember the promise I gave him, just before the two of you set off?'

'He wanted you to make sure that his boss knew what he had done here. I can help you with that. It shouldn't be too hard or take too long to set up a godspeaker relay. My father can arrange it with the Free State embassy in Delos-Chimr.'

'I'd rather talk to the fellow directly,' Lyra said.

'If you want to travel to the Free State after we get back to Patua, I can help to arrange that, too,' Orjen said.

Here it was. The hard thing Lyra needed to say. The decision she had made.

'You were right in thinking that heading straight to Simud is most likely going to get us killed,' she said. 'But going back to Patua isn't the answer either.'

'Of course it is,' Orjen said. 'I have to get back to work as soon as I can.'

'To help the army defeat the invasion.'

'As far as possible, given its nature.'

'And do you really think that, when you're done with the invasion, the army and the government will allow you to come back here, let alone go on to Simud?'

'Why wouldn't they, when the benefits are so obvious?'

'People in power gave philosophers a free hand in the fight against the invasion because it was the only way of defeating it. And when that fight is over, those same people will put a stop to anything that threatens them and theirs, same as they always have.'

'Thorn really turned your head, didn't he? You've forgotten that the government of the Free State controls philosophical inquiry as closely and rigidly as it controls everything else.'

'That's what we've been told to believe. The old man helped me to understand that it isn't true. That it's propaganda. The Free State government doesn't rule for the sake of ruling, and it doesn't suppress knowledge to stay in power.'

'Except that it very often does,' Orjen said.

'It has to find the best ways of using its resources to benefit everyone as fairly as possible, according to the wishes and desires of its people. And two centuries after the revolution, the Free State still doesn't have much in the way of resources, and is still beholden to Patua, which is why that faction was so eager to hand over Remfrey He. You mentioned the old man's legacy. I can't think of anything better than making sure that his country has an equal share in what we've found here. So if we really can get these flying machines working,' Lyra said, 'I intend to take one of them to the Free State. Not only because the old man's boss deserves to know what he did here. How he died, and what he died for. But also because I think the Free State should benefit from everything we've learned about the invasion and the omphalos. And if that gives it more muscle in its dealings with Patua, it might be able to broker a deal with the rebels, help Patua push back the invasion, and maybe help to save the world too. I don't know if that last is likely or even possible, but I do know that if it's left to Patua no one will ever try.'

They were sitting cross-legged, knees almost touching. Orjen studying Lyra coolly, saying, 'It's a nice little dream, but that's all it is. We'll fix two of these machines, and we'll survey the area and take as many samples as we can, and then we'll fly home and begin our real work.'

'You've forgotten that rank and privilege don't apply here,' Lyra said, as gently as she could. 'We're no longer in Patua, and you don't get to tell me what to do any more. If I help you fix these flying machines, and help with the surveys and all the rest, it's only because I want to. And when we're done here, I'll get to choose where I want to go.'

'You'd betray me, after all the time we have worked together? And betray your country, too? What could you possibly hope to gain?'

Orjen didn't sound angry, seemed to be puzzling it out. Lyra took that as a good sign.

'The old man told me something his wife once told him,' she said. 'Only try to fix what can be fixed, and let the rest go. That's what I did, working for you, and it's what I'm trying to do now. Because this isn't just about helping the Free State. It's also about helping you get what you want. If both of us fly back to Patua, if you help the army deal with the invasion and things go back to how they were, you can forget about coming back here, let alone re-establishing contact with Simud and all the rest. The flying machines will be mothballed in some secret warehouse, and we'll go back to collecting beetles. But if we share everything we find here with the Free State, help it join forces with Patua and deal with the invasion on equal terms, it'll change the balance of power. Change it permanently, and for the better. The old men who want to keep everything as it was won't be in charge any more. You'll be able to do everything you need to do.'

'Good luck with trying to use one of these machines without my help. To begin with, they only understand trade pidgin.'

'See, that's how I know you're tired, and not yourself. Else you'd remember who taught you trade pidgin in the first place.'

'And what will you do if we can't fix the flying machines? If we have to wait for rescue?'

'I hope you aren't wrong about those machines. When it comes to that kind of thing you generally aren't. But if we can't fix them, if we have to be rescued, I hope you'll do the right thing and let me do what needs to be done. That's why I'm telling you about it now. Because I trust you, and reckon you deserve to know. Because we both owe the old man and should do right by him. And because I'm trying to do right by you, as I always have.'

'If you defect, the government could force the Free State to hand you over, as they did Remfrey He.'

'The faction that handed him over did so against the wishes of the people, and have been punished for it. I reckon the old man's boss will speak for me, and after I've explained the importance of all we've discovered, what it means, how it can be used, there's no way the Free State will want to let me go. And if it all works out as I hope it will, I'll be able to come back here with you, and go on to Simud.'

'I need to think about this,' Orjen said, and got to her feet and walked off towards the far end of the strip.

Lyra stood too, picking up the long gun, keeping Orjen in sight. Remfrey He was dead and the shatterling had been defeated, but there were still plenty of monsters about. The mirror arc was setting in a glory of red light and the column of cloud caught and concentrated it, a candescent umbilical cord joining world and sky. The flying machines, giving off the day's heat to the dusky air, faintly creaked and rustled. They were slender, fragile-looking things. Hard to believe they could cross thousands of leagues of water, yet here they were. Although Lyra didn't much like the thought of winging across the restless ocean through every kind of weather, out of sight of land for days and days, she reckoned that it was better than putting their trust in the army and waiting for a rescue that might never come. Orjen's father was a power, but there were limits to his influence, especially if the army believed that it already had the key to gaining control of the invasion.

At last, Orjen came back, saying, 'If I agree to it, it's only because it's the best way of making sure that we can find out everything we need to know about the invasion, and the true nature of the omphalos and the mirror fragment.'

'Isn't that what I have been talking about?'

'And this isn't the end of the discussion. Far from it.'

'It'll end right here and now if some stray monster catches us in the open,' Lyra said. 'We should find this other settlement and its caretaker, and get some rest.'

As they started up the slope in the afterglow of arcset, brushing through tall red grasses and skirting tumbles of red vine, Orjen asked Lyra if she remembered how they had first met Thorn.

'I remember you were eager to show off your work to this ragged old mercenary,' Lyra said.

'To make a point about the superiority of Patuan philosophy. He'd think it funny, wouldn't he, if I ended up conspiring to help the Free State.'

'He'd think you'd made the right choice.'

They topped the rise and walked on to a fence that circled the hollow of the hilltop and a clutch of cylindrical buildings. Small round windows glowing with warm welcoming light. The unfathomable silence of the darkening alien land all around.

'You won't be able to ever return to Patua,' Orjen said. 'The government will claim that you are a traitor, and try and sentence you in your absence. They might think me a traitor too, for letting you go.'

'Maybe they will, at first. But I hope,' Lyra said, because she really, truly wanted to believe that Remfrey He's plans had died with him, the shatterling would stay safely caged in its pit, and they stood at the threshold of something new and amazing, 'I hope, if we can put what we've learned here to good use and fix what needs fixing, that soon enough they'll realise that we were right.'

Acknowledgements

An article published by Ibrahim Semiz and Selim Oğur, 'Dyson Spheres around White Dwarfs' (arXiv:1503.04376v1), was the inspiration for the lucidor's world; needless to say, all faults and improbabilities in its construction are my responsibility.

My agent, Simon Kavanagh, provided much-needed advice, encouragement and support from conception to publication. Stephen Baxter, Pat Cadigan, John Clute, Judith Clute, Barry Forshaw, Judith Forshaw, Jon Courtenay Grimwood, Elizabeth Hand, Kim Newman, Alastair Reynolds, Josette Reynolds, Russell Schechter and Jack Womack were there to help when help was needed. My thanks to Marcus Gipps for his exemplary patience and understanding during the novel's long gestation, and for critical editorial advice which spurred many essential improvements. Thanks also to John Garth for his scrupulous copy-editing, Henry Steadman for the cover, and all at Gollancz who helped to shepherd this book into publication, including Brendan Durkin, Stevie Finegan, Craig Leyenaar, Jen McMenemy, Charlie Panayiotou and Gillian Redfearn. Especial thanks to Malcolm Edwards, who was there from the beginning.